A COSY CHRISTMAS WITH THE VILLAGE VET

ELIZA J SCOTT

Storm

Copyright © Eliza J Scott, 2022, 2025

The moral right of the author has been asserted.

Previously published in 2022.

Ebook ISBN: 978-1-83700-371-6
Paperback ISBN: 978-1-83700-372-3

Cover design: Rose Cooper
Cover images: Shutterstock

Published by Storm Publishing.
For further information, visit:
www.stormpublishing.co

ALSO BY ELIZA J SCOTT

Welcome to Micklewick Bay Series

The Little Bookshop by the Sea

Summer Days at Clifftop Cottage

Finding Love in Micklewick Bay

Christmas at the Little Bookshop by the Sea

Cupcakes and Kisses in Micklewick Bay

A Snowy Seaside Christmas

A Wedding at the Little Bookshop by the Sea

Life on the Moors Series

The Letter – Kitty's Story

The Talisman – Molly's Story

The Secret – Violet's Story

A Christmas Kiss

A Christmas Wedding at the Castle

A Cosy Countryside Christmas

Sunny Skies and Summer Kisses

Heartshaped Series

Tell That to My Heart

For my family. Thank you for all of your support, and the supply of perfectly-timed cups of tea that appear through the door of my little writing room xxx

ONE

BROGAN

Monday 5th December

Giving in to a wide yawn, Brogan Hopwood opened the rickety door of the porch at Pond Farm and was instantly greeted by a savage blast of cold December air. It snatched her breath away, taking with it any final, lingering dregs of sleep. 'Brrr!' She gave a shiver, snuggling down into her dressing gown as her black Labrador pushed past and hurtled his way into the yard. 'Don't mind me, Wilf,' she said, watching as he commenced his usual morning ritual of sniffing intently around the farmyard. She smiled to herself as she savoured the warmth of the mug of tea she was nursing in her hands, steam rising in a thick plume.

With her shoulders hunched against the cold, and her wild, auburn hair falling over her face, Brogan braved a step outside, her green eyes taking in the thick hoar frost that sparkled under the glow of the outside light. It took mere moments for the cold of the ancient flagstones to start seeping through her slippers. She wiggled her toes instinctively in a bid to keep them warm, not that it made the slightest bit of difference. She cast her gaze around the broad valley of Great Stangdale. At a quarter-to-seven on a winter's morning, it was still swathed in darkness, lights from the surrounding farmsteads twinkling back at her. A tawny owl hooted from the cluster of trees nearby. Moments later, a reply travelled from the other side of the valley, clear as a bell on the still, frosty air. Wilf paused, raising a front paw off the ground, ears cocked as he listened for more, making Brogan chuckle. He glanced across at her, wagging his tail before resuming his investigation of the yard, sniffing out clues to the nocturnal wildlife that had ventured onto his territory.

She took a sip from her mug as thoughts began spilling into her mind, the first one being of an unexpected encounter she'd had with a handsome stranger a couple of weeks earlier. Releasing a sigh, she closed her eyes, a smile playing over her mouth as she savoured the delicious memory of him and his urgent kisses; it was something she'd found herself indulging in regularly since that day. Her heart rate took off at a gallop. *Woah! Calm your jets, woman! Save that for later. Your mind should be focusing on other things this morning.* A cluster of nerves started up, squirming away in her stomach and scattering her daydreams, reminding her of the significance of the day ahead.

Monday the fifth of December. The first day of her new job as a veterinary nurse at Danskelfe Vets. It seemed to have been in a hurry to get here. She'd been looking forward to joining the practice ever since Yvonne Peirson, the practice manager, had called, offering her the role. But as the day had drawn closer, a feeling of trepidation had taken up residence inside her, not least because it had been a few years since she'd last worked in a veterinary environment. What if her training was seriously outdated, or she'd forgotten how to do everything? What if everything had changed? What if she turned out to be not what they were looking for? What if she was useless? What if they didn't like her? What if she didn't like *them?* 'Ughh!' She paused and rubbed her brow with her fingertips, reminding herself that she wouldn't have been offered the job if they didn't think she was capable. Yvonne had already explained that they had plans in place to ensure Brogan's skills were refreshed and brought up to date. The only thing she'd been required to do before today was re-register as a vet nurse with the Royal College of Veterinary Nurses and pay the annual fee, which she'd already done. So what was the worry? She heaved a sigh. She needed to stop thinking like this. Needed to stop her mind from getting swept away on a wave of negativity and self-doubt, which was something she'd found, over recent years, could very easily happen if she let it.

Why, at the age of twenty-six, had she become so down on herself? she wondered. She never used to be like this. She'd always been confident; comfortable in her own skin. Her friends used to describe her as fun and bubbly with a dash of feistiness thrown in for good measure. So what had made her self-confidence do a disappearing act? An image of her ex appeared in her mind as if she'd conjured him up specially. Archie. His expression was the very one he'd worn the last time she'd spoken to him. When he'd uttered *those* words. She swallowed; she could hardly bear to be reminded of them.

Nevertheless, they managed to force their way into her mind. 'You're not enough... I don't love you anymore.'

Not enough. That had somehow felt worse than him telling her he didn't love her anymore. Brogan squeezed her eyes tight shut as her heart twisted at the reminder of the hurt those words had inflicted that day – the hurt they still had the power to resurrect, albeit to a much lesser degree. At the time, she'd been inconsolable, had cried for days. *Days?* Who was she kidding? She'd sobbed for weeks; couldn't imagine the pain ever easing its grip, thought she'd never be able to move on.

But she had. And today was proof of that.

TWO

NICK

'Blast! How the heck's it got to that time?' Nick Heuston took a final bite of toast, washing it down with a quick glug of unpalatably cold tea. 'Bleurgh!' He pulled a face; he'd been heavy-handed with the milk again. He quickly set the mug back down on the worktop. One day, just *one* day, it would be good if he could manage to be on time – or early even. Fat chance of that, he thought. He'd been exactly the same for all of his thirty-three years; he doubted he was going to change now. No matter how hard he tried, it never seemed to happen. And even on the occasions he was ready on time, he wouldn't be able to find his wallet or his keys, or his phone. A time-sucking hunt for them would ensue, making him late, which was something he'd become infamous for. He'd set his alarm for six o'clock that morning – a whole hour earlier than necessary – and yet, somehow, that time seemed to have just trickled away with him faffing about and having nothing to show for it. 'Procrastination is your middle name, son,' his dad regularly joked. And, Nick had to admit, he was right.

Maudie, his black Labrador – well, she wasn't strictly one hundred percent Labrador, there was a dash of Labradoodle in there too, giving her a slightly wavy coat and fluffy tail – eyed him with interest from her bed. She seemed to have sensed there was something different about this morning. He dashed over to the sink, adding his mug and plate to the growing pile of dirty pots. The pile of dirty pots he'd hoped to have tackled in the extra hour he'd given himself. He'd run out of clean crockery and cutlery and had had to give some a cursory rinse under the "hot" tap so he could have his morning tea and toast – the word "hot" being misleading since only icy water had flowed from the tap since his arrival at Willow Cottage; he really must get to grips with the water heating system, or at least contact the landlord about it.

'Come on, Maudie, if we don't get a wriggle on I'm going to be late for work.' Nick smoothed down his dark-blond hair, which had a habit of sticking up at the front thanks to the cow lick he'd inherited from his dad, before reaching for his jacket.

Maudie blinked, looking at him as if to say, 'And whose fault is that? I've been ready for hours, you're the one who's been "faffing about", as you call it. As usual.' Four-year-old Maudie was well-known – and well-loved – for her expressive face and haughty manner.

Her look tickled Nick and he chuckled. 'I know what you're thinking, and you're right; I don't know how I manage to do it either.' He pushed his arms into his padded waxed jacket, glancing around at the poky kitchen, his eyes sweeping over the stack of cardboard boxes that were still waiting to be unpacked. There were similar piles in the tiny living room, his bedroom too, and another couple that annoyingly made the narrow hallway difficult to navigate; they were first on the list to be tackled. There was so much to do! He puffed out his cheeks and blew out a noisy sigh, making Maudie's ears twitch.

'Right!' he said, purposefully. In the next moment, he strode across the room, taking her lead from the hook on the back of the door. She shot up and was beside him in a flash. 'Ready to face the day?' he asked her.

She looked up at him and gave a wag of her tail.

'Come on then, young lady; let's see what our first day at Danskelfe Vets has in store for us.'

He'd just eased his way around the boxes in the hallway when it dawned on him that he hadn't got his keys. 'Blast!' He manoeuvred his way back into the kitchen, with Maudie giving what sounded convincingly like a sigh of disapproval. Nick scanned the room, lingering on the tiny pine dresser where mail addressed to the previous occupant was piled up alongside a small fruit bowl – still empty – and a mug containing the dregs of yesterday's cup of tea. But there was no sign of his keys. 'Where the heck are they?' he said to himself, scratching his head impatiently; he felt certain he'd put them on the dresser after he'd locked up last night. A disappointing sense of déjà vu crept over him. He'd promised himself he'd be different when he moved here, be more organised. So far he was failing in an epic way.

Maudie heaved another sigh and sat down. Nick glanced across at her to meet a gaze that said, "This again?"

'I know, I know,' he said, pushing his fingers into his hair, making his fringe ping up once more. 'I should've hung them on the hook over there like I said I was going to when we first moved in.' If he didn't know better, he could have sworn Maudie had just rolled her eyes at him. 'Little madam,' he said, sotto voce, a smile twitching at the corners of his mouth as he began rummaging amongst the letters; she certainly had bags of personality which was what he loved about her. In fact, since the recent events that had turned his life pretty much upside down, he'd been glad to have her companionship. Granted, she may be haughty and aloof, but when there was just the two of them sitting in front of the telly of an evening, him stroking her head that she'd rested in his lap, she really was the best company. Nick was naturally predisposed to be upbeat and positive, but Loretta's betrayal had really knocked the stuffing out of him. There was no way he would have been able to pull himself round as quickly as he'd done if it hadn't been for Maudie's presence in his life, nudging his hand as the tears had fallen, or trotting over, a ball in her mouth, her eyes pleadingly saying, 'Come on, Dad. Please be okay. Let's play!'

Yes, it was fair to say, she'd helped him move on, helped him drag his sorry butt out of bed each morning, able to face the day. Well, that and a little unexpected interlude with a rather attractive stranger. The said rather attractive stranger he hadn't been able to get out of his mind since he'd met her a couple of weeks ago. Not that he was grumbling about it. On the contrary, it had been refreshingly pleasant to have something else to occupy his mind rather than his somewhat bruised heart. Which was exactly why Nick had been happy to let his mind wander to the attractive stranger who'd managed to make him smile again.

THREE
BROGAN

She'd thought he was her forever; that they'd grow old together. And she'd thought he'd wanted that too; at least, he'd certainly led her to believe that from all the conversations they'd shared, curled up on the sofa of their rented cottage, his arm around her, squeezing her tight. Archie had been the driving force behind their talks of the future; he'd had it all mapped out. They'd be engaged within the year, married the following one – at that fancy hotel over in the Dales. A year after that, they'd buy their own place – Archie had his eye on one of the spacious houses on the little estate of new-builds just on the edge of Skeltwick – and a couple of years after that, they'd start a family – two kids; a girl and a boy. By then, Archie would be driving a large, top of the range, four-wheel drive. 'We're perfect for each other, Broge, soulmates, and we're going to have an amazing life together,' he'd regularly said. Brogan had been thoroughly swept away by it all. And she'd had no reason to doubt him or worry that his words would be as flimsy as tissue paper. Until the Sunday evening he'd returned home from a business trip in a strange mood. He'd been distant and cold, and done all he could to avoid making eye contact with her. Brogan had been utterly thrown by it. 'I can't do this anymore. I just can't,' he'd said sharply when she'd asked him what was wrong. 'The more I think about it, the more I know it's not for me.' He'd headed upstairs and started throwing his things into a case. 'The thought of being tied down, married with kids for the next twenty years, fills me with the worst kind of dread. It's the last thing I want. I want to live life for *me*. Live it to the fullest without having to compromise for someone else.'

'Where's this come from, Archie?' she'd asked, a feeling of panic rising inside her. 'Why are you saying this?'

'I've just been thinking, that's all. Talking to Phil; he's got life sussed.' He'd looked at her with an expression she didn't recognise. 'We're over. Finished.' He'd followed up with the words that had haunted her for the last three years. 'You're not enough. I don't love you anymore.'

And with that, the bottom had fallen out of her world.

Looking back, she was pretty much certain *that* was when she'd become so down on herself. Her self-confidence had taken a thorough kicking, plummeting to an all-time low, one she'd thought she'd never be able to pick herself up from. It had been the reason she'd quit her job as a vet nurse and sought refuge at her grandparents' smallholding on the moors near Lytell Stangdale, where she could tuck herself away and lick her wounds in private.

Stan and Elsie had been wonderful, their love and care a soothing balm to her damaged heart. If it hadn't been for them, she wouldn't have managed to pick herself up. Of that she was certain. They'd been delighted when Brogan had accepted their offer to stay with them, having told her, since they were getting on, they could do with some help around the place. 'You'd be doing us a favour, lovey. Wouldn't she, Stan? Here's your grandad; he can tell you himself,' Grandma Elsie had said. She'd called her granddaughter, concerned that her low spirits were lasting so long. After a series of muffled sounds, and her grandma using a loud stage whisper, instructing her grandad what to say, his reassuring voice came down the phone.

'Aye, your grandma's right, flower, it'd be good to have a young 'un around the place. Truth be told, I reckon we need you just as much as you need us. We've actually been talking about having to sell up. We're not getting any younger; I'm not sure how much longer we can manage this place on our own.'

The thought of her grandparents struggling and having to sell their beloved home was all the encouragement Brogan needed. Two days later, her little four-wheel drive, jam-packed with all her worldly goods, had nosed its way into the yard of Pond Farm, her grandmother rushing out to meet her, a wide smile on her ruddy face.

There hadn't been a lot to do livestock-wise at the smallholding since most of the animals had been sold off. There'd just been a spot of fixing here and there, along with getting the house tidy – which, to neat-freak Brogan, had been something she'd been itching to do for years. Her grandparents hadn't been exactly what you'd call house-proud, with piles of old newspapers perched precipitously on a corner of the old pine dining table, carrier bags full of who-knew-what dotted about the place, things cluttering the kitchen worktops. The pair were hoarders, unable to bear the thought of throwing anything away. And she didn't know the last time a duster had been flicked around the place. This wasn't some-thing recent, brought about by ill health or old age; they'd always been that way, not that Brogan judged them. But she'd relished getting stuck in and tackling the mess –subtly, of course, telling her grandparents cleaning kept her mind off "things"; there was no way she'd hurt their feelings. In turn, her grandma had taught her how to make her infamous rhubarb crumble and killer chicken stew using the secret mix of herbs and the recipes that had been passed down through generations.

Brogan had flourished in their kindness, her heartache easing far more quickly than she'd anticipated. It was fair to say, Pond Farm had proved to be the perfect sanctuary, and Brogan hadn't regretted her decision to give up her job and say goodbye to her old life in Skeltwick one iota. In fact, she hadn't been there long when she'd decided she never wanted to leave.

Her grandparents had gone a step further in boosting her

happiness. Brogan had returned from a head-clearing walk on the moors to find a surprise waiting for her. After heeling her wellies off in the porch, she'd walked into the kitchen to see her grandma wearing an extra wide smile.

'Hi, Grandma. Everything all right?' she'd said, a quizzical tone in her voice. In the next moment, a chunky Labrador puppy had gambolled across the quarry tiles and started tugging at her socks, his tail wagging ten-to-the-dozen. Brogan had laughed, scooping him up and holding him out in front of her, gazing at the most adorable face. Her heart had melted in an instant. 'Hello there, little fella. Aren't you just gorgeous, eh?' The puppy had wriggled and she'd snuggled him close, breathing in his delicious puppy smell. 'What's his name?'

'Well, lovey, what you call him is entirely up to you.'

'Up to me?'

'Aye, flower. Your grandad and me took one look at him and thought he was a grand little lad, and that he'd be just what you needed. We remembered how you used to love all our Labradors when you were a little lass.'

'You mean he's mine?' Brogan's heart had raced with happiness. She'd snuggled the puppy into her neck, smoothing her hand down his warm, silky back. She could still remember how that first cuddle had felt to this day.

'Aye, he's all yours; he's eight weeks old. Got him from the same breeder we've always used, so he's from good stock. All the little lad needs is a name.'

Brogan looked down at the mischievous, wriggling bundle, a huge smile spreading across her face. 'Hello, little Wilf. Welcome to the family.' She'd headed over to her grandmother and kissed her on the cheek. 'Thank you, Grandma, he's perfect.'

'Aye, we thought you'd be chuffed with him.'

Brogan had been more than chuffed with Wilf; they'd been inseparable ever since, bonding over long walks and lots of cuddles.

Despite her responsibilities with Wilf and helping out her grandparents, Brogan still found she had an unhealthy amount of time on her hands, which had led to her mind wandering back to Skeltwick, and Archie. Which was why, when her grandmother had mentioned old Tommy Hind was under the weather and unable to take his sheepdog, Bess, for a walk, Brogan had offered to do it for him. It hadn't taken long for an idea to start germinating in her mind.

With a little bit of research, she'd been thrilled to discover a hole in the local business market: dog walking. It was perfect! There were plenty of folk who lived in the surrounding villages and commuted to work, feeling guilty about being unable to walk their canine companions. So she'd placed posters advertising Pond Farm Pooches dog walking services on the village noticeboards and in the windows of local businesses and, before she knew it, her new venture had mushroomed. She'd initially offered a limited doggy-day care service if an owner was going to be out for the full day, but more recently, she'd focused on the dog walking aspect of her business.

As well as being a way of earning some much-needed extra cash, it had also helped her get better acquainted with local people – particularly Anoushka and Kristy, with whom she'd become close and now called her best friends – which in turn, had led to her being offered a part-time job at the local pub, The Sunne Inne, where she worked behind the bar a couple of nights a week.

Before she knew it, she'd quickly settled into the rhythm of village life and her happiness had returned.

That had been just over three years ago, and though Brogan was pleased to say she was a very different person now, she hadn't been surprised to find that some dregs of her self-doubt still remained.

The only thing that had tainted her time there was the loss of her beloved grandparents. Even though it had been a year since – just a month apart – the pain sat as heavy as a lead weight in her heart and was still too raw for her to dwell on. Brogan had been stunned to find they'd bequeathed the smallholding to her, knowing how much she loved living there, unlike her mum, Cathy.

Instead, they'd left their daughter the surprisingly large sum of savings they'd had in the building society. Brogan had been relieved at how her mum had taken the news that Pond Farm hadn't been willed to her. 'Oh, thank heavens I won't have the hassle of it. And it's only right it went to you, lovey,' Cathy had said. 'It's your home and we all know how settled you feel there. And who knew how much they'd been squirrelling away all these years? With the sum they've left me, I'll be able to pay my mortgage off.'

But Brogan couldn't blame losing them for her current feeling of disillusionment with her dog walking business; that had crept up on her afterwards. It had made itself particularly noticeable when she'd been traipsing over the moors in torrential rain, a gaggle of dogs in tow. The cold she'd had at the time had developed into a nasty bout of bronchitis, knocking her off her feet for a couple of weeks. The accompanying cough had taken a while to shake off, compounding her desire for a change of career.

Which was why her interest had been piqued when she'd been told of the vacancy at the new veterinary surgery over in Danskelfe.

Brogan shook her head. Today was about looking forward and moving on with the next phase of her life, she told herself. The recent conversation she'd had with Anoushka and Kristy made a timely appearance in her mind. 'You're perfect for the job, Broge; you've got loads of experience; it'll all come flooding back,' Anoushka had said, beaming at her.

'You'll be brilliant, chick, that's why they offered you the role. And your love for animals just shines through,' Kristy had said, giving her arm a reassuring squeeze. Their kind words had gone some way to easing Brogan's doubts. Until this morning, when they'd come rushing back at her.

She sighed. 'Ughh! Let's hope you two are right,' she said to herself as she watched Wilf, still busy on his yard-sniffing quest.

It still didn't stop her feeling a twinge of guilt at telling her clients they'd have to find someone new to walk their dogs. Poor old Bert Hoggarth at Broad View Cottage – which was Pond Farm's nearest neighbour – had been devastated. A good friend of her grandparents, he wasn't very mobile on account of being desperately in need of a hip replacement and had been struggling to walk his fox red Labrador, Nell, for some time. Feeling concerned for his predicament, Brogan had arranged for her friend Ella Welford who ran the boarding kennels at Camplin Hall Farm to take over the exercising of Nell, which had pleased Bert and gone some way to assuaging Brogan's guilt.

Wilf trotted over, interrupting her thoughts, looking up at her expectantly, his tail wagging. She couldn't help but smile at him; his upbeat nature always elicited a feeling of happiness. 'Not just yet, lad; I'll take you for a walk when I've got dressed.' Though his ears had pricked at hearing the "w" word, her tone seemed to appease him and he wandered back into the oak-beamed kitchen. Brogan followed, watching him give a harumph as he flumped down onto the clippy mat in front of the old cream Aga. Thanks to the stove, the kitchen was toasty warm, unlike the rest of the cottage with its draughty, rattly windows, threadbare carpets and radiators that had just about given up the ghost.

Brogan felt the pull of another yawn. She flopped down onto the stick-back chair, adjusting its squishy cushion, and cast her gaze around the room. Evidence of the cottage's seventeenth century origins was everywhere, from the deep, squat stone mullioned windows, and the sandstone inglenook fireplace that housed the Aga, to the chunky, age-darkened beams supporting wide elm floorboards, and quarry tiles, worn smooth by centuries of feet passing over them. The uneven walls were a couple of feet thick in places, except for the flimsy porch which was a later addition and looked like it was ready to be blown down by the next gust of wind that hit the moors. Though the décor rocked a tired nineteen-eighties vibe with an abundance of floral patterns everywhere – just as her grandparents had left it after they'd passed away – the cottage oozed potential and Brogan loved the place. She knew she'd have to update it at some point, but she couldn't contemplate that right now. The décor of the cottage made her feel as though her grandparents were still with her which she found comforting. Changing it would feel like she was erasing their memory. And, right now, that was the last thing she wanted.

Besides, there were other things to occupy her mind today, like getting ready for her new job. She glanced up at the clock on the wall. *Yikes!* Time to get cracking. The nerves in her stomach leapt to attention and gave another wriggle.

FOUR

NICK

'There they are.' Nick's eyes landed on a glint of something that looked promisingly like his bunch of keys. They were almost hidden from view by a precarious stack of mugs by the draining board. 'What are they doing behind that lot? I don't remember leaving the flaming things there,' he said under his breath. 'I reckon you must've moved them, Maudie.'

Maudie blinked at him, unamused.

'Yeah, sorry, not funny.' He stooped to ruffle her ears just as his mobile phone rang from somewhere over by the kettle.

He loped across and scooped it up, the number flashing on the display sending a surge of mixed emotions through him. None of them good. Loretta. *Oh, jeez.* His heart plummeted. He didn't need this right now. He knew what she was going to say. Knew that she'd be annoyed. *Ughh.* Scraping his teeth over his bottom lip, he toyed with the notion of ignoring the call, quickly deciding against it. She'd been on at him every day since he'd moved in here, leaving a slew of increasingly irate voicemails. Last night's sprang to mind and he winced; she'd been particularly scathing. No, it'd be better to get the earbashing out of the way. 'Right, here goes, Maudie. Wish me luck.' Nick breathed out a sigh and swiped the screen to answer the call. 'Loretta. To what do I owe this pleasure?' His heart was hammering.

Maudie looked on with interest. She'd never liked Loretta; or so Loretta would have Nick believe.

'Nick!' Loretta sounded exasperated. 'Why don't you ever answer my calls?'

'I've been b—'

'You still haven't done it. Honestly! How hard can it be to get a pair of shoes back to me? It's not like I'm asking you to traipse halfway across the country with them; Arkleby must only be about ten miles away from Middleton-le-Moors. Anyone would think you were being deliberately difficult.' Nick winced at her icy tone. He'd put money on it being frostier than the weather outside.

Pushing away the sadness hearing her voice had triggered, and hoping she hadn't detected it, he said, 'I know. I'm sorry. I promise you, I'm not being difficult, it's just been a bit hectic, what with me moving house and—'

'I could always come and get them myself. It's not as if I haven't offered.'

Panic surged through him. The last thing he needed was for Loretta to see the pitiful place he'd moved to; to regard him as being down on his luck. He wasn't ready to deal with her criticism or her pity or worse, see her take pleasure from it. 'There's really no need for that, Loretta. My cottage is a pain to find. I'll drop them off, but—'

'Just do it, Nick, preferably tonight. I'm not asking a lot of you; I just want you to return my shoes, okay?' Her voice was laced with irritation.

Return them! 'Loretta, I didn't take them. You were the one who put them in a box of my stuff and left them piled up outside the house. I didn't even know they were there 'til you told m—'

'It was a mistake! Okay? I didn't deliberately put them in the wrong storage box; I must've picked them up by accident when I was... getting your stuff ready.' Her voice tailed off.

'You mean when you were packing my stuff up, neatly

removing me from your life?' he said, not caring that he sounded bitter.

'It wasn't like that. I was helping you; making it easier.'

Easier? Who was she kidding? Nothing about leaving the home he'd shared with the woman he'd expected to spend the rest of his life with had been easy. In fact, he'd go as far as to say it had been one of the hardest things he'd ever had to do. 'Easier for who exactly?'

Ignoring his question she steamed on. 'Anyway, I need them; I'm at a party this weekend and I don't want to have to go traipsing around the shops hunting for a new pair this close to Christmas.' She paused, releasing a noisy sigh. 'Just drop them off here, Nick. Today. There's no need for all this fuss. And there's no need to knock, just leave them in the porch. That way we don't have to see each... well... just in case I'm not in.'

Her words landed like a blow to the chest. She didn't even want to see him, didn't want to speak to him face-to-face. But what hurt even more was that he knew why Loretta needed the shoes. She was having a weekend away with *him*. Aaron; the bloke who'd been his best mate until he suddenly decided to relieve Nick of his fiancée. They'd be at Aaron's company's Christmas party at some fancy hotel in the Lake District and she'd want to show off her expensive designer shoes. No doubt she'd be wearing them with the clingy, sparkly dress she'd bought last month, the one she'd told him was for a girls' night out. Nick had had his doubts at the time, but hadn't said anything. More fool him. And to rub salt into the wound, she wanted Nick to leave the shoes at the house he'd, no *they'd*, called home until recently. The home he still jointly owned with her. Didn't she realise how hard that would be for him? How much it would hurt? It was as if she had no conscience; that she didn't care what she asked of him as long as she got what she wanted.

'Nick! Nick!' Loretta huffed out an impatient breath. 'Why aren't you answering me? I don't have time for this; I need to go. Just tell me you'll drop them off ASAP.'

The sharp tone of her voice pulled him back to the conversation. 'Yeah, don't worry; I'll make sure you have them in time.' He gave a weary sigh.

'Good. Be sure you do.'

Before he could reply, the line went dead.

Nick stared at his phone, myriad thoughts running through his mind. He still couldn't believe they'd come to this.

Sensing things weren't right, Maudie ran across to him, nudging his leg with her head and giving a little whimper. He couldn't help but smile. 'Ahh, at least I've got you, eh, girl?' He crouched down and she pushed her head onto his shoulder, her tail wagging as he ran his hand over her back. She knew when she needed to show her softer side.

Feeling his mood lift, Nick gave Maudie one last ear ruffle before pushing himself up. 'Right then, Maudie. Keys. Where did I see them? Ah, yep, over there.' He strode over to the draining board and scooped his keys up before heading back into the hallway and the obstacle course of boxes. As he squeezed around them, he wondered if it was one of these that contained Loretta's precious shoes.

Her call had dampened his mood big time, making him wish he hadn't answered it. But at least it had stopped him from forgetting his phone, he thought. 'Yep, think positive, Nick, it's the way ahead for you,' he said, keen for his previous enthusiasm to return to face his first day at his new job.

FIVE

BROGAN

After the third attempt, the engine of Brogan's ancient little four-wheel drive spluttered into life. She heaved a sigh of relief, her panic skittering away. 'Thank goodness for that.' The last thing she wanted was to be late for her first day at work; she was eager to create a good impression from the get-go. She turned the fan on full blast, directing all the air vents towards the windscreen in a bid to speed up the defrosting process before she set off. Not that her car ever produced much heat, except for in the summer when it blasted out hot air. In winter months, it seemed to switch to Arctic temperatures. Like today. Brogan could swear it felt colder inside the car than it did outside. She jumped out and sprayed de-icer liberally over the windows. Right now, she was still absolutely nithered from her quick dog walk with Wilf, and Bert Hoggarth's Labrador, Nell – it was her last one before Ella took over since her friend hadn't been able to do this morning. The wind on the moors had been particularly cruel, but despite the biting cold, Brogan had got the impression Bert would have been happy to chat on the doorstep for hours when she'd popped Nell back. It had been hard to pull herself away, and she'd felt guilty about doing it; the old chap was obviously feeling lonely. She'd made a mental note to still call in on him regularly, make sure he was okay. He'd lived on his own for as long as she could remember and he'd never mentioned family. On top of that, he didn't go very far owing to the pain in his hip he complained of. No wonder he was lonely.

Brogan knew what it was to feel lonely. Much as she loved living at Pond Farm, it was in a remote spot and since her grandparents had passed away, the long winter evenings sometimes dragged. The cottage seemed empty without her grandparents going about their daily life. She missed her grandma's infectious laughter ringing around the place, the way she'd hum when she was busy with whatever task was in hand. And much as her grandma used to grumble – albeit good-naturedly – about her husband's whistling, calling it a 'bloomin' tuneless racket', Brogan missed the way her grandad's chirpy notes filled the yard. Instead, an echoing silence took their place, closing in on her at times. She could understand why Bert would want to hang on to a visitor for as long as he could. Though, unusually for him, he'd seemed somewhat agitated about an unfamiliar dark-grey van he'd seen loitering outside his cottage the day before which, like Pond Farm, was in an isolated corner of the moors.

'Had a great big dent on his right-hand passenger door. I managed to get the number plate down, mind, lass. Just in case there's any bother in the area.' Brogan had been relieved to hear that; she'd spotted a similar vehicle at the end of the lane to her home the other day. She'd noted there were two people in the front but hadn't been able to get a glimpse of either of them since she'd got the impression they'd been hiding their faces. It had sent a prickle of unease running up her spine. Since then, she'd made sure to be extra vigilante about locking up the outbuildings, and she made doubly sure to lock the door of the rickety porch when she went to bed. She made a mental note to get in touch with the local bobby, PC Snaith, and share her concerns about the van with him.

As a rule, there was very little crime in the area; what little there was usually occurred in spates, with criminals coming in from the towns, taking advantage of the villagers' complacent attitude to security, raiding outbuildings, stealing quad bikes, lawnmowers and the like. A couple of years earlier, someone had reported the theft of a trials bike, a strimmer and a stash of cooking apples, the latter item raising local eyebrows.

With what Bert had told her still running through her mind, Brogan pulled her woolly bobble hat down further over her ears before she set about liberally sprinkling salt over the old uneven flagstones in the yard. It gave a satisfying sound of cracking ice as it took effect. That done, she turned her attention to scraping the thick layer of frost from the windscreen, working at it briskly, the bitter cold nipping at her face and her fingers. Wilf looked on with interest from his place on the front passenger seat as if to say, "Come on! Hurry up! Have you any idea how bloomin' cold it is in here?' She eyed her grandparents' well-loved Land Rover parked in the far corner, wishing she'd been able to afford to have its rusted chassis replaced, but the quote from Jed at the new garage in Danskelfe had been prohibitive and, in turn, the vehicle had failed its MOT. Brogan had loved driving it; it had made her feel safe, as if she could tackle all weathers in it. Her grandparents had bought it brand new donkey's years ago and it had been a real workhorse, but they hadn't exactly taken good care of it, and decades of not getting things fixed, and standing out in so many moorland winters had taken its toll. *Maybe one day...* she thought.

By the time she'd finished scraping ice from the car windows, her fingertips were completely numb.

'Right, Wilf, I expect you to be on your best behaviour when we get to work, okay?' she said, her frozen hands struggling to click her seat belt in the dock. Wilf looked across at her, giving a quick wag of his tail. He seemed thrilled to be joining her for this new adventure. Chris Crabtree, one of the partners at the surgery, had told her she could take Wilf to work as long as he behaved himself, declaring he'd be welcome company for his wirehaired Dachshund, Oscar. This had been music to Brogan's ears who'd been loath to leave Wilf at home all day, nipping back at lunchtime to check on him. That would have been too awful for the poor lad, not to mention lonely for him; he was a sociable little chap and thrived on company. The alternative was to drop him off at Ella's boarding kennels for the day, but though Ella's rates were reasonable, the cost would still eat a great chunk into her wages, which again wasn't ideal. And even more reason for Brogan to be thrilled when Chris had said Wilf was welcome.

Everything seemed to be falling into place with surprising ease. It was as if this new job was meant to be. Until her doubts about her ability had set in, that is.

Brogan made her way carefully along the bumpy track from Pond Farm. Her stomach was performing somersaults, making her regret the toast she'd had for breakfast. It was times like this when the loss of her grandparents hit her hardest. Yes, she'd been over the moon to get this job, but it would have been so much better if they'd been here to share her news. Her mum had been pleased when she'd told her, of course she had, but Cathy was busy leading her own life as a busy conveyancer at a firm of solicitors in York. Nothing would ever be able to match the enthusiasm of her grandparents, nor the pride that would have undoubtedly shone in their eyes. She pictured her grandmother's kind, plump face, the gentle smile she would have worn, of how her grandad would have beamed down at her. Brogan felt a pang of longing. How she wished they were still here. What she'd give to feel the warmth of her grandmother's embrace right now as she wished her luck, waving her off on her first day at her new job.

Feeling the sting of tears, Brogan blinked quickly and sniffed, wiping a gloved hand under her chilly nose. 'Come on, Brogan, pull yourself together, lass. Now's not the time to get all maudlin,' she said to herself. The car was still freezing and her words came out in a puff of steam. 'Flippin' 'eck.' She gave a shiver; the cold had got right into her bones. Wilf glanced across from his place in the front passenger seat and gave a little whimper. 'It's all right, lad; s'just me being daft, that's all.' She reached across and gave him a reassuring ear ruffle, making his tail wag.

The country lanes to Danskelfe Vets were thick with ice; though the gritter had been out on the bigger country roads the previous evening, it clearly hadn't ventured out to these more remote parts. Glad to have winter tyres fitted to her car, Brogan took it steady, her heart lurching when the vehicle skidded on a stretch of thick ice that ran across the road from one of the many springs.

At just before eight o'clock, she was pulling up beside Chris Crabtree's smart new Land Rover in the courtyard of the Danskelfe business "units" as their landlady, Lady Carolyn Hammondely, referred to them. The word "units" didn't do the old sandstone buildings justice, with their beautiful arched windows and thick, broad doors. But it was good to see the once dilapidated property restored and being put to good use after so many years of standing unloved and empty.

'Right, Wilf, here we are.' She glanced across to the vets' surgery where the lights were glowing in the windows. Her heart was lurching for a different reason now.

Brogan pushed open the heavy door, the smell of disinfectant rushing at her, making her nostrils twitch. Everything looked pristine and new and white. Chris Crabtree was leaning over the reception desk in mid-conversation with a young woman dressed in pale-green scrubs. Brogan recognised her from nearby Arkleby, her name temporarily evading her. The pair were poring over a computer monitor. Chris looked up and beamed. 'Ah, morning, Brogan.'

'Morning.' The young woman greeted her with an equally wide smile.

Wilf lunged forward, pulling on his lead, eager to make friends. 'Morning,' Brogan said, smiling back.

'Welcome to Danskelfe Vets; we're delighted you've joined our team.' Chris strode across the waiting room to her. 'And this must be Wilf.' He got down on his haunches, rubbing the Labrador's head. The vet was rewarded with a sweep of Wilf's tongue across his face. 'Well, aren't you a friendly fella?' Chris said, with a hoot of laughter.

A moment later a whiskery-faced miniature dachshund appeared, trotting over to them in a jaunty manner. He had quite possibly the shortest legs Brogan had ever seen. 'Oh, my goodness, he's so cute!' She bent down, offering Oscar her hand to sniff before giving him a scratch between the ears which, judging by the tail wagging, he enjoyed enormously.

Wilf pulled towards the little dog and a bout of sniffing commenced, each apparently meeting with the other's approval.

'Meet Oscar,' said Chris. 'What he lacks in size, he makes up for in personality. And you're right, he is a cute little guy; been desperate for a canine companion since we lost his buddy and part-ner-in-crime, Giles, which is why I thought you bringing Wilf here would be a good idea. Actually they should be joined by another friend any minute; my new business partner's bringing his dog too. The three of them can curl up together in front of the stove in our little staff room at the back; they'll be fine out of the way there.'

'Sounds perfect. Wilf will be glad of the company too.' Brogan really couldn't believe her luck.

'I'm Jules, by the way; I'm the receptionist, well, one of them. The other one's Jo; she's part-time; works Wednesdays and the odd Saturday morning.' The young woman, who Brogan guessed was in her mid-thirties, had come round and was now fussing Wilf who was enjoying every moment of the attention.

'Oh, I do apologise, I got so distracted by this wonderful lad, my manners failed me,' said Chris, giving another laugh. 'Brogan, meet Jules, Jules meet Brogan.'

'Hi, good to meet you, Jules,' said Brogan.

'Likewise.' Jules smiled broadly.

'Morning, Brogan. Ready for your first day with us?' Brogan peered round Jules to see Yvonne Peirson. She was the practice manager who'd also sat in on her interview alongside Chris and another of the practice's vets, Georgia Collier, who was mum to two young boys and worked part-time at the surgery. In her early fifties, Yvonne was wearing a friendly smile and scrubs in the same shade as those worn by Jules.

'Hi, Yvonne, yes; I'm really looking forward to it.' Brogan's stomach gave a quick lurch at the reminder.

'Well, that's good to hear.' Yvonne made her way over to Wilf, giving him a tickle on the tummy. 'Hiya, handsome.'

'I take it you're talking to Wilf and not me,' said Chris, a mischievous glint in his eye.

Yvonne gave a throaty chuckle. 'I hate to disappoint you, but, yes.'

'Fair enough.' Chris grinned.

Yvonne pushed herself up. 'Right then, I'd best get back to it.' She turned to Brogan. 'I'll catch up with you a bit later on; we can run through everything then; discuss the training courses I've got in mind for you. But in the meantime, if you have any questions, please feel free to shout up. Becky should be here any minute – she's one of the other vet nurses along with Mia – she'll be happy to help too. And I heard Chris say Jules was going to show you round the place.'

Brogan nodded. 'Yeah, that's right.'

'Good.' She gave a friendly smile. 'You'll be settled in and feel part of the team before you know it; everything'll come flooding back.'

'Thanks.' Brogan felt reassured by Yvonne's words and the friendliness everyone had shown her. Her biggest worry about resuming her role after such a long break was if her mind went blank or if she had an obvious gap in her training. The last thing she needed was for clients to think she didn't know what she was doing; they needed to feel confident and secure in the knowledge that their precious pets were in good hands. She'd hate to let the surgery down, especially when it had only been running for a few months. But Yvonne's confidence was already rubbing off on her. Brogan had done the job before, and done it well if what her previous employers had said was anything to go by – at her inter-view, Chris and Yvonne had said her old boss had given her a glowing reference, saying they'd been sorry to have lost her – there was no reason why she couldn't do it again. She'd loved being a vet nurse; it had been her dream job, a true vocation, and it felt suddenly exciting to be resurrecting it. And, if things went as she hoped, once her training was up to date, she was keen to pick up where she'd left off and gain further qualifications, which both Chris and Yvonne had been pleased to hear at the interview.

'By the way, everyone calls me Vonnie,' the practice manager said, heading towards her office. 'And I've got your new scrubs here – one to wear and a spare set for when it's in the wash – you can get changed in the bathroom just off the staffroom.'

'Oh, okay. Thanks, Vonnie.' Brogan felt a thrill rush through her at the thought of wearing scrubs again.

'Right then.' Chris got to his feet, pushing his blond hair back off his face. 'I'll leave you to go and get changed. When you're ready, Jules can show you round the place while I make us a cuppa, which is the way we always start our day, before the chaos kicks in. Clinic begins at eight-thirty during the week – nine on a Saturday where we finish at one – and Jules has just informed me we've got a jam-packed day ahead of us, involving a visit from a Labrador who has a habit of eating things he shouldn't, which should be interesting.'

'Yes, we know all about Labradors who do that, don't we, Wilf?' Brogan said, looking down at Wilf. On hearing his name, he glanced up at her, an innocent expression on his face as his tail swished across the floor. 'We won't tell Chris and Jules all about the poached salmon you swiped from the table at Tinkel Bottom Farm the other week, will we?'

Chris roared with laughter. 'Sounds like Wilf has a very discerning palate.'

'Not so sure about that,' said Brogan, chuckling. 'He's a shame-less opportunist; grabs whatever's going; he doesn't care if it's the finest salmon or cold pasta.'

'Well, Oscar would be very jealous to hear of such table swiping escapades; his legs are too short to pull a stunt like that. Not that he doesn't give it a damn good try.'

Brogan smiled. She had a good feeling about working here. A really good feeling. Everything was going to be all right; she could feel it in her bones.

Locking the door of the little rented cottage that still didn't feel like home, Nick made his way cautiously down the icy path. He'd resolved to push his conversation with Loretta right out of his mind and concentrate on getting to work, which from the look of things, was going to be something else to hold him up that morning. He cursed himself for not setting the engine away of his large four-wheel drive. The frost was thick; it would take ages to demist the windscreen. On top of that, he dreaded to think what the roads from here in Arkleby to Danskelfe would be like. All he knew was that they were narrow, full of twists and turns and more worryingly, steep in places. Not to mention the parts he'd spotted with eye-wateringly sheer drops right down the valley side. It would be so easy to find yourself hurtling down one of those. All it would take would be one unfortunate skid of a tyre. It didn't bear thinking about. At least he didn't have to get Maudie to Ella Welford's boarding kennels at Camplin Hall Farm over at Lytell Stangdale, which had been his original plan. That would have been something extra to factor in and make him even more late. Chris, his new partner at the vets, had suggested he bring Maudie to the surgery where she could curl up with Oscar in front of the little stove in the staff room. His suggestion had been a huge relief – not that Ella didn't come with glowing recommendations; she absolutely did – but Nick didn't like to think about the sulking that would ensue once he'd picked Maudie up in the evenings. Maudie was highly skilled at the silent treatment if he dared do something to meet with her disapproval. And, boy did she know how to drag it out, sitting with her back to him, acting as if he wasn't there. She was definitely entertaining, but the thought of her being too sulky for cuddles on the sofa held no appeal. She may be a flouncy little madam, but he appreciated her companionship. She made his empty cottage feel more homely; he dreaded to think what it would be like without her.

Nick had been shocked at how icy the roads to Danskelfe had been and had tackled them with great caution which meant his arrival at his new job at twenty-past eight, was a good twenty minutes late. 'Here we are, Maudie,' he said, breathing a sigh of relief when the stone building that was home to the surgery came into view. It really was impressive, occupying a large corner spot, with ample room for parking.

Moments later, he was pulling up by the other staff vehicles parked there, a feeling of first-day nerves making themselves known in his stomach. His life really had taken an unexpected turn. Maudie peered out of the window with interest, before casting him a suspicious look.

'It's not what you're thinking, Maudie. I haven't brought you here for any injections or thermometers in unmentionable places. I promise.' He gave her a reassuring pat.

Maudie didn't look convinced.

It took him a good five minutes to manoeuvre her off the passenger seat and out of the car; she really was a dead weight when she made up her mind she wasn't budging. And though it was bitterly cold, Nick was now sweating, beads of perspiration prickling over his brow as he tried to tempt Maudie to move from her spot by the car. 'Help me out here, Maudie, you know I'm already late,' he said, tugging at her lead, still gasping after his struggle. 'Now's really not the time to be difficult. I promise you, you'll love it in there.' But Maudie remained rooted to the freezing cold ground. 'Look, I'll do a deal with you. If you move your backside, there'll be a treat for you, okay? A big, fat *treat*.'

The word "treat" got her attention. Her ears pricked up and her bushy eyebrows lifted simultaneously.

With an inward cheer, Nick seized the moment. 'Come on, let's get out of this cold.' He walked briskly over the frosty gravel, Maudie trotting along beside him.

'Nick! Welcome!' Inside the surgery, Chris strode over to his new colleague, his hand outstretched, a friendly smile on his face.

'Sorry I'm late, Chris.' Nick pulled an apologetic face as he took his friend's hand.

'Hey, no worries, mate; you're here now. I should imagine the road from Arkleby was a bit dicey with the gritter not venturing this far out last night.' He pumped Nick's hand enthusiastically, his smile growing wider. 'Ready to begin our new business venture?'

Forgetting his nerves, and his less-than-happy start to the day thanks to Loretta, Nick couldn't help but return Chris's smile. 'I sure am,' he said, a surge of enthusiasm filling his chest.

'And how are you, young lady?' Chris stooped to ruffle Maudie's ears and she gave a happy tail wag. 'Oscar's looking forward to seeing you, and there's a new friend for you to meet. He's called Wilf and I think you'll like him; he's a very handsome black Labrador; belongs to our new nurse.'

'Oh, he's so cute; a great big softy with bags of character,' said Jules.

'Hear that, Maudie? A cute black Labrador,' Nick said with a wink.

Maudie gave him an unamused, side-long look which made Jules and Chris burst out laughing.

'Maudie doesn't look very impressed,' Jules said through her giggles.

'No, she won't be until I give her the T.R.E.A.T. I promised her,' said Nick, smiling down at her. 'She never forgets, and she bears a grudge, trust me.'

'Ah, we can soon remedy that.' Chris reached into the jar of dog biscuits that was kept on the shelf at the back of the reception desk. He handed one to Maudie who sniffed it before taking it gently. 'Good, lass.' He gave her a pat.

Nick looked on, smiling fondly at her. 'Right, then, I supposed I'd better get cracking and check the computer for details of my first patient.' He turned towards the door that had his name plaque fixed to it, a strange mix of excitement and trepidation swirling around inside him. Much as he was looking forward to joining his old friend in this new venture, and though his natural predisposition was to be upbeat and happy, a hint of sadness had sneaked in as the circumstances that had had brought him here popped into his mind. There was no getting away from the fact that Loretta's untimely phone call that morning had put a bit of a dampener on things. Had she done it on purpose? he wondered. Probably not, she'd be too wrapped up in her own life to give much consideration to his now.

Oblivious to the thoughts whirling around Nick's mind, Jules checked the screen of her monitor. 'That'd be Fudge Simpkins; he's a guinea pig. Mrs Simpkins is bringing him in. Says in the notes here he's got a problem with overeating.'

That lifted Nick's mood in an instant, his smile pinging back. He chuckled and patted his stomach. 'I know the feeling. I was the same with my dinner last night.' That wasn't strictly true. In fact, it was actually pretty wide of the mark. Nick's dinner the previous evening had been a tasteless microwave meal masquerading as chicken tikka masala and fragrant rice with a garlic and coriander naan bread for dipping in the, supposedly, "mouth-watering sauce". It was a poor imitation of one of his favourite meals, having about as much flavour as shredded cardboard and the texture to match. He'd only been able to eat half of it before scraping it despondently into the bin. His mind sprang to the last time he'd had a decent chicken tikka masala. It was at Cardamom, the Indian

Restaurant in Middleton-le-Moors and it had been sublime, the best he'd ever tasted. He'd been with Loretta, and though the meal had been delicious, the atmosphere between him and his then fiancée had been so thick you could cut it with a knife. Nick hadn't known why at the time and had blamed it on the fact he'd lost his keys just before they'd left, resulting in them arriving late for their booking. Even so, Loretta's pinched expression and the heavy cloud of awkwardness between them had seemed out of proportion to his "misdemeanour". *Funny how a bit of hindsight can shed a whole new light on things,* he'd thought later when he'd found out she'd rather have spent the evening with his best mate.

'Right, that's the kennels cleaned out and given fresh bedding; everything seems okay there.' Pulled out of his musings, Nick turned to see a vet nurse with a blonde crop. She was dressed in purple scrubs and had a cheery expression.

'Nick, this is Becky,' said Chris. 'She's one of our three vet nurses; she and Bro—'

He was unable to finish his sentence thanks to the door bursting open, admitting a blast of bitterly cold air and a kerfuffle as a huge Great Dane hurled itself through the door dragging a petite woman on the end of its lead.

'Tiny! Heel!' said the petite woman. Tiny obeyed, stopping so abruptly his owner crashed into him.

Tiny? thought Nick, amused.

'Ah, here's my first patient,' said Chris. 'Morning, Mrs Winter-bottom, if you and Tiny just take a seat, I won't be a moment.

The gentle giant surveyed the room, his gaze settling on Maudie who looked on, adopting a superior air.

Chris glanced from Maudie to Nick and flicked his eyebrows, entertained by Maudie's response. 'Right, hope you have a good first day, Nick. Catch up with you later this morning,' he said as he headed towards his consulting room.

'Thanks.' Nick looked down at Maudie. 'Right, miss, let's get you settled before my first patient arrives.'

SEVEN

BROGAN

Adjusting her auburn ponytail, Brogan gave one last check in the staffroom mirror. Being in scrubs again gave her a bigger thrill than she'd expected, gave her a sense of purpose. The love of her old job came rushing back. She felt like a different person; a more confident version of the one she'd been for the last three years. She released a happy sigh, smiling at her reflection. Her life was back on track.

A moment later, she was following Jules on a quick tour around the surgery which was even more spacious than it seemed from the outside. Lady Carolyn Hammondely's plan to convert the buildings for business use had been genius. The surgery really was state of the art and must have cost a fortune for the vets to kit out. As well as the reception area, and the two consulting rooms, there was an operating theatre, a lab, kennels and recovery rooms, as well as the staffroom which was fitted out more like a comfy living room, complete with a little kitchenette and cosy stove. Jules pointed out a washing machine and tumble drier where they could launder their scrubs rather than risk contamination by wearing them out of the surgery and taking them home. Brogan liked that standards were high.

Wilf had taken no time to get comfy with Oscar, settling down in front of the stove. 'Someone looks right at home,' Jules said, making Brogan smile. Another good sign.

Jules gave her a run down on the surgery's routine and the rest of the staff. 'It's a great team, we all muck in. And you'll love Georgia,' she said of the part-time vet. 'Well, I suppose I would say that since she's my cousin, but it's true.' Jules flashed her a wide smile. 'She moved back to Arkleby from York six months ago; works two days a week – Wednesday and Thursday. She's got two little boys – they're a real handful, but don't tell her I said that! – and she's really bubbly and friendly. Oh, and she's horse mad. In fact you've probably seen her trotting around the moors on her mare.'

'Mm, I have. I didn't realise she worked here until I came for my interview and she was part of the panel. She seems lovely; I'm looking forward to meeting her properly,' Brogan said, an image of a woman she'd encountered with whilst walking her canine charges out on the moor, appearing in her mind. They'd nodded and said hello, exchanged brief pleasantries about the weather, but that had been it. Still, Brogan remembered thinking the young woman had a friendly face. Another good reason to work here to add to her list.

With the tour over, Brogan had one last check on Wilf to make sure he'd settled. Content he had, she smoothed down her tunic and drew in a deep breath, pushing down the jangle of nerves that had started to surface. 'Right, here goes. You've got this; it's going to be all right.' She turned to Wilf who was watching her from his toasty place in front of the stove. 'You be a good lad, okay? I'll pop back and see you soon.'

Wilf responded with a wag of his tail.

Pulling the staffroom door shut, Brogan gave the handle a quick jiggle, making sure it was closed properly; it wouldn't do to have Wilf escape and get up to mischief, especially on their first day. Heading towards the reception area, she could hear Jules chatting away, a deep voice joining her lighter tone. No doubt the first client had arrived. Brogan's nerves jumped back to life. *No going back now* she thought as she headed through the door to see Jules in conversation with a tall, broad-shouldered man with dark-blond hair.

'Ah, talk about perfect timing, here's our new vet nurse,' Jules said.

The tall man turned round, his smile faltering and his mouth falling open as he clocked Brogan.

Brogan gasped, her eyes growing wide. It was as if a thunderbolt had struck her with such force it made her heart perform an enormous flip. Just like the one that had knocked the wind out of her sails when she'd first set eyes on the tall, blond man two weeks ago.

'Brogan!'

'Nick!'

They both spoke at once, each looking at the other in disbelief.

'But I thought... I mean... You're a vet nurse? Here?' he asked as his eyes ran over her scrubs, his brow creased in confusion. 'When did?... I had no idea you lived round here. Oh wow! This is... *great* news,' he said, as the penny obviously dropped, a smile spreading across his handsome face and lighting up those clear blue eyes she remembered all too well.

Realising her mouth had been hanging open for what felt like too long – which she was certain couldn't be an attractive look – Brogan clamped it shut. She took a big swallow, marshalling the thoughts that had sent her careering back to *that* day. *Oh, jeez. Ahem. Never mind that day! What about that night?* said a little voice. She rubbed her brow, as if hoping to erase the memory that had been scorched on her brain. Erase the memory that was, at this precise moment, excruciatingly embarrassing. This couldn't be happening, could it? He was supposed to be moving out of the area, or so he'd told her. And she'd never expected to see him again, which was exactly why she'd behaved so... so... out of character, for want of a better expression. *Ughh! Don't go there!* She could feel her face growing hotter by the minute, her knees going suddenly weak. *Get a grip and pull yourself together, woman!* Which, after a shock of this magnitude, in her small, quiet life where nothing out of the ordinary ever happened, was easier said than done. Especially when *that* day had been extremely out of the ordinary.

While her brain was scrambling for something to say, Brogan became acutely aware of Jules glancing between them. 'Um, I er...' She cleared her throat. 'I work here; it's my first day.'

'So it would seem. You didn't mention it when...' Still smiling, Nick's gaze flicked over to Jules. 'I mean, same here; it's my first day too. I'm the new vet.'

'Oh.' If Brogan wasn't mistaken, he seemed happy about this sudden revelation. And it looked suspiciously like the shocked expression in his eyes had been replaced by a twinkle. The very twinkle she remembered from *that* day, and the very one that had made her heart behave with such wild and reckless abandon. *'It wasn't just your heart that behaved with such "reckless abandon", lady, the rest of you didn't do so badly either,'* said the little voice, making Brogan squirm inside. She sincerely hoped Jules hadn't spotted the twinkle too.

'Don't tell me you two know each other?' Jules was evidently entertained by their surprise.

'You could say,' said Nick, his smile pulling wider.

'Yeah, we met once, not long ago actually; just briefly though.' Relieved to have been able to formulate a coherent sentence at last, Brogan was now having a battle to make eye contact with either of them as an image of herself and Nick together took centre stage in her mind. *Jeez!* Was it possible for her face to get any hotter? she wondered.

'Yeah, that's right.' Nick's eyebrows did an amused dance. She could see he was biting down on something mischievous to say. 'It was a brief encounter.'

For a fleeting moment, their eyes locked, unspoken words passing between them as they both recalled that day; an invisible thread linking them to a moment of intimacy. Brogan's heart took off with a gallop. *A brief encounter? Did he really just say that?*

Mrs Winterbottom made herself comfortable in her seat, folding her arms as she and Tiny looked on with interest.

'So we can dispense with formal introductions, then,' said Jules, grinning.

'Er, yeah, I suppose so,' said Brogan. Even she could hear the hesitancy in her voice, heaven knew what Jules must be thinking. She was dreading the questions that would inevitably follow once the two women were on their own.

'No, none necessary.' Nick shook his head. 'It's really great to see you again, Brogan.' He sounded like he meant it.

Brogan blinked several times in an attempt to regain her composure. Something told her she should reply with a similar sentiment, but her mouth couldn't form the words. Instead, she shifted her attention to the fluffy black Labrador-type dog on the end of the lead Nick was holding. The said Labrador-type dog was looking up at Brogan with a level of interest she found disconcerting; it was almost as if she *knew*! 'Who's this?' she asked, adding a faux breeziness to her voice. Talking about dogs put her right back in her comfort zone.

Seemingly reluctant to pull his eyes away from Brogan, Nick followed her gaze. 'Ah, this is Maudie. She's a Lab with a dash of Doodle thrown in, and despite her snooty expression, she's actually very friendly with those who've gained her seal of approval.' He glanced at the clock on the wall. 'Actually, I need to get her settled in the staffroom before my first patient arrives.'

'Hello, Maudie, you're very pretty,' said Brogan.

'And doesn't she know it?' Nick said, a laugh in his voice.

Brogan was torn between wanting to approach Maudie and give her a fuss, and feeling intensely awkward about moving closer to Nick – which, after their "history" seemed a little strange. In the end, the urge to stroke Maudie won out. 'Hello, girl,' she said, offering her hand for the Labrador to sniff before giving her a tickle behind the ears. 'Ooh, aren't you lovely and soft, eh?'

Maudie wagged her fluffy tail vigorously, apparently thrilled by the attention from this new person. All the while, Brogan was aware of Nick's eyes on her as her mind raced over the implications of what she'd just learnt.

He was the new vet here? Really? The very place she'd just got a new job. He was going to be her *boss*. How had this happened? More importantly, how on earth was it going to pan out? Her brain was in turmoil. Was she going to be able to keep her job here? She really hoped so. Or was it going to be too excruciatingly uncomfortable? The thought of going back to walking dogs over the moors in the depths of winter sent her heart plummeting. She'd been so looking forward to resurrecting her career as a vet nurse. Where had her head been when she... *Ughh!* She couldn't even bear to think about it. She'd never behaved so recklessly before. She cringed inwardly at what her grandparents would have thought of her if they'd known. Her actions that day had been so utterly out of character. And now look what had happened; it had come back to give her a great big bite on the backside. Typical! He could be a player for all she knew, wouldn't be able to wait to share the details of their "brief encounter" with Chris. What would her new boss think of her after hearing that? That thought sent a wave of nausea rushing over her.

Nick's voice pulled her back to the present.

'Well, this is a first. Maudie doesn't normally give strangers the time of day; she takes a long time to get to know folk, as a rule.'

Brogan risked a glance up to see Nick looking down at her, his eyes soft. She quickly looked away. 'In that case, I'm very honoured, Maudie.' It was somehow easier to communicate through Maudie who was savouring the attention from Brogan, nudging her hand for more ear ruffling when Brogan paused to listen to Nick.

Just then, the main door opened and a lady holding a plastic pet carrier stepped inside, a cold breeze sneaking in with her.

'Morning, Mrs Simpkin. Just take a seat,' said Jules, cheerily. 'Nick, here's your first appointment.'

'Right then, I'd best get Maudie settled in the staffroom. Come on, miss.' Nick clicked his tongue and Maudie followed.

As soon as he'd left the room, Jules didn't waste a moment. She beckoned Brogan over to her and dived right into her interrogation.

'So, how come you know Nick?' she asked, her expression saying she knew there was more to the situation than met the eye, with the possibility of some juicy gossip. 'Have you known him long?'

'Oh, I just met him at a—'

At that moment, the phone rang. *Thank goodness!* Brogan felt her insides sag with relief.

'Stay right there,' said Jules, snatching up the phone and answering in her best "telephone" voice. 'Good morning, Danskelfe Vets, Jules speaking. How can I help you?'

Jules was still on the phone when Nick came back into the waiting room, wearing what looked like an "I-can't-believe-this-is-actually-happening" smile. Brogan tried to ignore the somersault in her stomach as she met his blue-eyed gaze, which wasn't easy when images of the last time she'd seen him had rather inopportunely pushed their way back into her mind.

'Right then,' he said, rubbing his hands together, before briefly switching his attention to his first appointment. 'Won't be a moment, Mrs Simpkin.' He turned back to Brogan, lowering his voice. 'I wouldn't mind a hand for a minute.' He raised an enquiring eyebrow as he headed into his consulting room, holding the door open for her to join him.

Brogan followed, her heart rate upping its speed. *Uh-oh.* How should she play this? Act thrilled to see him? Act indifferent? She needed more time to think; more time to get her head around this whole new situation.

Closing the door, Nick spun round, his eyes wide with wonder. 'Brogan! I can't believe this. I had no idea you lived around here.' He pushed his fingers into his fringe. 'How've you been? – you look beaut... er, you look well, by the way.'

Oh, that deep, rich voice, it had the power to turn her legs to jelly. She met his gaze shyly, anticipation crackling in the air around them. And those blue eyes were every bit as vivid as she remembered... that strong, square jaw. Ooh, and don't mention the way his generous mouth had felt on hers; all warm and soft and delicious. *Mmm.* Even the thought was enough to turn her insides molten. She felt the burn of another blush, the memory knocking her off kilter for a moment. She needed to take control of herself. 'I, er... yeah, I'm fine thanks. I live just out of Lytell Stangdale, on a smallholding.' She wanted to add, '*And I didn't know you lived round here, never mind worked at this place! You didn't breathe a word about that!*' but she couldn't seem to get the words from her brain to her mouth. Instead, she just looked at him, as scenes from their first encounter continued to play out in her mind. It may have been brief, but the impact it had made on her had been something else, as had the feelings he'd stirred in her – and if the way she was currently feeling was anything to go by, he clearly still did. Truth be told, she was slightly embarrassed to admit that he'd occupied her daydreams for an inordinate amount of time since then.

'I live in Arkleby; just moved there actually. I'm renting a cottage that thinks it's a fridge; it's absolutely freezing. I can't seem to get the place warm.'

'Oh, right.' Nick's words pulled her out of her musings. Frowning, she said, 'So what happened to moving to the Dales?' She was sure that's where he'd told her he was going. In fact she distinctly recalled him referring to it as a "fresh start".

A shadow flitted across his face, making her regret asking him. 'Er, yeah, I was; change of plan.' He pushed his smile back up.

'Oh, right.' *Oh, right? Is that all you can say, woman?* She really needed to expand her vocabulary, but it was difficult when there was so much to absorb and her brain was struggling to play catch up.

'Yeah. Long story short, I bumped into Chris who told me Paul Jenkins, who was supposed to be joining him here, had backed out at the last minute. We got chatting and he asked me if I fancied taking Paul's place. It was an offer I couldn't refuse. Didn't need to think twice about it actually. I hadn't signed a contract with the new place I was supposed to be heading to – in truth, I hadn't been able to shake the feeling that something just hadn't felt right about joining that practice. And, much as I love the Dales, my heart had never been in moving there; it was a classic knee-jerk reaction.'

She couldn't help but wonder what the catalyst to his "knee-jerk" reaction had been.

'It's as if my bumping into Chris was meant to be... for lots of reasons. I like to think of it as serendipity,' Nick said with a smile, making Brogan wonder what exactly he meant by that. 'So, how come you're working here? I thought you had a dog-walking business.'

'Well, it's kind of similar to what happened to you, I suppose.'

EIGHT

NICK

Nick listened as Brogan gave him an abridged version of how she'd heard there was a new vets' surgery opening up in one of the recently converted Danskelfe Castle Estate units and had been hopeful of applying for a job there. She'd been disappointed to find all the vet nurse positions had been filled. However, just a few months after, she'd been surprised to receive a telephone call from Chris Crabtree. By a stroke of luck, the husband of one of the vet nurses had been offered a lucrative job working down south which meant, as the family were upping sticks and moving, she'd handed in her notice.

'Which is when he rang me, asking if I was still interested in the job,' Brogan said. 'I couldn't believe my luck.'

Nick nodded, his mind going back to Chris mentioning there was a new vet nurse starting who'd made a good impression on him; he'd said he thought she'd be perfect for the practice, had a nice way about her. It was clearly Brogan he'd been talking about.

'Sounds like serendipity has struck twice,' he said, looking into her dark-green eyes, edged with thick lashes; they were every bit as captivating as he remembered when he'd first looked into them two weeks ago.

He watched as two spots of colour bloomed on the apples of her cheeks. Seeing her here like this, so unexpectedly, had lifted his spirits inexorably after his doomed call with Loretta. He'd never expected to see her again, but now, here she was making his heart beat faster, just like before. She looked so beautiful, her face all fresh and free of make-up, her freckles on display in all their glory. He recalled her saying how she hated them, but he thought they looked lovely.

'So, is this a permanent move? I mean, do you plan on staying here, at Danskelfe Vets?' Brogan asked.

It took a moment before his thoughts got back on track. 'Er, yeah, that's the plan.' He nodded. 'With a view to going into partnership with Chris if everything works out.' Right now, he really hoped it did. 'And you? Do you see this as being permanent for you?'

'Yeah, I do.' She gave a small smile that triggered a surge of happiness through him. 'At least, I hope so.'

There was something about being around this young woman that made things feel right, made him feel uplifted. He couldn't put it into words, but he'd felt it when they'd first met. It had made him glad he'd decided to go to the wedding. They'd clicked instantly; something unspoken had made him feel he could just be himself with her. He'd never felt so at ease with someone, especially someone he'd only just met. Though he wasn't certain of where she was from, it was what had originally made him question his decision to go to the Dales. Until she'd just disappeared, leaving him with no way of contacting her. His newly uplifted spirits had taken a nose-dive then.

Nick had been in two minds about going to the wedding on his own since he and Loretta were no longer a couple, but his older brother, Matt, had talked him into it. A couple of days before the ceremony was due to take place in a swanky hotel on the outskirts of York, the pair were chewing the fat over a pint in The Golden Fleece pub in Middleton-le-Moors.

'You'll have a great time, Nick. And it'll do you good; you could do with letting your hair down after what Loretta did to you. And you never know, you might get lucky with one of the bridesmaids,' Matt said, waggling his eyebrows and giving Nick a teasing nudge. 'You know what they say about getting back on the horse...'

'Hmph! Not so sure about that, or your analogy.' The bridesmaids in question popped into Nick's mind. One had a reputation for being prickly and, from what he'd heard, she was no stranger to throwing the odd right hook when she'd had a few drinks down her. He didn't relish getting involved in anything like *that*. Two, he knew, were already married. Which had left Nina, who, as far as he could gather, was single. The downside – and it was a really big downside – was that she worked with his ex, which put her firmly out of the equation. From what Loretta had told him, she and Nina couldn't stand the sight of each other. After introducing them at her work's Christmas function, Loretta was convinced Nina had the hots for Nick, which, as far as he was concerned, was even more reason to steer clear. The mere thought of what Loretta would have to say if she got wind that he'd been up close and personal with Nina was enough to make his toes curl. It wouldn't matter that they'd broken up, she'd accuse him of hooking up with her nemesis just to get back at her. He wasn't strong enough to face Loretta on the warpath. No, Nina was to be avoided at all costs. And besides, he really wasn't in the mood for a dalliance of any kind. His heart was wounded, as was his pride. Plus, he'd be rubbish company.

'You've got to go, Toby's a good mate of yours. And you don't have to hang around for the evening do, as long as you show your face at the wedding and the reception afterwards; that's the main thing – trust me, I know from what it cost Brooke and me at that place we got hitched, the amount they'll be forking out per head for the food will be eye-watering; it'd be seriously bad form not to turn up. At least they had time to arrange someone to take Loretta's place, but three days before the big day is too short notice, I'm afraid, Nick. Once the reception's over and done with, you can get the hell out of there if you find you're really not enjoying yourself.'

Nick dragged a hand down his face. The sooner he moved on, got on with his life and put Loretta out of his mind, the better. He heaved a sigh. 'Yeah, I suppose you're right. I'll go.'

'That's the spirit.' Matt gave him a sound pat on the arm.

Toby hadn't been too surprised nor devastated when Nick had told him Loretta wasn't going to be joining him. In fact, Nick could've sworn he looked relieved. 'Hey, no need to apologise, mate. Me and Ciara heard what had happened. We feel really bad for the way she treated you; it's shameful. And we'd rather have you at the ceremony than her,' he'd said, a sympathetic expression on his face. 'Honest, don't give it another thought. I think Ciara has someone in mind who might be able to fill her shoes – I don't mean as a date for you,' he'd said, hurriedly. 'It's mainly for the meal at the reception; it'd be a shame for it to go to waste.'

'Thanks for being so understanding, Tobes.' Nick had been relieved to hear they'd got someone lined up to take Loretta's place; they'd obviously discussed what to do if she wasn't going to join him, and he'd been able to understand their situation. He only hoped it wouldn't be too short notice for the "someone" they had in mind.

Still, he couldn't help but think what he'd much rather do on Saturday was take Maudie for a cobweb-clearing walk on the moors and get lost in his own thoughts, running through his mind the things he still had to do in preparation for his new life in the Dales. His "fresh start" – which actually didn't feel very "fresh" at all. It felt more like he was running away, but, hey, maybe that would be better for him; put some distance between him and Loretta. He could finish the day off nicely with a takeaway from his favourite Indian restaurant in Middleton-le-Moors. Yep, that was way more appealing than going to a wedding in some fancy hotel and socialising with a bunch of people he hardly knew or had never met before; making small talk was way down his list of things he'd like to do. Having a romantic encounter with a stranger was even lower. In fact, it was so low, it hadn't even made it onto the list.

NINE

NICK

Saturday 19th November

Nick ran his finger around his collar; he was feeling decidedly uncomfortable in the stiflingly hot ceremony room, his plus-one glaringly noticeable by her absence. Classical music burbled away softly in the background. He cast his gaze around, taking in the registrar who was standing before a large bay window that was festooned with elaborate swagged curtains. There was a huge floral display in the centre, its heady perfume filling the room. The registrar was smiling as she said something to Toby and his brother – who was also his best man – and the three of them laughed. Nick turned his attention to the congregation, his eye alighting on a pretty young woman in an emerald-green silk dress who was sitting over on the bride's side. She had full lips and striking auburn hair that fell over her shoulders in luxurious waves. As if sensing him watching her, she turned and met his gaze, their eyes locking for a moment. She smiled and a bolt of attraction shot through him with such force it took his breath away. *Wow! What the heck's going on here?* This was a first for him. Transfixed, he returned her smile, his heart taking off with a gallop.

The ceremony passed by in a blur, with thoughts of the

beautiful redhead and the feelings she'd aroused taking up every inch of space in his mind. He'd been unable to resist the urge to steal another look at her – well, several actually – and, each time, that same feeling came rushing back, surging through him. He raked his fingers through his hair. It was intoxicating. She'd caught him watching, but he still couldn't stop himself, couldn't tear his eyes away from her. The only time his thoughts had been occupied by someone else was when it was time to sing along to one of the songs in the Order of Service. The lady standing behind him had a voice so loud and so eye-wateringly harsh, Nick had almost jumped out of his skin when she'd started singing. She'd let rip with such force, he'd actually been able to feel her breath on the back of his neck. He'd caught the redhead's eye and they'd both struggled to stifle their giggles like a couple of mischievous kids in a school assembly. And judging by the snorts that were going on around them, they weren't the only ones.

Before the ceremony was over, Nick had found himself determined to seek out the beautiful stranger, but as they'd all filed out and made their way into the garden for photos, he'd lost sight of her and had found himself drawn into a conversation with the lady with the "voice" and her husband, all the while scanning the garden for the mystery redhead. He couldn't recall a word the couple had said, his mind had been so full of this captivating stranger. Before he knew it, it was time for the reception and he was cursing that he still hadn't seen her.

Nick was the first one to his table and had just sat down when his eyes alighted on the mystery redhead, who rather fortuitously, appeared to be heading his way. He watched as she worked her way around the seats before picking up the name card at the empty space next to him. 'Oh, at last! I was beginning to think they'd forgotten to include me.' She smiled, holding up the card that said "Brogan Hopwood" in a cursive hand. 'I've so been looking forward to the meal; I'm absolutely starving.'

His spirits soared as he watched her pull out the chair and sit down. He sent up a silent thank you. Maybe coming here wasn't such a bad idea after all, he mused.

'Hi, Brogan Hopwood,' he said, holding out his hand. 'I'm Nick. Nick Heuston. Good to meet you.'

'Wow! Nick Heuston, that's a really cool name. You sound like you're an astronaut or have a job in something wildly exciting like space exploration.' She gave him a wide smile and took his hand. 'Good to meet you too.'

Her small hand felt soft and cool in his, her touch sending a frisson of excitement through him. 'Ah, I hate to disappoint you, but I'm afraid I'm not an astronaut. In fact, I'm nothing even remotely like an astronaut, nor do I have anything to do with space exploration, but it was one of the jobs I wanted to do when I was a little boy, if that counts?'

'Hmm.' She pursed her lips and tipped her head to one side as if giving his suggestion some serious consideration. 'You know, I reckon it could just about scrape through.' The throaty giggle that followed was delicious and made his stomach leap.

'Well, thank goodness for that,' he said.

Brogan tucked her bag under her seat and turned to him. 'So, the burning question is, have your ears managed to recover from the "singing" – or should I say caterwauling?'

'Only just,' he said, laughing. 'It really was quite something.' And it's not the only thing, he thought as he admired Brogan's dark green eyes, flecked with burnished gold.

'Your face when she first started was hilarious! It made me want to burst out laughing more than the singing itself.' She pressed her hand to her mouth to suppress a bubble of laughter.

Oh, there was that giggle again. It instilled an instant feeling of joy in him, and it was infectious. 'Sorry about that, but her voice came out with such force it just about took the skin off the back of my neck,' he said, laughing and catching her eye.

'Wow! That's some talent; exfoliate the person in front while you sing. Novel.' She nodded.

'Indeed,' he said, his eyebrows raised in agreement, his eyes drawn to her full mouth.

'Don't see it catching on though, do you?' she asked, resting her elbows on the table and picking up her name card, fiddling with it. He noticed she had short, neat nails, free of varnish. In fact, she didn't appear to be wearing much make-up at all, maybe something on her lips; they looked glossy. Not that he was an expert, of course, but he recalled all the kit Loretta would use to get ready for a night out. She'd had brushes for this, brushes for that; she even had odd-shaped sponges – he hadn't a clue what she'd used them for. He'd found it mind boggling, especially when, in his opinion, she didn't need it. He much preferred her fresh-faced rather than all sculpted with huge "coloured-in" eyebrows that sat above her eyes like a couple of chunky caterpillars. Not that he'd ever voiced this to her. His eyes ran over Brogan's face, taking in her fresh complexion and the crop of freckles that ran across her nose and cheeks. *Mmm.* She was clearly unaware of how attractive she was.

Realising it might look like he was staring, his mind pinged back to her question with a start. 'The singing would have to be at least in tune if I was to consider it again,' he said with faux serious- ness, though he couldn't stop his smile from growing wider.

'Yes, I think that's vital.' Brogan nodded, giving him a sidelong look, a twinkle of mischief in her eyes. A second later, the pair of them burst out laughing again, heads turning beside them.

Before he knew it, they'd been talking non-stop for hours, and had barely conversed with the other guests sitting either side of them. In that time, he'd managed to establish that she was single, which had cheered him up no end – though he'd found it hard to believe that her last relationship had been a whole three years ago. The plates had been cleared, speeches delivered and glasses raised in toast, all seemingly in the blink of an eye. Darkness had fallen without him realising and now the thud of music could be heard, heralding the start of the disco in the function room next door. It didn't take long for the guests to be drawn to it, with Toby's sisters performing a slightly merry conga as they made their way there. Soon just Nick and Brogan remained with staff clearing away around them, the clink of crockery in the background. His brother's suggestion of leaving after the meal couldn't have been further from Nick's mind right now. And neither could Loretta. Nick couldn't remember when he'd last felt this lighthearted.

Turning to Brogan, he said, 'Don't suppose I can tempt you to a whirl around the dance floor, can I?'

'A *whirl?*' she asked with another of her infectious giggles that set his heart stampeding. 'Sounds like something my grandad would've said to my grandma. "Fancy a whirl, our lass?"' She exaggerated her North Yorkshire accent.

Nick laughed and cringed at the same time. 'Yep, sorry about that. I have been told I'm seriously uncool at times. In fact, I'd go as far as to say, I've honed being uncool to perfection.' He gave a light-hearted shrug.

'Well, it's lucky for you I'm rather fond of "seriously uncool". I'm no stranger to it myself.' She grinned. 'And, yes, I'd love a "whirl", but just let me go and freshen up first, my hair feels all frazzled like it needs taming.' She smoothed it down with her hand and straightened one of the sparkly hairslides beside her ear. 'I bet I look like a lion that's been caught in a wind-tunnel.'

Nick chuckled, attempting to picture her analogy. 'You really don't, your hair's lovely.'

'Thank you,' she said shyly, her face growing pink. 'I'll be really quick.'

They arranged to meet at the sofa by the large Christmas tree in the hotel foyer, rather than risk struggling to seek each other out in the darkened function room which was packed with dancing bodies. Nick hoped she'd return, and hadn't just used the excuse to freshen up as a means of escaping him. But something told him she wouldn't do that; that he'd see her again. His heart fluttered at the thought.

And just ten minutes later he was proved right when he glanced up to see her making her way over to him, her hair freshly brushed, the light picking out golden highlights. He felt a little flame ignite in the pit of his stomach. There was something inordinately special about this girl.

'Hi,' she said, beaming. 'Ready for that "whirl"?'

He gulped. *More than you'll ever know.* He cleared his throat, recalibrating, inhaling the spicy perfume she'd obviously spritzed while she'd been away. 'Er, yeah, I sure am.' He noted she was wearing a pair of flat, green satin ballet pumps, adorned with sequins, which meant, at six-foot-three, he towered above her. He held out his hand and led her to the disco.

'Oh, I love this song,' she said, her voice raised to be heard over the music. She pulled him onto the dancefloor as one tune segued into the next. 'Come on, Nicky Boy, let's "whirl"!'

They danced non-stop for a good half-a-dozen songs, Nick's tie loosened, his brow glistening with perspiration. 'Fancy a drink?' he asked, bending to speak in her ear. Her hair brushed against his face, stirring up the scent of her perfume. His pulse took off again.

'Love one! I'm gasping,' she said, her eyes shining.

The queue at the bar of the function room was three deep with no one getting served any time soon so Nick suggested going to the main bar in the hotel. 'Good plan,' said Brogan, following him, the music muting as the door closed behind them.

As he'd expected this bar was quiet and he was served quickly. He handed Brogan her glass of chilled Pinot Grigio, saying, 'Don't know about you, but I could do with a breath of fresh air.' The heating at the hotel had been cranked up to compensate for the recent cold snap and everywhere was stiflingly warm. It didn't help that he'd kept his suit jacket on while he'd been dancing.

'Actually, I'd love some.'

'That's settled then.' Smiling, he held out his hand which she took almost shyly. He liked how her hand felt in his.

By the door was a basket filled with neatly folded fleece blankets. Nick handed one to Brogan before taking one for himself. 'Thank you. They've thought of everything,' she said.

Outside, they found a covered, paved area set out with all-weather rattan furniture. Fairy lights were twinkling everywhere.

They were strung from the timbers of the roof, wrapped around the chunky oak posts, draped over shrubs and the Christmas trees in pots, their glow sparkling over the frost. The effect was magical.

'This looks perfect,' said Nick. 'You okay to sit here for a bit?'

'Oh, it's so pretty. I'd love to.'

She wrapped one of the fleeces around her shoulders and sat down on the rattan sofa. Nick, still needing to cool off, didn't feel the need for his fleece just yet. He sat down beside her, acutely aware of her presence next to him. How could a woman he'd just met arouse such feelings in him? The urge to put his arm around her was overwhelming, but he wasn't sure she'd welcome it, so he took a sip of his beer instead, casting his eyes up to the inky-blue sky that glittered with stars. He was suddenly gripped by the feeling that there was something special about this day; something that would have a seismic impact on his life. There was no way he could ever say it out loud – at least, not without running the risk of sounding absolutely bonkers – but he just *knew*, could feel it in his bones, that this moment with this beautiful girl beside him was going to be momentous. He smiled, feeling inordinately happy, and released a contented sigh.

Brogan turned to him. 'You okay?'

He looked into those big green eyes, taking a moment before he answered, his gaze dropping to her full mouth. 'Brogan, can I ask you something?'

'Er, yes, course.' She nodded, looking directly at him, the hint of a frown creasing her brow.

'Can I kiss you?'

She grinned. 'Yes, please.'

TEN

BROGAN

Brogan hadn't expected today to turn out quite the way it had. Getting a phone call from Ciara (who she knew from when she used to live in Skeltwick) a few weeks ago with a last-minute invitation to her wedding had been a big enough surprise, but this situation with Nick had capped that. Big time. To think her initial feeling had been to turn Ciara down, but she'd been persuasive. 'I've checked and the hotel's still got a couple of rooms available so you could stay over, wouldn't have to drive,' she'd said. Feeling at a low ebb, the prospect of spending the rest of her life alone taking up way too much of her headspace recently, and thinking it would be a change of scenery at least, Brogan finally agreed. Her best friends, Anoushka and Kristy had encouraged her too, telling her she could slip away to her room if she felt things were getting too much for her, treat herself to a luxury bubble bath using the specially created toiletries the hotel was noted for. And now she was really rather pleased she'd taken their advice.

Nick was easy to talk to. They'd connected straightaway; it felt like she'd known him for years, which was bizarre because she was usually quite reserved with strangers, not letting her guard down until she felt comfortable with them. But with Nick it felt different. She felt like she could be herself with him, didn't need to put her barriers up. And it was nice flirting with him too. She thought she'd forgotten how – not that she'd had much practice! She hadn't dated anyone since her split with Archie three years earlier. He'd been the last man who'd had the full extent of her flirting repertoire, and she'd been with him for four years. Yep, in any ordinary situation, chatting and getting flirty with a bloke, she would, without a doubt, be as rusty as an old garden gate. But it didn't feel that way with Nick. It helped that he had the most gorgeous clear blue eyes; she'd found it hard not to gaze into them. His fringe was cute too, with its cow lick that made it stick up no matter how many times he tried to flatten it down. She'd never been a big believer in fate, and would probably call herself a sceptic, but something deep inside her told her he was the reason she was meant to be at the wedding. She didn't question how she knew; she just did. Which was why she didn't hesitate when he asked if he could kiss her; she wanted it more than anything else in the world at that moment.

Feeling Nick's lips on hers was utterly mind-blowing. They were warm and soft and... boy, did he know how to use them. She'd never been kissed like that before; the surge of feelings it aroused were all-encompassing. With a groan, she pushed her fingers into his hair, kissing him harder. She was tingling all over, including the places she'd forgotten could tingle! Before she knew it, they were making their way back to his room, and the door had hardly clicked shut behind them before they were tearing each other's clothes off, their kisses growing more urgent by the second. The thought that she was glad she'd treated herself to some new lacy underwear flitted through her mind. She was relieved that she wasn't wearing her usual misshapen belly-whackers.

Afterwards, they lay in a tangled mass, sheets knotted, legs entwined, clammy skin against skin, a warm, sultry glow around the room. Brogan's head was resting on Nick's chest; she could hear the solid thud, thud of his heartbeat, feel the warmth of his toned body as he absently ran his fingers over the top of her arm. How was it possible she'd only known him for a few hours when it felt like she'd known him for years? She'd never felt such contentment, as if this was exactly where she was meant to be.

Nick pressed a kiss to her head before tucking his fingers under her chin and tilting her face to his. He kissed her again, rolling onto his side, propping his head up on his hand. 'I just wanted to look at you again, remind myself how beautiful you are.'

Brogan felt her face burn crimson. Feeling suddenly shy, she pulled her gaze away from him. 'Don't be daft. I'm not beautiful, I'm ordinary; you've got beer goggles on.'

'I have not! And you are most definitely not ordinary. I couldn't stop looking at you the moment I first set eyes on you.'

'I think that's called morbid fascination,' she said, self-deprecatingly, following her words with a giggle. 'I've got wild red hair that I can't tame no matter how hard I try, more freckles on my face than any person needs, there's a bump on my nose, I've got pasty skin, oh, and a big bum for good measure. And that's just for starters.'

Nick leant down and kissed her tenderly. 'I think you must look at yourself through some sort of wonky comedy mirrors. I can't see anything of the person you've just described. Like I said, you're beautiful, and your hair's stunning.' He ran his fingers through it. 'It's your crowning glory.'

'Hang on a minute, are you sure you're a northern man? 'Cos if you are, you should know that's not the way northern blokes are supposed to talk. I was led to believe it was more comments like, "By 'eck, you scrub up well, lass", that kind of thing. And if you don't mind me saying, you're in danger of sounding a little bit cheesy.'

Nick threw his head back and laughed. 'Point taken. And, yes, I'm very definitely a northern man – born in York actually, got the birth certificate to prove it – and I have to confess, I've never spoken to a woman like this before. Not that I've told any of my girlfriends they "scrub up well", but nor am I the caveman type with a habit of clubbing any woman who takes my eye over the head and dragging her off to the nearest cave. But in truth, I've never had the compulsion to say the things I've said to you.' He took a moment, as if considering this. 'Which can mean only one thing: it's your fault, you've brought it out in me. I hold you entirely responsible.'

'It that right?' She smiled, gazing up at him.

''Fraid so.' His eyes twinkled.

'Well, you don't want to let your mates hear you talking like that, or they'll be chasing you out of town and confiscating your flat cap.'

'Hmm. Good point.' He grinned down at her and kissed the tip of her nose. 'How did you know I have a flat cap?'

Brogan found this banter enjoyable; it was far easier to navigate than having compliments bestowed upon her. She wasn't good at accepting them, didn't know how to respond to them. She snuggled into Nick. He felt solid and safe and warm. She didn't ever want this night to end.

Nick flopped back on the pillow, pulling her closer to him. 'Don't know about you but I'm not in a hurry to re-join the celebrations downstairs. I'd much rather stay here with you.'

Brogan's heart swelled with happiness and she sighed contentedly. 'I'd rather stay here with you too.' *Is this really happening? How is it possible to feel this happy with someone I barely know?* She closed her eyes, savouring the moment. Much as it felt surreal, it also felt intrinsically right.

'In that case...' he said, leaning over her and pressing a tantalizing kiss to her lips, 'I've got a very good idea of how we can spend the rest of the evening.' He kissed her again and she felt her insides dissolve into a puddle.

ELEVEN

BROGAN

The first thing Brogan became aware of when she woke the following morning was how warm and comfy the bed was, the duvet soft and puffy. She blinked drowsily. The room was in darkness but for a shaft of light reaching in from the ensuite bathroom. *Ensuite bathroom?* Her bedroom didn't have an ensuite bathroom the last time she looked. Was she still asleep? Was she dreaming? Her feeling of disorientation was exacerbated by what appeared to be an arm covered in dark-blond hair thrown across her. Brogan blinked, trying to make sense of this. The owner of the arm stirred, making small murmuring sounds as he snuggled into her. Slowly, she turned until her gaze landed on... *Nick!* She froze momentarily, the events of the previous evening rushing back at her. 'Oh, my God!' She mouthed the words silently, clamping her hand to her forehead. She squeezed her eyes tight shut, trying to calm her stampeding heart. *What have I done?*

As carefully and stealthily as she could, Brogan began the delicate process of extricating herself from Nick's embrace. Each minuscule movement seemed to take forever but the last thing she wanted was to disturb him. How could she face him after *that*? She'd only just met him, for goodness' sake, and she'd spent the night with him. What must he think of her? What if his words of the previous night meant nothing and he wanted her gone as soon as he woke? *Oh, jeez!* How humiliating would that be? She needed to get out of there, get back to her room, and quick.

Holding her breath, she eased herself off the bed, her pulse thrumming loudly in her ears as she crept around the room in the semi-darkness in search of her clothes. They'd been scattered far and wide and, as she scooped them up, she felt herself blush at the memory of how urgent things had been once they'd arrived here the previous evening. She remembered Nick's kisses travelling down her neck... *Arghh! Don't go there!*

After wriggling into her dress, she tiptoed across the floor, her shoes in her hand, and very slowly pressed down on the door handle, hoping with all her might the door wouldn't squeak when it opened. She felt a huge surge of relief as it clicked shut on the other side, and she scurried silently back to her room.

She flung herself down on her neatly made bed, the sheets unruffled, unlike the one in Nick's room – they'd had a bloomin' good ruffling if her memory served her right. With a groan, she clapped her hand over her eyes as if to erase the images that had forced their way into her mind. Why did she have to go and remind herself of that? She pushed herself up on her elbows. What should she do? There was no way she could go down for breakfast later, risk seeing him there. That would be way, *way*, too embarrassing. He probably wouldn't want to have anything more to do with her now that they'd... *No! Stop thinking about that!* He might even ignore her, which, when she thought about it, would be excruciatingly awful. The feelings that had encompassed her body and mind last night hadn't simply withered and died; she hadn't imagined them. They were still surging round her but, in the cold (almost) light of day, she felt exposed and foolish. Foolish for letting herself get carried away with them. Foolish for believing his words – those wonderful things he'd whispered in her ear, the way he'd made her feel. *Oh!* She felt the memory rush over her in a shimmer. There was no way that could be real, no way he could have meant it; it was just part of his repertoire to get a girl into bed with him.

That was all. But in the moment, with all the heady emotions flying around, it had made her feel so incredibly good. 'Ah,' said a little voice, throwing cold water over her memories, 'you know what your grandma used to say: if something feels too good to be true, you can usually guarantee it is. And she was hardly ever wrong.'

With all these thoughts whirling around her mind, Brogan leapt to her feet. She glanced at the illuminated numbers of the clock on the phone by the bed. It was five-past-six. There was only one thing for it. She had to get away from here and, if she was quick, she'd could be changed and gone before he surfaced.

Hurriedly, she peeled off her dress and pulled on her jeans and jumper. Then she grabbed her overnight bag and threw her things in with little regard to how badly they'd be crumpled and creased which went against her usual "everything had to be folded neatly" way. She had no time to waste on that; she could sort it out when she got home.

Downstairs in reception, Brogan was a jittering ball of nerves, glancing around her as she settled her bill. She wouldn't feel calm until she was in her car and on her way home.

The one thing that hit her as her car bounced along the track to Pond Farm was that at least she and Nick hadn't had a chance to exchange numbers. She hadn't told him where she lived either, so he wouldn't be able to just turn up, trying to seek her out. Relief washed over her at the thought. Rather bizarrely, it hadn't cropped up in the conversation; probably because they were too busy talking about so many other things. She knew he was leaving for the Dales, but she didn't know where he was leaving from, nor did she know what he did for a living. Thinking about it, all she really knew about him was that he was called Nick Heuston and he was single – well, at least he'd told her he was single. Her heart plummeted. What if he was just a player? What if he'd just used her and she was just another conquest? Nausea churned in her stomach.

That thought was just too horrible to bear. She thought they'd had a connection, but had she just been fooling herself?

As her four-wheel drive nosed into the yard of the isolated smallholding, the realisation that she had more than likely been fooling herself hit her full on. She felt cheap and alone. The loneliness she'd felt since losing her grandparents suddenly engulfed her, reminding her how keenly she still felt their loss. What she'd give to talk to her grandma right now. She'd know the right things to make Brogan feel better; her words served up with a huge chunk of the latest cake she'd baked. Tears blurred her vision and she blinked quickly, wiping her hand under her nose with a sniff. 'Get a grip, Brogan,' she said to herself.

With a heavy sigh, she pushed open the porch door, silence rushing at her. The first thing Brogan decided she was going to do when it got to eight o'clock – which was the opening time for Ella Welford's kennels – was jump back in her car and go and get Wilf. She defied anyone not to feel happy around him, even the thought of him made her smile. Then she was going to message Anoushka and Kristy, see if they fancied heading to the Sunne that night. Wilf, Anoushka and Kristy, the three individuals guaranteed to make her feel better. Well, as long as Wilf hadn't been rolling in fox poo, that was.

TWELVE

NICK

Nick turned over in bed, the sheets rustling. His eyes opened slowly as sleep slipped away. He lay a moment in the soft light as memories of the previous evening filtered their way into his mind, a smile spreading across his face as he remembered. 'Brogan,' he said softly, turning to the pillow beside him, a wave of happiness filling his chest. In the next moment, his heart gave a leap. She'd gone!

Pushing himself up, he glanced around the room before snapping on the bedside lamp. He listened a moment, to see if there was any movement in the bathroom, but all he heard was the thudding of his heart and the muted sound of car tyres crunching over the gravel in the parking area outside.

He fell back onto his pillow, his bubble of happiness burst. He glanced at the clock; it was just after seven. When had she left? he wondered, rubbing his brow. He wasn't such a deep sleeper that he wouldn't have felt her get out of bed; she must have been deliberately quiet, not wanted him to hear her leave. He pushed his fingers into his fringe despondently. He'd been certain she'd felt the same connection that had driven him to act the way he had last night; been sure she'd felt the same frisson of being on the cusp of something special; something that came along only once in a lifetime – if you were lucky. He gave a mocking snort at his own foolishness. *Special connection. Pah!* He'd clearly been so desperate to hide the hurt Loretta had caused, he'd been kidding himself, allowed himself to get carried away on some crazy notion of finding the person he was so utterly convinced he was meant to be with; his soulmate. He slapped his hand down on the bed, cringing at how cheesy that sounded, hardly daring to believe that thought had actually run through his mind the previous evening – several times – that he'd actually believed that's what had happened. 'Another example of you being seriously uncool, mate,' he said aloud, throwing the duvet back and climbing out of bed.

Making his way to the bathroom, picking his way around last night's cast off clothing, something on the floor glinted, catching his eye. He stooped to pick it up, turning it over in his hand. It was one of the hairslides Brogan had been wearing. His pulse quickened. It must've fallen out of her hair when they'd been in the clutches of passion, tearing at each other's clothes.

As he'd drifted off to sleep last night, with Brogan wrapped in his arms, thoughts had tumbled into his mind. How he'd suggest spending the following day together, maybe go for a walk in the countryside, enjoy a hearty pub lunch afterwards. She'd utterly captivated him and he'd been eager to get to know her better. But her unexpected disappearance had scuppered those plans.

With happiness deserting him, he threw his stuff into his overnight bag and shrugged on his coat. He couldn't face breakfast; he just wanted to head straight home, continue with the final preparations for leaving for the Dales. Last night with Brogan had been a happy interlude, he told himself. He'd been an idiot to think it was anything more. The sooner he pushed her out of his mind, the better. There was no point mooning over something that might have been when he had a house move and a new job to contend with. But something told him Brogan wasn't going to be so easy to forget.

He was loading his bag into the boot of his car when his phone pinged from his jacket pocket. He fished it out to see a text from

Loretta, his frown deepening as he read it. If he thought his heart couldn't sink any lower, her message proved him wrong.

> Had an offer on the house. Cash buyers, no chain, keen to move quickly. It's a bit below the asking price but I've accepted it. Means we can get this over and done with. You need to get the rest of your stuff out ASAP.

"Means we can get this over and done with." Ouch! Talk about kicking a man when he was down. Nick re-read the text, a prickle of annoyance running over him. Why did Loretta think it was okay to accept the offer without discussing it with him? After all, they were joint owners of the house; decisions like this should be made jointly. And how much below the asking price was it? he wondered, thinking it slightly suspicious she hadn't put the amount. He momentarily toyed with the idea of contacting the estate agent, telling him he refused to accept the offer, before quickly dismissing it. He scrunched up his face. The shouty phone calls that would ensue from Loretta didn't bear thinking about. The sooner this was over and done with, the sooner she would be out of his life and he'd be free to move on. Weariness engulfed him. He'd had a gutful of negotiating with her, of treading on eggshells every time they spoke, wary of incurring her wrath if he said the wrong thing. At times it was as if she got a kick out of taking his words and distorting their meaning to make it sound as if he was being unreasonable. He couldn't keep up with the mental gymnastics. He'd had enough of them. He just wanted this situation over with.

THIRTEEN

BROGAN

Bang on seven-thirty that evening, the horn of a Land Rover tooted in the yard of Pond Farm. Wilf jumped up from his place by the Aga while Brogan grabbed her bag, quickly followed by his lead. 'Come on, lad,' she said, her spirits lifting at the prospect of catching up with her friends.

Outside, the Land Rover belonging to Withrin Hill Farm was waiting, its engine rumbling, steam curling from its exhaust. Ben, Kristy's boyfriend jumped out and headed round to the rear. 'Ey up, Brogan, how're you diddlin'?' he asked, smiling as he pulled open the large rear door. Wilf didn't wait a moment and jumped right in.

'Hi, Ben, I'm good thanks. You?'

'Aye, grand, thanks,' he said.

Brogan followed Wilf, clambering into the back of the Land Rover and plonking herself down on the bench opposite Kristy.

'Hiya, Broge.' Kristy beamed a smile at her.

'Hiya.'

'Now then, Brogan,' said Camm, who was at the wheel. He had a woolly hat pulled down over his dark curls.

'Hi, thanks for picking me up, I really appreciate it.'

'Ey, it's no problem. I was giving Ben and Kristy a lift into the village; it's no hardship to scoop you up on the way, lass,' he said with a smile as Ben climbed back in at the front.

'Yeah, Ben's going over to Tom and Adam's to talk Belted Galloways.' Kristy rolled her eyes, making Brogan giggle. Tom was Ben's twin who lived with his partner, Adam, at Rowan Slack Farm just out of Lytell Stangdale.

'Don't knock it, Kris, rare breeds are the way ahead,' said Ben good-naturedly. 'And Belties produce fantastic beef.'

'Aye, and diversification's key,' said Camm. 'Those woodfired hot tubs we got installed at the campsite have been a big attraction.'

'They so have,' said Kristy, nodding.

'Actually, while I remember,' Brogan said, 'keep your eyes peeled for two people in an unfamiliar dark-grey van loitering round the moors. I saw one at the end of my lane the other day and Bert Hoggarth mentioned seeing one near his cottage at Broad View. From his description it sounds like it's the same one; has a big dent on the right-hand side rear door. Both driver and passenger seemed to be at pains to hide their faces, left me feeling there was something a bit shifty about them.'

'Now you mention it, I saw a van fitting that description parked up on the end of the lane to Danskelfe Castle the other morning,' said Camm. 'I remember thinking the two blokes in it looked a bit suspicious.'

'Great, this is all we need on the run-up to Christmas,' said Kristy.

'I'm going to mention it to PC Snaith, just in case. Bert says he wrote the registration number down.' Brogan felt suddenly anxious at the thought of going back to an empty house. She quickly reminded herself she had Wilf who, though he was a big softy, could look pretty fierce when the need arose. She gave him a quick pat and he nuzzled into her.

'Aye, and in the meantime, we'd best spread the word locally so we can all be vigilant,' said Ben.

'I'll post a warning on the village social media pages. I'll mention we could do with a photo of the van, then everyone'll know what to look out for,' said Kristy. 'I mean, it might be innocent, but I think you get a feeling about these things.'

'Too right,' said Camm.

Before long, they'd pulled up outside the quaint thatched building of The Sunne Inne. Set in the centre of Lytell Stangdale, soft light spilled from its stout mullioned windows, and smoke curled up from its squat chimney. Kristy and Brogan jumped out of the Land Rover to a chorus of "goodbyes" and hurried over the road to the characterful fifteenth century pub. Local blacksmith Jimby Fairfax and his glamorous wife, Vi, were making their way along the trod, holding hands and heading in their direction.

'Now then, ladies,' said Jimby, giving one of his familiar broad smiles.

'Hi there.' Vi gave them a warm smile too. She looked as immaculate as ever in her emerald-green velvet coat, cinched in at the waist, and her contrasting plum-coloured leather boots. She always put Brogan in mind of a fifties movie star, with her cat flick eyeliner and impossibly glossy hair sculpted into aubergine waves. 'We've got a pass out for the night. My parents offered to babysit Pippin for a few hours, so we jumped at the chance.' Vi's green eyes shone happily. Jimby had given their little daughter, Elspeth, the nickname "Pippin" owing to Vi's craving for apples while she was carrying her and it had stuck.

'Don't blame you,' said Kristy. 'By the way, while I remember, be alert to a dark-grey van with a dent in the rear passenger door on the right.' She went on to give the couple a brief rundown of their recent conversation. 'So spread the word. Oh, and on a much happier matter, I hear you got the commission to make the wedding dress for that lifestyle vlogger from York.'

'Who's this?' asked Brogan, only half listening. Her mind had started drifting off to the happenings of the previous night and her moment with Nick. The word "wedding" had made her heart lurch and her face flood with colour, fearing they'd touched on the subject of yesterday's event.

'Savannah Lesker from "At Home with Savannah", she does

those gorgeous lifestyle vlogs. We were watching one of them about how she designed her zen garden only the other week,' said Kristy. 'She's a really popular influencer, Vi. You realise Romantique Designs is going to go crazy with orders once everyone's seen her dress.'

'It's already started,' said Vi. Vi was a partner in a thriving business, designing and making wedding dresses along with Jimby's sister, Kitty, and the local GP's wife, Livvie. Their small studio was located in the back garden of Vi's parents' house. 'Kicked off pretty much as soon as she'd announced it on social media. We're going to have to advertise for someone to join us, especially since Livvie's on maternity leave with the twins.'

'Aye, our Kitty said the phone's been ringing non-stop and they've been bombarded with emails from brides-to-be making enquiries.' Jimby smiled proudly as he pushed against the chunky oak door. 'After you, ladies, but mind you'd best be quick or folks'll complain about me letting a draft in.' He held the door open and they stepped inside to join the jovial chatter and burble of the locals that mingled with the delicious aroma of landlady Bea Latimer's wholesome home cooking.

'What a gent you are, Jimby,' said Vi, patting him affectionately on the backside as he smiled down at her. He responded with a wink.

Wilf tugged on his lead, his nose shooting up in the air as he sniffed appreciatively. 'Steady on there, lad,' said Brogan.

As usual, a huge fire was roaring in the vast inglenook fireplace, its woodsmoke lingering in the air, adding to the cosy vibe of the place. Already, the bar was busy. Brogan scanned the room to see Anoushka sitting at a table for three over by a window that was hung with thick tweed curtains in subtle shades of the moors, a sturdy radiator beneath it. Wearing a pale blue chunky-knit jumper that set off her long, blonde hair, Anoushka looked up from scrolling through her phone and waved at them, her face lighting up.

'Enjoy your night, lasses,' said Vi as she and Jimby headed over to the bar.

'Aye, have fun,' said Jimby.

'Looks like Noushka's got the drinks taken care of,' said Kristy as they made their way over to their friend.

'Hiya,' said Noushka, flicking her hair over her shoulder and putting her phone down.

Brogan shrugged off her coat, slipping it over the back of the chair. Kristy followed suite.

'We've just been hearing about Savannah Lesker commissioning your mum's company to make her dress,' said Brogan. 'How awesome is that?'

'I know! They're chuffed to bits. They're going to get loads of exposure and heaps of orders off the back of it.' Anoushka smiled proudly. 'But anyway, Broge, what's happened with you? I was most intrigued when I got your text. Did the wedding go okay?'

'Yep, come on, spill, flower. Noushka and me are dying to know what's got you dragging us out on a Sunday night – not that I'm complaining, but I can tell there's something.' Kristy grinned as Anoushka filled their glasses with Pinot Grigio.

Brogan drew in a deep breath. 'Well... uhh! I can't believe I'm about to tell you this, but...' She went on to share the details of her time with Nick, covering her burning face with her hands as she recalled heading back to his room. 'Oh, my God, I really can't believe I did that!' she said, her voice muffled. An image of Nick looking down at her before his lips touched hers filled her mind, making her stomach flutter.

'Wowzers!' said Anoushka. 'Sounds like he was really into you, Broge.'

'It *so* does,' said Kristy. 'But I can't understand why you crept out of his room the way you did; didn't give him the chance to let you know if his feelings were genuine – which I reckon they so were, by the way.'

'Yeah, me too. He sounds lovely and it's time you had someone like that, chick; you deserve it.' Anoushka rubbed her hand up and down Brogan's arm, smiling kindly at her.

'You do,' said Kristy. 'And you could definitely do with some more of that bedroom action if he's as good as you say he is.' The three friends burst out laughing, Brogan's face burning brighter than ever.

With their giggles under control, Anoushka took a sip of her wine. 'And it sounds like you had a *genuine* connection which, trust me, is a two-way thing. I know from Gabe and me, even though I fought it for ages.'

'Tell us about it.' Kristy rolled her eyes jokingly. 'But, seriously, love always finds a way.'

'I'm not so sure about that, he's moving to the Dales.' Giving a regretful shrug, Brogan glanced between them.

'Which is hardly a million miles away, flower,' said Kristy.

'If something's meant to be, you'll make it work,' said Anoushka, looking at her intently.

'Er, hold your horses, you two, you're getting a bit ahead of yourselves.' Despite her words, Brogan felt the warm glow of hope her friends had given her. They'd raised her spirits and helped ease her dreaded self-doubt, just as she knew they would. 'But, if it's as you say it is, all he needs to do to track me down is ask the groom about me; get my contact details from him.' Why had this just dawned on her? Her heart gave a jolt; he could find her – if he wanted to. 'There's no way I'm going to ask them about him; the ball's very firmly in his court. So, we'll see,' she said, more lightly than she was feeling.

'And, mark my words, he will.' Anoushka's blue eyes twinkled at her.

'Noushka's right; I'd put money on it that you'll hear from him before the end of the week,' Kristy said, resolutely.

Brogan's heart started to thump a little louder. Dare she hope he would?

She was momentarily distracted as a rattle of raucous laughter went up from the table by the fire where a noisy game of dominoes was taking place between octogenarian local artist Gerald, his wife Big Mary and retired farmer Hugh Heifer – Hugh's real surname was Danks but he'd been given the nickname "Heifer" owing to the prize winning heifer he still kept and walked daily around the village. He was dressed in his habitual flat cap and overcoat, tied round the middle with a length of blue twine, a pair of wellies that had seen better days on his feet. He seemed inordinately pleased at winning the round.

'It's a bloomin' fluke!' said Big Mary in her sing-song County Durham accent. She gave a hearty cackle.

'Like 'ell it is. It's down to skill and tactics. Pure and simple. A fluke's got nowt to do with it,' said Hugh, looking very pleased with himself as he swept the pile of pennies towards him. 'Look! I'm raking it in. You lot need to up your game; you're making it too easy.'

'Skill and tactics, eh?' Gerald threw his head back and gave a gummy roar of laughter.

Brogan, Anoushka and Kristy looked back at each other and giggled. 'That'll be us one day,' said Anoushka.

'Maybe, but I'd like to think I'd have more teeth than Gerald,' said Kristy dryly, making the three of them splutter with laughter.

FOURTEEN

NICK

The following Sunday, Nick was at a low ebb, walking Maudie along one of the country lanes that led out of Middleton-le-Moors, when he bumped into Chris Crabtree. He knew Chris from working in Middleton-le-Moors where there were two veterinary surgeries. Chris had worked at one, and Nick the other.

'Nick, good to see you, mate. I thought you'd left for the Dales,' Chris said with a smile and a note of surprise in his voice, his nose red with the cold.

'Hi, Chris. It's another week before I go.'

'Right.' Chris nodded, thoughtful. 'I could be getting the wrong end of the stick here, but you don't sound too thrilled at the prospect.' He gave Nick a questioning look.

The thought of staying in a B&B until he found somewhere more permanent was losing its appeal by the day. 'Yeah, I'm beginning to wonder if I haven't been a bit too hasty,' Nick said, rubbing his hand over the dark-blond stubble of his chin as they strolled along, their feet crunching over the blanket of frosty autumn leaves that covered the path. Oscar and Maudie trotted along jauntily up ahead. 'Don't get me wrong, I don't regret handing in my notice at my last practice, that feels right, but moving away? Hmm... I'm not so sure now.'

'Tell you what, if I'd had even an inkling you were looking for another job, I'd have got in touch to see if I could've tempted you to join me. You'll have heard I've set up a new practice over at Danskelfe in the old castle estate offices? Georgia Collier's part of the team; she works a couple of days a week. She's a brilliant vet; has moved back this way from York,' Chris said.

'Yeah, I'd heard that on the grapevine.' Nick nodded. He liked Chris, and respected him too; he was a good vet with a sound reputation, as was Georgia, though he didn't know her as well. 'So how's it going?'

'Well...' Chris went on to explain how his partner in the new business venture had backed out, leaving him looking for another vet to take his place. 'If you're seriously regretting your plans to move out of the area – and I know this is going out on a limb – I don't suppose you'd reconsider your decision to leave and maybe think about joining me and Georgia at Danskelfe? I think we'd make a good team.'

Nick listened quietly to what Chris had to say, his words circling around in his mind and gaining pace. He couldn't deny it, he found the offer tempting, and before he'd known what was happening, he was giving it real consideration.

'Listen, are you doing anything this afternoon?' Chris asked.

'Er, no, I don't have any plans. Why?'

'Why don't you meet me at the surgery?' Chris said. 'You can have a look around, see what you think? Then, when you've had time to weigh everything up, you can let me know what you've decided to do – though I'd prefer it if you didn't leave it too long to give me your decision; I'll need to start advertising for someone new if you think it's not for you. Having said that, I'm pretty confident you'll be impressed.' Chris grinned at him.

Nick was surprised to find he quite liked the idea of having a look around the surgery at Danskelfe. 'You're selling it well, Chris,' he said laughing. 'What time?'

'Well, there's no time like the present. How about we head there now?'

'Sounds good to me.'

As it turned out, Chris had been right, Nick was impressed. As soon as he set his foot through the door he felt his enthusiasm of old rush through him. As Chris gave him a tour of the place, explaining his vision for the future, Nick felt more and more fired up by the minute, his spirits lifting. He could see himself happy working here – and the potential for going into partnership with Chris made it even more appealing. Chris was a positive bloke, decent and hard-working too. Nick had a lot of respect for him. In truth, if he could have chosen anyone to potentially go into partnership with, Chris Crabtree would be top of the list.

'Like I said, have a think about it and let me know if you're up for it.' Chris smiled hopefully at him.

Tempted as he was to dive right in and accept Chris's offer straight away, Nick held back, telling himself not to be so impetuous over such a huge decision. But deep down, he knew he'd already made up his mind.

As he drove home, his head was brimming with it all. His heart was thumping; it felt so right.

Two hours later, he made the call, Maudie watching with her usual haughty interest. 'Chris, it's Nick.'

'Hi, Nick.' Chris sounded nervous.

'If it's still okay, I'd like to be a part of Danskelfe Vets; I'd like to accept your offer,' he said, a smile in his voice.

'That's absolutely fantastic, Nick mate. You won't regret it.' Chris sounded as over the moon about hearing the news as Nick was delivering it. 'When can you start?' he asked, laughing.

'How does Monday the fifth of December sound?' That would give him time to clear the rest of his stuff out of the house he'd shared with Loretta and find somewhere to rent closer to the surgery.

'Sounds good to me,' Chris said. 'I'll get the paperwork sorted and I'll be in touch.'

Chris's optimism had been infectious and Nick had ended the call feeling the happiest he'd felt all week. At least this new job would keep his mind off his failed relationship and potential house sale. He wasn't so sure it would keep his mind from straying to Brogan though, and how she'd slipped through his fingers. He hadn't been able to get her out of his head all week and it had been driving him crazy. How could he have got it so wrong? It had crossed his mind that he could do a bit of research, ask Toby if he could fish out Brogan's contact details for him, but he decided against it; if she'd wanted to get to know him better, she wouldn't have done a middle-of-the-night flit. She obviously hadn't felt the same connection he had; hadn't wanted to take things any further. He didn't fancy being hurt twice if she'd told him that night had been a one off. No, the more he thought about it, the more he felt things were best left alone.

FIFTEEN

BROGAN

Present Day

'Right, I'll just go and get Mrs Simpkin and Fudge. If you could just give the examination table a quick wipe down that would be great, thanks,' Nick said, flashing Brogan a smile before popping his head round the door. 'Fudge Simpkin, please.'

Dinah Simpkin came scurrying in, an anxious expression on her face.

'So, what appears to be the problem with Fudge?' Nick asked as he washed his hands at the sink in the corner.

'Well, he's my daughter's guinea pig and she says that recently, he's been getting really fat. And I have to admit, I agree with her; he's got *huge*. We wondered if he had something wrong with him that was giving him such a raging appetite, or if the poor thing had some sort of tumour.'

'Right then, let's take a look.' Nick opened the pet carrier, the sweet scent of hay filling the air. He carefully scooped a rather large Fudge up in his big hands. 'Hello there, Fudge,' he said, taking a quick look at the guinea pig's undercarriage. 'Hmm.' He caught Brogan's eye and she detected a barely discernible lift of his eyebrows. 'Does Fudge have a companion, or does he live on his own, Mrs Simpkin?'

Brogan had a feeling she knew where this was going.

'He lives with his brother, Toffee. Poor little Toffee can't be getting a look-in with the food; Fudge must be eating so fast. We've tried to separate them for a while, just so Toffee can get something to eat, but it doesn't seem to be making a difference. In fact, Fudge seems to be getting bigger.'

Nick set Fudge down on the table, checking the little creature's fur for fleas. Seemingly unperturbed, the guinea pig looked around inquisitively, chomping on a blade of hay that was disappearing into his mouth at great speed while Nick began palpating Fudge's rather rotund abdomen.

'And how old is Fudge?' asked Nick.

'I think he's about four months old,' said Mrs Simpkin.

'Well, I can confidently tell you that Fudge is in the best of health.' He gave Fudge a quick tickle between the ears. Brogan was struck by Nick's calm and gentle manner.

'Oh, thank goodness for that. I didn't know what I was going to say to my daughter if anything was wrong with him.' Dinah Simpkin sagged with relief. 'So, is he just greedy then?'

'No, *she* isn't greedy at all.'

Mrs Simpkin looked at Nick, her eyes growing wider as the penny dropped. It was in synchronicity with her bottom jaw. '*She?* No!' She pressed a hand to her chest. 'Does that mean...?'

'Fudge is a female guinea pig; a sow,' said Nick, smiling kindly. 'And a heavily pregnant one at that. I could feel a few pups having a good old wriggle around in there when I examined her; there's at least four.'

'*Four?* But... but... How did that happen? The pet shop we bought them from assured us they were both boys; told us they were brothers.' Dinah Simpkin glanced between Nick and Brogan, her face a picture of disbelief.

'Well, I can assure you that Fudge is very definitely a female. And I assume this will be her first litter, which is good news as her young age will be in her favour; sows over the age of seven months run the risk of having serious problems giving birth. But, happily that's not going to be the case for Fudge here.'

'Oh, thank goodness for that.' Mrs Simpkin was looking a little punch-drunk from all this information. 'And is it possible to tell how many babies she's going to have?'

'I can x-ray her to see how many pups are in there, if you like?'

'Is that necessary? I mean, are guinea pigs known for giving birth to a large number of babies?' She stroked her hand along Fudge's back.

'I wouldn't say it's crucial. And in answer to your question about litter size, they can give birth to as many as eight – but I don't think that'll be the case with Fudge here. The average is two to four which is more likely for Fudge; there might be another one hiding behind the others.'

'Oh, okay.' Mrs Simpkin nodded as Fudge made little chattering sounds as she sniffed the air.

'And you might be surprised to know guinea pig pups are born with their eyes open and are fully furred. They're also mobile straight away so are able to walk around. And I have to say, they're very cute.'

Mrs Simpkin nodded, continuing to stroke the guinea pig as she absorbed Nick's words. 'How have I been so stupid? It's kind of obvious looking at her now.'

'You're not the first person it's happened to, Mrs Simpkin,' said Brogan. 'Lots of people have been caught out that way.' She glanced across at Nick, a flicker of something passing between them, giving her a jolt and making her look away.

'Brogan's right,' said Nick, 'but it might be a good idea to get the word out, see if you can get some homes lined up for when the pups are old enough to leave Fudge. Guinea pig sows can start breeding as young as two months old; you don't want to be overrun.'

'Oh, my goodness, we certainly don't. Well, thank you, Mr

Heuston. Come on, Fudgy, let's get you home so we can break the news.'

'And it would also be a good idea to separate Fudge and Toffee too; you don't want them having a repeat performance; bizarrely sows can get pregnant straight after giving birth,' Nick said as he scooped the guinea pig up and carefully popped her back into the pet carrier. 'There we are, back to your snuggly bed, Fudge.'

'Ooh, perish the thought; poor Fudgy.' Mrs Simpkin gave a shudder as she walked towards the door Nick was now holding open for her.

Nick turned to Brogan and smiled, holding her gaze. 'Well, I don't know about you, but I've had worse starts to the day.'

Her stomach performed a somersault. Was he referring to the morning she'd crept out of his room? 'Oh, yes, me too.' She grabbed the disinfectant spray and gave the examination table a thorough dousing, her cheeks burning as she scrubbed away. She'd been momentarily distracted while Mrs Simpkin had been there, slipping into work mode with ease, but now the awkwardness of earlier between her and Nick had returned with a vengeance. If first day impressions were anything to go by, it wasn't going to be easy working in such close proximity to him. She sighed inwardly; she really didn't know if she could do it. But she'd been so desperately looking forward to this job. Why did things have to be so complicated? Already it was tying her up in knots, setting her stomach churning away.

She could feel his eyes on her, sense he was desperate to broach the topic of *that night*, tackle the elephant in the room. She wished he'd just get it over and done with, then she'd know where she stood, know whether he was going to be the sort of bloke who would blab to all and sundry about his "conquest"; tell everyone she'd thrown herself at him and tarnish her hitherto good reputation of keeping herself-to-herself as far as men and relationships were concerned – it definitely didn't include hot and steamy one-night stands.

She heard him draw in a breath beside her. 'Brogan, I know

now's not the right time, but I'd really appreciate it if we could talk, especially if we're going to be working together like this. I think we'd both benefit from clearing the air.'

She swallowed the ball of nerves that had wedged in her throat and raised her eyes to his. The earnest, clear blue gaze that met her made her pulse surge as the familiar electricity crackled between them. The feelings she'd had two weeks ago came rushing back at her, tugging at her insides. He looked every bit as handsome as the man she'd stored in her memory; the one she hadn't dared to take out and revisit. Taking a moment, she gathered herself together and said, 'Yeah, I get that. I'd like us to talk too, but I'd rather not do it here, if that's okay?' She didn't want to risk anyone overhearing what they'd been up to, nor did she want to set tongues wagging about them having a private conversation. That could very easily send her new colleagues jumping to conclusions and the last thing she wanted was unwelcome attention because of that, and to be the subject of office gossip, especially when she hadn't been there five minutes. On top of that, gossip had a habit of spreading like wildfire around the moorland villages, and talk of her and Nick would very likely reach Lytell Stangdale before she did. This "thing" between them needed handling very gently, of that she was sure. 'We need to go somewhere private.' She glanced up at him, gnawing at her bottom lip.

Nick raised his palms. 'Yeah, course, I totally get that.' He was looking at her intently, making her feel self-conscious. 'So, I don't suppose you're free tonight, are you? It'd be good to get things sorted straight away,' he said. There was a hopeful look in his eye.

'Sorry, I can't do tonight.' She pulled an apologetic face. With it being her last shift at the Sunne she definitely didn't want to talk about *that* night there, especially when she didn't have a clue what he was going to say about it. Tongues would certainly wag.

'Okay, how about tomor—'

He was silenced by the sound of dogs barking and snarling loudly in the waiting area – one belonging to a smaller breed, if the yappy pitch was anything to go by. In the next moment, their objections were joined by their owners' voices, yelling out orders to "heel" and "no!" and "sit!" but the dogs didn't appear to be taking any notice.

Nick's eyebrows hitched up. 'It would seem my next appointment's arrived,' he said dryly, a small smile lifting the corners of his mouth.

'Mr Blake and his Rottweiler, Patrick, are booked in for Patrick's boosters and Mr Jowsey's got his Jack Russell, Spud, booked in to have his nails clipped and an MOT. Take your pick.'

'Hmm. Judging by all the yapping out there, Spud doesn't sound to be in the best of moods,' he said.

'He's notorious for being snappy. I've taken him for walks before but all he was interested in was biting ankles; human and canine, he wasn't fussy. Little horror punctured two pairs of my wellies. I ended up refusing to take him.'

'He sounds like a delight.' Nick flashed her another disarming grin and she couldn't help but smile back.

'Totally.'

'Listen, I'd better go and get Spud, but when we get a quiet moment, can we organise that chat?' he said.

'Yeah, that's fine with me.' She gave another smile, not really sure if it was fine at all. She hadn't got a clue which way the chat would go. Which way did she want it to go? she wondered, her mind going back to the moment he first kissed her. Her heart was in no doubt as it responded with a leap.

'In the meantime, let's go and see if we can restore calm in the waiting room.'

'Hmm? Oh, yes, good idea.' His words pulled her back to the present with a start.

The day flew by in a blur and before Brogan knew it, it was gone six o'clock and time for home. Nick had been called out on a visit to Tinkel Top Farm which meant that she could slip out without the embarrassment of having to say goodbye to him, and face the awkwardness that would trigger. They hadn't had a chance to organise a time for "the chat" which she couldn't decide if she was glad or disappointed about. And besides, she needed to get home and get showered in readiness for her last stint behind the bar at the Sunne.

Once she'd changed out of her scrubs, she gathered up Wilf who seemed reluctant to leave his cosy spot in front of the fire with Maudie and Oscar. Brogan was pleased with how he'd settled today. 'You've been a good lad,' she said as she ruffled his ears. He responded with a happy wag of his tail. Brogan had already bid farewell to Vonnie who was now busy in her office poring over paperwork. And after asking after her first day, Chris had gone to check on a tabby cat whose paw he'd operated on to remove a shard of glass that afternoon. The cat was awaiting collection by his owner who'd been on the phone to say she was running late thanks to roadworks springing up just outside Middleton-le-Moors.

'So, how did you find your first day, Brogan?' asked Becky, zipping up her padded jacket. She was the other vet nurse who'd worked that day. 'And what did you think of our new vet? Nick's pretty delish, isn't he? Do you reckon he's single?'

Brogan busied herself rummaging for her car keys in her bag, hoping Becky and Jules wouldn't notice her blushes. 'Yeah, my first day's been brilliant, thanks. I've loved it.'

'You settled in really quickly, you'd never think it had been three years since you last did any vet nursing, you're a natural,' said Jules, smiling kindly. She turned to Becky. 'And as far as Mr Delish is concerned, from what I can gather, he's newly single – he was engaged, but it didn't work out; I don't know all the details, but from what I can gather his ex cheated on him.'

'What? She must've been bonkers! There's no way I'd cheat on him if he was my boyfriend.' Becky's eyes were wide with disbelief.

And there was the proof that news really did travel fast; not just on the village grapevine, but apparently on the veterinary grapevine too. Brogan felt the need to extricate herself from the conversation as quickly as possible. She felt it was straying into the realms of gossip and was beginning to make her feel uneasy. Not wanting to appear rude or unfriendly, she was relieved she had the excuse of having a quick turnaround at home. 'Right, I'd best be off or I'll be late for my shift at the pub which isn't the way I want to end things,' she said with a laugh. 'Thanks for showing me the ropes, and being so patient with me, both of you. I'll see you in the morning.'

To a chorus of cheery goodbyes, she clicked her tongue at Wilf and the pair bid a hasty retreat from the surgery and out into the frosty air. 'Brr! Bloomin' 'eck, Wilf, it's nippy out here.' A chilly wind had whipped up over the course of the afternoon. It carried with it the distinct smell of snow; well, that's what her grandad would have said, anyway, thought Brogan as she hurried over the gravel to her car, the wind nipping at her cheeks.

She drove home, frost sparkling in the headlights. She had the fan on full-blast to keep the windscreen clear, her teeth chattering ten-to-the-dozen thanks to the freezing temperature in her car. Though she was concentrating hard on the road, Brogan's mind crowded with thoughts from the day, each one vying for attention. She didn't know which to tackle first. It had been a huge relief to find everyone had been friendly, and even more so that everything had come flooding back, her three-year absence from working in a vets' surgery shrinking to almost nothing. Having said that, she couldn't wait to get started on the courses Vonnie had organised for her, fill in the gaps and update her skills; they'd definitely boost her confidence as well as her knowledge. But by far the biggest contender for taking up her headspace was Nick. Wow! How did that happen? Talk about coincidence! Never in a million years would she have guessed he'd turn up working at the same place as her. She couldn't wait to tell Noushka and Kristy, see what their take on it was. She puffed out her cheeks, Wilf glancing over at her; she still needed to get her head around all of that.

One thing she knew for certain was the feeling that had gripped her when she'd first set eyes on him at the wedding, that almost primal connection – she felt ridiculous thinking of it that way, but that's exactly how it had felt. It was still there, still as strong, if how her body had responded to him today was anything to go by. The burning question was, did he still feel it too? Or had it been something he'd made up that day? Had it been nothing more than lip-service, or blagging, so he could get her into bed with him? *Oh, jeez.* That's what really scared her. She didn't want to go making a fool of herself when they were having "the chat". Her heart leapt in her chest at the mere thought.

It had been a super-fast turnaround from getting home to getting ready for her last stint at the Sunne. By a quarter to seven, Brogan had changed into her black straight-leg jeans, black fitted sweater with a cream-coloured star emblazoned across the middle, and her favourite chunky boots. She jumped into her car, Wilf beside her – Bea had kindly said he could join her on her last shift. He regularly curled up with the landlords' dogs, Nomad and Scruff, and was never any bother. She turned the key in the ignition and was met with a half-hearted splutter that didn't have anywhere near enough power to ignite the engine. Her heart sank. 'Don't do this to me, tonight of all nights.' She waited a moment then tried again, only to be disappointed when the same thing happened. 'Oh, for, crying out flaming loud!' She felt her stress levels shoot up. It wasn't the first time this had happened; it had caught her out several times on and off over the last month. Each time, Brogan told herself she'd get the car booked in at the new garage over in Danskelfe. But it had behaved itself recently, which had lulled her into a false sense of security and, consequently, she'd postponed the call to Jed at the garage to ask him to give it a check over. And now look what had happened. She'd never get to work at this rate.

It took several attempts before the engine reluctantly spluttered to life. Brogan sighed with relief as she put the car into gear and drove off.

It was with mixed feelings that she headed to the Sunne that night. Much as she was relieved at the prospect of not having to turn herself out for work in the evening – especially over the winter months – and, worse, head back to a dark and empty house, she'd miss the camaraderie that went hand-in-hand with her job behind the bar. Bea and Jonty Latimer were wonderful bosses. They'd always been kind, treating her like a member of the family, particularly after her grandparents had died. They'd taken her under their wing then, inviting her to join them for meals, Bea packing up plates of food for her to take home, or wrapping her arms around her when she'd been overcome with grief after losing her grandparents, not minding as she'd sobbed hot, wet tears into her shoulder. Brogan would never forget such heart-warming generosity. And she loved chatting with the locals too. Working there had been a good way to get to know everyone when she'd first moved to the area, and now she felt like she'd been there forever.

She reversed into a parking place on the main street and stilled the engine, hoping there wouldn't be a repeat performance of earlier when it came to her going home. 'Right then, Wilf, let's go and see what Monday night in the Sunne has on the cards for us.' She doubted it would be busy, what with it being a freezing cold December Monday on the run-up to Christmas. She leaned across and gave him a pat, and he responded with a quick swipe of his tongue over her face. 'Hmm. Has anyone ever told you, you give the sloppiest kisses, young man?' she said with a laugh, hugging him close. He rested his head on her shoulder and wagged his tail. Brogan felt a rush of love for him.

She glanced across at the pub, which was looking achingly festive, with potted Christmas trees festooned with twinkling fairy lights positioned either side of the broad door, where a large festive wreath hung. 'Come on then, lad.' They made a quick dash over the road and into the pub, Brogan's head bowed against the nipping wind that was rushing round her ears. Inside, the warmth was a welcome relief as it wrapped itself around her. Her eyes went straight to the bushy Christmas tree that glowed in the corner. It looked stunning, dressed in shades of purple and gold. Bea, a former interior designer, had a good eye for tasteful décor. Sitting at the bar were the familiar "early doors" locals engrossed in chat with Jonty and his daughter, Portia. Portia's face lit up when she saw Brogan.

'Hello, darling. How's your day been? Tell all,' she said in her plummy accent, brimming with her usual enthusiasm. She was looking as well-groomed as ever in a black silk shirt printed with silver-grey roses, and black faux leather jeans, her long blonde hair hanging in a glossy curtain down her back.

'It was great, thanks.' Brogan smiled, pulling off her gloves and stuffing them into her pockets before bending to unclip Wilf's lead. He didn't waste a moment, and trotted over by the fire to be with his canine pals. 'It absolutely flew by.' Brogan slipped her coat off and went to hang it in the little room just off the bar.

'I'm so pleased it went well for you,' said Jonty, peering over his glasses. 'Though, I can't deny, we'll be sorry to lose you, my dear.' His kind smile tugged at her heart and a lump appeared in her throat, taking her by surprise.

'Oh, er—'

Everyone's attention was taken as Jimby Fairfax bowled into the pub, his hearty laugh breaking through the low hum of conversation. Jimby was one of the village's most exuberant characters, always upbeat and happy. In fact, Brogan couldn't remember the last time she'd seen him without a smile on his face. And she was enormously grateful he'd arrived when he did, saving her from having to tackle the tears that were threatening. His buoyant entrance had done a good job of chasing them away.

Jimby was followed by Ollie Cartwright, who was Anoushka's dad and Jimby's brother-in-law. Jimby and Ollie had been best friends since childhood and were regulars at the Sunne.

'By 'eck, it's brass monkey out there,' said Jimby, rubbing his hands together briskly.

'Aye, I reckon snow's on its way,' said Ollie.

'Ey up, Brogan, how did your first day up at the veterinary's go?' asked Jimby, pulling his woollen hat off his short crop of dark curls.

'Aye, our Noushka said you were starting there today,' said Ollie.

'It was brilliant, thanks; great to be back in scrubs. I loved it.' *Apart from the shock of seeing a certain person.*

By the time it had got to a quarter-past eight, she'd found herself answering similar questions many times over. It warmed her heart that people cared and were interested. She only hoped no one had detected any hint of the misgivings that were lurking at the back of her mind thanks to a certain tall, blond and handsome vet.

Considering it was a Monday evening in December, and not usually one of the busiest times for the Sunne, she was surprised at how busy it actually was. In fact, she suddenly realised, the place was as jam-packed as it if it were a Friday or Saturday night, which was why she and Portia hadn't had much chance for a catch-up. Brogan always enjoyed hearing about the clients her friend worked for as an interior designer – Portia had taken over Wisteria House Interiors from her mother when Bea and Jonty had moved to the pub, but popped back regularly and enjoyed helping out behind the bar. One of her more recent projects had been to design the interiors of the new lodges at Danskelfe Castle. Portia had worked closely with Lady Carolyn Hammondely, daughter of Lord Danskelfe whose family seat it was, and the two had become firm friends. But there'd been no chance for any of that kind of chat so far this evening. Nor had Brogan had the opportunity to grab much of a word with Anoushka and Kristy who'd been here for a good half hour already.

She was halfway through pulling a pint for Camm who'd come with his partner, Molly, when she glanced up to see a familiar pair of blue eyes gazing at her. Her heart gave a jolt and butterflies started fluttering wildly in her stomach. Nick! What was he doing here? *Please tell me he doesn't want to have "the chat" right now.* Her eyes flicked over to Anoushka and Kristy who, judging by their interested expressions, had clocked her surprise.

SEVENTEEN
NICK

It was just gone seven o'clock by the time Nick got back to Arkleby. His spirits had slumped considerably when he pulled up outside Willow Cottage and glanced up at the foreboding building. It was in total darkness and looked as cold and unwelcoming as was possible. A far cry from the well-insulated, contemporary new-build with underfloor heating he'd shared with Loretta.

'Home sweet home, Maudie,' he said, and opened the car door, a biting wind rushing in and stinging his face.

Stepping into the hallway, he wondered how it was possible that the temperature felt lower than outside. The heating must have failed to kick in again. 'Looks like we're in for another chilly evening, Maudie.' Nick sighed despondently as he flicked the hall light on, the naked bulb casting a harsh light around the outdated, slightly shabby décor. Undeterred, Maudie trotted straight to the kitchen while Nick closed the door on the night and inched his way by the boxes. As he did so, Loretta's phone call that morning hit him with a jolt, sending all thoughts of how cold his new home was scurrying away. 'Oh, blast! She's going to be livid!' he said out loud as he remembered she was expecting him to drop her shoes off. He wasn't sure when he was supposed to find the time; today had been full-on busy. Not that it would wash with her. Should he head over now? he wondered, tapping his key fob against his chin. He glanced at his watch, considering his options. There was always the risk they'd both be there – Loretta and Aaron – all cosy and warm, lights from the Christmas tree twinkling away in the window of the house that had been his home until recently. His jaw tightened as he felt bile burn in his stomach. Going there at this time of night, even if Loretta had instructed him to simply leave the shoes on the doorstep, was the last thing he felt like doing. Plus, he had no idea which of the dozen or so boxes the flaming things were in. Hunting them out wasn't going to be a quick job, never mind the mess it would make. No, he couldn't face that tonight. He wasn't being unreasonable; as far as he could see, the shoe situation was Loretta's fault, not his. And besides, he'd never agreed to drop them off today; he'd been *ordered* to "as soon as possible" by her, in no uncertain terms. And that was something else he'd noticed, she'd become quite adept at dishing out orders, rather than being willing to discuss anything with him. She'd call him, bark out a command, refuse to budge on anything, and shoot him down before he'd finished what he had to say. She'd been the one making all the decisions, with little regard to his feelings or opinions. Her acceptance of the offer on the house sprang to mind. She'd always been assertive and sassy, but she'd taken things to a whole new level now. He had to admit, doing what she wanted had been easier than the alternative of going down the blazing row route – confrontation was something he hated – but right now, it looked like these tactics had been making his situation worse.

Back to the matter in hand, he thought with a sigh. Right now, he felt tired and hungry and all he wanted to do was have a hot shower, shove a ready meal in the microwave and eat it while watching a bit of mindless telly with Maudie snuggling up beside him. He'd leave thinking about the repercussions of not getting Loretta's shoes to her to tomorrow. His priority for this evening was to get the temperature of this cottage above freezing. One thing he knew for certain, the cold would be the least of his worries once

Loretta got her hands on him. He gave a shiver, not sure if it was from the cold or from the thought of what she'd do to him.

Despite numerous attempts, the heating refused to work. Giving up on it, Nick went to turn the gas fire on in the living room, only to find it would appear the gas bottle had run out. 'Bloomin' marvellous.' He flopped onto the sofa dispiritedly, Maudie watching him with a suitably unimpressed expression. 'Don't say anything. I feel crap enough about myself as it is,' he said, leaning his head back.

He vaguely remembered his landlords, Gary and Jackie Trotter, saying something about a man who supplied calor gas bottles. They'd left his number on a piece of paper. The only problem was, he didn't know where the paper was, and even if he did, it wasn't going to solve his problem at this hour. With a weary sigh, he pushed himself up and dragged himself upstairs to have a shower.

He was halfway through washing his hair, thinking that at least the shower had some force behind it rather than the trickle he was expecting, when his body was bombarded with icy jets of water. 'Warghh!' It felt like he was naked in a hailstorm. Gasping, and with bubbles streaming into his eyes, he fumbled to turn the shower off but it wouldn't play ball. *Like the rest of the flaming house!* With goosebumps pinging up all over his skin at an alarming rate, he reached for a towel, realising he hadn't unpacked the bath size ones, and only had a hand towel to dry himself. 'No way!' Could this day get any worse? Shivering, he stepped onto the cold lino, his hair dripping down his back, while he rubbed the small towel briskly over his body. He'd almost finished when the house was plunged into darkness. He froze, waiting for the lights to come back on, but he was disappointed. 'You've got to be kidding me!' His heart plummeted to his chilly feet.

Nick rubbed a circle in the steam of the window and peered out to see lights from other properties still shining brightly. It would appear that only Willow Cottage was under a veil of darkness; there evidently hadn't been a power cut. Somehow that didn't surprise him. He'd have to find a torch, only he didn't have a clue which of the numerous boxes they were in. A thought pinged into his mind; he could use the torch on his phone. If only he knew where he'd left that. He threw his dressing gown on and picked his way carefully down the creaky flight of stairs in the pitch black. Shock spiked through him when he reached the bottom and his bare feet made contact with the freezing cold quarry tiles of the hallway. The kitchen was at least partially illuminated by the bright moonlight that shone in through the window, for which Nick was thankful. He started the hunt for his phone, feeling round the surfaces, reaching into the shadowy nooks. He heard the flutter of paper as the pile of envelopes on the dresser floated to the floor. He'd pick them up tomorrow. He finally managed to locate his phone in the pocket of his waxed jacket, a wave of relief washing over him. 'I know. You don't have to say anything,' he said to Maudie, who, just from her shadowy form, he could tell was giving him one of her 'I'm seriously unimpressed' looks.

Digging out some clean clothes, Nick dressed hurriedly, his fingers numb with the cold, his teeth chattering. There was a savage draught whistling through the gaps around the old York-shire sash window in the bedroom. He made a mental note to stuff it with paper in daylight hours. No doubt about it, it was going to be a bitterly cold winter living here.

Back downstairs, he sought out the electricity consumer unit and flicked the trip switch back on. It tripped out immediately. 'Blast!' Somehow, he'd guessed it would.

Nick's shoulders sagged. He was cold right through to his bones, and he was hungry. As if on cue, his stomach gave an obliging rumble. Up until he'd returned to the house of doom – and discounting his phone call with Loretta – today had been good. His first day at Danskelfe Vets had gone better than he'd expected; he'd enjoyed himself and, more importantly, he'd found Brogan! How unbelievable was that? The thought of her brightened his damp-ened spirits. He'd been looking forward to mulling over their conversations in his thoughts that evening, as well as working out what he wanted to say to her when they got round to *that* chat. He hadn't been able to tell if she'd been pleased to see him. There had been moments when he'd caught a certain look in her eyes that maybe gave him a hint she was. And he'd definitely felt that connection sparking between them again – there was no getting away from that – but then again, he reminded himself, there was a reason she'd done a disappearing act on him at the hotel. He'd be foolish to build his hopes up.

His stomach grumbled again, this time much louder and making Maudie's ears twitch, prodding him to have a think about his evening meal. The options at Willow Cottage weren't great since there was no way of heating any food, never mind heating the house, and he was really craving something warm to eat. A steak pie popped into his mind, with lashings of rich, dark gravy and piles of mashed potato. Mmm. He salivated at the thought. Classic comfort food, of which he was particularly fond. What he'd give to have a plate of that right now. An idea slipped into his mind, growing on him by the second. He and Maudie could go to the pub, get a bite to eat – maybe even a steak pie if there was one on the menu – and a warm through. It would be better than turning blue with the cold here with nothing better to eat than a limp ham sandwich with his hair sopping wet. He gave another shiver. And, he'd heard the food at The Sunne Inne in Lytell Stangdale was particularly good.

Just then, his phone illuminated and pinged simultaneously, heralding the arrival of a text. Nick glanced at the screen, his heart sinking. Loretta. He wasn't strong enough for her right now; he'd call her back tomorrow, sort out what to do about those blasted shoes, and maybe hunt out a couple of torches in the process. He'd call his landlords too, see what they had to say about the electrics.

After a surprisingly brief hunt around in the darkness for his keys – they'd conveniently jangled in the pocket of his waxed jacket as he'd gone to put it on – he was eager to get going. 'Coming, Maudie?' he said as he reached for her lead. She jumped up and trotted down the hall. Nick followed, knocking his knee on one of the boxes, sending an excruciating shot of pain through his leg.

'Ouch!' He rubbed his knee vigorously. He was beginning to think the house of doom had got it in for him.

Lytell Stangdale looked utterly charming as he drove along the main street searching for the pub, his windscreen wipers swiping away the sleety snowflakes that had started to flurry just as he'd set off. The village's chocolate-box pretty thatched cottages, illuminated by traditional-style street lights, looked all set for the festive season with Christmas trees twinkling in their windows and wreaths on their doors. Many had smaller Christmas trees in their gardens too, adding to the cosy scene.

By the time he'd pulled up outside the Sunne, Nick had managed to thaw out a little thanks to the car's heater and the heated seats. His hair was still damp though, and he knew about it as soon as he stepped out into the cold night air, the icy wind rushing over his skin and nipping at his ears. Squinting against the sleet, he walked briskly down the path to the pub.

The warm wave that hit him when he opened the stout oak door was more welcome than he'd expected, soothing him instantly. The place was surprisingly busy for a Monday evening in December, he thought as he cast his eyes around the sea of people. Maudie looked on with interest as a young girl hurried by with plates in her hands piled high with scrumptious looking food – one of which looked suspiciously like a steak pie, reminding him of just how hungry he was. *Oh, thank you, Lord!* It smelled mouth-wateringly good. Nick chuckled as Maudie's nose shot up in the air, sniffing enthusiastically. 'Smells tasty, doesn't it, lass?' She gave him a sideways look, wagging her tail.

The room was thrumming with conversation, the odd laugh floating over the top. From what Nick could see, most of the tables were taken and there was a huddle of people at the bar. But he was undeterred; he didn't care how long he had to wait, he was determined to savour the ambience of the place and, more importantly, sample some of that pie and gravy.

As he walked towards the bar, his heart gave a jolt. Surely that couldn't be Brogan pulling a pint? He paused, trying to make sense of what he was seeing. Did she work here as well as at the surgery? His eyes lingered on her. She looked beautiful with the mellow light picking out golden highlights in her dark auburn hair. She was laughing and chatting animatedly to a dark-haired man. As if sensing he was watching, she glanced up, her eyes locking with Nick's. If he wasn't mistaken, her smile widened, sending happiness surging through him.

In the next moment, a lady wearing chef's whites and a pair of tortoiseshell glasses perched on her blonde bob came from what he assumed was the kitchen. She was walking steadily and carrying a cake, its candles flickering away. A cheer went up and Brogan turned, her face a picture of confusion as the lady made her way towards the bar.

EIGHTEEN
BROGAN

Brogan didn't know what to think. Unless her eyes were playing some kind of trick on her, Nick, her new boss, had just walked into the pub with Maudie. Unable to tear her gaze from his, her heart started racing, that now familiar charge pulsing through her body. She wouldn't have been able to stop her smile from spreading across her face if she'd wanted to. Before she had chance to consider the reasons behind his unexpected appearance, an almighty cheer rang around the room and she turned to see Bea walking towards her with what looked like a large cake in her hands. Frowning, Brogan's mind scrambled to process what was happening around her, her hand stilled on the beer pump. What was this all about? Was it somebody's birthday? Was it an anniversary? If so, how had she forgotten? Or has it got something to do with Nick turning up, here, in the Sunne? Her mind was whirling.

'Brogan, my dear, you might have noticed the pub is a little busier than normal for a wintry Monday evening,' said Jonty, giving an enigmatic smile.

'Yes, I'd just been thinking that actually,' she said, confused, as she glanced around at the smiling faces looking back at her.

'Well, there's a jolly good reason for it,' said Portia, beaming broadly.

'There is?' Brogan's frown deepened; she was beginning to feel a little self-conscious.

'There is,' said Bea, setting the cake down on the bar. 'We couldn't let you simply slip away, my darling. We had to say goodbye to you properly. We've loved having you work for us and we'll miss you terribly.'

'Hear, hear,' said Jonty.

'We so will,' said Portia. 'And you've got to promise you'll still come and have a catch up with me; still pop in so we can go for a walk with the dogs.'

'Course I will.' Brogan felt a lump forming in her throat but she somehow managed to force a smile. *Keep it together.*

'Good,' Portia said resolutely, flashing a happy grin. 'Anyway, we thought we'd get a little cake organised for you; mention it to a few of the locals.'

Brogan looked on, speechless. When she eventually found her voice she said, 'You got me a cake?' The touching gesture had sent her emotions rising to the surface. Tears swam in her eyes and she fought to keep them at bay. Before she knew what was happening, she found herself engulfed in a cloud of sweet perfume as Portia swept her up in a hug, squeezing her tightly. 'And you've got to promise me you'll still call in for a bite to eat with us,' she said in Brogan's ear.

'Promise,' said Brogan, her throat tight. It was beginning to feel like she was heading to the ends of the earth, rather than just switching her job, but Portia always did love a bit of drama.

'Good. You're like a daughter to Mummy and Daddy; having you around stops their nest from feeling empty while I'm away.'

Brogan wasn't so sure about that, but she knew Portia meant well. A sob caught in her throat. She looked over to see Nick smiling at her just as a plump tear plopped onto her cheek and rolled down her face. 'Oh, that's so kind of you.' Her voice cracked and her bottom lip wobbled.

A collective 'Ahh" ran around the room, and she mustered up a shaky smile.

Get a grip, Brogan! 'I'll still be coming back in as a customer, so you haven't got rid of me that easily.' She laughed, swiping her tears away. 'But if it means I get a gorgeous cake like this one, then I'm not complaining.' Her words triggered a ripple of laughter around the bar. Making light of it was definitely the best way to go with this, especially with so many people she knew looking on. And, worse, Nick! Brogan had never been one for showing her emotions in public and her discomfort was beginning to make her squirm a little. She dreaded to think what her new boss would be making of all of this.

'We're not complaining either, chick, if it means we get a slice,' said Kitty, grinning broadly.

'Too right,' said Ollie.

'It's a gorgeous cake, Bea. Did you make it?' asked Kitty's cousin Molly.

'Oh, I wish,' said Bea. 'A very talented lady called Jasmine from Micklewick Bay made it. She'd done one for a friend of mine, which was absolutely divine. It was covered in sugar paste flowers that looked unbelievably lifelike, it got me thinking. I just had to ask her to make one for you. Anyway, you need to blow the candles out before they melt everywhere. Don't forget to make a wish, darling.'

Brogan gazed admiringly at the cake which was covered in green fondant icing. It featured a sugar paste girl with a wide smile and long auburn hair who appeared to be dressed in vet nurse scrubs. Around her were positioned a variety of sugar paste animals, including a dog who looked remarkably like Wilf, and mounds of what appeared to be sugar paste heather. The words "Good Luck Brogan!" ran around the base which had also been covered in fondant icing.

'Underneath is a chocolate sponge, filled with ganache, and the girl's supposed to be you, strolling over the moors with Wilf and lots of other creatures in tow,' said Bea, smiling at her.

Touched by the gesture, Brogan found herself suddenly overwhelmed by the wish that her grandparents had still been alive to witness this. She pictured their happy faces, how her grandma, who had a savagely sweet tooth, would have enjoyed tucking into a slice of chocolate cake with great gusto. The thought triggered an ache in her heart. She wasn't sure how much longer she could keep it together without crumbling completely. 'Thank you, it's beautiful.' She caught Nick's eye and his kind smile just about finished her off.

'Like Mummy said, don't forget to make a wish, Broge,' said Portia, clapping her hands together.

Brogan couldn't remember the last time she'd blown candles out on a birthday cake, never mind make a wish with a load of people watching. Feeling excruciatingly self-conscious, she held her hair out of her face, cleared her throat and closed her eyes. It took a couple of attempts before the candles were extinguished and Brogan could breathe a sigh of relief. A round of applause went up, sending her embarrassment levels soaring.

'Bet we can't guess what you wished for,' Kristy said, giving Brogan a saucy wink which she followed up with a dirty chuckle.

Though Brogan shot her a warning look, she couldn't help the smile that twitched at the corners of her mouth. She may not have wished for what Kristy had alluded to, but it had certainly featured Nick.

'Tell you what, my dear, why don't you go and have a break with your friends. We can manage here,' said Bea, gently directing her to the customers' side of the bar.

'Are you sure?' Brogan asked, turning to look at her.

'Yes, of course, it's a jolly good idea,' said Jonty.

'We'll slice the cake and bring some over to you,' said Bea.

'Oh, okay. Thank you. Oh, and Camm needs his beer, I've only half poured it,' Brogan called behind her as she was scooped up by Anoushka and Kristy and guided to a couple of tables by the fire that had been pushed together by Jimby and Vi. Her mind was suddenly filled with thoughts of Nick, and the reason for him being there. She should really go and say hello; it would look like she was being unfriendly otherwise, not to mention it really was rather nice being in his company. She glanced around her as she was being propelled along by her friends but he was nowhere to be seen. Maybe he'd left. That thought hit her with an unexpected pang of disappointment.

Moments later, she was sitting in front of the fire, tucking into the most sumptuous chocolate cake, listening while Jimby entertained everyone with a story of how he'd slipped on ice earlier that day and had just missed sliding into the village pond. 'I tell you what, I was millimetres away from a bloomin' icy dunking,' he said, following up with a hoot of laughter.

'It's not like you to go A over T, Jimby. You're not accident-prone at all,' Molly said, a generous dash of sarcasm discernible in her voice.

'Honestly, Moll, you should've seen him the other day. He did the splits when he encountered some ice on the path in the back garden,' said Vi. 'Squealed like a pig. Pippin and I howled with laughter.'

'Yes, thanks for rushing to my assistance, darling wife,' Jimby said, feigning hurt feelings and making everyone chuckle. 'I could've sustained a serious injury to my family jewel department for all you cared.'

'Enough!' Molly held up her hand. 'Now's not the time to bring your bits into the conversation, thanks very much, Jimby.'

'You're not wrong,' said Vi, pulling a face.

'Is there ever a time, Moll?' asked Ollie, chuckling.

'No!' said Kitty, shaking her head and rolling her eyes affectionately at her brother. 'Never.'

'On a completely different subject, Broge,' said Ella. 'Joss and me spotted a dark-grey van looking a bit suspicious, you know, like the one you mentioned before. We were heading along our track when we noticed it coming towards us. Joss got out of the Landie to see what they were after, but the driver did a quick about-turn and shot off like a bat out of hell, sliding all over the place in the slush.'

'Aye, from the glimpse I got of them, him and his mate looked very shifty; a right pair of wrong 'uns,' said Joss.

'Even more shifty by driving off like that,' said Ollie.

'I must admit, I was a bit worried when Joss was walking over to them. You never know what folk like them are thinking; how they'll react,' said Ella, looking concerned.

'Aye, we all need to be careful; keep our wits about us,' Molly said. 'And we don't want any of you fellas acting the hero, okay? It's better to let the thieving scumbags steal a quad bike, or whatever it is they're after, than risk any of you lot getting hurt – or worse – trying to stop them. The alternative doesn't bear thinking about.'

Everyone knew what Molly was alluding to. Six years earlier, Roger Scarth, a farmer from Arkleby, had been seriously injured when he'd tackled a couple of masked thugs who'd broken into an outbuilding in an attempt to steal his quad bike. He'd taken a severe beating for his trouble and had ended up on a life support machine. It had sent shockwaves around the rural community for some considerable time after. Too traumatised to continue farming, on his release from hospital, Roger had given notice on the farm he rented with his wife and they'd moved out of the area. No one had heard from them since.

'I agree with Moll,' said Kitty.

'Me too,' said Vi. 'If anyone sees or hears anything suspicious, they need to call the police, let them deal with it, and that includes you, Jimby.' She gave her husband a pointed look.

'Understood, Vi.' Jimby nodded, his smile slipping away, his tone uncharacteristically serious. Turning to his cousin he said, 'Don't worry, Moll, none of us'll do anything daft, will we, fellas?' He cast his gaze around the table as assurances from the menfolk followed. 'And, mind, that includes you, Moll. We all know how feisty you can be when you get going.'

'Don't you worry, I won't be doing anything daft,' she said.

Brogan glanced over at her, picking up the non-verbal messages flying around the table. She knew Molly had extra reason for not wanting Camm to tackle any potential villains. Having already been widowed at a young age, she wouldn't want to go through the heartbreak of losing a second partner.

'Oh, I nearly forgot to say, I managed to take a couple of photos with the camera on my phone,' said Ella. 'Only problem is, the shots are a bit blurry and half the rear number plate's missing; looks like it's snapped off, but I suppose it's better than nothing.'

'It definitely is, Ells, that's brilliant,' Brogan said. 'And are you okay to post them on all the local social media pages?' That was one of the good things about living round here, the way the villagers pulled together at times like these.

'Yeah, course, no probs. I'll do it tonight when we get back.'

Brogan was about to ask if they knew of anyone else who'd spotted the dodgy van when she felt something warm push itself into her lap. 'Ooh!' Startled, she looked down to see Maudie's brown eyes gazing up at her, her tail swishing back and forth. 'Maudie! Hello, girl,' she said, ruffling the dog's ears, feeling inordinately pleased to see her.

In the next moment, Nick was standing beside her. 'Hi, Brogan, I must apologise about Maudie, she's never usually this forward,' he said. 'But she seems very taken with you.'

'Honestly, there's no need. It's lovely to see her; I'm very taken with her too,' she said, her stomach performing somersaults as she looked up at him, his blue eyes making her heart melt.

'That's okay then.' He attempted to smooth his fringe down with his fingers, which Brogan noted hadn't made a jot of difference. In fact, it seemed to have had the opposite effect and his hair was now sticking up on end.

'I've just come for a bite to eat. The electric's gone off at the cottage I'm renting. It's absolutely freezing there and I've got no way of preparing food. It was a choice between either a pub meal or a dry ham sandwich. And after what I've been hearing about the food here, there was no contest, the Sunne won hands down.' He gave her a disarming smile.

'Good choice, Bea's food is awesome,' she said.

'So, you work here too?'

'I did; it's my last shift,' she said, aware of Anoushka and Kristy watching the exchange with interest. 'Though I do feel a bit lazy sitting over here and stuffing my face with cake while the others are rushed off their feet behind the bar.' From the corner of her eye, she saw Anoushka and Kristy exchange a surreptitious glance at one another.

'Ah, right.' Nick nodded.

'Who's your pal, Brogan?' asked Jimby, in his usual friendly manner.

Brogan flushed, embarrassed at not having thought to introduce Nick. 'Oh, yeah, sorry. Everyone, this is Nick Heuston, he's the new vet over at Danskelfe.' She didn't dare make eye contact with Anoushka and Kristy as she went around the table, introducing everyone. 'Nick, this is Jimby, he's married to Vi here, and next to him is Camm, he's Molly's partner – they live at Withrin Hill Farm. Then there's Ollie; he's married to Kitty opposite – they live at Oak Tree Farm and she's Jimby's sister; Molly's their cousin and Anoushka here is their daughter. And this is Kristy, she lives at Withrin Hill Farm with Ben who's one of Molly's twin sons. At the top of the table there's Ella and Joss; they live at Camplin Hall Farm – Ella's related to Kitty and Molly though I can't quite remember how.' She drew in a deep breath. Her self-consciousness had made her gabble and she wondered if she'd overloaded Nick with names and information. 'Phew!'

'Hi, everyone,' Nick said, smiling round the table and raising his hand in a small wave. 'It's good to meet you all, but I'll apologise in advance if I don't remember your names at first. I'm hopeless with getting to grips with human names; never animals, for some reason. Funnily enough, I can always remember what my patients are called but struggle to recall their owners' names.' He shook his head and grinned.

His comment made everyone chuckle. 'Don't worry, Nick, I answer to anything,' said Jimby.

'Just as well, mate,' said Ollie dryly, his hand around his pint.

'Aye, you're not wrong there,' said Jimby. 'Anyroad, Nick, you're very welcome to join us, if you fancy? I've kept a spare stool hidden here under the table for such eventualities. I can pass it down; there's room at the end there.'

Various sounds of encouragement followed and Brogan's heart took off at a gallop. She risked a glance at Kristy, who was sitting on the other side of the table, to see her friend looking highly amused.

'Oh, I really wouldn't want to intrude,' said Nick, his eyes switching to Brogan.

'Don't be daft, you wouldn't be intruding, would he, Brogan?' asked Ollie.

Brogan swallowed. 'No, you wouldn't. Not at all.'

'And it'd be good to get to know the new veterinary and welcome him to the village,' said Jimby. 'I think you'll find we're a friendly bunch. And you won't regret sampling some of Bea's cooking, I can promise you that; it's sublime.' He eased the stool out from its hiding place and passed it over to Nick.

'Well, if you're sure.'

'Course we are, sit yourself down,' said Anoushka, giving Brogan a loaded look.

'Thanks, Jimby.' Nick set the stool down opposite Brogan.

'And I'll just go and make sure Bea saves you a piece of cake,' said Kristy, sloping off.

'Oh, thanks. That's really kind,' said Nick, looking slightly bemused.

Brogan could feel her cheeks flame, struggling to meet his eye as he sat down. She had no idea how the rest of the evening was going to pan out, but she couldn't deny the feelings that were now racing around inside her.

NINETEEN

NICK

Nick couldn't believe how his evening had turned around. Talk about extremes. It had gone from him being blasted by an icy shower in a freezing cold cottage that had been plunged into darkness when he was in the said icy shower, to sitting beside a roaring fire in a cosy pub that positively oozed character with its low, oak-beamed ceiling and sumptuous tweed soft furnishings, in the warm embrace of a bunch of friendly locals, who included him in their banter like they'd known him for years. And if that wasn't enough, he'd just ordered a steak and mushroom pie with rich ale gravy and mashed potato, the thought of which almost made him drool. But most importantly of all, he was sitting opposite Brogan. Lovely Brogan. Could life get any better? he wondered. Hmm. Actually, it could, he thought as his mind wandered back to their time in his hotel room, her in his arms, her body pressed close to his.

'So, how are you finding it round here, Nick? Have you settled in yet?' asked Jimby.

Nick swallowed his mouthful of shandy and shook the image from his mind. 'Mmm. I haven't been here long, but first impressions are good – apart from the cottage I'm renting over in Arkleby, but I'm only staying there temporarily, so I suppose it's not too bad.'

''What's up with the cottage?' asked Molly.

Nick rolled his eyes. 'Ughh! Where to start?' He went on to tell them about the problem with the hot water, the heating and the lack of electricity. They listened, making various sympathetic sounds. 'So if anyone has the name of a good plumber or electrician, I'd be eternally grateful.'

'It's the landlord's responsibility to put those things right and make sure the house is safe to be rented out,' said Kitty.

'Kitty's right,' said Vi.

'Out of interest, what's the name of the property?' asked Camm, his thick, dark brows drawn together.

'Willow Cottage, on the main street in Arkleby.'

A chorus of groans and snorts ensued. 'Gary and Jackie Trotter,' said Molly.

'Why doesn't that surprise me?' said Jimby, rolling his eyes.

'They've been told about that place; it's a safety hazard. Apparently there was a gas fire in the living room that was as old as the hills and absolutely lethal by all accounts. The last tenants reported it, which resulted in it being condemned. The Trotters were supposed to have had it removed.' Molly shook her head.

This wasn't sounding good. 'Well, from what you've described, it's still in situ and it probably explains why it wasn't working when I tried to turn it on,' Nick said.

'Bloomin' 'eck, Nick, I wouldn't touch it again,' said Ollie, his face serious. 'In fact, I'd find some alternative accommodation as soon as you can. The Trotters have a few properties around here and have gained a reputation for not keeping them in good order. I wouldn't touch them with a barge pole.'

'There wasn't much choice, to be honest.' Nick scratched his head. 'The only other property available for rent had been snapped up the day before my appointment to view it.' An image of his shiny, new, contemporary home at Middleton-le-Moors bloomed in his mind. It stood in stark contrast to the pitiful, unloved cottage he was going back to that evening.

'Willow Cottage sounds dangerous, Nick. You really need to

find somewhere else. I heard recently from someone who was renting one of their properties in Danskelfe that a storage heater started smoking. Turned out there was a loose wire; could've caused a fire,' said Brogan, her forehead creased, her green eyes filled with concern. It touched him that she seemed to care.

'They're a disgrace. We'll ask around, see if anything suitable's about to come free; get you out of there,' said Vi.

'Thanks, I'd appreciate that.' Their kindness warmed Nick's heart.

The evening progressed with Nick tucking into his steak and mushroom pie, which had been delicious. Wilf had crawled commando-style undetected from his place in front of the fire to sit beside him, drooling prolifically and watching every forkful going to Nick's mouth, hopeful that a morsel might come his way, until Brogan noticed and sent him back to his friends. 'I don't think so, young man. You've had your tea. Go on.'

Conversation flowed freely, with Nick's new friends asking questions in an interested, rather than nosy, way. It felt like he'd been part of their group for way longer than a mere handful of hours. Nick learned that Ella and Joss not only ran a boarding kennels up at Camplin Hall Farm, but they also took in stray animals. That would be handy to know if he encountered any homeless creatures that needed a temporary place to stay. And of course, there was Brogan, whose leg kept accidentally touching his, her eyes opening wide whenever it did. Sitting near her had to be the bonus of the evening (even beating the steak and mushroom pie!). It was taking all his strength for his body not to react to her, to ignore the urge to reach across, take her face in his hands and kiss her full on the mouth. To be reminded of exactly how it felt, to be hit by that blaze of emotions once more. How would she react if he threw caution to the wind and did just that? he wondered. It would set tongues wagging, no doubt about it. The way her lips had felt on his, all warm and soft, came rushing back to him, making his heart take off.

'If you're serious about being keen to be part of the local

community, then you might be interested in joining our village committee, Nick,' said Camm.

'I definitely am,' said Nick, nodding enthusiastically and hurriedly squashing down his wayward feelings. There might be a use for that cold shower after all, he mused.

'Aye, we raise funds throughout the year so we can help support local causes. We're always trying to think of new ways to do it. We've done all sorts. The last one was an auction of promises to help raise money to go towards the local primary school's new extension. It was a bloomin' brilliant night,' said Jimby, taking a gulp of his beer.

'It so was,' said Kristy.'

'It did really well, raised loads,' said Anoushka.

'And the best part is the meetings usually take place here, in the pub,' said Ollie with a grin.

'It's sounding more and more tempting.' Nick chuckled.

'And the next one just so happens to be on Wednesday,' said Camm.

'In that case, how do I put my name down?' Nick beamed, making them all laugh.

Molly reached into the basket of logs by the hearth and threw one on the fire, sending sparks shooting up the chimney and the tang of woodsmoke into the air. The dogs watched with interest as flames started dancing in the grate. Nick found himself wishing there was an open fire at Willow Cottage, at least the house would be warm, electricity or no electricity.

'Oh, and while I remember, Jimby and I are having a party at our house on Friday; you're very welcome to come along,' said Vi.

'Thanks. That sounds great. Do I need to bring anything?' A smile lit up his face. It felt great to be included.

'Just a hot date, if you've got one, that is,' Jimby said with a chuckle.

Nick felt his eyes drawn to Brogan who hurriedly looked away, but not quickly enough and he'd still had chance to catch that same intriguing spark he remembered from their first meeting.

. . .

Jonty called last orders at the bar to the few stragglers that were left at the pub. Nick had been hanging back, hoping to snatch a quick word with Brogan and was relieved when he heard the landlord say, 'You might as well get yourself home, Brogan, my dear. I know you've got an early start; we can finish up here.'

'Oh, well, if you're sure,' she said, finishing stacking glasses on a tray.

With their goodbyes said, more quickly than Nick was expecting with it being Brogan's last shift – he got the impression she didn't want to hang around and risk getting emotional all over again – he and Brogan headed towards the door together, Wilf and Maudie in tow, his mind spinning with all he wanted to say to her.

Outside, the temperature had plummeted. The sleet that had been falling earlier had frozen hard and was now sparkling in the glow of the moon that poured over the village.

'Brr!' Brogan shivered, steam spilling from her mouth. Though the wind had dropped, it was still bitterly cold.

Now probably wasn't the best time to start a conversation, thought Nick feeling a pang of disappointment. He wasn't ready to say goodnight to her yet and he really wanted to set her straight on something.

'Brogan, before I head off, I just want you to know I wasn't stalking you by coming here tonight. I mean, I know I could've gone to the Fox and Hounds at Danskelfe, but their reputation for food isn't anywhere near as good as the Sunne's, and I really wanted something appetising to eat.' After the evening he'd had at Willow Cottage, he wasn't exaggerating and he really wanted her to believe him.

'Hey, you don't have to explain yourself to me, and Bea's food is awesome, I can understand why you were tempted to try it, especially with the problems you've had with the cottage.' She smiled up at him.

He felt relief wash over him. 'Right, well, I'll see you in the morning.' He gave her a bright smile, unable to think what else to say.

'Yep, see you in the morning, you too, Maudie.' She bent to ruffle Maudie's ears.

There it was, that unmistakable charge that filled the air when he was with her. Surely she could feel it too, he thought, as he struggled with the urge to ask her.

Nick let Maudie have a sniff around while he watched Brogan walk to her car, his mind going over the events of the evening. It had been fun; Brogan's friends were great and incredibly welcoming. For the first time since his split with Loretta, he hadn't noticed the empty feeling that normally engulfed him, made him feel totally rubbish about himself. Instead, he'd laughed and felt normal again. *Progress!*

Hoping she didn't think he was staring, Nick watched Brogan spray de-icer over the windows of her car. It was the sort of thing he'd always done for Loretta; he'd flick the engine on of her little smart car so it cleared the windows and was warm when she was ready to climb in and set off for work. She'd come to expect it; didn't seem that grateful. Not that he minded, he was happy to do it.

He made his way over to his own car and opened the passenger door for Maudie who didn't waste a moment before she jumped in. As he was walking round to the driver's side, he noticed a spluttering sound echoing down the road from Brogan's vehicle. He stopped, listening while the same thing happened again, and again. This didn't bode well.

As he was crossing the road, she jumped out of her car, frustration written all over her face, her breathing heavy. 'Bloomin' car! Why did it have to do this to me now?' She threw her arms up in the air.

'Hey, it's no trouble, I can drop you home.'

She stood looking at him, her hands on her hips, clearly mulling over his offer. 'But it's out of your way.'

'Like I said, it's no trouble.'

She frowned, nibbling on her bottom lip. 'But how am I going to get to work in the morning when my car's here?'

'I can come and get you,' he said. Again she took a moment to consider this.

'I could always ask Kristy or...'

'There's really no need, I honestly don't mind.'

She huffed out a noisy breath, mist curling around her face in the glow of the streetlight. 'Well... if you're sure? I'll ring the garage first thing.'

'I'm very sure. Come on, let's get out of this freezing cold and into my car.'

Even in the darkness, with only the pale moon illuminating the dale, the pin prick lights of the farmsteads peppering the surrounding fields and moorland, it was easy to see that Pond Farm was in a stunning location, set in the sweeping valley of Great Stangdale. Nick had driven carefully along the unfamiliar, icy roads and down the bumpy tractor track that led to the smallholding. He noted the frost had tightened its grip the further into the exposed dale they'd driven, the headlights of his car picking out snow that lined the hedges and dry stone walls. He could appreciate why folk around here were described as hardy.

'I'm really grateful for this, Nick,' Brogan said, turning to him when he came to a halt in the farmyard.

'Like I said, it's not a problem. How else were you going to get home? It's a long walk from the village.' He grinned and his heart leapt at the charge that crackled between them.

She laughed. 'Yeah, I've done it loads of times, but it's a bit of a trek for this time of night, I suppose.'

'I guess it would be.'

A few beats passed and an awkward air sprang into the space, quickly filling the car. 'Um... right, well, thanks again. I'll see you in the morning,' she said.

He watched as she unclipped her seat belt and cast a quick glance his way.

'Yep, see you in the morning.'

She hesitated before she opened the door. 'As long as you're sure you don't mind...'

'I really don't mind, Brogan. I'll be here at quarter-to-eight. Oh, and don't forget Wilf in the back there.' He nodded in the direction of the boot. 'I don't think he'd be too chuffed at swapping his warm bed for a night at the house of doom,' he said with a laugh.

The giggle she gave made his pulse quicken. 'I won't,' she said, climbing out of the car. 'Though judging by the way he spent the day gazing at Maudie like a love-struck teenager, I don't suppose he'd mind that much.'

'You could be right,' he said with a chuckle, recalling how Maudie had been utterly indifferent to Wilf's adoring looks.

He waited until Brogan unlocked the porch door, giving one last wave before disappearing into the farmhouse. Nick felt the pull of a huge smile spreading across his face. What a day it had been. The word "roller coaster" sprang to mind. It had felt like he'd been careering perilously around on one today, and he could safely say, the high points had definitely outweighed the low ones. He'd felt optimistic about starting his first day at Danskelfe Vets, as if he'd turned a corner, was moving on – to use the appropriate clichés – but to see Brogan there... Wow! Just wow! He shook his head in disbelief. Knowing he was going to see her again, hoping upon hope that he hadn't been wrong about the connection they'd had at the wedding flickering back to life – that she'd felt it too – made going back to a freezing cold house, with even colder water, worth the while.

'Well, Maudie, what do you make of all that then?' He didn't have to look at Maudie to know the expression she was wearing and it made him chuckle. 'I know, I won't go doing anything hasty.' He put the car into gear. 'You like her too, don't you? And we all know how chilly you can be with people you've only just met; even colder than Willow Cottage.'

Back at the house of doom, Nick's spirits sank down to his chunky boots as soon as he put the key in the door. He flicked the light switch in the hallway, hoping that by some miracle the electricity had come back on, despite common sense telling him he'd have to at least try to turn on the trip switch before that stood a chance of happening. 'Oh, well, no surprises there,' he said with a sigh.

It was going to be a long, cold night, but at least he had a little nugget of hope. Brogan's reappearance into his life would help him through it, of that he was sure, even if he didn't know exactly how she was going to feature.

TWENTY

NICK

The next morning, Nick was awake before the alarm went off, his body stiff from sleeping curled up in a tight ball in a bid to conserve what little precious heat he'd managed to miraculously generate. He'd slept fitfully thanks to the cold that had crept in and burrowed its way under the duvet, sneaking right into his very core. And it hadn't helped that the window had rattled persistently in its frame as the wind had howled around the cottage. He'd thrown the rule book out as far as having pets sleeping on the bed were concerned and had let Maudie upstairs to cuddle up with him. She'd snored shamelessly, but he hadn't cared; her presence had been a comfort.

He rubbed his eyes and Maudie stirred beside him before quickly snuggling back down, apparently as reluctant as he was to move and let even a tiny scrap of warmth escape. It was still dark outside but for the light from street lamp that filtered in through the thin curtains, casting shadows around the room. Nick lay staring at the shapes on the ceiling as thoughts started filtering into his mind. The first one being Brogan and her welcome arrival back into his life. Wow! That chased any residue of sleep away. That she'd turned up at Danskelfe Vets – and her first day being the same as his –was more than just a coincidence, he was sure of it.

He couldn't help but smile as he pictured her face, animated as she chatted away to her friends the previous evening, her eyes expressive. A happy glow spread through him, his heart giving a gentle squeeze. In the next moment, he bumped unceremoniously back down to earth as Loretta and the shoes elbowed their way into his thoughts, quickly followed by the lack of electricity and hot water at the house of doom. Adding salt to the wound, he remembered what he'd been told about the gas fire being condemned. Nick groaned and clamped his hand over his forehead, unsure of which problem to tackle first, never mind how he was going to fit it all into his day.

After seeing a slew of text messages and missed calls from Loretta when he'd got home last night, he'd turned his phone off, not wanting to take the happy edge off the time he'd spent with Brogan and her friends. He was dreading listening to what she had to say today. Reluctant to dwell on that, he pushed back the duvet that was heavy thanks to the clothes he'd piled on top for extra warmth. He grabbed his dressing gown – which was conveniently on top – and braved the chilly air of the bedroom, a feeling of doom descending on him. He went to peer out of the window to see a thin layer of ice had formed over the glass; confirmation of just how cold the night had been – as if he needed any.

Since there was no way to make a cup of tea, nor make any toast, Nick had a quick shave and got dressed, telling himself he'd grab something at the surgery. He'd take Maudie for a walk once they were there too. In the meantime, he needed to get a move on; get to Brogan's to scoop her up for work. Determined not to have his usual last minute panic before he left the house that morning, he'd made a concerted effort before he'd gone to bed by putting his keys and his phone in the pockets of his waxed jacket. That would, at least, eliminate the risk of not being able to find them in the semi-dark. Plus, the cottage being so bone-numbingly cold meant he wasn't keen to hang around; the sooner he got to the warmth of the surgery and thawed out, the better. He couldn't remember ever being this cold in a house in his life.

Nick opened the front door, the crisp air filling his lungs and spreading across his chest as he breathed in. There'd been a covering of snow overnight, and a lone set of tyre tracks ran down the middle of the road, illuminated by the streetlight.

Up above, dawn was breaking, and thick, pewter clouds hung low in the sky, threatening the moors with a fresh assault of wintry weather. Nick couldn't imagine it getting properly light all day. The lack of electricity at the cottage jumped into his mind again and he groaned inwardly. He really needed to get onto the Trotters about that as a priority. He pulled up his collar and headed to his car, letting Maudie in the large boot area. Then he set the engine away, the vents on full, heat turned up to the max, as he made a start on scraping the snow from the windscreen, all the while, the cruel wind slicing at his face and ears.

The journey to Brogan's hadn't been as dicey as Nick had expected thanks to the roads being ploughed – the previous evening Nick had learnt that Camm had the contract for ploughing around the Great Stangdale area stretching to Danskelfe, Arkleby and leading up to the main moor road. Local farmers had also helped by spreading grit from the bins dotted about along the roadside.

Before long, Nick pulled up in the yard of Pond Farm, lights glowing from the downstairs windows. He saw Brogan peer out from one. A moment later she was locking the front door while Wilf trotted over to the car, leaving a trail of paw prints in the snow, his tail swishing happily.

Nick got out and let the Labrador in beside Maudie who gave him one of her indifferent looks. Wilf was oblivious and looked absolutely thrilled to be in her company again as he nudged at her face.

'Hi, Nick. Thanks for this,' said Brogan, the wind whipping the words from her mouth as she headed over to him, her wellies crunching over the snow.

'It's not a problem at all,' he said, his heart lifting at the sight of her all snuggled up in her padded jacket, tendrils of hair from her ponytail blowing around.

Once in the car, she said, 'Jeez, it's bloomin' freezing this morning, but it's nice and toasty in here. My car never warms up in winter. Anyway, how was it at the house of doom? Not too cold, I hope. And is the electric back on?' She rubbed her hands together vigorously.

He was pleased to see there was no awkwardness between them this morning. 'I'm afraid I have to report that the house of doom was pretty cold. And, sadly, the electric's not back on. I tried it again before I left, but something's tripping it out and I don't know where to start looking for the cause, though I've got a sneaking suspicion it might be something to do with the central heating boiler which doesn't seem keen to fire up.'

'Right.' She was thoughtful for a moment, gazing out into the semi-light at the snow covered fields. 'And are you sure there's enough fuel – I mean calor gas or oil – to run the heating? That could be why it's not working.'

'Hmm. According to the bumf that came with the cottage, the central heating runs on oil. But now you mention it, checking the level's not a bad idea.' It was another thing to add to his list for the dratted cottage.

Brogan turned to face him. 'You really need to find somewhere else to live, you know, Nick. That place sounds like a death trap. The Trotters should be reported for renting out a cottage that's not fit to live in. They have one hell of a nerve, charging people for that.'

He glanced across at her to see she was wearing a serious expression. It touched his heart. 'It really didn't seem that bad when I first looked around it; just a bit dated, but it was always going to be a short-term stay for me until I found somewhere more suitable. And I put the fact that it was cold down to it having been empty for a while and the heating not being on.'

'Warghh! Look out!' Brogan gripped onto her seat, her eyes wide.

Alarmed, Nick quickly swung his gaze back to the road to see a deer leaping out in front of his car.

'Wha—? Oh, blast!' He slammed his breaks on, the skidding tyres setting the car spinning around full circle. Brogan let out a squeal as they just avoided colliding with a dry stone wall, before gliding slowly to a halt.

Nick puffed out his cheeks and released a slow breath, his heart hammering in his chest.

'Phew! That was close,' said Brogan, her breathing heavy.

He craned his neck to see the creature bounding away across the field. 'You're not kidding. Remind me to keep my eyes very firmly on the road around here. I missed clipping it by a nano-second.'

'It's a hazard of driving round here, I'm afraid. You'll find you're always dodging something; sheep, rabbits, pheasant...'

'And, as I've just discovered, deer,' he said, hitching his eyebrows as her eyes met his.

'Yep, deer,' she said. 'And what happened to you keeping your eyes on the road? That didn't last long, did it?' They both chuckled at that.

'Point taken.' He jokingly cast her a sideways look.

'Eyes back on the road, please,' she said, delivering a gentle backhander to his arm.

They were the first to arrive at the surgery – being the first to arrive anywhere was a novelty to Nick and he found he quite liked the calm feeling it instilled rather than arriving late and flustered as he usually did. He checked the appointment list while Brogan headed off to get changed into her scrubs. He'd turned his phone on just before he'd left Willow Cottage and stuffed it straight back into his jacket pocket as the missed calls and messages filed in. He'd been aware of it buzzing away for most of the journey here; checking the messages had been filling him with increasing dread. He didn't need to look to know who the bulk of the communication would be from. And he knew he'd have to face Loretta at some point today. He might as well get it over and done with, the sooner the better. With a heavy heart, he called her number.

'Nick!' she said, her snappy tone making him wince. 'What excuse do you have this time for not dropping my shoes off? I really am intrigued to know. Anyone would think you were being deliberately awkward about it.'

'Loretta, I'm honestly not being awkward. I'd planned on dropping them off last night, but I had a stinker of an evening. The electricity's off at my—'

She huffed impatiently down the phone. 'I don't want your excuses, Nick, I want my shoes. Tonight. I've already told you how desperately I need them. I don't know what you think you've got to gain by dragging it out. You're being childish. And infuriating! You need to get used to the fact that we're over; hanging onto my shoes isn't going to make us get back together. Quite the opposite, in fact. As I've said repeatedly, leave them on the doorstep. Oh, and make sure it's done today or I'll be forced to come and get them myself.' With that she ended the call.

Nick felt the start of a stress headache brewing at his temples. Since their split, he'd lost the will to stand up to her; it was too much like hard work. She'd got so that she'd never back down. Over the last six months, he'd found himself getting dragged into her way of arguing and point-scoring. It didn't sit well with his easy-going personality and now he'd had a gutful. Slipping his phone into the back pocket of his jeans, he closed his eyes and sucked in a deep breath just as Brogan walked in with a mug of tea.

'Oh! Is everything okay?' she asked, concerned. 'I wasn't sure if you'd had breakfast, what with the power being off at your cottage, so I wondered if you fancied some toast, but if you'd rather I...' She hesitated by the door.

He looked over at her pretty, earnest face. It was touching that it had crossed her mind that he might not have eaten. But he'd been so wound up about speaking to Loretta, it had quashed any feelings of hunger and left his stomach churning instead. The thought that Brogan was the polar opposite of this new Loretta he was faced with rushed into his head. His ex had gone all hard and prickly since she'd hooked up with Aaron. He'd bet she didn't talk to his ex-best mate the way she spoke to him. She'd be all lovey-dovey, purring in his ear, not be able to do enough for him, saving her new cold side for conversations with Nick. And that hurt. Really hurt. Especially when they'd been together for three years and had been making preparations to get married mere weeks before she'd dumped him. Nick marvelled at how she'd been able to turn her feelings on and off so quickly.

He rubbed his hand over the back of his neck and puffed out his cheeks, suddenly gripped by the overwhelming feeling that he'd had enough of this whole damned situation. He was weary of feeling that he was always doing something wrong; never seemed to be able to get it right. Yes, he should probably have got the shoes over to her last night – it would certainly have saved him some earache – but if only she'd listened to why it was difficult for him with the state of the cottage, maybe she could have understood. But no, she wasn't even prepared to listen to his explanation. It was beginning to feel like Loretta got some kind of pleasure out of him "failing"; seeing it as some kind of victory over him. And boy, was he weary of the endless gut-churning confrontations with her. He didn't want to do it anymore; simply didn't have the energy. He'd get her precious flaming shoes to her tonight. Come hell or high water, he'd make sure she had them. That way, he wouldn't have to endure these phone calls any longer. Then they could focus on getting the house sold. And, yes, it could be considered irresponsible of him, and he might end up regretting it later if he didn't have enough capital to put down as a deposit on a house, but he didn't care if the house he'd shared with her went for less than it was worth. The prospect of being free from all this grief far outweighed the difference it would make to his pocket. Yes, he thought, he'd do all he could to hurry the sale through.

It took him by surprise, how much brighter reaching that decision made him feel, the relief tangible, giving him hope that he could move on.

He heaved another sigh, felt his shoulders relax and smiled at Brogan. 'I can't tell you what a welcome sight you are.'

'Oh... um.' Her face turned crimson, masking her smattering of freckles. 'I always feel that way when someone brings me a cup of tea too.' She giggled, the creases lifting from her brow. 'Here, get this down you. I bet you haven't had a warm drink this morning. I wouldn't be able to function without a cuppa to start my day, I'd be like a zombie. And how about that toast?' She smiled up at him.

It dawned on him he hadn't had any kind of drink that morning, never mind a warm one. No wonder his head was throbbing – he couldn't attribute all of the blame to Loretta. 'That would be lovely, though I can get it myself. I don't expect you to run around after me.'

'I'm happy to do it; we're here early, making toast doesn't take long,' she said with a shrug, her blushes fading. 'Jam, marmalade or just butter?'

'Hmm. Jam, I think, would be nice.'

'Jam it is. I'll give you a shout when it's ready; you might as well have it at the table in the staffroom, rather than wolfing it down standing up.'

'Thanks. And, Brogan...'

She turned to look at him, her big green eyes making his senses leap to attention. 'Yeah?'

He smiled. 'I really appreciate it.'

'That's okay.' She smiled back. 'It's only a couple of slices of toast,' she said with a shrug.

It may only be a couple of slices of toast, but the simple act of kindness at the very moment he needed it, gave him a bigger boost than she could ever imagine.

He watched her disappear through the door, her ponytail swinging. Whatever indefinable quality this intriguing young woman possessed, it reached inside him and touched his soul. And it made facing the problems at Willow Cottage a little less daunting.

Before he knew it, the comforting aroma of toast wafted its way to his consulting room, giving his appetite a kick-start. He picked up his mug of tea and followed the smell to the staffroom where Brogan was setting a plate piled high with slices of toast on the table. The dogs looked on hopefully from their place by the stove. Wilf was drooling shamelessly.

'Mmm. Toast has never looked so good,' Nick said, meaning it.

'Well, get stuck in before it gets cold. And please ignore Wilf over there, sucking his cheeks in like he hasn't been fed for a week; he's a right greedy guts. Oh, and the jam's summer berries, by the way. I hope that's okay. It's from the shop in the village; homemade by Lucy, she's one of the owners. I'm not sure if you've been before, but it sells everything, has a teashop attached to it too.'

'The jam sounds delicious. And I'll be sure to give the village shop a try.' Nick was happy to see Brogan talking easily with him, no hint of yesterday's awkwardness. He buttered a slice of toast, gave it a generous slather of jam and bit into it, his tastebuds dancing. 'Mmm. The jam really is good,' he said appreciatively through his mouthful.

Brogan beamed. 'I thought you'd like it; it's my favourite, especially on Bea's creamy rice pudding. Mmm-hmm.' She rolled her eyes as if in ecstasy. It made his pulse surge unexpectedly as the last time he'd seen her wearing that very expression exploded into his mind.

Wow! Down boy! He gulped and took a slug of his tea. Must be seriously good rice pudding, he thought.

Just then, Jules and Becky bustled in, wrapped up well against the cold, each sporting a dusting of snow flakes.

After a slew of "good mornings" and comments exchanged about the delicious smell of toast and the weather – according to Jules, the moors were due to be dumped with a load of snow from the Arctic later that week – Nick's wayward thoughts had been brought under control and packed away.

Oblivious to the emotions she'd triggered in him, Brogan said, 'Right, I'm just going to go and clean the kennels. I'll contact Jed at the garage about my car on my break later this morning.'

'Okay.' He'd momentarily forgotten about her car being stuck in Lytell Stangdale. 'I'll give you a lift to drop the keys off if you like, or I can do it for you? Oh, and thanks for this,' he said with a smile, raising the slice of toast he had in his hand.

Jules and Becky watched with interest, hanging up their coats, a "blink-and-you'll-miss-it" raise of an eyebrow from Becky.

Judging by the two dots of colour that had appeared on her cheeks, Brogan had spotted it. 'You're welcome,' she said, before scurrying off.

TWENTY-ONE
BROGAN

Her second day at Danskelfe Vets had whizzed by. Brogan hadn't stopped for a minute, and she'd loved it. The only thing left to do after checking on the pets that were staying at the surgery overnight, was to have a word with Vonnie. The practice manager had asked Brogan to give her a knock before she left, then she could give her a quick update on her training. She felt excited at the prospect of refreshing her knowledge, of feeling that she deserved this job.

Brogan had contacted Jed from the garage over at Danskelfe in her morning break. Much to her relief, he'd told her he needed to call at the surgery to get some worming tablets for his dogs so would kill two birds with one stone and pick up the car keys at the same time, which he'd done. It had removed the problem of her having to accept Nick's offer of a lift to drop them off, or of him doing it on her behalf, which would have run the risk of piquing Jules and Becky's interest further. Something she wasn't keen to do at all. Nor did she like to trouble Nick.

Since his visit to the surgery, Jed had taken a look at her car and mentioned a problem with some part he'd have to order in. Brogan was happy to tackle any range of DIY projects, but cars were a whole different matter and she didn't have much of a clue of what he was talking about, but he had a reputation for being honest and not ripping people off and she trusted him implicitly – unlike his cousin over at Middleton-le-Moors, who was well known for carrying out unnecessary work and charging people through the nose. 'Mind, Brogan, like I mentioned at the time, it scraped through its last MOT by the skin of its teeth, and things have got worse since then. I hate to say it, but I reckon it's going to cost more than the car's worth to put it right. You might be better off selling it for scrap and getting something a bit newer. I'll do what I can to get you by for now though, but I can't guarantee it'll last for long,' Jed had said. She'd thanked him, releasing a despondent sigh when she'd ended the call.

It wasn't the news Brogan had hoped for on the run up to Christmas, especially with all the extra expense the season entailed, but she supposed it could have been worse; he could have said her ancient little car was beyond repair right now – which she'd secretly half-expected. It also meant that she would need a lift home after work, and back here in the morning, which wasn't ideal, especially for someone who was so resolutely used to being independent and loathed relying on anyone for anything. She only ever asked for help as a last resort, when no alternative was available, and it always pained her to do so. Indeed, she was regularly told by Kristy and Anoushka that she never asked for help when she should, that they would be happy to help, *wanted* to help. 'That's what friends are for, Broge,' Anoushka had said, quickly followed by Kristy who'd said, 'Yeah, you don't need asking twice when we need help; you're always the first to jump in and offer, so why should it be different for you?' But old habits died hard, and even though Brogan totally got this, something deep inside her made it difficult to push herself and take that step. She never wanted to run the risk of being viewed as a nuisance; the mere thought was utterly repellent. It was probably why her dog-walking business had got so out of hand; even though there'd been barely enough hours in the day for her to exercise all her canine charges, letting any new clients down and saying she was too busy was unthinkable in her book. Which was why she'd been so glad when Ella Welford had offered to help out.

But the loss of her beloved grandparents had changed Brogan's outlook on life, and a seed of disquiet had taken root inside her. It had triggered a little voice that whispered in her ear, telling her life was too short to do things that didn't make you properly happy. That she should grab the bull by the horns and go for it; put her own wishes and needs first for a change. Which she, blushingly, thought probably explained why she'd acted so out of character with Nick the first time they'd met. She'd unequivocally put her needs and wishes first that day! Big time. On a more serious note, it was also the very reason she'd brought her dog walking business to an end, and now had her wonderful job at Danskelfe Vets, which was something she couldn't imagine regretting for a moment.

There was only one thing that had the potential to be a spanner in the works and that, sadly, was Nick Heuston. But, after giving it some thought, Brogan came to the conclusion that the best way to manage their "situation" was to carry on as if their "brief encounter", as Nick had referred to it, simply hadn't happened, hoping it would eventually fade away to nothing and become a distant, dusty memory. And she hoped Nick would follow suit without her having to say anything; hoped he'd forget about the "chat" he'd mentioned. Much as she liked him – *really* liked him – the more she thought about it the more she believed adopting this tactic would be easier for everyone. It would make everything way less complicated, which is just how she liked her life.

There was only one flaw in her plan. Nick Heuston seemed to be occupying more and more of her thoughts, with her mind regularly slipping back to the day they'd first met. Of how he'd made her feel, not to mention the emotions he kick-started inside her when they were together, the electricity that sparked around them. She'd never experienced anything like it before. It wasn't going to be easy to ignore.

Despite this new change in her career and outlook, it still didn't mean Brogan was any better at asking for help. Even as it sank in that she'd be without a car for a few days at least, her mind was working to find a way to get to and from the surgery without troubling anyone else, least of all Nick. She didn't want him to start thinking of her as a burden or a headache. She shuddered at the thought. The old Land Rover sitting in the yard at home had crossed her mind, and she'd wondered if Jed could take a look at it with a view to fixing it, but she'd quickly discounted that; he'd already told her he was rushed off his feet and had squeezed her little car in as a favour because his parents had been good friends of her grandparents. Plus, fitting a new chassis would involve stripping the vehicle right down and that wouldn't be cheap. She'd even considered making the journey on foot, her heart sinking as she realised it would put her back to traipsing over the moors in awful weather conditions. Much as it went against the grain, maybe she'd just have to bite the bullet and accept Nick's offer of help.

Brogan had grown up to be fiercely independent and was accustomed to fending for herself without giving it a second thought. Her dad, Steve, had walked out when she was a toddler. His contact while she was growing up had been sporadic until it had petered out to virtually nothing when Brogan was in her early teens, leaving them little opportunity to form any kind of relationship. Brogan had lost count of how many years it had been since she'd last seen him. As a consequence, her mum, Cathy, had become a hardworking, single parent who had striven to forge a career for herself, gaining promotion after promotion, working long hours so she could provide Brogan with the best of everything, which she had. A downside of this meant that, growing up, Brogan hadn't seen much of her mum and had learnt how to be self-sufficient at an early age. Looking back she didn't feel any bitterness about this or felt that she'd missed out. Her mum had always been loving and affectionate when they'd spent time together which, to Brogan's way of thinking, more than made up for it. Rather, she felt the experience had made her stronger. She'd been letting herself in with a key, helping with the washing and ironing, and making her own tea when she got in from school since she was twelve years old – though she'd been made to promise not to tell her grandparents, who Cathy knew wouldn't approve.

Brogan had been okay with this arrangement but it didn't stop her from being thrilled when the holidays came round and she'd go to stay at Pond Farm, which she'd loved, especially the long six weeks over the summer when she'd stay the full stretch. In that time, when she wasn't tearing about outside or jumping on bales of hay stacked in the barn, she'd learn to bake with her grandma and tackle DIY jobs under the watchful eye of her grandad – she'd become a whizz at doing repairs around the smallholding which had come in handy when she'd moved there full-time. They were the happiest of times. She'd forged a close relationship with her grandparents, particularly so her grandma. On the days Brogan was too ill to go to school, her grandparents would scoop her up and take her back to Pond Farm where her grandma would dote on her, making her restorative bowls of chicken soup and dole out some much needed TLC. They'd made her feel she was the centre of their world and utterly loved.

'So, that's me done for the day,' said Nick, wandering out of his consulting room and into the reception area where Brogan was speaking to Vonnie about the training course she was booked in for the following month. At almost quarter to seven, they were the only ones left at the surgery.

Brogan glanced across at him, feeling a flutter in her stomach as they made eye contact.

'Yep, we're all done here too,' said Vonnie. 'It's late, you get yourself home now, Brogan. And can I just say how pleased I am that you're settling in so quickly.'

Thanks.' Brogan beamed, hoping to calm her surging pulse. 'Everyone's been very welcoming and friendly.'

'That's what I like to hear. And hopefully that little car of yours will get fixed soon,' said the practice manager. Brogan had told Vonnie how Nick had offered to give her a lift owing to her car breaking down, hoping to allay any gossip before it got legs and started racing around the practice.

'I hope so too. See you in the morning, Vonnie, and thanks for booking those courses.'

'No problem, flower.' Vonnie smiled kindly at her as she headed towards her office.

With Wilf and Maudie scooped up, Brogan and Nick braved the weather outside. Frost glittered over everything in the outside lights. The wind had dropped a little but it was still bone-numbingly cold, with a clear, star-strewn sky up above.

As they were pulling out of the carpark Nick turned to Brogan and said, 'Can I be a real pain in the bum? Would you mind if I called at Willow Cottage before I drop you off? I've got to pick something up then head over to Middleton-le-Moors, and it would save me doubling back on myself.'

'Not at all. I'm grateful of you giving me a lift, I don't expect you to double-back on my account.' Brogan glanced across at him from the gap between her thick, woolly scarf and bobble hat as she snuggled down against the cold. She couldn't help but wonder what made him need to go over to Middleton tonight. A girlfriend, maybe? She felt a prickle of jealousy at that thought, quickly batting it away as she reminded herself of her resolution to act as if nothing had happened between them.

They chatted away as they drove steadily along the twisting roads to Arkleby, Brogan savouring spending time with him. He really was good to be around. They laughed about Terence the ginger tom cat who'd escaped his owner's clutches and taken off around Nick's consulting room. He'd smugly perched himself on top of one of the cupboards, mewing pitifully while they tried to coax him down. In the end, Terence had leapt onto Nick's shoulder where the vet acted speedily and managed to grab the cat and, with Brogan's assistance, had manoeuvred him round so he could hold him steadily while his owner described why she'd brought Terence to the surgery. Nick had earned himself an array of angry scratches for his trouble. 'I reckon old Terence had an inkling Mrs Ventress had come to talk about having him neutered,' he said with a chuckle. 'Come to think of it, I'd be tempted to put myself out of harm's way if I was threatened with the procedure.'

It wasn't long before they were pulling up outside Willow Cottage. Brogan peered out of the window at the small property. There was no doubting it had the potential to be quaint if it didn't look quite so foreboding in the dark.

Nick pulled on the handbrake and stilled the engine. 'I might be a while – I've got to find something; it's, or should I say, *they* are in one of the boxes I've yet to unpack.' He paused a moment, chewing on his bottom lip. 'Actually, it might be best if I take you home. I don't know why I thought to come here first, it makes no sense. The house is in darkness, I forgot to pick up a torch; I've only got the light from the torch on my phone. It's probably going to take me ages to find what I'm looking for.' He scratched his head. 'I'd suggest you come in, make yourself comfortable, but that's the last thing the cottage is; it's freezing and decidedly uncomfortable; I can't expect to you wait in those conditions while I rifle through a load of boxes. No, I'll take you home.' He started the car up again.

'I can help, if you like? There's the torch on my phone and I've also got a little one on my house keys; it's got a really strong beam. With two of us looking we'll be able to find whatever it is twice as quickly.' She didn't like to see Nick look so sad and stressed.

She watched his face in the warm glow of the street light, his expression changing as he ran her suggestion over in his mind. He turned to her. 'Are you sure you don't mind?'

'Not at all. Come on, let's get cracking. You can tell me what it is you're looking for. The sooner we get started, the better.' She opened the car door and stepped out.

'Okay. Though I suggest we leave Wilf and Maudie where they are, they'll at least be warm in the car,' he said as he headed towards the short, icy path to the cottage.

Nick put his keys in the door, giving them their usual jiggle about before the lock relented with a loud clunk. He went to push the door open but it didn't budge. 'Must've swelled with the damp,' he said as he put his shoulder to it. On the third push, it finally opened. In the next moment, he released a loud gasp as icy cold water rushed over his feet. 'What the—?'

'Arghh!' Brogan, who was standing right behind him, squealed as a mini river gushed down the step and onto the path, making her glad she was wearing her wellies. Nick appeared to be rooted to the spot, his hand clamped to his forehead. She peered around him and flicked her torch on, shining it into the hallway, her eyes alighting on a row of cardboard boxes standing in several inches of water. 'Oh, dear.' Whatever was in them would very probably be ruined.

'I can't believe it! Where the heck has all this water come from?' Nick said, exasperated as it continued to rush by, the step creating a little waterfall.

'I suspect it's a burst pipe.' Brogan shifted the beam of her torch to the ceiling to see an array of watermarks spreading across it.

'You're kidding me? Could anything else possibly go wrong with this cottage?' He huffed out a noisy sigh.

Brogan felt a pang of pity for him which sent her straight into coping mode. 'Right then, we need to keep the door open, let the water run out; see, the level's sinking already. The water supply needs turning off as quickly as possible. It's a good thing the electricity isn't working, or we might've been faced with bigger problems. I'm guessing the kitchen's through at the back?' she asked, sloshing through the water and inching by the sodden boxes in the hallway.

'Oh, right, yeah, it's through there.' Nick was rubbing his hand over the back of his neck, his eyes fixed on the boxes. He started muttering something that Brogan could have sworn sounded like he was yet to face his biggest problem. She briefly wondered what that could mean as she reached the kitchen and her attention was taken by the sound of pouring water. She shone her torch in the direction of the sound to see an impressive water feature running down the wall by the oven. 'Oh heck!' She needed to act quickly. 'At the risk of asking a stupid question, you didn't leave a bath running this morning, did you?'

'No, there was no hot water and I'm not in the habit of starting my day with an icy dip.'

'Good point. If you have a sweeping brush and know where it is, can you grab it and start swilling the water out onto the path?'

'I can't remember seeing a sweeping brush but I'll go and check in the shed outside.' Brogan heard him sploosh his way to the backdoor.

With her torch in her mouth, she squatted in front of the cupboard under the sink, relieved to see it wasn't full of cleaning equipment or junk like the rest of the cottage appeared to be. With the sound of running water reminding her of the urgency of the situation, she pushed the bottle of washing-up liquid to one side and reached in. Grasping the stopcock, she went to give it a twist but it was stuck fast. 'Typical!' After a brief but unsuccessful struggle, not helped by her clumsy hands that were seizing up with the cold, she reached for the tea towel she'd seen hanging by the sink. She hurriedly wrapped it around the stopcock handle and tried again, her face distorted with the effort, but still no luck. She took a moment's break, gasping, before going in for another try. There was no way she was going to let a pesky little stopcock defeat her. Mustering every ounce of strength she had, she sucked in a deep breath and went for it. 'Waarghh!' After several drawn out seconds, the tap finally turned. Oh, the relief! Her heart was racing. She puffed out a steamy breath and twisted it as fast as she was able until it was shut tight.

Sitting back on her haunches with her chest heaving, she took the torch from her mouth, rubbing her hand over her dry lips. 'The water's off,' she called to Nick who she realised must have found a sweeping brush since she could hear the sound of him swooshing the mini river out onto the front path. Already, it was making a difference to the level.

Nick appeared in the doorway. 'Oh, thank God for that. And thank you for acting so quickly. My head was all over the place when I saw those boxes, the state of them totally threw me.' His breath hung in a cloud as he spoke. Even in the semi-light she could see he wore an air of defeat. Her heart squeezed for him. He hadn't had much luck with this place, that was for sure.

'Yeah, it can't have been easy to see.' Brogan dreaded to think how she'd have felt if she'd returned home to find Pond Farm in a state like this. She eased herself up, grabbed the washing-up bowl from the sink so she could help bail the water out, and made her way over to him, her legs stiff from squatting. She suddenly became aware that her jeans were drenched, the wet denim sticking to her goosebump-covered skin. Her teeth began to chatter violently; she couldn't ever remember feeling this cold.

'Crikey, Brogan, you look freezing. Here, have this.' He took his jacket off and placed it over her shoulders.

'There's honestly no need,' she said through chattering teeth. 'I'll help you bail the rest of the water out; that'll warm me up.'

'I think there's every need; you look like you're turning blue,' he said. 'There's no way you're going to do anything else; we need to get you out of here quickly.'

Brogan couldn't argue with that. She had a sneaking suspicion water had lapped in over her wellies when she was working on the stopcock, but her toes were so cold she could no longer feel them to tell. 'I don't think you can live here anymore. It's not habitable; you'll die of hypothermia. I don't think Maudie would be very impressed if you brought her in here.' Shivering, Brogan managed a laugh.

'Oh, Lord, she so wouldn't.' Nick gave a hoot of laughter just as part of the ceiling collapsed onto the sink.

'Wargh!' They said simultaneously, directing their torches towards where yet more water was cascading from the bathroom.

'Bloody hell, Brogan, you were over there only seconds ago! It could have fallen onto you; you could've been injured.'

In the next moment, she felt two strong arms wrap around her, pulling her close. With her head pressed against his chest she could hear his heart beat, it was pounding as hard as her own. She briefly closed her eyes, the warmth of his body comforting, taking her back to that night of just a few weeks ago, but the cold was becoming increasingly permeating as an icy wind blew in through the open door, quashing her musings.

Nick was the first to pull away, resting his hands on the top of her arms. 'I'll get locked up here, then get you home. I'll give Chris a ring, see if I can crash at his place for the night. Then I'll call the Trotters, let them know what's happened here. I'm not going to get across to Middleton now,' he said despondently.

Brogan felt a twinge in her heart. 'You can stay at my place. I've got a spare room. You can use it 'til you get somewhere else sorted out.'

TWENTY-TWO

NICK

Nick took a moment to absorb her words. 'Are you sure?' he asked her. 'I mean, I kind of got the impression you weren't keen to—'

'I wouldn't offer if I wasn't sure,' Brogan said, her tone suggesting she didn't want to hear what impression he'd got. 'Though I should warn you, the kitchen's nice and toasty, but the rest of the house isn't what you'd exactly call cosy. But it's a damn sight warmer than this place – drier too,' she said with a shivery laugh.

'Well, that wouldn't be difficult.' He laughed too, hesitating a moment before he said, 'Are you absolutely positive? I mean, I'm sure Chris wouldn't mind.'

'I'm positive. Now if you wouldn't mind, it's absolutely freezing; please can we get out of this place before anything else goes wrong with it?'

'Good point,' Nick said, thankful that the water had stopped pouring.

He helped a shivering Brogan into his car and set the engine away, turning the heat as high as it would go. Maudie and Wilf looked on with interest. 'I know it seems counter-intuitive given the temperature, but it might be better if you get those wet jeans off.

I've got a couple of blankets on the back seat, you can wrap one of those around yourself.'

'Bet you say that to all the girls,' she said, mustering up a grin.

'Yep, never fails.' He grinned back, reaching behind him for a blanket. 'While you're doing that, I'm just going to pop back into the house of doom, pick up some essentials before we head off.'

Inside the cottage, he had a quick scrabble inside the storage boxes, assisted by the light of Brogan's torch. If he did nothing else, he needed to find Loretta's shoes. He started with the boxes in his bedroom, hoping they'd turn up in one of those, safe and dry. He knew there was no chance he was going to get them to her tonight, but at least if he found them, he could drop them off tomorrow, put an end to the tortuous text messages. And it wasn't as if she needed them right now.

'Typical,' he said when he'd been through all the boxes in the bedroom to find there was no sign of the shoes. During his rummage, it hadn't escaped his attention that Loretta had given him a selection of their engagement presents he knew she didn't like, including the print with some obscure piece of modern art she'd said reminded her of an angry red elephant and the vase hand-painted in garish colours by one of her aunts. Rather bizarrely, she'd also included a framed photo he'd taken of her in a white bikini when they'd holidayed in Greece last year. 'Why would you do that, Loretta?' he said aloud. The message it appeared to send was "This is what you're missing". Nick wasn't quite sure why he'd need to feel that way. Did she still want him to pine for her? His mind snapped back to the cold that was seeping in, making him feel crotchety. He threw the photo back in the box, pushed himself up and made his way carefully downstairs where he eventually found the elusive shoes in one of the storage boxes in the living room. Tentatively, he lifted the saturated shoe box out, watching in disbelief as the cardboard fell apart in his hands revealing the champagne-coloured satin shoes. Nick's stomach clenched. Even in the torchlight it was easy to see they were heavily stained with watermarks. They were ruined. 'Oh, no.' He swallowed, feeling his heart sink all the way to the icy depths of his boots as Loretta's reaction to hearing the news crowded his mind. She was going to go absolutely ape.

By the time they pulled up in the yard of Pond Cottage, the car had warmed through and Brogan had finally stopped shivering, the heated seats helping the process. She pushed her feet back into her soggy wellies while Nick let Maudie and Wilf out of the boot. They seemed pleased after being cooped up for a while, and trotted busily around the yard, leaving a smattering of paw prints on the crisp, white snow. Wilf, who was giving something a thorough sniffing, gave a loud snort, shook his head and followed up with a slew of sneezes after inhaling a nostril full of snow. 'You okay, Wilf?' Brogan asked with a giggle. He looked across at her, wagging his tail as she hurried over to the porch. She was holding onto the blanket she had wrapped around her with one hand, whilst unlocking the door with the other. As soon as she pushed it open, Wilf shot inside with Maudie in hot pursuit.

'Don't mind me, you two,' she said, chuckling.

'I don't think they do.' Nick gave a laugh as he followed her into the wooden porch, the prospect of spending the evening in Brogan's company filled his heart with warmth.

She eased off her wellies. 'Oh, I can't tell you how much better that feels,' she said, wiggling her toes that had turned a vivid pink with the cold.

'I can imagine.' Nick set his overnight bag down on the floor and removed his wet boots. She was right, it did feel better.

The porch led to a cosy-looking kitchen with a gently undulating floor of quarry tiles that, though they looked centuries old, were polished to a rich amber. Warmth from the Aga wrapped itself around him and he sighed gratefully, though he couldn't ignore the slightly surreal feeling of finding himself standing in the kitchen of her home. If Brogan felt the same, she wasn't letting on.

'Right then, here we are,' she said, smiling up at him. 'I'll stick the kettle on, make us a nice, hot cuppa.'

'Ah, I do like a girl who gets her priorities right,' said Nick. Their eyes met and they exchanged a smile. There was that frisson, shimmering between them again.

'Of course; a cup of tea always comes first,' she said. 'When my grandparents were still here, the teapot was never empty.'

Nick noted her grandparents featured regularly in her conversation, but not so much her parents. In fact, he couldn't recall her mentioning them at all, but, then again, they hadn't had that many opportunities to chat, he figured. And he probably hadn't mentioned his either; he'd had no reason to.

Weariness suddenly crept up on him. What a day it had been. Was it really only this morning Brogan had been making him tea and toast? Today had been so long, with so much being thrown at him, the tea and toast could easily have been forty-eight hours ago.

Nick glanced around the pin-neat room. Though the décor was dated and there were loads of knick-knacks dotted about, taking up every bit of available shelf-space – the dark oak dresser particularly so, which was cluttered with a mix of blue and white china, and little pottery animals – it was spotlessly clean and positively oozed homeliness. It wasn't difficult to conjure up an image of noisy family dinners around the old pine table where a jug of holly, festooned with bright red berries, currently sat in the centre. The thought made him feel instantly brighter.

'Please excuse the décor, it's how my grandparents had it – not that I'm criticising their taste but it's been pretty much the same as far back as I can remember. I'm sure it was the height of fashion in the eighties or nineties but I haven't had the heart to decorate since they passed away last year. My grandma loved the wallpaper in here; she was big on blowsy flowers – inside as well as outside the cottage.' She gave a small smile.

Nick noted a hint of sadness in her voice and his heart went out to her; he hoped nothing in his facial expression had made her feel embarrassed about her home or the need to apologise. 'I'm so sorry to hear about your grandparents, Brogan, but if this room's anything to go by, they created a lovely, cosy home.' He smiled down at her, giving her arm a squeeze. 'It actually reminds me of my own grandparents' house; I spent many happy times there.'

'Oh, really?' She beamed up at him. 'I used to spend all my holidays here as a kid, hated tearing myself away to go back home to Skeltwick. It's why I came back when...' Her smiled dropped. '... um, when I had the chance.' She pushed her smile back up.

What had she been going to say? he wondered, studying her face, noting her smile didn't quite reach her eyes. 'I can imagine it was hard to leave.'

'Yeah, it was,' she said, just a little too breezily, giving a shrug. 'Right then... kettle... Hmm. Actually, it might be better if we got changed first. I can show you to your room, if you like?'

'Sounds like a plan,' said Nick. He couldn't wait to get into something warm and dry. He looked round for Maudie to see she'd taken up residence on a large, cushiony dog bed that he assumed was Wilf's. Poor old Wilf seemed perfectly content to sit on the tiled floor and just gaze happily at her while Maudie looked down at him wearing one of her superior expressions. 'I feel a little embarrassed to say a certain someone's made herself right at home.' He nodded towards the two dogs.

Brogan followed his line of vision and burst out laughing. 'Oh, dear, looks like he's got it bad.' She went over and ruffled Wilf's ears. 'You're a great soppy lump, aren't you, lad? But it's good to see you're a gentleman and letting Maudie have your bed. I'm very impressed.' Wilf responded with a vigorous wag of his tail.

'I don't think the poor fella will've had much choice in the matter if I know Maudie.'

'Ah, well, you know the saying, "treat 'em mean to keep 'em keen"; maybe Maudie's using those tactics,' said Brogan as she made her way to a door on the other side of the room.

'Maybe she is,' said Nick, the cogs of his mind whirring. Did Brogan employ these tactics too? If so, it could explain her sudden reluctance to talk about their "brief encounter", explain why she appeared to be keeping him at arm's length emotionally speaking. *Hmm.* The thought gave him a little glimmer of hope; maybe their encounter wouldn't be so brief after all. There was an extra spring in his step as he followed behind her. He'd be careful not to push things, though. He didn't want to scupper any potential chances of picking up where they'd left off that day at the wedding. But he knew one thing for certain, he definitely wanted to get to know Brogan better, find out what made her tick, hear stories of her days here when she was a child. From the little time they'd spent together, and as corny as it seemed, he already knew there was no one he'd rather be with.

Upstairs, Nick followed Brogan down a long, narrow landing covered with a Persian-style runner, the ancient elm floorboards creaking underfoot. 'So, you should be okay in here. I'll fill a couple of hot water bottles to air the bed.' Brogan pushed open an old pine door with a brass handle and stepped in, Nick close behind.

He scanned the room which was small but full of character. Being in the eaves, it had a sloping, heavily beamed ceiling, a sweet dormer window and a floor-level stone mullion on the gable wall. Brogan went over and drew the floral curtains that matched the floral wallpaper – more evidence of her grandmother's love of flowers, he thought. His eyes alighted on the cast iron bed with plump pillows and a patchwork quilt thrown over it. He dearly hoped it was as comfy as it looked. Beside it was a bedside table upon which sat a lamp with a floral shade and a small bowl. The furniture was mismatched antique pine, which only added to the quaintness of the room. It comprised of a single wardrobe, a chest of drawers and a dressing table. The carpet – another testament to Brogan's grandmother's love of all things floral – appeared to be a little worn in places, not that it mattered. But most importantly of all, the room looked so much more welcoming than his bedroom at Willow Cottage, and Nick was in no doubt he'd enjoy a good night's sleep here.

'I did warn you my grandma liked flowers,' Brogan said, smiling apologetically up at him.

'I think it looks very cosy.'

She went over to the radiator beneath the window and fiddled with the thermostat. 'I'm not so sure cosy's the word I'd use, but I've turned the radiator up to full; it won't get red hot but you'll be warmer here than the place at Arkleby, which I know isn't saying much, I reckon a fridge would be warmer than that. And you won't find yourself knee-deep in icy water – at least, I hope you won't.' She gave a small laugh. 'Anyway, I'll leave you to it. See you downstairs when you're ready.'

'Thanks, Brogan, I really appreciate you doing this.'

'Hey, it's no problem. You helped me out by giving me a lift.'

'It's hardly the same.'

''Tis in my book. A favour's a favour,' she said with a shrug and closed the door.

Is that all this was? A favour? He'd hoped because of their previous connection, offering him a place to stay might actually mean more to her than that. 'Oh, well,' he said under his breath. Whatever her motivation, however she viewed it, he was grateful of it.

By the time Nick landed back downstairs Brogan was standing over the Aga, stirring something in a large pan that was filling the kitchen with the most delicious aroma. His stomach growled loudly.

'Hi. Feel better now you're all dry?' she asked as she turned, greeting him with a broad smile. His heart responded with a flip. She looked cute in a pair of black jogging trousers and a bottle green hoodie, a pair of chunky sheepskin slipper boots on her feet. She'd piled her hair up on top of her head, and tendrils were hanging down, showing off her delicate bone structure. He had the sudden urge to nuzzle the nape of her neck. She was tiny, he thought, not much over five feet. It made him want to wrap his arms around her, take care of her. Though something told him that would be the last thing she'd want; from what he'd seen of her, she seemed fiercely independent. It would probably be safer if he kept his feelings and his hugs to himself for now.

'Much, thanks.' He'd swapped his wet clothes for a dry pair of jeans and a navy V-neck sweater with white T-shirt underneath. 'How about you? Have your toes thawed out yet?'

'Just about,' she said, giving her infectious giggle, making his heart beat faster. Everything about this girl tapped into his senses, making them tingle.

'Whatever's in that pan smells seriously good.' He headed towards her. 'And those two rascals seem to think so too.' He looked at Maudie and Wilf who'd directed their laser beam stares at Brogan, determined not to miss a move she made. He noted Wilf was perched on another large cushion that had appeared alongside the one Maudie had taken up residence on.

Brogan turned to face him. 'It's chicken stew; my grandma's secret recipe. It's a favourite of mine. I always used to ask her to cook it whenever I came to stay. She showed me how to make it myself when I was fifteen.' Her smile fell a little. 'You do like chicken, don't you? I forgot to ask.'

'I love it, and if your chicken stew tastes anything like as good as it smells, I'm going to be in for a real treat.'

Her smile grew wider. 'Thanks. There's herby dumplings too, with grated cheese on the top.' She gave the pan a quick stir before replacing the lid. 'I thought we could do with something warming and hearty after our earlier escapades.'

'You're not wrong there.' Nick was struggling to take his eyes off her, just as he had the first day he'd seen her. 'Is there anything I can do to help? Set the table?'

'Er, okay, yeah. Mats are in the dresser – the drawer on the left – cutlery's in the one beside it. I'm not much of a drinker midweek, but I don't know about you, I think a glass of wine would go down well tonight.'

'I think a glass of wine would go down very well.'

'In that case, the glasses are in the cupboard on the right. I'll get the wine, you can pour.'

'Deal.' He beamed at her. Despite the lousy day he'd had, being with Brogan somehow made everything seem so much better, smoothed away the harsh edges, gave his spirits a much-needed boost. He only wished he knew what she was thinking. If she felt the same way about him. She wasn't an easy one to read, that was for sure. But one thing he was certain of was the burgeoning feelings he had for her; they were growing stronger the more time he spent in her presence.

TWENTY-THREE

BROGAN

'Mmm. This is seriously good,' said Nick.

'Thanks. It's a bit later than I usually eat, but hey-ho, that's just the way it's gone today.'

'Yeah, it's definitely up there as one of the more challenging days I've had. Well, part of it, at least. I don't suppose I'd be getting stuck into your grandma's glorious chicken stew if Willow Cottage hadn't flooded. That's definitely not challenging!'

'Yep, every cloud...' Brogan said lightly, her gaze catching his, her heart responding with a leap. He really did have the most amazing bright blue eyes; they seemed to look right into your soul, which is exactly what they seemed to be doing at this very minute. She looked away, focusing her attention on her plate as a blush stained her cheeks. 'So, did you manage to get hold of the Trotters?' She pushed another forkful of chicken into her mouth.

'Ughh! It's a total nightmare.' Nick rolled his eyes. 'They never pick up when I call them. The phone rings out then goes to voicemail every single time. I left them a message, told them what happened, explained how bad it was. I should be surprised they haven't called back, but for some reason I'm not. I kind of half-expected it. I'm still waiting for them to reply to my other messages telling them about the heating and lack of hot water. I don't know what it would take for them to actually have a conversation with me. They were very keen when they wanted me to sign the tenancy agreement. They were always on the phone then. Practically hounded me about it.'

Brogan looked across at him, her fork poised. 'They're shocking. You should ask for your money back. That house was unsafe and they knew it when they rented it to you. There must be laws about that sort of thing.'

'I think there are.' He set his knife and fork down on the plate and dragged his hand down over his face. 'I could really do without dealing with that sort of thing right now. I've had a lot on recently and... well, it would've been nice to have a break from the hassle for a while.'

Brogan felt for him. He looked drained. 'I'm really sorry to hear that.'

'Hey, it's not your problem. I'm sure things'll get sorted eventually.' He mustered up a smile.

'Is there anything I can do to help?' she asked. She quite liked helping people sort out their problems and was regularly asked for advice by her friends. Anoushka had confided in her and sought her counsel when she was having relationship trouble earlier in the year. Years of sorting through her own problems, thanks to her independent upbringing, when she'd spend hours mulling things over, trying to work out the best course of action, had made her pretty good at it.

'You're already doing loads; giving me somewhere to stay for the night, feeding me with this delicious stew. I can't tell you how much I appreciate it.' Nick's face brightened and he flashed her his heart-melting smile before taking another mouthful of his dinner.

The words that he could stay as long as he needed were on the tip of Brogan's tongue, but something made her hold back. She didn't want to act hastily and end up regretting it, especially with them working together and Nick being one of her bosses. If things got tricky here she couldn't exactly withdraw her offer, and risk the awkwardness spilling over into work. And he still hadn't brought up that "chat" he'd been so keen to have. Thought of that sent nerves jittering in her stomach. She couldn't quite work out what path that would take and was glad he seemed to have forgotten about it.

With the food eaten and the dishes washed – Nick dried and put away – they went into the living room. Brogan had lit the fire in the vast inglenook once she'd got changed when they'd first got back and the scent of woodsmoke lingered in the air. The room didn't have the wrap-around warmth of the kitchen, but with the sofa and chairs pulled up close around the fire, it could almost pass for cosy. Brogan usually stretched out on the old sofa of an evening, wrapping a fleece blanket around her on chillier nights while she watched the television or read a book.

'What a lovely room,' said Nick, looking around him at the dark oak beams and seventeenth-century panelling on the back wall. A thick bressummer beam ran across the ceiling just before the fireplace, while a fixed wooden settle, backed with dark oak panelling that ran right up to the ceiling, was tucked in at the left-hand-side of the inglenook, affording a toasty warm seat for whoever was lucky enough to occupy it. On the other side of the fireplace a spice cupboard with the initials WL and the date 1645 carved into the door was set into the wall, with a smaller salt box below.

'As you can see, my grandma didn't waste an opportunity to get yet more florals around the place.' A floral border ran around the room that matched the paper on two of the walls as well as the three-piece-suite and cushions. A multitude of knick-knacks were dotted on every available surface. The word "busy" could have been coined for it. Brogan took a log from the basket and threw it on the fire, sending sparks flying up the chimney, the thought that she really should get round to tackling the décor at some point soon crossing her mind. She hadn't had the heart to face it yet; to change things still felt tantamount to eradicating the memory of her grand-parents, and there was no way she was ready for that. Having her grandma's trinkets and floral décor around her made it feel like they weren't too far away, still within reach. In fact, the prospect of getting rid of or changing any of it made her feel almost panicky.

'I think it's lovely,' said Nick.

Brogan wasn't so sure she believed him, but all the same, it was kind of him to say.

The next couple of hours passed companionably with them chatting about a whole variety of innocuous subjects, skirting around the day they'd first met. Wilf and Maudie were curled up together on the rug in front of the fire as if they were old friends, Wilf's head resting on Maudie's back. Nick had made himself comfy on one of the armchairs and Brogan had her legs tucked beneath her on the sofa while she listened to stories of when he was a little boy, visiting his grandparents' farm over by York. It was where he'd developed his love of animals and it had been their encouragement that had led him to want to train to be a vet. The more he told her, the more Brogan realised they had much in common.

She was enjoying his company. In fact, she'd found herself thinking that she'd quite like to be snuggled up to him here on the sofa on more than one occasion that evening, her head resting on his chest, his arm around her. Bliss! She felt completely at ease with him, just like she'd done that Saturday at the wedding. It made her realise why she'd fallen for him so easily that day and it hadn't been a case of her simply throwing herself at the first available man who'd shown her attention. Which is what she sometimes talked herself into believing when she was reliving the memory in the wee small hours. But him being here tonight, their laughter and chatter bouncing around the room, made the place seem brighter again; made it seem alive. It also made her realise how lonely she'd become since her grandparents had gone. Why couldn't she let herself take the plunge and be guided by her feelings for him? She was sure she wasn't imagining that connection sparking between them. Granted, she'd never experienced anything quite like it before, but she was sure it couldn't just be her imagination that was making her feel this way. The emotions Nick aroused in her were way too strong for them not to be real.

Brogan drew in a deep breath, her thoughts tumbling around her mind. If that was the case, then she shouldn't let what had happened between her and Archie affect her forever. Couldn't let it hold her back. She hadn't dated anyone since he'd so unceremoniously dumped her; she'd been too scared to dip her toe in the dating pool. In fact, Nick had been the first man she'd kissed since Archie and there'd been no comparison between the two. Wowzers! Nick's kisses had blown her socks right off! They should've come with a warning! The thought made her giggle. And while she remembered Archie's as being kind of *nice*, they'd never aroused the strength of feeling in her Nick's had – and she was absolutely certain it wasn't just because it had been a long time since she'd been that close to a man! She felt her face flame and her pulse race as she recalled how Nick's lips had felt on hers. *Wow! Just wow!* It had rocked her to her core. If that was how he'd made her feel, wasn't it time she opened up her heart again? Three years was a long time to keep it locked away. She was in serious danger of the door permanently seizing up, never to be opened again. From what she could tell, Nick seemed to genuinely like her, unless, of course, she was reading things all wrong.

She froze, her stomach squeezing, as she ran the possibility over in her mind. Maybe she *was* reading him all wrong. Maybe she was so out of practice, she couldn't read the signals properly anymore– not that she'd ever been any good at it anyway, and had never been able to tell when a boy fancied her. Maybe she was seeing things she wanted to be there, or at least *hoped* were there. *Oh blimey.* It was a minefield, and way, *way* too confusing for her to navigate. She needed to calm herself down, think about something else.

She breathed out slowly and glanced over at Nick, her heart taking off again. *Well, that didn't last long!* The way he was looking at her right now, the way his gorgeous blue eyes had gone all soft, made it impossible to doubt for even the tiniest second he had feelings for her. Surely he couldn't fake that kind of expression? One thing she couldn't doubt was that she sure had feelings for him. Feelings of the extremely strong, lose-yourself-in-the-moment variety. And at this very moment they were coursing around inside her, making her heart thump hard against her chest and her skin tingle in the most delicious way. *Oh my days!* This was heady stuff. She was in serious trouble of falling head-over-heels in love with him if she wasn't careful.

A little voice piped up in her mind, asking if it would really be so bad for her to fall for him. It was quickly followed by another, telling her it had the potential to be monumentally disastrous. *Oh jeez!* Talk about confusing. Why couldn't things be simple for a change? She tried to steady her wayward heart, feeling completely and utterly torn.

'You okay?' Nick asked, bringing the battle that was raging inside her head to a halt.

'Uhh? Oh, umm… yeah, I'm fine, thanks. Just a bit tired, that's all.' A yawn made a timely appearance as if to prove her point. She covered her mouth with her hand. 'Oh, excuse me.'

'Of course, I'm not surprised, it's been quite a day. I shouldn't have kept you talking for so long.' His smile fell a little.

'Oh, I didn't mean… I've really enjoyed our chat and hearing about your grandparents' farm.' She smiled at him. She hadn't wanted to make him feel guilty, she'd just said she was tired as it was the first thing that had popped into her head.

'You sure you're not just being kind? Sure you're not in danger of being bored to sleep by my stories. "By 'eck. I remember t'day…",' he said, emphasising his North Yorkshire accent.

'Not at all.' She giggled, just as his phone started vibrating with a call, as it had done several times that evening. 'Who calls at nearly eleven o'clock at night?' she asked, watching as he picked it up and looked at the screen.

His smile dropped.

'Ughh. My ex, that's who.' He ran his hand over his chin. 'She's the reason I was supposed to head over to Middleton-le-Moors tonight. Flaming heck! I shouldn't be such a coward, I should take the call, get my bollocking over and done with. I won't be long.' He got to his feet and pressed the phone to his ear. 'Loretta,' he said as he walked towards the door, his head hung low.

Brogan couldn't help but feel for him. He hadn't mentioned what the situation was with his ex, but she sensed things were far from resolved between them. It made her wonder if the vibes she'd picked up from him liking her were nothing more than rebound feelings.

The thought was enough to dampen her mood.

Despondently, she pushed herself up and reached for a log in the basket by the hearth, stepping around Maudie and Wilf as she threw it on the fire. It caught light instantly, flames leaping up the chimney, sending out a welcome blast of heat.

The bedroom she'd given Nick was located directly above the living room and, with such low ceilings, she couldn't help but overhear his side of the conversation, in which he mostly appeared to be apologising profusely. Feeling uncomfortable, as if she was eavesdropping, Brogan reached for her wine glass and headed for the kitchen, her spirits sinking as she went.

TWENTY-FOUR

NICK

Nick listened as Loretta wiped the floor with him. She hadn't given him an opportunity to explain why he hadn't managed to get the shoes to her. As he absorbed more of her tirade he could feel his stress levels rising, his chest squeezing. If she was this livid about him not showing up, he could only imagine what she'd be like when he'd told her that her shoes were ruined. Which was something he hadn't been able to do because she hadn't given him a chance to get a word in edgeways. And the longer she went on, the more he wanted to get it over and done with. The only problem was, since he'd first seen the damage, he'd been running through his mind how best to broach the matter, but now his carefully prepared explanation had deserted him, and his brain was scrabbling about to find the right words to break it to her.

'Loretta, I need to tell you someth—'

'I've told you a million times, Nick, I don't want your pathetic excuses. I just want my shoes! It's not difficult, but you seem to be getting a great deal of pleasure out of hanging onto them.'

'But I've been trying to—'

'The only thing you should've been trying to do is to get them here. End of.'

'But if you'd just give me chance to explain—'

'I don't need a pathetic explanation, I just need my shoes. By dragging it out like this you're being nothing more than puerile and irritating. I don't need this stress. I'm too busy to have to keep reminding you how much I need them. They'd better be here by the time I get back from work tomorrow or I'm going to—'

'That's the thing, I'm not going to—'

'You'd better had, or I'll contact my solicitor and get...'

Oh, my God! Was she for real? Nick zoned out. Had it really come to this? Not that long ago she'd been busily making plans for their wedding, and now here she was threatening him with a solicitor over a pair of shoes. He couldn't ever remember feeling so frustrated. And the way the conversation was going, he seriously doubted he was going to get the chance to explain what had happened to the damn shoes.

'Nick! Nick!' Loretta's voice jabbed into his brain. 'Are you listening to me? I need my shoes.'

He closed his eyes and hissed out a sigh, not hearing whatever else she was saying. 'They're ruined,' he said flatly.

She stopped mid-rant. A loaded silence travelled down the phone line; he could sense her bristling. 'What did you just say?' she asked, barely containing the anger in her voice.

'I'm afraid they're ruined.' He'd made up his mind he wasn't going to apologise for what had happened to them anymore. There was only so many times you could say sorry for something, particularly something you hadn't done. He wasn't the one who'd packed them into the boxes by mistake. In fact, he hadn't packed his boxes at all. Loretta had done it, packing them up, getting rid of him as quickly as she could. It had hurt at the time. Really hurt, but in recent weeks, the pain had eased and he'd started to feel differently about their relationship.

'Ruined?' She barked the word.

'Yes.' He swallowed, he'd always hated confrontation with her; she could battle for hours.

'What do you mean? How did they get ruined?' He could hear her breathing heavily.

'Well...' Nick gave a brief outline of what had happened, conscious of her fury simmering away.

'If you'd got them to me when I asked, or if you'd let me come and get them, they'd still be okay. They wouldn't have had the chance to get ruined.' He could tell she was talking through gritted teeth.

'And I could counter that by saying if you hadn't put them in the box in the first place, they'd still be okay; wouldn't have been at the cottage to get wet,' said Nick. It was revealing of what little regard she held him in that she hadn't shown an ounce of sympathy for his situation, hadn't asked where he was staying, if he was okay. It was on the tip of his tongue to add, 'And if you hadn't gone and cheated on me with my best mate, then given me no alternative but to leave the home we'd shared, your precious shoes wouldn't have ended up in a box and got soaking wet. They'd still be okay.' But he thought better of it. And anyway, he was beginning to feel glad they weren't still together after all. This hard, unfeeling side of her was something he didn't find attractive.

'Don't think you've got off the hook that easily. I still want them! They might be salvageable, so you can drop them off here tomorrow. And I'm warning you, Nick, no more excuses.'

Nick clenched his jaw and ran his hand over his head, frustration twisting his insides. She made him feel like a naughty schoolboy on the receiving end of a telling off from the headmistress. What made her think it was okay to talk to him like that? Didn't she realise how much he had on his plate right now? In fact, he'd reached the stage where he really didn't care if she saw what sort of place he'd been reduced to living in. 'If you're so desperate to have your shoes, then you can come and get them yourself. I don't have time. Goodbye, Loretta.' He ended the call before she could say anything else.

He stood in the middle of the bedroom, his chest heaving as he waited for the fingers of tension to release their grip. Today, he'd been bombarded with stress from a variety of angles. He didn't want to go back downstairs and inflict his change of mood on

Brogan. That wouldn't be fair after the kindness she'd shown him. From what he'd gathered, there was a thread of sadness running through her despite the fact she'd been doing her best to hide it. It was obvious to him she missed her grandparents desperately but she'd been coping as well as she could and getting on with her life. She was evidently made of strong stuff and he already admired her for that. And he couldn't imagine her making a fuss about a pair of shoes.

He closed his eyes and steadied his breathing before returning downstairs to join her.

Hearing movement in the kitchen, he headed towards it to find Brogan sitting on the floor by the Aga. She was fussing Wilf and Maudie, who appeared to be enjoying it enormously if the enthusiastic tail wagging was anything to go by. Nick couldn't help but smile as he stood in the doorway watching Maudie nudge Brogan's hand to resume a bout of ear ruffling. He'd never seen his canine companion so taken with another person before and it gladdened his heart. A spluttery laugh escaped as he spotted Wilf, who was gazing with unbridled affection at a totally oblivious Maudie.

His laughter made Brogan look up. 'Hi,' she said, flashing him a wide smile, making his heart flip. It struck him how his growing affection for her had the power to quash the negativity that had swamped him only moments earlier.

He leaned against the door jamb, smiling, his happiness levels rising. 'Hi, looks like you've got your hands full there.'

'Just a bit. They're both very fond of ear ruffles, aren't you, eh?' she said to the dogs. 'They're a right pair of softies.'

'From where I'm standing it appears it's not only ear ruffles Wilf's fond of; he looks somewhat smitten with a certain someone.' He nodded towards Maudie.

Wilf wagged his tail harder at hearing mention of his name. Brogan smoothed her hand over his velvety head. 'Ah, you in love, lad?' He gave a quick glance her way followed by a swipe of his tongue across her cheek, making Nick laugh again. 'I'll take that as a yes, shall I?' she said.

Their attention switched to the sound of the wind whipping up outside, howling around the cottage and making the porch door rattle. Next, hailstones started drumming hard against the windows. Both dogs sat to attention, ears cocked.

'Wow! Looks like winter's reminding us of its presence,' said Nick. 'And I can't tell you how grateful I am you've let me stay here tonight.' He looked from the window back to Brogan who was getting to her feet.

'Hey, it's not a problem.' She met his eyes and gave a shy smile. 'I've enjoyed your company.' It didn't escape Nick's notice that her cheeks suddenly flushed pink. 'Maudie's too, and I think we both know how Wilf feels.' She giggled. 'Anyway, whenever the weather was like this my grandma always used to make a creamy hot chocolate. Don't know about you, but I quite fancy one?'

Nick didn't need much tempting; he had an infamous sweet tooth. 'Hmm. You know what? I'd absolutely love one.' His stomach started performing somersaults as his eyes roved over her face. He felt the last vestiges of the evening's tension slip away and found himself overcome with the urge to hold her in his arms. *Calm your jets, man!* Pulling himself together, he asked, 'Can I give you a hand?'

'You can grab the milk from the fridge, if you like.'

'Course.'

As they sipped their hot drinks in the comfort of the kitchen, elbows resting on the old, scrubbed table, Nick couldn't remember the last time he'd felt this relaxed, this contented. Actually, scrap that, he could. He'd felt this way the first time he'd met Brogan, when they'd spent the afternoon at the wedding reception chatting away like they'd known each other forever. They slotted together perfectly. Then, as now, running through his mind had been just how much he'd like to kiss her. However, tonight, he was going to hold back. It wouldn't be right; he didn't want her to feel he was taking advantage. But it didn't mean he couldn't savour spending time in her company.

'What a day,' Nick said, wrapping his fingers around his mug.

'You're not kidding,' said Brogan. 'You know there's no way you can go back to Willow Cottage with the state it's in, don't you? On top of everything else that's wrong with it, it'll take months to properly dry out, you'd get ill.'

'I know.' He heaved a sigh. 'I'd ask to stay with my parents or my brother, Matt, but with them living way over on the other side of York it's not exactly ideal for commuting over here, never mind being on call for the surgery. There's the winter weather to think about too. I'll just have to intensify my searches; I'm sure I'll find something.'

A beat passed before Brogan spoke again. 'You know, you and Maudie are welcome to stay here as long as you need. I appreciate how difficult it is to find rental property round here.' She took a sip of her hot chocolate, her green eyes peering over the top of her mug.

Nick was touched by her offer and, much as it was tempting, he said, 'That's really kind of you, but I don't know how long it's going to take to find somewhere new, and I wouldn't want to put you out, or for you to regret offering. I mean, Maudie hadn't been here five minutes and she'd kicked poor old Wilf off his bed.'

Brogan laughed, the pair of them turning to the dogs who were spread across both cushions, Wilf's leg resting on Maudie's as they slept contentedly. 'Ahh, I don't think Wilf's complaining much, do you?' she asked.

A smile spread across Nick's face as he observed how settled Maudie was, suddenly realising it had been a whole day since she'd treated him to one of her haughty looks. 'I don't think Maudie is either, come to think of it,' he said fondly.

'Well, then, you've both had a rotten few days, so if it helps take the pressure off, my offer to stay here stands. It's just Wilf and me rattling round the place on our own; somehow seems a bit wrong not to let you have use of a room 'til you get sorted with somewhere new.'

'Are you sure?'

'I am.' She nodded.

'Well, in that case, I think I can speak on behalf of Miss Snooty-Pants over there when I say, we'd love to take you up on it – but we'll be sure not to outstay our welcome; I'll get onto house-hunting right away.' The relief he felt was palpable, like a huge weight being lifted from his shoulders. It had been a day of contrasts, that was for sure.

'That's settled then. And I'm happy to help you bring your stuff over from Willow Cottage. Hopefully, most of it will be salvageable.' She beamed at him.

Nick beamed back, thinking that whatever it was that had brought this extraordinary woman into his life, he'd be eternally grateful. She truly was a breath of fresh air, there was no edge to her, no hidden agenda. She was kind and decent, and her presence in his life made it a better place, that was for sure. He hoped she'd be in it for a long time.

Before long, Brogan was declaring she was tired and needed to get to bed. Much as Nick was reluctant to leave her company, he had to agree; he felt suddenly exhausted, the events of the last few days catching up with him.

After helping her wash their mugs, he bid goodnight to Maudie and Wilf then glanced across at Brogan who'd just finished checking the porch door was locked properly. 'Thanks again for your offer, Brogan. You've no idea how much easier you've made things for Maudie and me.'

She met his gaze, looking up at him. 'Hey, don't mention it, I'm happy to help.' She flashed him a smile.

'Not many people would offer a roof over their head to someone they barely know. I really appreciate it.'

'I feel as if I do know you,' she said, almost shyly.

His eyes roved over her face, his heart started pounding. What was she saying? Was she referring to their time at the wedding? Or did she feel it too? This powerful connection that almost over-whelmed him, pulling them together? He didn't dare ask, not wanting to get it wrong, not wanting to risk making things awkward between them. 'Yeah, I know what you mean,' was all he could think of to say, his mind all over the place. Before he was tempted to elaborate, he bent and kissed her cheek, her auburn waves brushing his face, her soft skin and the scent of her shampoo adding to the heady mix of emotions that were swirling like crazy inside him. 'Night, Brogan. Sleep tight.'

'Night, Nick. You too.' She smiled up at him.

He smiled back before turning and taking his wayward thoughts to bed.

TWENTY-FIVE

BROGAN

Brogan woke with a start, her eyes pinging open and her heart pounding as she lay still, listening in the darkness, the sound of her pulse whooshing in her ears. She was sure she'd heard Wilf barking downstairs in the kitchen and couldn't work out if that was what had roused her from her sleep or something else; something that had caused him to bark. She had a nagging feeling in her sleep-fuddled brain she'd heard the sound of a car door closing. But with Wilf now silent, the only other noise was the bed creaking in the next room as Nick turned over.

Her mind went to the van the locals had been talking about and her pulse rate surged. She felt suddenly glad that she wasn't on her own tonight.

Reaching for her alarm clock on the bedside table she saw it was twenty-past two; she'd only been asleep for a few hours. She slipped out from beneath her duvet and crept silently over to the window in her pyjamas, avoiding the floorboards she knew would complain at being stepped on. Cautiously, she peered through a chink in the curtain to see that the wind had dropped and feathery snowflakes were falling steadily from the sky. The light in the yard revealed nothing unusual. Beyond, the surrounding area was swathed in darkness, but she couldn't see anything that looked suspicious; no flashing torch lights, no unfamiliar sounds.

After spending ten minutes at the window, the cold was starting to creep in and she was shivering. Content that it was probably just some nocturnal creature hunting around for food that had woken her and made Wilf bark, she tiptoed back to bed, snuggling down under the duvet, thankful it had retained some of its warmth. She closed her eyes, but her mind decided it would be a good time to take a trip down the road that led to Nick's ex and the reason for her call. It kept sleep at bay for a good forty-five minutes, Brogan finally convincing herself them getting back together was inevitable. Why else did she keep getting in touch with him? She clearly wanted his attention. Since her split with Archie, Brogan hadn't contacted him once.

Bundled up well against the cold and with the fans blowing out much-needed warm air, Brogan and Nick trundled down the track from Pond Farm, tyres crunching over the snow. Maudie and Wilf were in the boot space where they'd curled up together straight away. Up above, the first glimmers of daybreak were just becoming visible in the still-dark sky.

Though she'd been a little surprised when she'd found herself overcome with the urge to offer Nick somewhere to stay, Brogan hadn't regretted it. It had felt like the right thing to do, but more than that, she'd really enjoyed being in his company. The cottage had somehow felt happier having him there; *she'd* felt happier, and Wilf certainly seemed to be enjoying having Maudie around.

They were almost halfway down the lane when Brogan picked out what appeared to be traces of tyre tracks and foot prints in the snow. Her heart clenched as she peered out of the windscreen, her eyes straining to get a better look. From what she could tell it didn't seem to have snowed much more since she'd been woken in the early hours, and the imprints had been frozen as the temperature had plummeted.

'Oh, my God! I knew I'd heard something last night,' she said, anxiety creeping up her spine. 'Somebody's obviously come this far down the track then doubled back.'

'What do you mean, you heard something last night?' Nick brought the car to a slow halt and looked across at her, his eyebrows drawing together in a frown. 'After we'd gone to bed?'

'Yeah.' Brogan explained how her sleep had been interrupted. 'I dismissed it as an animal having a mooch about the yard, but it obviously wasn't.'

'I didn't hear anything; I fell asleep straight away and woke up when my alarm went off,' he said.

'Sound travels really clearly round here; I'm used to all the familiar noises, it must've been something different to wake me up.'

'Are you sure they're not the tracks made by us yesterday?' Nick asked, following her gaze, the car headlights illuminating the road ahead.

'No, they're more recent than ours, which you can barely see now; they've been pretty much covered by the snow. But those there, they're much more visible, and it's got nothing to do with how the snow's been drifting either; this part of the road's just as exposed as the rest of it, so if those tracks had been covered, then these would too.'

'Yeah, I take your point.' Nick nodded, driving steadily on. 'I suppose it could've been someone who got lost, took a wrong turn and realised when they got so far down the track. Doesn't explain what they'd be doing out and about in the early hours though.'

'No, it doesn't. But I don't think it was someone lost; we're off the beaten track. Who'd come down here? I think whoever it was knew where they were heading and I've got a horrible feeling it was the blokes in that van people have been talking about in the village.' Goosebumps prickled over her skin as she uttered the words.

'Right. And do you think Wilf's barking scared them off?'

'Maybe. But it could be because they were worried about getting stuck in the snow. It was coming down pretty heavily when

I looked out; must've stopped not long after though.' Brogan really didn't like the uneasy feeling this was giving her.

'Well, try not to worry about it too much for now. We can check the local social media pages, and ask around. And maybe text your friends, see if they've heard of anyone getting lost and asking for directions. I'm sure there's a logical explanation for the tyre tracks; you're probably feeling a bit jumpy about things like that with the reports about the van. It's understandable.'

Brogan turned to him and smiled, his words and calm tone of voice making her feel instantly better. She needed to keep her worries in check, not let them get carried away. It was another reason to be glad to have Nick staying at the cottage, and not just that she felt happy being around him and that his presence appeared to be taking the edges off the pain of losing her grandparents. 'Yeah, I'm sure you're right.'

The smile he returned filled her with warmth and made her heart skip a beat. Was it wrong of her to secretly hope that it would take him a while to find somewhere new to rent? she wondered. That he and Maudie would have to stay with her and Wilf for a long while yet? She snuggled down into her scarf and turned to look out of the window, her mind drifting back to when he'd asked if he could kiss her. It filled her with a warm glow.

The morning flew by with Brogan squeezing time in her break to text around, asking if there'd been any further sightings of the suspicious-looking van and its occupants. She'd checked all local social media beforehand, noting a few reports of them over at Arkleby. Nobody had heard of anyone asking for directions, which, much as she tried not to let it, had worried her a little.

It was the first day she'd worked with Jo, the part-time receptionist, and Mia, the other vet nurse. She'd warmed to both instantly, particularly Mia with her straight-talking and down-to-earth sense of humour. 'Tell you what, the new vet's a bit of all right, isn't he?' she'd said in her gravelly North Yorkshire accent, a mischievous glint in her eye. 'And from the way he looks at you, I reckon he thinks you are too.'

Brogan had felt her cheeks grow hot. 'He's definitely easy on the eye, but I think you've got it wrong about him liking me; he's just friendly.' What would Mia say when she found out he was staying with her at Pond Farm? She'd no doubt have some fun with that piece of information.

'Hmm. We'll see about that.' Mia had eyed her knowingly.

It was also the first time she'd worked with the part-time vet Georgia who proved to be every bit as friendly and bubbly as Brogan had guessed she would be.

With morning surgery finished, Brogan was walking into the waiting room with Nick, the pair of them laughing about the escapades of a house rabbit he'd tried to examine as a newly quali-fied vet. Nick rested his hand on her shoulder as he told her how the buck rabbit had sprayed his scent all over him. 'It went in my hair, everywhere. I stank of it for days. I learnt my lesson sharpish, I can tell you. My girlfriend at the time dumped me, said I had hygiene problems. I was mortified.'

'I know the smell's intense, but that's a bit drastic. Though, I have to admit, it must've been hilarious to see,' said Brogan, looking up at him and giggling.

'Well, isn't this cosy?' said a female voice, heavily laced with sarcasm.

Brogan turned to see a tall, slim woman with blonde hair pulled back into a severe ponytail. Her glamorous clothing, perfect makeup and high-heeled boots looked at odds in such a rural setting.

'Loretta! What are you doing here?' asked Nick, his face falling.

Brogan glanced between them, sensing the growing tension as it dawned on her that the woman was Nick's ex. Mia and Jo looked on, eyes wide with interest.

Loretta's red, glossy lips were pulled into a sneer which made

Brogan bristle instantly. She clenched her teeth in a bid to stay calm as Loretta arched an eyebrow and snorted a laugh.

'You were the one who told me if I wanted my shoes, then I'd have to come and get them myself, which is exactly what I've done, only you neglected to share your address with me so I had no choice but to come here.' She tapped her foot impatiently. 'And judging by what I've just witnessed, I'm beginning to see what made you so reluctant to tear yourself away and head over to Middleton-le-Moors.' She looked Brogan up and down and gave a disapproving sniff.

Nick blew out a sigh. 'Loretta, I've tried numerous times to explain why I was struggling to get your shoes to you. I've been having a nightmare of a time, what with—'

'So I see.' Loretta looked pointedly at Brogan before turning back to Nick, pinning him with her icy gaze. 'And my shoes are?'

'They're still at Willow Cottage.'

Loretta's nostrils flared. She looked ready to explode. The last time Brogan had seen anyone look so annoyed it was Anoushka's ex when he was being attacked by Jimby's wayward cockerel, Reg. 'They're still at the place that flooded?' Loretta asked, barely containing her anger.

'Yes. Like I said, they looked pretty ruined to me. At the time, I didn't think you'd want them back; couldn't see you wearing them.' His voice sounded weary.

Loretta nodded, pushing her lips into a pout. She was eyeing Nick like a cat ready to pounce on an unsuspecting mouse.

Brogan fought the urge to say something in his defence which wasn't easy, but she didn't want to run the risk of making things worse for him. From the look of things, it wouldn't take much. But she really didn't like the way this woman was speaking to him with such arrogant disdain. Had Nick really been engaged to such a cold, hard person? Brogan found it difficult to imagine them together, never mind committing to getting married. Sensing his discomfort, she said, 'I'll just go and check on the kennels.'

'Yeah, okay. Thanks, Brogan.' He gave a weak smile.

'Ah, Brogan is it?' the woman asked, placing her hand on her hip, as Brogan walked away. 'Not your usual type, is she?' she heard Loretta say, her sneering tone getting Brogan's hackles up. A little thorn of hurt made itself known; she was only too aware she wouldn't match up to someone like Loretta.

A few minutes later Nick appeared behind her. 'I'm really sorry about Loretta, please ignore her. I don't know what's got into her, she never used to be like this.' He pulled an apologetic face.

'You've got no need to apologise,' she said.

'Not sure Loretta would agree with that. Anyway, I'm just going to nip over to Willow Cottage and get her shoes. Hopefully that should pacify her.'

'Okay.' Brogan nodded, noting the drained look in his usually happy eyes. A sudden thought hit her, making her stomach churn. 'You're not leaving her here are you?'

He gave a small laugh, touching her arm reassuringly. 'No, don't worry, she's going to follow me then head home once she's got her shoes. It shouldn't take long; I'll make sure I'm back for surgery this afternoon.'

'Okay. Well, good luck, then.' She pushed her mouth into a smile, hoping he didn't detect the misgivings Loretta's presence had created.

'Thanks. I've got a feeling I'm going to need it.' He puffed out his cheeks and headed through the door.

Brogan waited until she heard the sound of car engines driving off, before she headed back into the waiting room.

'Well, whoever she was, she was a right hard-faced piece of work,' said Mia, with a look of disgust.

'Wasn't she just?' said Jo. 'It was just as well we didn't have any clients here to witness that. From what I've seen of Nick, I can't imagine him marching up to her place of work and behaving like that. So unprofessional; she should've saved that for a private conversation.'

'Aye, you're right there. I hope the shoes are worth the fuss she was making. Flippin' 'eck anyone would think they were gold-plated,' said Mia.

'Looked to me like she was on a power trip,' said Jo.

'Hmm.' It had looked that way to Brogan too.

'Daft moo. Anyroad, missus, you and Mr Sexy Vet seem to be getting along pretty well. Don't suppose you can shed any light on what was going on with them two?' Mia turned her attention to Brogan, her eyes glinting mischievously.

'Me?' Brogan asked, her eyebrows lifting.

'Yep, you.' An amused smile twitched at the corners of Mia's mouth. 'Jo and me have already spotted the chemistry sizzling between the pair of you and you haven't even been here five minutes. Surely he's shared some deets of his ex with you.' Her smile became a full-on grin as she caught Jo's eye.

Colour rose in Brogan's face. 'You've got the wrong impression; he really hasn't said much about her.' She was saved from any further interrogation when Chris bowled in on a blast of wintry air.

'Brrr! It's bloomin' parky out there. I'll need to get some more grit on the path before it gets too slippery.' He glanced around, looking puzzled. 'Have I missed something?'

TWENTY-SIX

NICK

As he drove the icy roads to Arkleby, Nick felt a strange mix of stress and relief swirling around inside him. The stress, he knew, could be attributed to a variety of reasons. At the forefront of his mind was the thought of yet more verbal sparring with Loretta, never mind what she'd have to say when she saw the shoes. He knew from what he'd seen of them the previous night, there was no way she'd contemplate wearing them. In fact part of him was beginning to think her turning up like this was her way of exerting an element of control over him. He wondered if she'd soften at all if she knew what he'd been dealing with. Somehow, he doubted it.

As far as the relief was concerned, he knew without doubt that was creeping in courtesy of the prospect of finally handing Loretta her precious shoes, bringing an end to the stream of hostile texts and voicemails. He couldn't wait to be free of them. Couldn't wait to be able to look at his phone without the feeling of dread that had started to take hold of him whenever it pinged or rang.

Owing to the recent ploughing, snow was banked up on the verges making the road narrower. Nick slowed down as he carefully negotiated a sharp bend. He released a long sigh as the sign for Arkleby appeared, his eyes flicking to his rear view mirror catching a glimpse of Loretta's car reflected back at him, her stern face in the windscreen. Dread pooled in his stomach. Facing Willow Cottage again and the prospect of how Loretta would react at seeing her shoes wasn't an ideal combination. 'Oh, blast!' he said under his breath.

He parked outside the cottage and regarded it, a sense of doom washing over him. 'Right, let's get this over and done with,' he said aloud. Trying to ignore the stress headache that was beginning to pulse at his temples, he climbed out of the car.

'Is this it?' asked Loretta, her nose turned up in distaste as she took in the peeling paintwork, and the gaps between the bricks where the pointing had long-since crumbled.

'There wasn't much choice,' Nick said flatly as he felt in the pocket of his waxed jacket for the keys. They weren't there so he tried his trouser pockets. They weren't there either. *Oh, no!* He had a horrible feeling he'd left them at Brogan's place. In fact he could see them in his mind's eye on the dresser by the little ceramic donkey where he'd set them down last night.

'In case you haven't noticed, it's freezing out here.' Loretta was standing on the pavement, her shoulders hunched against the cold wind.

'Er, yeah, I know.' He bit his bottom lip, wishing he hadn't been so hasty in taking the keys off his keyring.

He headed back to the car, checking the little space he sometimes chucked bits and bobs, but he was disappointed to find they weren't there.

Loretta threw her head back and gave an impatient groan. 'Oh, don't tell me, Nick-I-Lose-Everything has struck again. How typical.' She looked daggers at him.

'In fairness, I had no idea you were going to turn up at the surgery. If I had, I would've made sure to have brought the keys with me.'

'You were the one who told me to come and get the shoes,' she said snappily. 'And anyway, why aren't they on your keyring? Who doesn't fix their house keys to their main set? Oh, yes, silly me; *Nick* doesn't.'

Nick pinched the bridge of his nose between his forefinger and his thumb. He was getting pretty fed up of hearing Loretta speak to him like this. He tried counting to ten, but had only reached three when he found himself saying, 'Actually, if you hadn't been so wrapped up in yourself, you'd have stopped to listen to me explaining to you that, as of yesterday evening, this cottage became uninhabitable. A small matter of a flood – on top of everything else, i.e. no heating, no hot water, no electricity. It's been hell, Loretta. Absolute hell. And I've been put in this position by you, so please don't give me any more grief about your shoes. Okay? There's no way you would've put up with something like this without throwing a hissy fit like the princess you've become.' His words poured out in a torrent, his chest heaving. And now he'd started, he found he couldn't stop himself. 'I took the keys off because there's no way I'll be living here again – which some people may think is a stupid reason but, hey, it's just what I felt like doing last night. I've been trying to contact the landlords but they don't seem to want to know. I'm feeling pretty brassed off with the whole situation, and your snide comments aren't helping.'

'I am not a princess,' she said, glaring at him, her lips pushed into a pout.

'That right?' he said, giving her a pointed look before launching into one last check of his jacket for the keys. He reached into a side pocket, feeling a pulse of hope as his fingers touched something that felt distinctively like a set of keys. He pulled them out to see they were the very ones for Willow Cottage. *Thank you!*

The door had swelled up even more, and he had to put his shoulder against it before it would budge. Nick took a tentative step into the hallway. In the stark winter light things looked distinctively worse than they had in the torch light of the previous evening. His nose twitched at the tang of damp that pervaded the air as he inched past the soggy boxes in the hallway and headed into the living room, his boots squelching over the carpet. It had been a cold house before the flood, but now it was bone-numbingly so.

'Oh, my God. I can't believe you actually pay money for this place, it's a dump.' Loretta's breath floated out in a plume of condensation. She gave a shiver, and pulled up the collar of her coat as she looked around her, making no attempt to hide her disdain.

Nick was finding it hard to believe too, but he wasn't in the mood for one of her critiques. 'Like I said, I didn't have much choice if I wanted to live near the practice.' He reached into the box that held the ill-fated shoes, his spirits slumping. They looked worse than he remembered and were now peppered with black dots of mildew. There was no easy way of doing this. 'Here they are.'

'My shoes!' Loretta snatched them out of his hand, looking at them in disbelief. 'They're ruined!'

'That's what I've been trying to tell you—'

'Yes, well, I didn't think you were serious. I thought you were just being bloody minded; making me suffer because I... because we broke up.' She stole a sideways look at him.

'You know that's not my style. And besides, I'm done with all the grief. It's the run up to Christmas and I'd like to get my life a little more settled and...' It suddenly struck him that he'd never felt more settled than he had last night with Brogan, an image of the two of them chatting away like they'd known each other forever blooming in his mind.

'And what?' Loretta asked, her eyes narrowing.

Nick gave a shrug. 'It's been an unsettling time, that's all.' He made his way to the kitchen to survey the damage there, conscious of Loretta's eyes boring into him as she followed behind.

'So where are you staying now? Have you got somewhere permanent sorted out?' He'd been dreading her asking this.

'It happened yesterday; I've hardly had chance to get anything permanent sorted, especially when vacant rental property is in such short supply.' He lifted his gaze to the gaping hole in the ceiling, the legs of the ancient cast iron bath peeking through. Jeez, it was grim; everything looked so much worse than he'd been expecting. A shudder ran through him as he recalled how Brogan had been seconds away from it collapsing onto her.

'So where did you stay last night then?'

He sighed, a cloud billowing out of his mouth. Was she ever going to give up? It dawned on him that he didn't have to answer her, didn't need to explain what he was doing. 'It really doesn't matter where I stayed, Loretta. What's important is you've got what you wanted. Now, if you don't mind, I need to get back to the surgery.'

She leaned away from him as he stepped past her, her gimlet gaze never leaving him. 'It's her, isn't it? That dumpy girl with the wild-looking, auburn ponytail you were flirting with. You've shacked up with her, haven't you?' she said mockingly. She gave a scornful laugh. 'Talk about being a fast mover, Nick.'

'I don't know who you could possibly mean from that description.' He felt a shard of annoyance spike through him at Loretta's bitchy comment.

'Oh, come on. Of course you do, you were all over her when you came into the waiting room. Laughing together like a couple of children.' She waved her hand dismissively. 'Bregan, I think someone called her.' Spite was dancing in her eyes, setting Nick's hackles up.

'If it's Brogan you're referring to, I find her curves attractive. And as for her hair, it was the first thing that struck me about her. I think it's stunning.' He headed towards the front door, his anger boiling.

Loretta's smile faltered. 'Well, I suppose there's no accounting for taste.'

Nick stopped in his tracks, turning back to his ex. 'Since when did you got so nasty, Loretta? You never used to be like this, all prickly and spiteful. You seem unable to say anything pleasant about anyone now. All I can think is that you must be feeling pretty unhappy with yourself to speak about other people the way you do.' He went to open the door; the sooner he could get away from her, the better.

She set her mouth in a hard line and glared at him, her eyes blazing. 'If you hadn't been so difficult about giving me my shoes, I wouldn't have had the need to get nasty; it's you who's made me behave this way, having to fight for my property.' Seconds later, her sneer returned. 'But judging by your overly defensive reaction, it looks like I guessed right, doesn't it? You've wormed your way into Bregan's sad little affections. What's that saying? Desperate men take desperate measures?'

Nick froze, his hand on the door knob. 'Wow! You really are a nasty piece of work, aren't you?' He was struggling to recall a time when he'd felt this way about someone. It struck him that the pernicious rivalry Loretta had with her younger sister, Catriona, had spilled over to encompass Brogan.

Loretta always wanted what Catriona had which Nick had struggled to understand; his relationship with Matt couldn't be more different, they'd always looked out for each other, supported one another. Yes, they'd scrapped at times, but their disagreements had always blown over, quickly forgotten. But that wasn't the way with Loretta and Catriona. He recalled a time when Catriona had turned up at their house with a new designer handbag. Loretta had been so consumed with envy, she'd barely been able to look at her sister. Catriona had only just closed the door behind her before Loretta was on her laptop, looking for a handbag to outshine her sister's, saying Catriona was just showing off and had only called round to 'flaunt her stupid bag'. It had been the same with cars, houses, and, it transpired, getting engaged, the stakes getting higher every time.

When Catriona and her wealthy, nightclub owning boyfriend, Calvin, announced their engagement, Loretta had been apoplectic. 'It's wrong! They haven't been together five minutes. It's making a mockery of what an engagement is supposed to mean; the commitment it's supposed to represent. It's not a fashion statement or something disposable. And did you see that smarmy look on her face? I know full well she's only doing it to get at me. She treats everything like a competition, always has to be the first to do anything out of the two of us. It's ridiculous! I'm the older sister. I should be the one to get engaged first! They won't last, I can guarantee it.' She'd huffed and pushed her mouth into a tight pout. 'And how come you haven't set up your own business by now? Calvin's the same age as you and he set his up four years ago, he's even expanding it with a new wine bar.'

Though he'd grown used to the sisters' competitive relationship, Loretta's bitter diatribe had shocked Nick. Things had moved up to a whole new level.

It had taken Loretta a couple of months to get Nick to agree that it was the right time for them to get engaged. The subsequent party she'd organised to celebrate had been bigger and glitzier than Catriona and Calvin's, her party dress costing twice as much as her sister's. And as for the ring she'd chosen… jeez! It had been eye wateringly expensive. The word "ostentatious" didn't cover it. Nick had actually felt embarrassed when people had asked to see it.

It had come as a shock the first time he'd witnessed the sisters' competitiveness – over a pair of earrings, he seemed to remember. He'd tried to convince Loretta not to let it get to her, but to no avail. Though he'd developed a better understanding of it when he'd discovered the cause: their father.

Catriona was a proverbial chip off the old block. Just like Donald, she was a high-achiever who always seemed to do well at everything with very little effort, from taking exams, to passing her driving test first time (Loretta had passed on her fifth attempt) or baking cakes for the Middleton-le-Moors summer fayre (Loretta's cake had collapsed so she hadn't been able to enter it). Their father seemed to relish pointing out his daughters' differences, particularly highlighting Catriona's successes. He didn't seem to notice how efficient and highly-regarded Loretta was at her place of work, or how she'd climbed up the ranks far more quickly than anyone else. It had resulted in her being head-hunted by Nick's then best mate Aaron to work at his company. That didn't seem to count in Donald's book (turns out Nick hadn't been too pleased about it either, but for a completely different reason!). There was no wonder Loretta had developed a hard exterior; she was clearly horrendously insecure which had manifested itself in this unpleasant side of her. She hadn't been this way when they'd first got together, but things had got progressively worse once Catriona had started dating Calvin. In fairness, Nick thought it couldn't be much fun having her nose constantly rubbed in everything little thing her sister did.

He felt a sudden pang of pity for his ex. He glanced over at her to see her face set hard as she glared back at him. His sympathy quickly leached away.

'Might be a good idea if you head back before the roads get too icy. We're due more snow,' he said, no trace of his previous anger in his voice.

His change of tone seemed to wrong-foot her. She blinked, a frown disappearing as quickly as it arrived. 'Right, I'll do that.' She stepped out onto the pavement as he closed the door – it took a good couple of yanks before it shut properly. Once he'd locked it he made sure to fix the keys to his keyring. *One less pair to lose!*

'Right then.' He was itching to get away.

'You still need to collect the rest of your stuff from the house.'

'There's loads of boxes in the cottage, so I can't imagine there's much of mine left at the house,' he said, keeping his voice cool.

'You still need to collect it. If you let me know when that's going to be I'll put the bags in the shed and leave the key under the lid of the recycling bin; you can post it through the letter box when you're done. That way you can just take them.'

'That's fine. I'll be over on Sunday afternoon.'

'Okay, though I doubt we'll be back from the hotel. It's Aaron's company's Christmas party over in the Lake District.'

'Yeah, I know, you told me before.' He walked over to his car and opened the door. 'Bye, Loretta.' He climbed inside. Usually, he'd offer a few friendly words about her looking after herself, but not today. Today he'd had enough.

'Bye,' she said, watching with a frown as he drove away.

. . .

An afternoon spent in the surgery's operating theatre had been a welcome distraction for Nick, his mind emptying of all the stressful things that had been troubling him while he focused on his patients.

Before he knew it, Jo was locking the door and turning the sign to closed. 'Right, time to collect my two gremlins from the child-minder. I'm hoping they haven't been up to too much mischief today. They're eight and ten, and snow seems to send them absolutely hyper.' She feigned a worried face as she pulled on her coat.

Nick laughed. 'Ah, well, if they're anything like my brother and me when we were that age, they'll have worn themselves out running around and having snowball fights.'

Just then, the door to Vonnie's room opened to reveal the practice manager talking to Brogan and Mia. Vonnie had her hand on the door, the three of them laughing about something she was saying. Jo went over to them. 'I'm heading off now, folks so I'll see you on Saturday. Nice to meet you, Brogan.' She gave a friendly smile.

'Nice to meet you, too,' Brogan said, smiling back.

'Right then, after that busy day, I think we should all be heading home and cosying up in front of the fire,' said Vonnie, tucking a pen behind her ear in her usual habit. 'Everything seems all right here. Mia and Brogan have checked on all our overnighters and Chris has been in touch to say he should be back within the next half hour. So all that remains for me to say is, I'll see you tomorrow, Mia.' She turned to Nick and Brogan, saying, 'Enjoy your day off, the pair of you, and I'll see you both on Friday.'

'Will, do, thanks, Vonnie,' said Brogan. As she headed through to the waiting room, Nick watched Mia lean into her, her eyebrows raised and an amused smile on her face. She whispered something into Brogan's ear, following up with a throaty giggle and an elbow nudge. Whatever she'd said, it made Brogan's face flush and she shot her colleague a mock warning look, at the same time fighting the urge to smile. Something told him that other people were picking up on the chemistry between them. Loretta's words sprang into his mind; she'd clearly spotted it too, though he'd assumed she'd been bluffing at the time, lashing out with a spiteful comment to get at him. Well, she'd succeeded in that. He could take anything she said about him, but it had really rankled when she'd had a pop at Brogan.

'Oh, and keep a look out for that van. I've had a few people mention seeing it loitering around today. It might be nothing, but it's best to be vigilant,' said Jo. She gave them a wave and headed out into the darkness.

Nick's thoughts went back to the tyre tracks he and Brogan had seen on the lane to Pond Farm, and to what she'd said about being woken in the night. He hadn't wanted to frighten her, but he had an inkling she was right to be suspicious. A few of his clients had mentioned the van to him today too.

After letting Wilf and Maudie have a quick run around outside, Nick and Brogan bundled into his car, glad to get out of the cold. The temperature had dropped again, making the snow crunchy underfoot.

'Well, that was a busy day,' said Brogan as the car headed down the lane from the surgery, frost sparkling on the roadside.

'It was; just the way I like it.' He smiled across at her in the darkness, his face illuminated by the dashboard lights.

'And, dare I ask, how did things go with your ex over at Willow Cottage?'

'Ughh! Not great I'm afraid. She was pretty livid about her shoes being wrecked, but at the end of the day, she put them in the box, so...' He gave a shrug. 'Anyway, at least she's got them now.'

'True.' Brogan gave him a sympathetic smile. 'And on a brighter note, I don't know how you feel about heading to the Sunne tonight? I had a text from Noushka reminding me it's the Village Committee meeting – Noushka, Kristy and me all joined earlier in the year – I think Camm mentioned to you that it was on tonight. It's usually a pretty good night, and the members are all a good laugh.'

'Yeah, why not? I'd like to get to know them all a bit better. Tell you what, why don't we grab a bite to eat there? My shout.'

'Ooh, I like the sound of that – not about it being your shout,' she said with a giggle. 'I'm more than happy to pay for myself, but I could murder one of Bea's boozy beef casseroles.'

'Well, that's settled then,' he said, his spirits lifting at the prospect. 'Boozy beef casserole at the Sunne it is.'

TWENTY-SEVEN
BROGAN

'Now then, you two, that was good timing,' said Jimby, giving Brogan and Nick one of his customary wide smiles as they joined the Village Committee members at their usual table by the fire. Maudie and Wilf shot off and curled up beside Nomad and Scruff by the hearth. A chorus of welcoming hellos rang out from the rest of the group.

'Ey up, come and sit yourselves down. We've saved a couple of seats for you,' said Ollie, smiling.

'How's the job going, Broge?' asked Anoushka, indicating towards Nick with her eyes as Brogan sat down on the banquette beside her. Nick took the stool opposite.

'It's great thanks, I'm loving it.' She ignored her friend's non-verbal hint.

'Good to see you, chick,' said Kristy, peering around Anoushka, her long dark hair falling in a curtain. 'And I knew you'd settle in straight away; you were made for the role.' She waggled her eyebrows.

'Thanks, Kristy.' Brogan couldn't help but smile as she gave her friend a warning look before setting her glass of Pinot Grigio down on the table. She knew what both Kristy and Anoushka were alluding to: Nick. She leaned into the tweed-covered back of the banquette, savouring the warmth of the fire that danced in the grate. The delicious aroma of Bea's cooking was making her feel suddenly very hungry.

'No regrets about giving up dog-walking, then?' Molly grinned at her.

'Pfft! None! Especially now winter's taken hold. Mind, I have to say, I do miss all the lovely dogs, but at least I'm getting a fix of all sorts of animals at the surgery and I'm loving that.'

'And how's things with your car?' asked Anoushka.

Brogan rolled her eyes and groaned. 'Still not fixed. Jed rang me today, saying he was having trouble getting the part.'

'Oh, no, what a pain. Hopefully he'll get it soon, but if you need a lift anywhere, flower, just holler,' said Kristy.

'And how about you, Nick? How've you settled in?' asked Camm.

'I'm really enjoying it,' said Nick. 'Best decision I ever made.'

'That right?' asked Vi. She caught Brogan's eye and gave her a wink, making Brogan's heart jump. Did Vi know something? And if she did, who else knew? Brogan's mind started running riot.

She was distracted by Nick who, thankfully, didn't seem to have picked up on that exchange. He leaned across to Brogan and said quietly, 'The bloke at the end of the table, sitting next to Jimby, is the double of Gabe Dublin. You know, the Irish indie-rock singer? If I didn't know better, I'd swear it was him.'

Brogan chuckled, as did Anoushka who'd overheard him. 'He's not only the double of Gabe Dublin, he *is* Gabe Dublin,' Brogan said.

Nick's eyes grew wide. 'No way?'

'Yes, way,' Brogan and Anoushka said in unison, both laughing.

'He lives in the village; recently bought The Manor House. He and Anoushka are an item.' Brogan couldn't help but giggle at Nick's changing expression as this information sank in.

'Wow! Really? I had no idea. He seems pretty low-key, not at all how I imagined a famous rock star to behave.'

'Gabe is very low-key; prefers a quiet life and is enjoying being part of the community since he moved here full-time,' said Anoushka. 'He uses the recording studio up at Danskelfe Castle when he's song writing.'

'Wow, a recording studio. You really do have everything round here, don't you?' said Nick.

'Pretty much,' said Brogan.

'Right, then,' said Jimby, 'has everyone got a drink?'

'Actually, I hope you don't mind, but Brogan and I haven't eaten yet; we hoped to grab something here. Is that okay?' asked Nick, waving the menu he was holding.

'Course it is. We were going to get a few nibbles ordered before we got properly started, so feel free,' said Jimby. 'In fact, why don't we do that now?'

With the food devoured – both Nick and Brogan tucked into hearty portions of Bea's boozy beef with a side of herbed green beans and creamy boulangère potatoes – Jimby opened the meeting. 'Right then, Zander texted me, saying he'd try to get here but he doubted it; said we should get started without him.'

'I'm not surprised, what with a one-year-old and new-born twins to contend with,' said Molly. 'It's a wonder he can even think about anything else.'

'I saw Rhoda earlier today, she said she's been nipping up there to give Livvie a hand,' said Kitty. 'She looks over the moon to be a step-grandma again.' Rhoda had moved to the village a couple of years earlier to be near her stepdaughter and family.

'She does, she looked ready to pop with happiness when I saw her the other day,' said Vi, triggering a slew of 'Ahhs'.

'Right then, you lot, Lady Caro sends her apologies but said she's happy to help with whatever she can. Ella and Joss send their apologies too, said something about not being keen to leave the farm on account of that suspicious-looking van. Apparently, Ella saw it on their lane last night, and was convinced there was someone snooping around their boarding kennels. For all everything's locked up, it's made them a bit twitchy about leaving the farm unattended.' Jimby glanced round at them, his face serious for once.

'Can't say I blame them,' said Molly who was busily scribbling down notes in her capacity as committee secretary.

'Neither can I,' said Lucy. 'It's why Freddie's not here. We didn't like to leave our property empty. We had someone really shifty in the shop today. He spent ages just skulking around but didn't buy anything. Had his hood pulled right over his face, so I couldn't get much of a look at him; made me feel really nervous.'

'That doesn't sound good, Luce,' said Camm.

'It made Freddie and me actually have a discussion about getting cameras fitted, which doesn't feel right in a little village shop, but that man really freaked me out.'

Brogan gave a shiver as goosebumps prickled over her skin. 'Something woke me in the middle of the night too, and there were tracks halfway down our lane this morning.'

'Aye, and I've seen the van parked up a couple of times while I've been out ploughing the roads,' said Camm. 'There's definitely something not right about it.'

'Well, if that's the case, we need to be extra vigilant. I think we should post on all local social media whenever we see the van or anyone acting suspiciously. That way, we'll stand more of a chance of keeping track of it. Shame we have to resort to this out here, but needs must,' Jimby said, shaking his head.

'We could maybe text each other too,' said Ollie. 'Nothing's happened yet, but I kind of get the feeling whoever it is, is casing the area, trying to get an idea of our habits.'

Kitty gave a shudder. 'I don't like it. Makes you think it's only a matter of time before something happens,' she said, her elfin face troubled.

'I know what you mean,' said Molly, 'but at least we're aware of them, and keeping an eye out'll make it more difficult for them to get up to no good.'

'True,' said Brogan. Molly's words offered a nugget of reassurance, though she still intended to check round at home, make sure everything was locked properly.

'Right then, on a happier note, I'd like to welcome Nick as a new member of the committee.' Various utterances of agreement followed. 'Thank you very much for putting yourself forward, Nick, I think you'll find we're a friendly bunch, though our Molly can be a bit scary when she puts her mind to it.' Jimby chuckled mischievously.

'Funny,' said Molly, pulling a face at her cousin. She turned to Nick. 'I'm only scary when I'm provoked.'

'Fair enough,' Nick said, laughing before casting his gaze around the table. 'Thanks for having me, everyone.' He was greeted with a sea of friendly smiles.

'So, the reason we're all here,' said Jimby, rubbing his hands together, 'is that I've been thinking about how Christmas can be an amazing time, but it can also be quite a lonely time for some folk roundabouts here.' There was a collection of nods and murmurs of agreement.

Bert Hoggarth sprang into Brogan's thoughts; he didn't seem to have any family looking out for him. 'What do you have in mind, Jimby?'

'Well, I've been mulling a few things over actually. The first one is something that could run throughout the year, so it doesn't really focus on Christmas, but I still think it's something the committee should consider and, if we all like the sound of it, we can get the ball rolling.' He paused, scanning their faces. 'I know there's a load of activities on offer in the village, what with all the groups that've been set up, you know, like the knitting group and the book group. But what I've be running over in my mind involves organising regular outings, you know, maybe a weekly trip to Middleton-le-Moors, a monthly one to York, garden centres, local stately homes. That kind of thing. There's quite a few of the older members of our community who don't seem to set foot outside this village, and I'm sure they'd like the chance to go further afield. I know we're served by a bus and a train, but I think to go on a trip out with other folk from the village, so they wouldn't be on their own, would go down well.'

'I like the sound of that,' said Ollie, nodding.

'Me too,' said Molly. 'But we're going to need a minibus and that won't come cheap. And we'll need a rota of folk to drive it, which means we'll need to sort out proper insurance and the like.'

'We could maybe look into getting a grant. I'm sure there'll be something available,' said Brogan.

'Good idea,' said Jimby. 'Every penny counts, and we'll need to crank up the fundraising, but I still think it's doable.' He glanced around the table, a twinkle appearing in his eye. 'It got me thinking just how successful our calendar was, fellas.' A grin spread across his face.

A series of groans followed. 'Oh, you've got to be kidding me,' said Ollie, throwing his head back and closing his eyes, making them all laugh. 'There is no way I'm getting my kit off for a calendar again, Jimby. No way!'

'What's this?' asked, Nick, grinning. 'Are you saying you posed naked for a calendar, Ollie?'

Ollie clapped his hands over his eyes and groaned again, while everyone hooted with laughter. 'It's not how it sounds, but for some reason we can't seem to have a committee meeting without Jimby dredging up the bloomin' calendar,' he said, making Kitty giggle.

Brogan was tickled by Nick's bemused expression. 'It was to raise funds for a defibrillator. Jimby organised a calendar with volunteers having their photo taken, posing naked with a strategically positioned item that referenced their line of work.'

'There wasn't much volunteering as I recall,' said Ollie. 'In fact, I don't remember being given a choice.' He flashed Jimby a look, making everyone laugh again. 'We're not all exhibitionists like you, you know, mate.'

'Hey, I'm a finely tuned specimen of manhood. The least I can do is share what I have with the world.' Jimby grinned again.

'Purlease,' said Molly, curling her top lip.

'No one wants to know about your manhood, Jimby, thanks very much,' said Vi, rolling her eyes and snorting a giggle.

Brogan caught Nick's eye and they shared a laugh together.

'It was hilarious on the day of the shoot,' said Molly. 'It's destined to become the stuff of Lytell Stangdale legend.'

'Great, that's all I need; can't say I'm overjoyed at being remembered for that!' Ollie shook his head good-naturedly.

'Yeah, I can just imagine the stories. "Oliver Cartwright, local carpenter, well-remembered for getting his chopper out for charity,' said Molly, her words triggering a raucous bout of laughter.

'Warghh! Molly, please! That's my dad you're talking about. I don't want to hear any more stuff like that!' Laughing, Anoushka put her hands over her ears.

'Sorry, flower,' said Molly, chuckling.

'You're outrageous, Moll.' Ollie shook his head, laughing despite himself. 'And I wasn't holding a chopper, it was a wood-plane.'

'That's splitting hairs, Oll,' she said.

'It's not the only thing it'd split by the sound of things,' said Nick, which raised yet more giggles.

Brogan glanced across at him. He looked relaxed, as if he'd always been part of the group. She noted the tension that had dulled his eyes earlier that day had gone. Just then, as if sensing her watching him, he turned, catching her eye. His smile widened, making her pulse rate zoom. She couldn't help smiling back. From the corner of her eye she spotted Kristy give Anoushka a nudge with her elbow. She knew they'd be quizzing her when they were next on their own together, but for some reason, she didn't mind.

'Anyroad, I'm deadly serious about doing another calendar next year,' said Jimby, bringing proceedings back in order. 'We're too late to get one organised for the coming year, and we need to maximise sales, so I suggest we get one ready for sale by early next September. Gives you fellas time to get yourselves into shape.'

'Something to look forward to, Oll,' said Camm, flashing him a grin.

'Can't wait.' Ollie rolled his eyes.

'You could make other merchandise, you know, like coasters of your favourite man of the month, notebooks with their photo on the front, or book marks even,' said Molly, giving a dirty cackle.

Ollie gave Molly a pointed look and shook his head. Nick roared with laughter.

'I reckon your cousin's doing a grand job of winding your husband up,' he said to Kitty.

'I reckon you're right,' she said, chuckling.

'So, forgetting about the calendar for now,' said Jimby.

'Thank the Lord,' said Ollie.

'I've been toying with the idea that we should maybe get something organised for Christmas Day for the folk who'd be on their own. I've had a couple of things running round my mind. I don't know how you'd feel about inviting someone to share Christmas Day with you? I mean, we all know everyone, it's not like you'd be entertaining a stranger. Or, an alternative might be to have a massive get-together and hold Christmas dinner at the village hall. Just so no one was on their own for the big day. Not sure how that'd work though.' He glanced around at his fellow committee members.

To look at Jimby, who was fondly regarded as the village joker, someone who didn't take life too seriously, who was accident-prone, with stories of his mishaps regularly entertaining everyone, Brogan mused that you'd never guess at the thoughtful, and at times serious, person that lurked inside. But that's exactly what he was. Yes, he was a larger than life character but he was one of the most kind-hearted people she'd ever met. In fact, she found herself thinking he pretty much summed up the local community, always looking out for one another, making sure folk were okay. She knew village life and all it entailed wasn't for everyone, but she savoured being a part of it. She regularly found herself grateful she'd made the decision to settle here after her break up with Archie. She'd have been very much on her own if she'd stayed in Skeltwick.

'You realise you're going to have to tread carefully on this one? You don't want to risk offending or embarrassing folk,' said Molly.

'Mmm. That's true,' said Brogan. She tried not to think too much about Christmas; the second one without her grandparents. Her mum was jetting off to a villa in the Canaries with her boyfriend Alan as she usually did. Like last year, the pair had said she was welcome to join them, but it wasn't for her and Brogan had turned them down. Besides, there was Bert to consider. He'd always spent Christmas Day with her grandparents; there was no way she'd leave him to be on his own. He'd been set to join her last year – the first one without Elsie and Stan – until he'd picked up a nasty vomiting bug and ended up being rushed to hospital on Christmas morning, pale faced and weak. Brogan had spent the day alone with Wilf and Nell, the significance of the day highlighting the loss of her grandparents, making her feel inexorably lonely.

Anoushka and Kristy had been up in arms when they'd found out, telling her she would have been welcome to join their large family gathering. But Brogan hadn't wanted to be a nuisance to anyone and had spent the day quietly with the two dogs, watching festive films and having lots of cuddles.

'Yes, Moll's right, we need to treat this sensitively,' said Lucy, bringing Brogan back to the moment.

'How do you plan on finding out who would want to be involved?' asked Camm. 'I mean, not everyone's on social media.'

'True,' said Kitty.

'How about putting a short note through everyone's door, with a couple of contact numbers for those who are interested? That way no one would get missed out,' said Brogan, her eyebrows raised in question. 'It's getting close to the big day, so we'd need to act quick. I wouldn't mind popping them through letter boxes.'

'Same here,' said Nick.

'Good plan.' Jimby smiled.

'I could type it up and get a load printed off tonight when I get home,' said Lucy.

'Well, it's my day off tomorrow, so I could call in at the shop to collect them; make a start straight away,' said Brogan.

'I'm happy to help; I'm off tomorrow too,' said Nick.

'And I can take some; hand them out at my dance lessons,' said Anoushka.

'Brilliant!' said Jimby. 'All we need to do now is decide what to say.'

The next twenty-minutes was spent fine-tuning the note and settling on using the contact numbers of Molly and Camm and Lucy and Freddie.

With that done, Jimby looked at his watch. 'Right, unless anyone has any objections, I think I'll declare the meeting closed. Thanks for coming everyone. I'll be very interested to hear the outcome of the notes. I reckon we'll need to have another meeting pretty soon, maybe next week, but we'll see if we've had many responses before we decide. Might be a last-minute one, but I've got a good feeling about this.'

Before long, Brogan and Nick were getting ready to leave, saying their goodbyes and gathering up Wilf and Maudie.

'It's been a great night. Thanks for suggesting it,' Nick said as they headed towards the car, the snow crunching underfoot.

'You're welcome. I knew you'd enjoy it. They're a sound lot.' Brogan smiled across at him, the icy air stinging her cheeks. She'd had a great time too, a feeling of happiness rushing through her at the thought of going home with Nick. She couldn't deny it, being with him felt so right. Just as it had done the first time they'd met, not that she wanted to think too much about it right now.

TWENTY-EIGHT

NICK

There'd been a light dusting of snow since they'd left Pond Farm, and Nick was relieved to see there were no fresh suspicious tyre tracks. There was also no evidence of unusual activity in the farmyard, the only footprints belonging to the wild animals that had sneaked in – he spotted rabbit and stoat tracks.

A tawny owl hooted from a nearby oak tree. It was followed by a shuffle in the hedgerow. Another hoot made Maudie cease her sniffing of the ground, looking around her, before glancing at Nick. 'S'alright, lass. It's just an owl.' His words seemed to pacify her and she ran to the porch where Wilf was waiting by Brogan who was unlocking the door.

'Hot chocolate?' Brogan asked once they'd divested themselves of their coats and boots.

'Thought you'd never ask.' Nick grinned at her.

'I'll just go and get my pyjamas on, then I'll get started on making them,' she said.

'I can do it. If you don't mind that is?' Nick asked. He didn't want her to think he was being presumptuous.

'That'd be great. I think you know where everything is after helping with the washing up last night.'

Five minutes later, Nick turned from the Aga where he was

whisking the hot chocolate in a pan to see Brogan coming back into the room, smiling. She looked adorable in a pair of oversized tartan pyjamas, her stunning hair hanging loose around her face, her green eyes shining. His pulse rate surged. Yet again, he found himself fighting the urge to go over to her and wrap his arms around her.

'Mmm. That smells so good,' she said, tucking her hair behind her ears and padding over to him, a pair of chunky woollen socks on her feet.

'It's just about done, I think.' Nick turned his attentions back to the pan, emotions hurtling around his body. She looked so beautiful. So natural. How he desperately wanted to press a kiss to that rosebud mouth. Take her up to his bedroom... *Ey up! Calm your jets, matey!*

'Fab. I'll go and put another log on the fire in the living room and we can get comfy through there, if you like?' She smiled up at him, making his heart leap.

He swallowed, doing his best to rein in his wayward thoughts. 'Yep, sounds good.' It was going to be a struggle not to bring up what had happened between them at the wedding but, all the same, he didn't want to set things back, especially when everything had been going so well. He reminded himself that they worked together, that he didn't want to affect their professional relationship, create any awkwardness such that Brogan would feel obliged to leave. He'd heard her enthusing to her friends about how much she was loving her new job. There was no way he could spoil that. He'd just have to let Brogan take the lead in their unusual situation. He hoped she would take them in the direction his heart was heading, and that it wouldn't take too long.

Nick woke early the following morning, darkness lingering outside. For the second night on the trot he'd slept well. The first thought that filtered into his mind was that he'd be spending the day with Brogan. He threw his arm above his head as a smile spread slowly across his face, a feeling of happiness blooming in his chest. He released a contented sigh. His second thought was that there'd be no angry texts or voicemails from Loretta to contend with now that she'd got her shoes. Boy, did that feel good. He hadn't realised just how much that had been dragging him down, no doubt made worse by the prospect of dropping them off at their former home at Middleton-le-Moors, with the risk of seeing her there. And as for the Trotters and that disaster of a cottage, he wasn't going to worry about that today. He'd done all he could. He'd informed his land-lords of the problems and if they didn't have the courtesy to respond to him, then there was nothing he could do about it right now. All that was left for him to do was to get the rest of his stuff out of there as soon as possible; he'd deal with getting the bond he'd paid them returned later. He didn't want to dwell on the niggle that they'd try to blame him for what had happened to the cottage, nor the fact that he might have to get his solicitor involved. No, after all that had been going on, today he was going to relax and enjoy spending time with Brogan and Maudie and Wilf. And he was determined that nothing was going to spoil that.

He was the first to arrive downstairs, feeling more refreshed than he'd done in a long time. After letting Maudie and Wilf out into the yard, he set to getting breakfast ready. In the fridge, he found everything he needed to make a hearty Yorkshire breakfast, and in the pantry was a loaf of wholemeal bread, perfect for making chunky slices of toast. As he was beating the eggs, he made a mental note to pick up some supplies from the village shop by way of his contribution to stocking the cupboards. He didn't want Brogan to think he was taking advantage of her hospitality. It was part of the reason he'd wanted to pay for their meal at the pub last night; a way of saying thank you, that he appreciated her letting him stay at Pond Farm.

Hearing a scratch at the door, he let Wilf and Maudie back in and they scurried to their bed, watching him attentively as he continued with the breakfast preparations, Wilf drooling spec-tacularly.

'That smells amazing.'

Nick turned to see Brogan walking over to him, rubbing her eyes. His heart gave its usual leap. 'Morning, sleepy head. Thought I'd start us off with a hearty breakfast seeing as though we've got a busy day ahead of us, delivering the notes. I hope you don't mind?' A sudden thought shot through his mind that she might think he was taking liberties by going through her cupboards and taking it upon himself to make breakfast.

Wilf and Maudie managed to tear their eyes away from the bacon sizzling in the pan and trotted over to welcome Brogan, their tails swishing. 'Morning, you two.' She smiled down at them affectionately before looking back up at Nick. 'Trust me, I'll never mind being woken by the delicious smell of a cooked breakfast wafting upstairs.' Her smile widened. 'It's ages since I indulged in one; I just usually grab a couple of slices of toast or a bowl of cereal.'

Wilf and Maudie trotted back to their bed and resumed their breakfast preparation observations.

Nick beamed, a feeling of relief in his chest. 'In that case, if madam would care to park herself at the table, I'll be happy to bring her a rather large mug of builder's brew.' He went over to the table he'd set for them earlier, and pulled out a chair, indicating for her to sit down.

'Thank you,' she said with a giggle as Nick tucked her chair in under her. Being so close, her hair brushed against his face and he caught a waft of her shampoo, its fresh floral scent triggering a somersault in his stomach.

'You're welcome,' he said, picking up the teapot and pouring her a mug of tea, doing all he could to calm his racing pulse.

'Ooh, I need this.' She took a generous gulp. 'Mmm. And it's the perfect temperature. Thank you.' She took another mouthful.

'My pleasure,' Nick said, making his way back to the stove. He placed a couple of slices of bread in the wire Aga toaster and set it on the hotplate. Soon the smell of toast joined the other mouth-watering aromas that swirled around the kitchen.

Brogan let out a splutter of laughter. 'Oh, my days! Look at the state of Wilf,' she said.

Nick turned, wire toaster in hand, to see that Wilf's drool had returned with a vengeance. The Labrador was now shivering with anticipation, making the strands of saliva quiver alarmingly. Nick let out a peal of laughter. 'Typical Labrador, driven by his belly.'

'He's shocking; from that performance, anyone would think he hadn't been fed for a week,' said Brogan, still giggling.

'I have to agree, it's very convincing. And the award for best actor goes to Wilf Hopwood!' said Nick, adopting a presenter's voice. Wilf wagged his tail at the mention of his name, glancing between Brogan and Nick, the drool swaying. Maudie looked on, unimpressed.

'You do realise you'll have to give him something now you've mentioned an award, don't you? He takes his drooling skills very seriously. And I should warn you, it'll have to be food based or he won't be impressed,' said Brogan.

'Already thought ahead; there's a particularly juicy sausage set by for him, one for Maudie too.'

'Phew! I didn't want him to get all diva on us.'

'Heaven forbid,' said Nick, raising his eyebrows as he walked over with a plate piled high with slices of golden toast. 'There you go, you might as well make a start while it's warm. I'll just be a moment with the rest.'

'That was delicious. Thank you. I feel very spoilt.' Brogan patted her stomach.

'Not at all. I can't thank you enough for giving me a roof over my head. I dread to think where I would've ended up staying if you hadn't.' Nick stood and headed over to where two sausages were cooling, breaking them up and putting them into the dogs' food bowls. Wilf devoured his enthusiastically, while Maudie took her time, sniffing it thoroughly beforehand. 'I'm not so sure Wilf tasted that, he wolfed it down so quickly,' said Nick, amused.

'I don't think he tastes anything, but he doesn't seem to care,' Brogan said with a chuckle. She pushed herself up, her chair scraping over the quarry tiles, and reached for her mobile on the dresser. 'I've had a text from Lucy, telling us she's printed off a load of notes and they're ready at the shop whenever's good for us to collect them.'

'In that case,' said Nick, 'we'd best get cracking. I reckon it's going to take us quite a while.'

'I reckon you're right. I'll just reply to Luce, then I'll go and get dressed.' She paused a moment, pressing her lips together as if something had crossed her mind.

'Everything okay?' he asked.

'I just remembered about my car, I wonder if I'll hear anything about it being fixed today?'

'Well, if you don't, I'm happy to play chauffeur 'til it is.'

'Does that mean you're going to doff your cap for me?' she asked, amusement dancing in her eyes.

'Only if you want me to.' He grinned, giving a quick demo.

'Hmm. I'll have a think about that one and get back to you.' She slipped her phone back onto the dresser. 'Won't be long. Oh, and thank you – for the yummy breakfast and the offer of being my chauffeur.' She flashed him a mischievous smile

'No problem.' Nick watched her go, his mind reeling with the feelings that engulfed him whenever he was around her. He wished he knew if she could feel it too. It was driving him crazy. There was a glint in her eye that suggested she did, but he didn't want to rely wholly on his instincts. After all, he'd never experienced anything like this before; he didn't want to misjudge the situation and for everything to blow up in his face. He winced at the thought. But all the same, he didn't know how much longer they'd be able to carry on like this without bringing up their time at the wedding. It was beginning to feel very odd tiptoeing around it.

He filled the washing up bowl with soapy water and made a start on the dishes, his mind full of the prospect of spending the day with Brogan, a warm glow of happiness spreading through him.

TWENTY-NINE

BROGAN

'Oh, my days,' Brogan said to herself. Nick was growing on her more and more by the minute. How considerate of him to make breakfast for her. And from the sound of the pots clinking down in the kitchen, he was now washing up. She felt a little spike of guilt as she brushed her teeth; she wasn't used to having people do stuff for her. It felt odd. There was no way she could leave all of the washing up to him; she'd feel like she was being a princess. When her grandparents had been alive, Brogan had always done the washing up with her grandma, the two of them chattering away as her grandma washed and she dried.

Brogan hurriedly got dressed and dashed downstairs to find the kitchen pretty much tidy. 'Wow! Talk about a fast worker,' she said, instantly regretting her choice of words, the heat of a blush warming her cheeks, her mind rushing back to the wedding. *Nice one!*

Nick laughed, his eyes locking on hers, setting a flutter away in her stomach. 'Yep, you could say.' He was clearly thinking along the same lines.

'Right,' she said, struggling to pull her gaze away, 'I'll give Maudie and Wilf a quick run around outside, then we can set off. Do you think we should take them with us?'

'Don't see why not.' He gave a shrug.

There was something about the way he was looking at her that was making her feel all unnecessary, like he knew what she was thinking.

'Oh, and in case you were wondering where your keys are, I've hung them on the meat hook on the beam by the dresser. That way, you can't lose them.' She hitched her eyebrow at him; she'd already cottoned on to him being slightly disorganised.

He followed where her finger was pointing and gave an amused laugh. 'Anyone would think I had a reputation for losing my keys.'

'Funny that,' she said with a cheeky smile before disappearing into the hallway.

Brogan had scattered a load of grit around the yard when she'd exercised the dogs earlier and it had done a good job of melting the thick layer of ice. Nick had just finished scraping the windscreen and the two of them set off, Wilf and Maudie in the back, looking out of the rear window with interest.

As they made their way steadily along the track, Brogan anxiously scanned the ground for fresh tyre tracks, but there didn't appear to be any. She sat back in her seat, the anxiety seeping away, her shoulders falling with relief.

'You okay?' asked Nick, quickly looking across at her, concern in his eyes.

'Yeah. Just relieved to see no evidence of unwanted visitors, you know, like yesterday morning.'

'Mmm. Maybe the weather put them off heading this far out. Judging by the amount of ice on the windscreen this morning, there was a hard frost overnight. It'll have made driving pretty dicey. I daresay whoever they are, they aren't from this area and won't be used to these conditions, and they probably won't have thought to get winter tyres on their vehicles.'

'True. Hopefully, it'll make them leave the area all together.'

'Here's hoping,' he said, flashing her a smile that unleashed a flurry of butterflies in her stomach.

She cast her gaze around the dale, taking in the clear blue sky above the stunning moorland landscape that was cloaked in a blanket of pure white. It sparkled in the pale winter sunshine. She couldn't ever imagine tiring of this scenery; whatever the time of year, it always looked breathtakingly beautiful.

Soon they turned onto the road to Lytell Stangdale, heading cautiously downhill, driving by huddles of sheep, their thick fleeces covered in a layer of snow. A grey squirrel darted across the road in front of them when they were – thankfully – on a straight stretch. 'Woah!' said Nick, lightly touching the brakes. They watched as it effortlessly leapt up a dry stone wall before scampering up a rowan tree whose naked branches stood stark against the white backdrop. A little further along, they pulled in for a tractor that was trundling towards them, giving a wave when they saw that it was Ella Welford's dad, Pete. His face ruddy with the cold, he gave them a cheerful smile and waved his thanks.

'Lytell Stangdale really is a beautiful spot. It looks just like a scene from a Christmas card,' said Nick as they made their way into the village.

The thatched longhouses with thick walls that sat either side of the wide road looked achingly cosy, smoke unfurling from their squat chimneys, snow covering their roofs and the lights from Christmas trees twinkling in their mullioned windows. Their little front gardens resembled winter wonderlands in miniature, sparkling snow dusting the hedges. On the village green was a cluster of snowmen of varying shapes and sizes, one wearing a brightly coloured scarf, another with a wide-brimmed hat set at a tipsy angle.

'It regularly gets described that way,' said Brogan, looking around her, and that description suited it perfectly, she thought.

The air was crisp and still, perfect for walking, which Brogan found herself looking forward to. Though the trods and road had been cleared and gritted, snow was piled up at the sides and in the gutters where it was turning to slush. They'd left Wilf and Maudie in the car until they'd collected the notes and had just crossed the road to the village shop when they encountered Little Mary walking cautiously along the ancient sandstone trod, her feet encased in a pair of fleecy boots. She was wrapped up warm against the cold, a bright red hat pulled down over her white curls. As usual, she had her large shopping bag over her arm.

'Hi there, Little Mary. I haven't seen you for a while. How are you doing?' asked Brogan, pleased to see her.

'Oh, hello, lovey. I'm fair to middlin', thanks. I'm just heading to the shop to get my bread order and a packet of custard creams to have with a cup of tea. How about you?' She gave a half-hearted smile.

'I'm fine, thanks.' Brogan noted the elderly lady seemed in low spirits which wasn't like her at all; she was always chirpy and cheerful. She scrutinised Little Mary's face in search of clues, but from what she could gather, she didn't seem to be ailing for anything. She simply looked sad.

'Well, that's good.' Little Mary nodded, casting a curious look Nick's way.

'Ah, let me introduce you to the new vet. This is Nick Heuston.' Brogan gestured towards Nick. 'He started work at the surgery the same day as me. Nick, this is Mary, but everyone calls her Little Mary to distinguish her from the other two Marys who live in the village.'

Nick gave a broad smile and held out his hand. 'Hello, Mary, it's lovely to meet you.'

That appeared to brighten the older lady up a little. 'Hello there, young man. And how are you enjoying your new job? Aren't you working today?' She glanced between them as she took his hand and gave it a gentle shake.

'I'm loving it, thanks. Though today's my day off, Brogan's too, and we're putting notes through all the letter boxes in the village on behalf of the Village Committee.'

'Oh? And what's that all about, then?'

Brogan noticed the older lady was beginning to look chilly; the paper-thin skin on her cheeks was red and there was a droplet of water dangling off the end of her nose which was also rather rosy. And if the cold was seeping through Little Mary's boots anything like it was Brogan's wellies, her feet would be bloomin' freezing. 'Tell you what, we're heading to the shop too, why don't we tell you all about it in there?'

'Yes, now you come to mention it, it is a bit raw today; I'm beginning to feel a bit nithered.' Little Mary gave a shiver as if to prove it.

The bell above the door gave a cheerful jangle as Brogan held it open for Little Mary to step inside. The delicious aroma of fresh baking wafting through from the adjoining teashop hit Brogan's nostrils. If she hadn't been so full of Nick's hearty cooked breakfast she'd have been tempted to talk him into heading there for a pot of tea and a slice of one of Lucy's yummy cakes. Maybe they could do that later, she thought; they'd no doubt work up an appetite traipsing their way around the village in the cold.

At the counter Rhoda's gentleman friend, Len Thornton, was paying Freddie for a newspaper and a carton of milk. It was odd to see him out of his usual cycling gear, but the roads were a bit too dicey even for a die-hard biking enthusiast like him to tackle.

'Ey up,' Len said, giving the three of them a friendly smile. 'I reckon this must be the new vet I've been hearing so much about.'

Nick shot Brogan a questioning look before holding his hand out to Len. 'Hi, I'm Nick Heuston, and you're spot on, I am indeed the new vet. And I hope it's all good things you've been hearing about me.'

'I'm Len, it's grand to meet you, Mr Heuston.' He took Nick's hand and pumped it hard.

'Nick, please.' Nick smiled at him.

'Aye well, Nick, everyone's been singing your praises. Apparently, you're the best thing since sliced bread.' Len's eyes briefly flicked to Brogan before returning to Nick.

Brogan's heart jumped in her chest. Had folk been talking

about her? *Please tell me I'm not the subject of gossip.* She really wasn't keen at the prospect of that. What had people been saying? she wondered, her mind searching for what they could possibly have found to talk about. *How about the small matter of Nick staying with you? That'd be more than enough to set tongues wagging round here!*

'Well, that's very kind. I must say, I've been made to feel very welcome,' Nick said bashfully.

'Aye, folks are very welcoming around here.' Len put his change in his pocket and tucked the newspaper under his arm. 'Anyroad, I'd best be off. Rhoda and me are heading to the cinema over at York; there's a film she fancies seeing, so I thought I'd treat her. Wouldn't do to be late, mind, especially with the way the roads are. Nice to meet you, Nick.' He nodded at the vet.

'You too, Len,' said Nick as the cyclist left in a chorus of good-byes and warnings to drive carefully.

'Now then, Nick and Brogan were just about to share some news with me,' said Little Mary.

'They were?' said Lucy, her eyes widening with interest.

'Really?' said Freddie, his expression matching his wife's.

'The notes,' said Brogan, quickly jumping in, hoping to direct Lucy's thoughts away from any gossip she might have heard about her and Nick. It suddenly dawned on her that the village shop was the perfect place for little rumours to start, with locals using it as a place to catch up with one another. And though well meant, it didn't take long for the little rumours to spread, growing bigger with each re-telling. 'You know, the ones Nick and I have come to collect from you so we can start posting them through the letter-boxes in the village and roundabout.'

Little Mary looked on, puzzled.

'Ah, right, yes. I've actually got them right here.' Lucy reached under the counter and lifted out a box. She pulled out one of the notes. 'There, what do you think?'

'Oh, you've done such a lovely job,' said Brogan, her eyes alighting on the small piece of paper Lucy and Freddie had decorated to look festive and eye-catching. 'It must've taken you both ages to get them all printed off and cut to size.'

'It did take a while and meant a rather late bedtime, but we wanted to get them done for this morning; Christmas isn't that far off if we're wanting to get something organised,' said Freddie.

'So what exactly is it all about? What are you wanting to get organised for Christmas?' asked Little Mary, peering at the note through her glasses.

Between them, Brogan and Nick, and Lucy and Freddie gave her an outline of Jimby's suggestion from the meeting. Brogan noticed Little Mary's face visibly brightening as she listened.

'Oh, my, how lovely,' said the older lady, her hand on her chest.

'It just means that everyone will have the option of spending Christmas Day with someone, rather than being on their own,' Lucy said.

'Well, I have to say, that's just typical of young Jimby Fairfax to come up with something like that. He's always been such a thoughtful lad. And, it comes at a very good time for me, since I've only recently found out that I was going to be spending Christmas Day on my own. I can't tell you how sad that made me feel – not that I'd let on if I hadn't heard about this. My nephew and his family, who I usually spend it with, are off to Australia to be with his wife's sister. Told me they're going to be having their Christmas dinner on the beach. A barbecue! Can you believe that?' she said with a chuckle, turning to Brogan. 'Anyroad, lovey, where do I put my name down?'

Brogan's heart squeezed at the thought of Little Mary feeling sad on Christmas Day. She caught Nick's eye, and he pulled a sympathetic face; he'd been touched by it too.

'We've got a book right here. We're keeping a list of everyone interested and you're top of the list, Little M,' said Freddie, kindly.

'Oh, how exciting!' Little Mary beamed around at them all, sending a wave of happiness through Brogan.

Just then, the door opened, the bell jangling cheerily as Molly's mum, Annie, stepped inside, a thick burnt orange scarf wrapped around her neck, a matching hat pulled over her dark wavy bob. With her large brown eyes, there was no mistaking the family resemblance between her and her daughter, not to mention Kitty and Jimby. 'Crikey me, it's perishing out there,' she said with a shiver. She pulled off her gloves and stuffed them into her pockets before retrieving a shopping list from her bag then scooped up one of the wicker baskets that were stacked by the door.

After a chorus of 'good mornings', Freddie said, 'You're not wrong, Annie, and if the forecast is to be believed, it's set to get even colder before the week's out.'

'Aye, so I hear.' She turned her attention to Nick. 'Hello there, you must be Nick, the new vet our Molly was telling me about.' Annie gave him a friendly smile. She and her husband Jack lived in a barn conversion on land belonging to Withrin Hill Farm where Molly and her family lived.

'Yes, that's me,' said Nick, smiling.

Brogan groaned inside as she wondered exactly what Molly had said to her mum.

'Our Moll says you're staying with Brogan for now 'til you get somewhere more permanent sorted. And I have to say, after hearing about that dodgy pair with the dark-grey van, I'm relieved to hear it; it wouldn't do for a young lass to be on her own when there's folks like that sneaking about the place. Jack and me saw them when we were heading down our lane yesterday. They'd pulled in and were looking over the dale with a pair of binoculars. Had a right shifty air about them, and most certainly didn't strike me as birdwatchers.'

'Ooh, I really don't like it when this sort of thing happens. Thankfully, we don't see that sort round here much, but when we do, they don't half make their presence felt.' Little Mary's smile had fallen.

A spike of unease shot up Brogan's spine. She couldn't shake the feeling that something bad was about to happen, though she kept her thoughts to herself, not wanting to add to Little Mary's concern.

'I get the impression that everyone's being extremely vigilant and keeping an eye out, reporting on local social media whenever they see anything out of the ordinary. If the pair are planning on doing something, then that should make it more difficult for them. Seems to me we're keeping a step ahead,' Nick said.

'True,' said Lucy.

Brogan couldn't help but agree. There had been an increase in the reported sightings, with plenty of people taking photos, though no one had yet managed to capture a facial shot. She felt sure it was only a matter of time before someone did. Plus, PC Snaith was on it too, which was reassuring; he always took people's concerns seriously.

'Right then,' said Annie. 'I'd best get started with this shopping list. I've got a dozen mince pies to bake for my reading group this evening, and a lamb stew for Jack and me for dinner, and I'm short of ingredients for both.' She waved her list at them as she shot off down the shop.

Brogan felt her gaze drawn to Lucy to see the shop owner wearing a look of mock horror. Brogan found herself having to stifle a giggle. Annie was a lovely lady, but she was infamous locally for her dreadful culinary "skills", her reputation helped in no small part by Molly who regularly shared entertaining stories of the inedible meals she and her brother had to suffer growing up. 'Honestly, it's a wonder we weren't seriously malnourished or didn't have rickets since most of the muck she churned out ended up in the dogs – and even they'd been known to turn their noses up,' Molly had said on more than one occasion. Most of the village had experience of Annie's fruit scones from when she baked for the fundraising coffee mornings that regularly took place in the village hall. They were known for being as hard as rock with a strong fishy aftertaste thanks to her liberal addition of bicarbonate of soda, but no one had the heart to tell her.

'I suppose we'd best get started dishing out these notes,' said Brogan, turning her attention to Nick.

'I think we'd better had,' he said.

'And we'll keep you informed of the Christmas Day details, Little Mary.'

'Looking forward to it, Brogan lovey. Now, mind you both have a grand day.'

Starting from the top end of the village, Brogan and Wilf worked their way along one side of the main street, while Nick and Maudie took the other, diligently delivering the notes through letter boxes. It took longer than expected, thanks to the icy pathways that led to some of the cottages, rendering them extremely slippery underfoot. Frozen fingers didn't help either, nor did gloves, especially when it came to separating the pieces of paper. But, eventually they got the job done, re-grouping beside the vintage telephone box just outside Oak Tree Farm where Kitty and Ollie and their family lived. The sound of children, shrieking and laughing in the playground at the village primary school on the hill floated down on the frosty air, mingling with the inharmonious squawks of Jimby's cantankerous cockerel, Reg. He was notorious for terrorising strangers – as well as the occasional local – and had an intense dislike of walkers, particularly those sporting a backpack. If one dared to stray onto his "territory", he'd hurl himself at them, spurs brandished, his sharp beak delivering spiteful pecks. And though he was getting on a bit, the bird showed no sign of mellowing.

'Which street next?' asked Nick, his face glowing red with the cold.

'Church Street, I reckon'd be best,' said Brogan. 'Then we can work our way along the shorter ones.'

'Okay.' He glanced up at the sky, his brow furrowing. The broad splash of blue had shrunk and the rest of the sky had taken on a strange purple hue where it was being encroached upon by clouds that slumped low in the sky. 'Looks like the weather's about to change. If those clouds are anything to go by, I reckon we're going to have a load of snow dumped on us before long.'

Brogan followed his gaze. 'Aye, we'll have to work quick.'

'Yep, let's get cracking.'

Just as they were setting off down the trod a Range Rover pulled up beside them and Lady Carolyn Hammondely climbed out, smiling cheerily. She was sporting a sheepskin duffle coat with matching hat and a friendly smile.

'Morning, Lady Caro,' Brogan and Nick said together.

'Morning you, two,' Lady Caro said in her cut-glass accent. 'I spoke to Jimby this morning, just to see what I'd missed at last night's meeting, and I have to say I think his idea is fantastic. He explained that you'd volunteered to drop notes through all the doors in the village. It's jolly decent of you, especially in this biting cold. Anyway, I spoke to my father and Sim and we're in agreement that we'd like to offer a place for a couple of people to spend Christmas Day up at the castle.' She beamed at them.

In recent years, Lady Carolyn had been tasked with the job of turning Danskelfe Castle – the family seat of the Hammondely family – into a viable business. It was something she'd done with flair and to great success. Along with converting the estate's old office buildings and renting them out to local businesses – like Danskelfe Vets – she'd organised the opening of several of the castle's rooms to the public, hosting weddings, arranging music events in the woods on the Danskelfe estate, as well as having the luxury lodges built. Business was booming, and it was having a positive knock-on effect for the local economy.

'That's really kind of you,' said Nick. He knew her from having previously treated her horses and Labradors when he worked at the surgery in Middleton-le-Moors.

'It is,' said Brogan, though she noted how Caro hadn't mentioned her mother being involved in the conversation. It didn't surprise her though; Lady Davinia could be a sour faced old boot. Brogan could imagine she wouldn't be keen on doing much festive hosting.

'Oh, darling, I'm absolutely positive. The thought of people we know being on their own for Christmas is simply too dreadful to contemplate. And besides, there'll only be a handful of us up at the castle; we'll be rattling around the place by ourselves. I can assure you, having some guests join us at the old pile would be far more exciting than watching Mummy getting squiffy on the gin before passing out in front of the telly.' She leaned towards them. 'But please don't tell her or anyone else I said that.' She gave a mischievous giggle.

'I promise I won't.' Brogan couldn't help but laugh too as an image of a sloshed Lady Davinia, sprawled out on a sofa sprang into her mind, her stiffly coiffed hair all skew-whiff, her trademark bright pink lipstick smeared.

'That's something interesting to add to the pot, Caro. I'm sure folk would be thrilled to spend Christmas Day at the castle,' said Nick.

'Just let me know when the next meeting is, and I'll do my best to be there. But for now, I need to pop into Ollie's workshop and have a chat about my next project, which is *top secret*.' She tapped the side of her nose and hitched her eyebrows mysteriously.

'Sounds intriguing,' said Brogan.

'Oh, it is, and I can't wait to share it with you all.'

'No one could ever accuse you of sitting back on your laurels, Caro,' Nick said as she headed to her car.

'No time to sit down, Nick! There's far too much to do, which is just the way I like it.' Caro grinned as she opened her car door. 'Oh, and before I forget, I saw that van this morning.' Her smile dropped and she rolled her eyes. 'You know the one that's been arousing everyone's suspicion? It was lurking on the rigg road opposite Camplin Hall Farm. There was a scruffy looking man, dressed all in black, standing on the roadside, and I'd swear he was looking through binoculars. He put them down as soon as he saw my car. I slowed down to get a better look at him, but his hood was pulled too far over his face to see anything, same with his equally dodgy-looking pal.'

Adrenalin surged through Brogan's veins as she recalled being disturbed the other night and the tyre tracks on their lane. She couldn't shake the feeling it had something to do with the dark-grey van. 'I don't like the way they're just creeping around. That sense of waiting for something to happen is really unnerving.'

'Yes, it's got me on high alert too, but according to PC Snaith, there's nothing we can do. They haven't done anything illegal, *yet*. He says we're to just keep a look out and not be as complacent about locking our cars and outbuildings as we usually are.' Caro shook her head. 'I wish they'd just clear off and leave us alone.'

'Yeah, me too.' Brogan breathed out a heavy sigh.

'I assume you've posted all this on the local social media pages?' said Nick.

'Not yet, but I'll do it on my phone now.'

It crossed Brogan's mind how glad she was to have Nick staying with her. And the reasons why were increasing by the day.

THIRTY

NICK

Snow had been falling steadily for the last hour and by the time they'd finished posting the notes through all the letterboxes in the village the temperature had dropped significantly. As Brogan crossed the road to join him, Nick noticed she was shivering. A layer of snow had settled on her hat and shoulders, her face was pinched red and she looked frozen to the core. As she reached him a snowflake landed on her cheek and without thinking, he gently brushed it away. Brogan's eyes met his, electricity sparking in the frosty air around them. Not for the first time he thought how beautiful she was as he felt the strong pull of attraction in his gut. His breathing deepened. He was seconds away from stepping closer and placing a kiss on her plump, rosy lips when Wilf charged by, kicking snow everywhere, crashing unceremoniously into their moment.

'Wilf!' said Brogan.

The Labrador seemed oblivious to the cold and was snapping playfully at the snowflakes while Maudie looked on, joining in occasionally. Despite his disappointment, Nick couldn't help but smile. Wilf had definitely brought out Maudie's playful side, though she could still muster up a haughty expression when the need arose.

'Do you still fancy that trip to the tearoom?' he asked, his eyes roving Brogan's face, taking in the damp curls that had escaped from beneath her hat. Much as he'd like nothing better, he knew it was pointless trying to step back to where they'd been before they'd been interrupted by Wilf's enthusiasm. The moment had gone.

'I'll go if you want, but to be completely honest, I think I'd prefer to head home and get changed into something warm and dry,' Brogan said through chattering teeth, acting as if nothing had happened between them. 'I've got some homemade soup in the fridge, we could have that. It'd help us thaw out.'

'Mmm. Sounds good.' He felt a wave of relief. Much as he'd love to sample some of the delicious-smelling food at the teashop, his feet felt like blocks of ice and his fingers were so cold, he was struggling to use them. He'd been secretly hoping she'd choose to go home. And the thought of a bowl of steaming soup was enough to start the thawing process.

They trudged up Church Street, two solitary figures and their dogs, their feet sinking into the freshly fallen snow. 'Jeez, I don't think I could get much colder. I can't feel my toes,' said Brogan, smiling when her eyes met Nick's which made his pulse jump to attention. He wasn't sure how much longer he could go on like this without saying something.

By the time they reached the main road, large feather-like snowflakes were swirling around them. They hurried towards the car, heads bowed. Nick would be glad to get back to Pond Farm and get parked up for the rest of the day. He was used to Middleton-le-Moors winters, and though the town wasn't that far away from Lytell Stangdale, the weather never got as extreme as it did out here on the moors, where it was more exposed and could change in a heartbeat.

They'd just got Maudie and Wilf ensconced in the boot space when their attention was taken by the unmistakable sound of the snow plough scraping along the road. 'Sounds like Camm's out and about,' said Brogan. A moment later, the man himself rumbled by, waving cheerily as he went, the plough making short work of the snow, pushing it out of the way. 'He does a brilliant job of keeping the roads round here clear. It's mostly so the milk tankers can get through to the dairy farms, but he's been known to plough the smaller lanes to farmsteads when the snow's got really bad.'

'Yeah, he's a decent bloke,' said Nick, as he brushed snow from the windscreen of his car while Brogan busied herself clearing the rear window.

'Yeah, he is, and he's been so good for Molly since Pip passed away.'

'Oh?' said Nick as the pair climbed inside. Nick set the engine away, the fans blowing bitterly cold air at them.

'Yeah, Molly's first husband died in an accident a few years ago now. As you can imagine, Moll was devastated. Apparently Camm – who's not from round here – came along at just the right time, made her smile again.'

Nick waited a moment for the condensation to clear from the windscreen. 'Right. I'd never have guessed she'd been through something like that. It must've been hard for her and her kids.'

'I can't even begin to imagine. From what I can gather Kitty and Vi were really supportive; did their best to make sure she was okay.' The passenger window had steamed up and Brogan rubbed a circle clear with her gloved hand.

'Now that I can believe. In fact, I don't think I know anywhere that has such a strong sense of community as the villages round here. Jimby's idea for Christmas is awesome, and the fact that the other committee members were keen says it all really. Everyone seems to look out for each other.'

'It's pretty close-knit, that's for sure.' Brogan's voice tailed away as she peered out of the window. 'Which reminds me, I wouldn't mind calling in on old Bert Hoggarth over at Broad View Cottage at some point before it gets dark today,' she said. 'It's not far from Pond Farm so won't take me long to walk. Only, I had a text from Ella who's taken over walking his Labrador, Nell. She thought he seemed a bit out of sorts when she saw him this morning. Though she said he did his best to reassure her otherwise when she asked if he was okay. It'll give me chance to remind him he and Nell are still welcome to spend Christmas day with Wilf and me.'

'I'll drive you over, if you like? Save you having to adopt the abominable snowman look again.' Nick glanced over at her.

'Are you saying I'm abominable?' she asked, her eyebrows arched in mock outrage.

'Perish the thought.' He chuckled.

'Well, that's all right then. And are you sure you wouldn't mind? Taking me over to Bert's?'

'Course not. I know Bert and Nell from my time at the surgery in Middleton. It'll be good to see him again.' Nick smiled at her, a hint of warmth finally blowing through the fans.

'That's great, thanks.' She beamed at him.

Back home, and changed into warm, dry clothes, Nick found Brogan in the kitchen. She was leaning over the Aga, stirring a pan of soup, its mouth-watering aroma making him salivate.

Wilf and Maudie, fresh from a thorough drying with the towel – which had made Maudie's coat look extra fluffy – were sat keeping watch from their usual position, the familiar drool dangling from Wilf's chops.

Nick chuckled, shaking his head as he wandered over to the Aga. He peered in the pan at the rich, red liquid that was simmering gently. 'Mmm. That smells seriously good.' And he couldn't help but think that it also felt seriously good to be standing this close to Brogan.

'Tomato; homemade, has a little hint of chilli so it should be extra warming.' She glanced up at him and smiled, sending a charge through him. 'There's some crusty bread over there if you fancy slicing it?'

'No problem.' He smiled, reluctantly pulling his eyes away from hers. If they were going to carry on like this, pretending that nothing had happened between them, then he was going to have to make a concerted effort to rein his feelings in. Which, judging by the emotions she stirred in him, was going to get more challenging by the day.

They were halfway through their lunch, chatting away, when Brogan said, 'I think I'll take some soup for Bert when we call in on him. I'm not sure he does much in the way of cooking for himself. I don't want to offend him, but just with Ella saying he didn't look his usual self, there's a chance he might be glad of it. I'll take him some bread too, something to fill him up.'

'I'm sure he wouldn't be offended; might be glad of it.'

'Mmm. True.' She nodded, thoughtful.

An hour later, it had finally stopped snowing and the wheels of Nick's four-wheel drive were making their way over the newly fallen snow on the lane to Broad View Cottage. Brogan sat with a basket on her lap. It was filled with soup, bread, and a few other provisions she'd rustled together. They'd agreed to leave Wilf and Maudie at Pond Farm; three high-spirited Labradors in Bert's small cottage had the potential to be chaotic and very probably not what Bert needed.

Nick drove slowly, keeping in a low gear and being careful to avoid the banked up areas where the snow had drifted in deep swathes. Dusk was already creeping in, and all around them the broad expanse of moorland was swathed in a thick eiderdown of snow, lights twinkling cosily from the farmsteads that nestled in the dale.

'Wow, it's beautiful, but it really is a remote spot for an elderly man to live on his own,' Nick said. Though he could appreciate its beauty, there was no getting away from the harsh bleakness of a moorland winter.

'He's never lived anywhere else; told me he was born there.'

'And did you say he doesn't drive?'

'He's waiting for a hip replacement. Hasn't driven for years as far as I'm aware. My grandparents used to take him wherever he needed to go; I took their place when... when they passed away.'

Detecting the note of sadness in Brogan's voice, Nick was keen to change the subject, hoping to stop her mood from slumping. 'It'll have been a wonderful place to grow up, with the moors as his playground.'

'Oh, he's got some fabulous stories about his adventures with his brothers and sisters, I love listening to them. Times seemed so much more innocent then, more carefree. I'll have to make an extra effort to pop in to see him, hear some more of his childhood tales, they're so wholesome,' she said, her smile reappearing, much to Nick's relief.

'I wouldn't mind joining you,' said Nick, bringing the car to a halt.

'I think Bert'd love that.'

The snow was deep along the path to the front door of Bert's cottage, and the lack of new footprints suggested he hadn't been out, and judging by the lack of paw prints, nor had Nell.

Brogan knocked on the door, pressing down on the latch to go straight inside. 'Oh,' she said when it didn't yield. 'Bert doesn't usually lock his door. Mind, with that dodgy pair in the van lurking around, I'm pleased he has.'

She knocked again and called through the letter box, 'Bert, it's just me, Brogan, and I've got Nick, the vet, with me.'

A bark from Nell emanated from the depths of the cottage, followed by a bout of chesty coughing as Bert made his way down the hall to the door. Though Bert seemed pleased to see them, Nick found himself agreeing with Ella's assessment that he didn't look himself; his complexion had a grey pallor and his eyes seemed dull.

'Now then, it's grand to see their pair of you,' said Bert in his broad moorland accent.

Nell nudged at their legs, her tail wagging, as they bent to fuss her. Nick ruffled her ears. 'Hello, lass, it's good to see you again.'

'Sorry I kept you hanging about in the cold, but I can't move as fast I'd like on account of my gammy hip.' Bert shuffled back, letting them inside. As they passed, he took a large cloth handkerchief from his pocket and wiped his nose, stuffing it back in his pocket when he'd done.

'No worries, Bert,' said Nick as he and Brogan followed the elderly man into his small living room. Nick was pleased to see it was toasty and warm thanks to the open fire that was glowing in the hearth.

'Sit yourselves down.' Bert gestured to the sofa while Nell curled up in front of the fire.

'You've got it cosy in here, Bert,' said Nick, looking around the room. He couldn't help but notice it would benefit from a bit of a tidy round, the flick of a duster, a quick vacuum. He made a mental note to ask Brogan if the elderly man had anyone going in to help him with housework. It couldn't be easy for Bert to do it himself with his mobility issues. Not that he would say anything of the sort to Bert!

'We've brought you some soup, Bert. You know what I'm like, I made too much as usual; I've got gallons of the stuff. Thought you might be able to help out and take some of it off my hands, rather than me having to eat it 'til it comes out of my ears!' Brogan said with a giggle. 'It's the spicy tomato one you like, and there's some other bits and bobs I've got too much of and need your help with, including that fruit cake you're partial to.'

Bert gave a hearty chuckle. 'By 'eck what are you like, lass? Actually, don't answer that. I can tell you. You put me in mind of your grandma, God rest her soul. Elsie was always making too much stuff so I had to help out and take some off her hands. Not that I'm grumbling, mind, she made bloomin' tasty grub, as you do. You're just like her, young Brogan.'

'Thanks, Bert. I've been using all her recipes so hopefully the standard hasn't fallen too dramatically since I've been doing the cooking.'

'To be honest, lass, it all tastes exactly the same as Elsie's; you've inherited her culinary talents, make no mistake.'

'That's very kind of you to say.'

Nick stole a look at Brogan to see a happy smile spreading

across her face. His affection for her was growing by the minute. Not everyone would have handled this situation as sensitively as she had. She'd managed to make sure Bert had something warm to eat without making it look like he was being offered charity, or made to feel she thought he couldn't cope.

'Have you got time for a cuppa, or do you need to head off? I know how busy you young folk are.' Bert looked from one to the other, hope gleaming in his rheumy eyes. He retrieved his hanky from his pocket again, giving a noisy blow of his nose.

'Bert, I've always got time for a cuppa with you,' said Brogan. 'Tell you what, why don't I go and stick the kettle on while you have a catch up with Nick? I'll get this lot put away, unless you fancy me warming you some soup now?'

'Ooh, well, now you come to mention it, are you sure you wouldn't mind?' Bert's face brightened.

'Not at all. I'll be two ticks.'

While Brogan was in the kitchen, Nick managed to glean from Bert that he'd been feeling under the weather for the last couple of days. And though the older man had described it as "just a bit of a cold" that was "nowt to worry about", Nick couldn't shake the feeling that it was causing him more discomfort than he was letting on, especially if his hacking cough was anything to go by.

Leaving Bert to enjoy his soup in peace, Brogan took Nell for a quick walk while Nick set to, clearing the path to the cottage and re-filling the coal scuttle before darkness properly settled in.

When they'd done, and had given Nell a good dry with an old towel, Bert insisted they stay for another cup of tea to "warm you through before you head off". Nick suspected it was more to do with him being reluctant to say goodbye to his company. He couldn't blame him. Much as Broad View Cottage was in a lovely spot, he guessed if it wasn't for Ella and Brogan dropping in, Bert could go for days without seeing another soul.

'So, Bert, Brogan tells me you've lived here all your life,' Nick said, as a way of inviting him to share the stories that Brogan had mentioned.

'Aye, lad, that I have. I was born here and I dare say I'll end my days here. Not that I'm grumbling, mind, I've got some right happy memories of the place.'

'I can imagine, and I bet you've seen some changes too.'

Bert blew out his cheeks and sat back in his armchair, his hands resting on his stomach. 'You're not wrong there. Take the winters, for example. They're nowt like they used to be. I dare say you think the snow out there's pretty bad today, but by 'eck, I've known a time when it's been piled right up as high as them windows.'

'Really?' said Brogan. 'That must've been something to see.'

'Oh, aye, it was, but it made for bloomin' hard work, what with the water freezing, never mind having to use an outside privvy. I tell you what, you didn't hang around when you needed to go.' Bert gave a hearty chuckle. Nick was pleased to see his face was animated and the colour had returned to his cheeks.

'I can believe that,' said Nick. He glanced across at Brogan, the pair sharing a smile as they nursed their mugs of tea, enjoying Bert's trip down memory lane.

'Mind, if the snow wasn't too bad, we'd still have to walk to school in the village; you know, the one up on the hill? I went to that very one. Took forever, trudging in the snow, but we had a right laugh, me and my brothers and sisters – there were five of us in total – having snowball fights with t'other kids on the way. We were soaked through by the time we got to the school, but you don't seem to feel the cold when you're a kid.' Bert released a contented smile, gazing into the distance. 'Aye, they were happy times.'

By the time they came to leave it was properly dark outside. Nick was pleased to see Bert seemed much brighter than he had when they'd first arrived.

'Right, Bert, we'll see you soon,' said Brogan, wrapping her scarf around her neck. 'And don't forget to keep your door locked while we've got unsavoury folk loitering in the area. I'm sure there's nothing to worry about, but it's always best to be on the safe side.'

'Aye, you're right lass, especially after what happened to poor old Roger Scarth.' Bert shook his head. 'Mind, I haven't seen owt suspicious since I saw that van with the dent in the side the other day. I'm hoping they'll realise I've got nowt worth nicking and not bother coming round again.'

'Well, you've got my mobile number now, as well as Brogan's, so if you see anything suspicious, or if you need anything, just call, okay?' said Nick.

'Will do. And ta very much for popping by, the pair of you. Me and Nell have enjoyed the company, haven't we lass?' He stooped to pat the Labrador who gave a quick swish of her tail.

'Well, I think we can say that was a resounding success,' said Nick as they drove away, the pale moon casting its ethereal glow over the snow-covered dale.

'It was, and he definitely looks brighter than when we first arrived. Though I'm a bit worried about his cough.' Brogan's brow crumpled. 'I'll make sure to check on him every day. And it's good that he's still happy to join me for Christmas Day,' she said, her expression lifting.

Nick glanced across at her. 'Will any of your family be joining you?'

'Oh... um, no. My mum's going to the Canaries with her boyfriend; it's what they always do.' She paused. 'It's been a while since we spent Christmas day together.'

Even in the dim light, Nick could see her frown had returned.

THIRTY-ONE

BROGAN

Though Nick had only been staying at Pond Farm for a few days, it felt as if he'd been there for far longer. The house felt somehow more comfortable with him in it, and Maudie too; she'd settled herself in quickly with her and Wilf becoming inseparable; even if she still bestowed on him the odd snooty look, which he didn't seem to mind. It was as if this was where she and Nick were meant to be; that this set-up, with Brogan, Nick, Wilf and Maudie, was the perfect fit for Pond Farm cottage. Brogan had begun to savour the time she spent with Nick, not wanting to think about how it would be when he found somewhere permanent to live. It made her stomach twist whenever it crossed her mind. His presence had made her realise just how lonely she'd become since her grandparents had passed away. It went without saying that Wilf was a good companion, but it wasn't as if she could have a conversation with him – well, she supposed she *did* actually talk to him, and from the way he tilted his head it was as if he understood her, which was true as far as the words, "biscuit", "dinner", "walk" and "treat" were concerned – but it didn't flow two ways.

If she was honest with herself, Brogan knew it wasn't just loneliness that made her enjoy Nick's company as much as she did. It ran way deeper than that. He was getting under her skin, burrowing his way into her heart. Yes, she couldn't deny it, she was falling for him. Falling hard. And it scared her a little. Scrap that, it scared her a heck of a lot! Especially after what had happened with Archie and how he'd pulled the rug so unceremoniously from under her feet. Since then, she'd kept her heart tucked safely out of harm's way and kept relationships firmly at arm's length. But that hadn't stopped her from yearning to find someone to love and to love her back when she'd let her mind wander in the darkest depths of the night when sleep eluded her. She'd give anything to have someone look at her the way Gabe looked at Anoushka; he adored her and didn't care who knew it.

Later that evening, Brogan and Nick sat chatting in the living room, discussing everything from keeping an eye on her elderly neighbour, to the feedback they'd already had from people showing an interest in the Christmas Day suggestions – Molly and Lucy had each been in touch with an update. It felt so easy to talk to him. The words just seemed to pour out, which was unusual for Brogan, being the sort of person who usually kept her innermost thoughts to herself and took a long time to get to know someone before she'd even consider sharing such personal stuff.

She told him about her parents, how her dad hadn't been around much when she'd been growing up and how they had no relationship to speak of now. When she explained about her mum, she noted his eyebrows shoot up when she'd told him about their after school arrangements. 'I don't want you to get the wrong impression,' she said. 'Looking back, I can see I was quite young to be doing that, but I didn't feel uncared for or neglected.'

'But what about Christmas Day. How come you don't spend it together?'

Brogan had gone on to explain how she'd been invited to join her mum and her boyfriend, but would rather spend the day with Wilf and Bert. 'It would mean Bert would be on his own for Christmas Day, and that would be awful.' Nick couldn't argue with that.

Conversation eventually found its way to their previous relationships with him asking why she'd been single for so long.

'Ah, well...'

Nick listened, his mouth falling open as she went on to explain about her ill-fated relationship with Archie and how he'd broken up with her.

'He actually said that? He actually told you that you weren't enough?'

Brogan nodded, feeling tears prickle her eyes at the memory. She blinked them away before they could take hold.

'No. How could he ever think that? He's a fool. If I were him, I'd think you were everything,' he said, his voice soft.

She cast her eyes down as the warmth of a blush rose in her face. 'Anyway, despite telling me he didn't want to get married and didn't want kids, he's now married to a girl I thought was my friend; she's now ghosted me.'

'You're kidding?'

'I'm not,' she said with a rueful laugh. She took a sip of her tea in a bid to hide any hurt that might sneak its way onto her face. 'Anyway, that's enough about me. I'm well and truly over him. It took a while, but looking back, I can see we weren't that well suited. I'm actually grateful he ended things when he did.' She mustered up a smile. 'So, how about you? What happened with Loretta, if you don't mind me asking? She's very beautiful, by the way.'

Nick heaved a sigh, blowing it out nosily through his lips. 'Yes, she's beautiful on the outside, though I'm not so sure she's as attractive on the inside anymore. She's barely recognisable from the girl I first met and fell in love with; the one I thought I was going to spend the rest of my life with. And funnily enough, she ended up ditching me for a mate.' His eyes met hers. 'Seems we have more in common than we realised.'

He went on to tell her how Loretta had been spending more and more time "working" late – he put finger quotes around the word – and how she'd become distant and snappy, spending more and more on expensive designer clothes, getting herself "glammed-up". 'And then, one evening, when she was out, I got a text from a total stranger, telling me Loretta was cheating on me with her boss – my best mate. She even sent a photo of them kissing, just in case I needed proof.' He rubbed his hand over his jaw. The flicker of pain that ran across his face hadn't gone unnoticed by Brogan; her stomach twisted for him. She couldn't imagine how seeing something like that must have felt.

'Oh, no! That must've been awful, and I'm not sure what I think of the woman who sent the text. I mean, I appreciate you needed to know, but what a horrible way to find out.' Brogan found herself overcome by an urge to reach out to him, touch his hand, but hard as it was, she resisted.

'Yeah, it definitely messed with my head that night. Turns out she worked at Aaron's company; she didn't get on with Loretta, blamed her for getting a verbal warning from Aaron.'

'And the photo was a way of getting back at her?'

'Yep, so it would seem. I know the breakdown of my relationship is more recent than yours, but strangely, I feel I'm at a similar stage to you. I can't deny it didn't hurt at the time, but now I'm actually relieved it happened. I can see Loretta and me would never have made each other happy; somewhere down the line we'd stopped following the same path, only I hadn't realised it; had a lot to do with the insane rivalry with her younger sister. Plus she was determined she didn't want kids; I thought I felt that way too, which maybe I did for a while, but not anymore. I know now I really want a family and I can't imagine not being a dad.'

They both sat quiet for a while, Nick's last sentence hanging in the air between them, the metronomic tick of the grandfather clock barely noticeable in the background.

'How about you? Do you see yourself getting married and having kids?' he asked, breaking the silence.

Brogan's usual answer when anyone put this question to her was to say that she enjoyed being single, enjoyed being able to suit herself, but her reply to Nick came out very differently. 'Yeah, I do actually. I'd love to have someone to talk to about what's happened in my day, to visit places with, see new things. And, yeah, I'd love to be a mum – and I'd like at least two kids; being an only child has its benefits, but I think it must be nice to have a sibling to play with when you're growing up.' Where had this openness come from? she wondered.

'Well, speaking as a sibling, I can tell you that despite my brother Matt and me having some fairly nasty scraps when we were kids, I'm really glad he was part of my childhood – and not just because I could try to pin the blame on him for my misdemeanours, not that it ever worked.' He grinned broadly and Brogan couldn't help but smile back. He'd lightened a conversation that had had the potential to turn a little heavy and looked as though it could venture down a path she hadn't been quite ready to tread.

They'd talked way longer than they should have done on a work night, all the while shared memories of their first meeting tangible in the air around them. She knew there'd been a couple of times when Nick had come close to saying something, but he'd hesitated, an uncertain look lurking in those clear blue eyes of his; he'd clearly had second thoughts and his words had remained unspoken. It had left Brogan feeling a mix of relief and regret. Part of her didn't feel ready to venture back to that day, face the wholly out of character way she'd behaved. But a big part of her wished he'd just gone for it, taken the plunge and got it out there. That way, she'd have no choice but to face up to what had happened between them, face up to the feelings he'd first stirred in her that day, the feelings that were currently gaining pace at a rapid speed. If only Archie's words would stop stalking her like some pernicious spectre. "You're not enough." They gripped her tight, squeezing the air from her lungs every time she thought about them, which had become more frequent recently as she'd wrestled with her feelings for Nick. The thought of not being "enough" for him, the thought that he might one day utter those words to her, was almost too much to bear. She'd rather their relationship didn't go any further than risk hearing that from Nick.

"You're not enough." *Ughh!*

By the time the grandfather clock struck midnight, the fire had become nothing more than a small pile of glowing embers in the grate. Brogan tried but failed to stifle a yawn which made Nick laugh.

'Looks like my scintillating conversation has struck again,' he said, amused.

'No, it's not that at all, it's all that walking about, delivering leaflets in the snow, plus I'm not used to such late nights; I'm such a granny, I'm usually tucked up in bed by ten o'clock.' She succumbed to another yawn, covering her mouth with her hand. 'Oh, no. I'm really sorry.' She laughed too.

As they were saying their goodnights, Nick placed his hands on the top of her arms, bending his head to meet her eyes.

'Brogan, you must never let anyone make you think you're not enough. I really mean it. Never, okay?' He gave her arms a squeeze as if to confirm his words.

'Um, oh, okay.' Her sleepy brain felt fuzzy as she tried to work out where this was going.

'I mean it. You're a wonderful, warm-hearted person, the way you look out for Bert is a perfect example of that. I've never met anyone like you, and I know I haven't known you long at all, but, you're enough for... What I mean is... what I want to say is, just don't let anyone make you feel you're not enough. Because there's no way that could ever be possible. That's all.'

'Oh.' Brogan braced herself, half-expecting him to pull her into a hug – she'd half-hoped he would. Instead, he held her gaze for several long seconds, before giving the tops of her arms another squeeze and kissing her briefly on the cheek.

She watched him disappear through the door, her hand going to where his lips had gently brushed against her skin. She got the feeling he was trying to communicate an unspoken message, but she felt too bone-tired to fathom it out. She scratched her head. Maybe it would make more sense in the morning, after a good night's sleep.

THIRTY-TWO

BROGAN

The ear-splitting screech of the alarm at six o'clock on Friday morning spliced through Brogan's slumber, waking her with a start. With her heart pounding, she reached her hand out from beneath the duvet and fumbled about for the clock, relieved when she'd managed to silence the blessed thing. She'd been in a deep sleep and the noise hadn't been at all welcome, especially with it still being so dark outside. Oh, what she'd give to have another hour snuggled up under her duvet.

The sound of Nick's bed creaking in the next room reached her ears. *And it would be rather nice if I could spend that extra hour snuggled up with Nick.* She blinked, realising that wasn't on the agenda for today, so she rubbed her bleary eyes and reluctantly dragged herself out of bed. She brightened as it dawned that tonight was Vi and Jimby's party.

The time from arriving at the surgery at ten-past-eight that morning to putting on her coat in readiness to leave at six-thirty in the evening seemed to have gone in the blink of an eye. They'd arrived at work slightly later than the previous days thanks to Nick forgetting where he'd put his keys. After a quick, but frantic search, Brogan had eventually found them in the utility room hung up alongside Maudie's lead. 'Hmm. Not quite sure why I'd hang them there, but never mind. Thanks for finding them,' he'd said, flashing Brogan an apologetic smile. Maudie had obliged by giving her dad one of her disapproving looks making both Nick and Brogan chuckle.

Brogan slung her bag over her shoulder as she waited for Nick to finish his conversation with Vonnie. She hoped he wasn't going to be much longer; they needed to get ready for the party. She felt a ripple of excitement; she'd been looking forward to it all week. She'd been keeping an eye on the sky all day and was pleased there'd been very little snow to add to the light dusting they'd had through the night, with the clear blue skies of the previous morning returning. It meant she and Nick wouldn't have to worry too much about the weather when they were trying to enjoy themselves.

It had been another good day at Danskelfe Vets, with Brogan feeling more settled. Already she felt she'd been accepted as part of the team; it was as if she'd been there for months, not just a week! The only spanner in the works had been another call from Jed at the garage saying he was still having trouble getting the necessary part for her car. 'No one seems to have it in stock, but I'll keep ringing round,' he'd said apologetically. Nick had told her not to worry, that he didn't mind driving her anywhere she needed to be, telling her it was the least he could do since she'd given him and Maudie a roof over their heads. His reassurances didn't stop Brogan from still feeling awkward at the prospect of having to accept help.

Old habits were hard to break, she told herself.

The emerald-green dress Brogan had worn to the wedding was hanging on the door of her wardrobe. She gazed at it, admiring the rich fabric and matching beading; it was the most feminine item of clothing she'd ever owned and she loved it. She'd toyed with the idea of not wearing it on account of the memories it might stir; the last time she'd worn it she'd been sneaking out of Nick's hotel room. But after a brief internal wrangle, she talked herself into it, reasoning it would be a waste if she just left it hanging in her wardrobe, never seeing the light of day again. It had been more expensive than any other item of clothing she'd bought; there was no way she could justify only wearing it once, and besides, she'd always intended to wear it to Vi and Jimby's party. Plus, she had very little else in the way of pretty party clothes, her wardrobe being mostly stuffed with practical items like jeans and jumpers, T-shirts and shirts. She had loads of those, but they would hardly do for tonight, and she didn't fancy dragging out the dress she'd worn to every smart do for the last however many years. Tonight felt different. Tonight, Brogan was thrilled with the idea of getting dressed up and celebrating the season, having a catch up with her friends at the same time. She felt a flutter of excitement at the thought. What could be better? Vi and Jimby were excellent hosts and their Christmas parties had a reputation for being fun and easy-going, with nobody ever wanting to leave.

She knew what had brought about this new lightness of spirit, what had eased the pain of the grief that still had her in its clutches. It was Nick. He'd brought the sparkle back into her life, no doubt about it. With a little help from Maudie too.

After a quick shower, she brushed her hair, smoothing it down with a squirt of anti-frizz serum, hoping to tame her wild waves. That done, she fastened a hairslide above her right ear – she'd been disappointed to have lost its partner after her trip to the wedding. Next, she applied her makeup, cursing the freckles that still managed to peek through her foundation. She'd just finished adding a flick of eyeliner when she remembered she needed to have another search for the pretty underwear she'd bought specially for the dress. The lady in the shop had advised her that the knickers would give her a sleek silhouette and avoid the risk of having a dreaded VPL – Brogan had never heard of the expression before then; she didn't even know such a "fashion faux pas", as the lady had described it, existed.

After a quick rummage through her underwear drawer she found the lacy bra but there was still no sign of the matching knickers and she didn't have the time to hunt around further for them. 'Looks like I'm going to have to resort to my trusty belly-whackers, VPL or no VPL,' she said to herself. *Just as well no one's in danger of getting a flash of them tonight.* She felt her mind wandering back to *that* night with Nick, the memories of how she'd felt like a completely different person. A more carefree, fun-loving version of herself. She quickly hauled it back, giving herself a stern talking to. She needed to steer well clear of going down that route tonight! Nick was her boss, she reminded herself. They were friends. And that's how it needed to stay.

She was popping her satin ballet flats into a bag, Wilf and Maudie observing her with interest, when Nick strolled into the kitchen, fiddling with the strap of his watch. She glanced up and her heart gave a wayward leap. He looked so handsome in his chinos and teal-coloured shirt. His fringe looked damp, like he'd been trying to flatten it, but his cow lick appeared to be doing a sterling job of fighting back. She was toying with the idea of saying something when he stopped in his tracks. His mouth fell open, and he stood looking at her for what seemed an inordinately long stretch of time.

'Is everything okay?' she asked, wondering what on earth could be the matter with him. Was her hair looking wild? She reached up her hand, smoothing it over her waves. It didn't feel too bad; she'd felt it far worse.

He closed his mouth and swallowed, then shook his head, as if ridding it of unwelcome thoughts. He cleared his throat. 'Oh... erm, yeah. Everything's fine thanks.' He gave an uncertain smile.

'That's good to hear. For a moment there, I wondered if you were going to have second thoughts about going to the party.' Much as she could understand if he didn't fancy venturing back out into the wintry night, she'd have been disappointed not to go.

'No, no. It's not that at all.' A wide grin was stretching across his face. 'It's actually the floaty dress and wellies combo. It's not something you see in many places.' He nodded to her feet that were encased in a pair of battered green wellington boots. 'You're the epitome of countryside glamour.'

'I like to think so.' She grinned back at him, waggling her foot. 'Just to clarify, I won't be wearing my wellies at the party; I've got my smart shoes in here.' She shook her bag at him. 'By the way, did you know Livvie had to wear wellies to get to her wedding to Zander?'

'Really?' Nick barked a laugh. 'That's brilliant.'

'Yeah, the snow got so bad, it actually looked like she might not even get to the ceremony.' She shrugged her coat on. 'But that's a whole other story.'

'I'm intrigued, you'll have to share it with me on our way to Jimby and Vi's,' he said, reaching for his waxed jacket. 'I love how you country girls aren't too stuck up or vain to get practical when the need arises. You just get on with things, unfazed.'

'Nothing gets in the way of having a good time round here, just ask any of the Young Farmers.'

'I can believe that,' he said, suddenly distracted. 'Anyway, you look lovely,' he said.

'Thank you.' She smiled, her mind hurtling back to the last time she'd worn the dress.

He glanced around the room, pressing his lips together.

'They're on the meat hook, over there.' Brogan nodded towards the beam in question where his keys were hanging, amusement glinting in her eyes.

'Ah, yes. Thanks.' He gave a sheepish smile and strode over to get them.

After giving instructions to Wilf and Maudie to behave while they were out, Brogan and Nick were soon on the road to Lytell

Stangdale, the air between them buoyant as they chatted happily. Brogan felt the tickle of excitement in her stomach.

'You'll have a great time tonight, though it's a shame you can't have a glass of wine or a beer. If my car had been fixed, I would've driven, then you'd have been able to,' she said as they bumped down the track.

'Hey, no worries. We're at work in the morning, so I wouldn't be indulging in much anyway.' He flashed her a smile.

Before long, they were knocking on the door of Rowan Tree Cottage, the muted sound of music and lively conversation audible from the doorstep. Brogan was admiring the wreath that was hung there in muted golds and rich shades of purple – a colour Vi was well-known for being fond of.

Seconds later the door was flung open and Jimby appeared, the sound from inside growing louder as it spilled out.

'Wayhay! You got here! Come and get yourselves inside where it's warm,' he said, holding the door open for them. He was looking smart but casual in a pair of navy chinos and a blue shirt flecked with tiny oatmeal-coloured roses. His broad beam was infectious and Brogan couldn't help but match it as she savoured the warmth of the cottage that wrapped around her.

After hanging up their coats, Jimby led them to the large state-of-the-art kitchen which was already brimming with people. Though Rowan Tree Cottage was a new build, Jimby and Vi had been keen for their home to be sympathetic to the older, vernacular houses in the village, rather than opting for something contemporary that would stick out like a sore thumb and look dated in a matter of years. They'd opted for exposed oak beams, inglenook fireplaces, and a heavy thatch for the roof. It was a fine example of contemporary living juxtaposed with traditional building techniques and styles.

'What can I get you to drink?' Jimby asked, his voice almost lost in a flurry of cheery hellos. 'Pinot, Brogan?'

'Mmm. Please.'

'Shandy for me, thanks,' said Nick.

'Coming right up,' said Jimby, dashing off.

'I'm so glad the snow held off so you could both get here.' Vi appeared, looking glamorous as ever in a figure-hugging deep-purple velvet dress with chiffon sleeves and matching fishtail hem. In her vertiginous purple satin high heels, she towered above Brogan who wondered how on earth she could walk in them without falling over.

'Snow or not, there's no way it'd stop me from getting here; I've been looking forward to it all week,' Brogan said.

'And it was kind of you to extend the invitation to me,' said Nick.

'Hey, no worries, you're more than welcome,' Vi said. 'Since we moved in here a few years ago, we always have a Christmas party, and we always say the more the merrier. My parents very kindly offer to have Pippin for the night so folk don't have to worry about keeping the noise down and can get on with having a good time.'

'There you go, mate,' said Jimby, returning with their drinks, thrusting a glass of shandy in Nick's hand. 'Mind she can sleep through owt, can our Pippin, but she's up with the larks, so we take Ken and Mary up on their offer so we can have a bit of a lie in.'

'And it goes without saying, my parents love having her,' said Vi.

'Aye, they do that; gives them the chance to spoil her summat rotten,' Jimby said affectionately as he handed Brogan a glass of wine. 'There you go, Broge. Right, I just need to go and pop some nibbles in the oven now everyone's here. I don't know about anybody else, but I'm that hungry I could eat a scabby hoss.'

'Jimby, you're always hungry,' said Vi.

'Hey, I'm a growing lad.' He patted his stomach, his abs made taut by many hours working at his forge.

Vi rolled her eyes, smiling as he dashed off.

A moment later, they were joined by Ollie, Zander and Camm. 'Now, then, mate,' said Ollie, patting Nick on the back. 'How's your first week at Danskelfe Vet's been?'

Brogan didn't get to hear his answer as Anoushka waved her over to where she was stood talking to Kristy, Ella and Livvie. Joining them, Brogan was swept up in an assortment of hugs and kisses on the cheek. She turned to Livvie who she hadn't seen for ages. 'Livvie, it's so good to see you, chick! Huge congratulations on the new babies. How've you been? You look gorgeous, by the way,' Brogan said, thrilled and surprised to see Zander's wife enjoying a night out just weeks after the birth of their twins. 'I have a little something for you but didn't want to intrude until you'd got settled in.'

'Ah, that's so kind, but you really shouldn't have. And it's fab to see you too, flower.' Livvie smiled. 'And it's kind of you to say, but to be honest, I don't feel exactly gorgeous. However, apart from having boobs the size of giant water melons, and a massive squishy tummy thanks to a c-section, I'm feeling better for sneaking out for the night, I can tell you. I couldn't give a stuff that I'm exhausted and am surviving on three hours' sleep a night if I'm lucky – as the black bags beneath my eyes that even a couple of inches of industrial-strength concealer have failed to hide will testify. But I'm determined to enjoy myself tonight.'

'Too right,' said Kristy.

'I don't blame you. So, is Rhoda on babysitting duty? And how are all your babies doing?' asked Brogan.

'Ahh, the babies are absolutely gorgeous. Zander's besotted.' Livvie pressed her hand to her chest, happiness shining in her eyes. It sent an unfamiliar pang ricocheting through Brogan, disconcerting her a little. She blinked, refocusing her mind.

'His parents are here for a few days, so they're looking after them. I'm not sure they fully appreciate what they've let themselves in for, with three little ones under a year old to contend with.' Livvie feigned a worried expression.

'Yikes,' said Anoushka, her eyes wide.

'I know, we did try to warn them, but they assured us they'd be fine, which I'm sure they will be; they're pretty chilled. And I'm not saying I jumped at the chance for a night out with Zan but... I jumped at the chance for a night out,' Livvie said, making them all fall about laughing.

'Actually, while I remember, lasses,' said Ella who'd come to the party on her own, 'someone was telling Joss that there's a couple of dogs gone missing locally.'

'No!' said Brogan, pressing her hand to her chest.

''Fraid so,' said Ella.

'Where from?' asked Anoushka.

'Ellerby Farm over at Arkleby. Titch and Sue Ventress were looking after their daughter's Labradoodle while she's on holiday and it went missing from their farmyard yesterday afternoon. As you can imagine, they're absolutely gutted.'

'Poor things. They'll be dreading having to deliver that news,' said Kristy, shaking her head.

'The other was a cocker spaniel. It vanished from a farm over at Danskelfe. And get this, apparently a dark-grey van was seen in the area around the time they went missing.'

'They've got to be linked. I'm going to tell my parents to keep a close eye on our dogs,' said Anoushka.

'I think we should all be keeping a close eye out. It's why Joss has stayed at the farm tonight. He didn't want to leave the dogs we've got boarding with us. His dad's there with him too. We're seriously considering getting security cameras fitted,' said Ella.

'It's a shame when we have to start thinking like that round here, but if it means we feel safe...' Kristy gave a shrug.

'Anyway, I didn't tell you that to bring down the mood of the evening, it was just to tell you to keep an extra close eye on your mutts. In happier news, have you heard about Joss's latest plans for the farm?'

'I haven't, do tell,' said Brogan.

Soon the delicious aroma of food started permeating the air, reminding Brogan of how hungry she was. She didn't have long to wait before Jimby was calling for everyone to help themselves from the appetising buffet set out on the large island. 'Tuck in, folks. There's plenty to go round.'

Brogan sat chatting with her friends, a plate of food on her knee. She glanced over at Nick who was sitting with Jimby, Camm and Ollie, the four of them listening to Zander who was talking animatedly. Her heart swelled with emotion. Nick had only been here a short space of time, but his easy way with people meant he'd slotted right in. There was no edge to him, no hidden agenda. People seemed to warm to him straight away. She was going to have to face up to her feelings for him sooner or later.

THIRTY-THREE

NICK

'So, Nick, you must have loads of funny stories in your repertoire about your time as a vet,' said Jimby, dipping a mini spring roll into a bowl of plum sauce. He popped it into his mouth and chomped enthusiastically.

'Yeah, I bet you have. What's the weirdest thing you've come across?' asked Ollie.

Nick got asked this question a lot. 'Yep, there's been a few entertaining moments, but the ones that always spring to mind involve Labradors, and me fishing a weird array of things out of their stomachs.'

'Sounds like it's not a good time to get stuck into this tempura prawn,' said Ollie.

'Yeah, you might want to finish your food before you hear it,' Nick said, nodding towards the plate in Jimby's hand, still piled high with food.

'Good point.' Jimby set his plate down on the worktop behind him and rubbed his hands together. 'Right then, fire away.'

Nick chuckled as the memories came flooding back. He went on to tell them of the time a man came into the surgery at Middle-ton-le-Moors with his Labrador. 'Charlie's owner complained that there was an alarming "rattling" sound coming from the Labrador's stomach whenever he moved about.' Nick looked around at the faces watching him intently.

'A rattling sound?' said Camm.

'Yes.' Nick nodded. 'He also told me Charlie had lost weight and his appetite had waned which wasn't like him at all. It isn't like a Labrador full-stop, but that's by the by. Anyway, poor old Charlie didn't look at all happy with himself.'

'Oh, dear,' said Ollie.

A subsequent examination and x-ray of Charlie's stomach had shown up a cluster of round masses, which had confirmed Nick's suspicions. He'd whipped the Labrador into the operating theatre and carried out emergency surgery. 'I'd heard stories of these things being consumed by dogs, but I hadn't actually encountered one, 'til I met Charlie.'

'So what was causing the rattling sound?' asked Ollie.

'Golf balls,' said Nick, matter-of-factly.

'*Golf balls?*' said Camm, his face a study of disbelief. The other's looked on agape.

'Yep.' Nick nodded. 'There were nine in total.'

'Bloomin' 'eck!' said Jimby. 'I bet poor old Charlie had one heck of a bellyache.'

'Oh, I should think the poor fella did.' Nick pulled a wry face. 'However, I'm very pleased to say, he went on to make a full recovery. And his owner promised to walk him well away from the local golf course.'

'Makes you wonder what possesses some dogs to eat what they do. I mean a golf ball would hardly be appetising,' Camm said.

'Oh, you wouldn't believe it. I removed three marbles, a rubber glove and a pair of crotchless knickers from another Lab.' Nick's mouth twitched.

'Aye, aye. Interesting combo,' said Jimby, a cheeky glint in his eye.

'It was a bit awkward actually, since I subsequently discovered that the knickers didn't belong to the owner's wife,' Nick said.

'Ey up,' said Camm.

'And how did you find that out?' asked Ollie.

'Well, owners are usually interested to see what I find after this sort of operation, so I always keep the items I've removed in a bowl for when they come to collect their pet. This particular lady was looking very puzzled and spent a long time scrutinizing the knickers, which I remember thinking was a little odd, until she announced that they weren't hers.'

'Uh-oh. I think I can see where this is going,' said Jimby.

'Oops,' said Camm.

'Her husband's face just drained of colour and he started spluttering some cringingly feeble explanation while his wife stood there, glaring at him. I didn't know where to look, or what to say. The next thing I knew, she'd given him a heck of a wallop across the face and stormed out.'

'Crikey,' said Jimby.

'But the good news is, the Labrador made a full recovery. Unlike its owners' marriage; I heard they divorced soon after.'

'No surprises there,' said Camm, taking a slug of his ginger beer. Like Nick, he was driving, so was on soft drinks. At this time of year, Camm had to be prepared to go out with the plough at the drop of a hat; the capricious nature of the moorland climate meant the weather could change without warning and he'd never risk having an alcoholic drink if there was the slightest hint of snow in the air.

'And the moral of that story is, don't take a Labrador with you if you're getting your leg-over with someone you shouldn't,' said Jimby. A round of hearty laughter followed.

Nick hadn't expected to enjoy the evening quite as much as he had. Everyone had been welcoming and friendly and he couldn't remember feeling more at home with a group of people. He couldn't actually believe he'd been chatting to Gabe Dublin. The singer exuded an easy-going air and proved to be every bit as down-to-earth and affable as Brogan had said he was. It was easy to forget his status as an internationally famous rock star.

People had migrated around the kitchen, talking in different groups, music playing in the background. Nick noticed Molly was now standing beside him, chatting enthusiastically to Kitty. On the other side of them were Brogan and Anoushka. He watched Anoushka whisper something into Brogan's ear that made her eyes grow wide and two dots of colour bloom in her cheeks as she shook her head vehemently. He was prevented from observing any further by Molly saying, 'So, when are you going to give us a song, Gabe?'

'Whenever folks think they're ready to put up with me,' he said in his warm, Southern Irish accent. 'Care to join me, Brogan?'

Nick glanced back to her before turning quickly to the others. 'Brogan can sing?' he asked.

'She sure can,' said Jimby.

'Oh, she's got the voice of an angel,' said Kitty.

Nick looked on as Gabe retrieved his guitar while Jimby busied himself, setting out a couple of bar stools at the back of the room for them to sit on. Brogan hoisted herself up onto her seat and Gabe leaned in. She nodded in response to something he said to her sotto voce. Seconds later he counted them in and they launched into a rousing, feel-good song Nick remembered as being one of the singer's early hits.

Soon, everyone had joined in, singing along with unbridled enthusiasm, tapping their feet and clapping their hands in time to the music. Nick couldn't take his eyes off Brogan. So transfixed was he, he was only half aware of the excited buzz in the room. His heart surged as he took in her rich auburn hair, a stunning contrast to the emerald colour of her dress, and her green eyes that were sparkling with happiness. He was utterly captivated.

Brogan was clearly oblivious to his thoughts as she threw herself wholeheartedly into the song; her voice, strong and pure, complemented Gabe's as she harmonised with his smoky vocals.

As Nick watched, it dawned on him right there, right then, he couldn't go another day without telling her exactly how he felt. How she'd captured his heart.

He only hoped his feelings wouldn't send her running for the hills.

THIRTY-FOUR

NICK

The party was winding down, everyone had reconvened to the stylish living room where flames were dancing in the log burner and fairy lights twinkled from the huge Christmas tree that scented the air. A mellow atmosphere had replaced the bubbly vibe of earlier. Nick felt relaxed, sitting on a large squishy velvet seat.

Vi had made a pot of tea for those who'd requested some, while Jimby was busy organising a tray of nightcaps of Molly's dad's infamous sloe gin for everyone else. 'Mind, sip this slowly now, folks, it's like bloomin' rocket fuel,' he said, handing out the tot glasses filled to the brim with the ruby-coloured liquid.

'Oh, my days, it is. I can vouch for that,' said Kitty, hugging a mug of tea. 'And they're very generous measures you're dishing out, Jimby. There'll be sore heads tomorrow.'

'Which is why I've opted for tea since I'm at work in the morning,' said Brogan. Nick cast his gaze to where she was sitting on the sofa between Anoushka and Kristy; the three clearly had a tight friendship. He briefly wondered if she'd told them what had happened between them at the wedding. He arrived at the conclusion she probably had.

'I've opted for a cuppa too,' said Molly, raising her mug. 'I'm taking Granny Aggie to Middleton-le-Moors tomorrow afternoon so I'll need my wits about me big time. Apparently there's something she *urgently* needs to look at in one of the shops there. I dread to think what it'll be.'

Granny Aggie was the grandmother of Molly's deceased husband, Pip. She'd moved to the village several years earlier and Molly, who'd always thought fondly of the old lady, still looked out for her, despite her mischievous ways.

'I saw her out and about on her new mobility scooter the other day. She was zooming along like a bat out of hell,' Anoushka said with a giggle.

It triggered a snort of laughter from Kristy. 'Honestly, she's lethal. She's like a flippin' wild woman behind the wheel.'

'Kristy's right.' Molly nodded. 'She nearly took the vicar out last week. He had to leap out of the way and ended up in Maneater Matheson's arms. The pair of them ended up in a heap on the village green.'

'That'd have been worth seeing,' said Ollie, giving a throaty chuckle as he sipped his sloe gin.

'Well, she wouldn't be complaining. I'll bet her hands were all over him; poor bloke'll have been traumatised twice over,' said Jimby, earning himself a round of laughter.

Anita Matheson was universally regarded as the village vamp owing to her predatory nature with the local men. She made no secret of the fact that she didn't discriminate between those who were single and those who were married. She favoured male company over female company, declaring that all women felt "threatened" by her.

'Too right. She's like an octopus when she gets going,' said Vi, arching a perfectly sculpted eyebrow.

'Tell me about it. I've still got the bruises from the last time she cornered me,' said Jimby.

'As if the poor vicar hasn't been through enough.' Though Molly shook her head, there was an amused smile hovering on her lips.

Jimby grinned. 'I can tell by our Moll's expression, Granny Aggie's been up to summat else.'

Molly rolled her eyes again, giving a sardonic laugh. 'Ughh. Just a load of the usual, you know; me having to get her out of scrapes with the vicar; tell him what she really meant to say in her naughty text messages.'

'She's hilarious,' said Ben.

'That's easy for you to say, son. You're not the one having to clear up her mess and witness Rev Nev's long-suffering expression when I have to deliver the old bat's bonkers excuses. Mind, she does tickle me sometimes.' Molly was struggling to fight a laugh. 'Anyroad, I was just heading through the door the other day when she rang to tell me Rev Nev had been round to have a word with her. Up in arms, she was, saying he'd asked her if she could be more careful with the texts she sends. Honestly, she was in a right old flap about it.'

'Well, it was only a matter of time; she's tortured him for years. In fairness to him, he's been very patient with her,' said Vi.

'He has.' Kitty nodded. 'In fact, he's probably made things worse for himself by being like that; might have made her think he was okay with her sending rude texts to him, that he found them funny.'

Nick listened, wondering where on earth this conversation was heading.

Molly rubbed her fingers over her chin. 'Hmm. That's a good point, actually. I might have to mention that to him. Anyway, would you believe she reckons he's the one with the problem, and has been taking her texts the wrong way? Told me he's got a dirty mind. And she reckons he should be more understanding. Says he should appreciate that an old lady like herself might struggle with technology and should at least give her credit for using it.'

'He does! But I think she's overstepped the mark a bit recently,' said Camm.

'Only recently?' Jimby said, chuckling into his sloe gin.

'Anyroad, according to Granny Aggie, she'd sent a text to

Penny Gaines, telling her how kind Rev Nev is and how only the other day he'd been round and had a good old rummage around in her undercarriage. Said she was sure he'd do the same for her mother if she fancied.'

'Crikey!' said Ollie, scrunching his nose up.

Nick looked over at Brogan to see her hand over her mouth and her shoulders shaking with mirth.

'Honest to God...' Vi shook her head. 'Granny Aggie is totally wild.'

'Tell me about it,' said Molly, while Camm laughed quietly beside her. 'Reckons she was talking about her "wheels" as she calls her mobility scooter. Anyroad, she's huffed with him, which might mean she'll leave him alone for a while. Here's hoping at least.'

'That was a brilliant night,' said Nick as they drove out of Lytell Stangdale, snowflakes curling down from the inky-black sky. 'It was hilarious hearing all those stories, especially the ones about Granny Aggie. Sounds like Molly's got her hands full with her.' He flicked the windscreen wipers on.

'I think she has, but Molly's got a real soft spot for her, and for all she gives off a vibe of being quite outspoken and feisty, Moll's actually very patient.'

'Yeah, I sensed that.'

'Vi and Jimby's Christmas parties are always the best. Mind, it's a shame Freddie and Lucy couldn't come, Lady Caro and Sim too.' Brogan's last words were almost swallowed by a yawn.

'It is; it would've been nice to get to know them better too.'

Lady Caro and Sim were busy overseeing proceedings ran smoothly at a wedding that had taken place at the castle that afternoon, while Lucy and Freddie had been too anxious to leave their premises unattended since the dark-grey van had been seen loitering outside their shop once darkness had descended earlier in the evening.

'And you didn't tell me you could sing!'

'Oh, well, I don't very often, just at the music night at the pub, and things like tonight's party,' Brogan said with a shrug.

'You should sing more; you've got a beautiful voice.'

'Thank you.'

He was distracted by the glare of a car's headlights on full beam approaching them. He squinted, his eyes dazzled. The vehicle appeared to be charging towards them.

'Blimey, I wish they'd dip their lights.' Brogan squealed as Nick was forced to swerve violently out of the path of the oncoming vehicle and into the side of the road. 'Oh, my God!'

How the vehicles didn't collide, Nick didn't know. His stomach clenched as he felt the wheels skid, the anti-lock brakes kicking in as the car shot over a thick patch of ice. 'What the—' he said, adrenalin coursing through him, making his heart pound as they narrowly avoided crashing into the metal post of a road sign.

The car came to an abrupt halt. Nick hissed out a lungful of air, his pulse racing. 'Who the heck was that?' he said, turning to Brogan whose chest was heaving, her breathing coming out in shallow bursts.

'I don't know. Their lights were too bright for me to see anything, but if I had to hazard a guess, I'd say it was that dodgy pair in the dark-grey van.' There was a discernible wobble in her voice.

'Are you okay?' Even in the dim light, he could see she looked shaken.

'Yeah, I'm fine, thanks. Just a bit shocked. How about you?'

'Same.'

She nodded.

'Let's get home,' he said.

THIRTY-FIVE
BROGAN

As they pulled up in the yard of Pond Farm Brogan tensed. Though there'd been no fresh tyre tracks on the lane, she knew instantly something was wrong. She swallowed nervously and peered out of the window, hastily scanning the yard. She gasped as the outside light revealed where numerous footprints had trampled over the light covering of snow that had fallen since they'd gone out.

'Oh, no! Wilf! Maudie!' Panic gripped her. Her heart rate gained pace and her pulse started thrumming in her ears, Ella's warnings looming large in her mind.

'It's them! It's them with the van! They've been here.' Fighting back tears, Brogan leapt out of the car, slipping and sliding over the snow, overwhelmed with relief when she heard the sound of Wilf and Maudie barking loudly from the cottage. 'Oh, thank goodness!' The tightness in her chest suddenly easing, she took a moment, glancing around her.

'Brogan, be careful!' Nick hurried towards her, but she barely registered his voice as her attention was caught by one of the sheds where the door was blowing open in the wind, bashing against the wall. Her stomach churned when her eyes alighted on the jagged splinters of wood where the lock had been forced.

Nick was behind her in a moment as she rummaged in her bag for the torch on her keys, her fingers rendered clumsy in the panic, her chest heaving.

'What can I do to help?' he asked, snow swirling around them.

'I'm just trying to find my torch.' She found his presence reassuring. She couldn't imagine how it would feel to face this on her own; she'd be terrified.

Snow started falling more quickly, the wind whipping up and whistling round the yard. Strands of her hair were blowing around her face, and her now wet skirt was slapping around the top of her wellies but she was too fired up with adrenalin to notice the cold.

'I'll turn the car so the headlights are shining in this direction.'

Nick went to head back, stopping when Brogan said, 'No need. I've found my keys.' She flicked on the torch and shone its beam around the cluttered space, strewn with thick, dusty cobwebs, revealing the contents scattered about haphazardly. It was full of years' worth of items her grandparents had hoarded and something she'd intended to tackle once she'd felt able to face it, but in this state of disarray, it was difficult to tell if anything was missing. She felt nausea curdle in her stomach.

'Has anything gone?' asked Nick.

'I don't know.' The cold was beginning to bite and her teeth started chattering.

After a quick check around the other outbuildings, Brogan discovered her bike was missing from one of the unsecured sheds, along with an ancient lawnmower, not that they were worth much, but that wasn't the point. The mere thought that someone had crept about her things felt like a violation. It sent a shiver running up her spine.

'At least the Landie's still there,' she said when they'd finished checking the outbuildings. 'But they'd have been hard-pushed to move it with the fuel tank being empty.'

'Well, that's something at least,' said Nick.

'I'll go in first,' he said when they reached the porch door of the cottage. Wilf and Maudie were still barking frantically from the kitchen. Brogan tried to protest, but Nick wouldn't hear of it. 'I'm sure they're long gone, and it was them in the van that nearly ran us off the road, but just in case,' he said, his tone suggesting he'd brook no argument. Reluctantly, she handed him her keys.

The door gave its familiar groan as he pushed it open. Brogan tensed. Growling and snarling now joined the barking from the dogs. They sounded quite terrifying, nothing like the soft pair she was used to. With her heart hammering against her ribcage and her legs shaking with fear, she held her breath as Nick placed the key in the lock of the kitchen door. Slowly, he turned it with a click before nudging it open a crack, allowing the dogs to pick up their scent. 'It's okay, Maudie, Wilf, it's just us,' he said.

'Wilf, everything's all right,' Brogan said. In a moment, the barking had ceased.

Once safely inside, Maudie and Wilf trotted about them, whimpering and nudging at their legs. They were visibly stressed by events. 'This isn't like Wilf at all, he's usually pleased to see me and eager for a tummy tickle when I get back, but this wound-up behaviour is unusual for him.' Brogan did her best to soothe the Labrador who remained twitchy, constantly glancing over at the window.

'Yeah, they're clearly agitated.' Nick went to calm Maudie, speaking in a soothing tone which helped a little, though she was still looking around, uncertain.

Satisfied that Maudie was all right, Nick said, 'Listen, if you don't mind, I'll just go and have a check around, make sure everything's okay.'

'Yeah, that's fine.' His words made her start, the suggestion that something might be amiss inside the cottage didn't sit easy with her.

The sound of her phone vibrating in her bag caught Brogan's attention. She'd put it on silent while she'd been at the party. She headed over to the dresser where she'd dumped it when she came in, the thought that it was late to be calling someone crossing her mind. By the time she'd fished it out of her bag it had stopped ringing. 'Typical.' She glanced at the screen, a deep frown crumpling her brow as she took in the tranche of missed calls. 'Oh no...' They were all from Bert. Bert who barely used his phone. Tapping on the screen, she saw that amongst the missed calls were a couple of voicemail notifications. Her stomach lurched. Brogan had a bad feeling about this.

She was listening to the messages when Nick came back into the room.

'Everything's fine, I didn't noti—' He stopped when he saw she had her phone pressed to her ear.

'Oh, my God! Oh, my God! It's Bert!' Fighting back tears, Brogan ended the call and pushed the phone into her coat pocket. She clamped her hand over her mouth, biting down on the emotions that were swamping her. It had been a long time since she'd felt so utterly distraught. Doing all she could to keep her voice steady, she drew in a fortifying breath. 'Nick, we need to get to Bert's. They've been round at his cottage. Nell's gone. We've got to help him.'

THIRTY-SIX

BROGAN

The distress in the elderly man's voice had been heart breaking, and wasn't helped by the fact that he'd been struggling to speak thanks to his wheezing and coughing.

Nick stood before Brogan, his face wrought with concern. 'Right, you need to get something warmer on, that dress won't do, the weather's getting worse out there.'

'There isn't time.'

'There is, it'll only take a couple of minutes to put a pair of jeans and a jumper on; you don't even have to take your dress off, just pull them over the top. Be sure to put some warm socks on too.'

She went to object again, but he said, 'You'll be no good to Bert if you're too cold to help him.'

She knew he was right. 'Okay.' With that she raced upstairs and flew into her bedroom, pulling on the clothes with lightning speed.

As Nick drove, Brogan couldn't get the distress in Bert's voice out of her head. She called his number several times to let him know they were on their way, but it just rang out, sending a spike of anxiety shooting up her. She dragged her hand down her face, aware of her pulse throbbing in her neck. Why wasn't he picking up?

Nick stole a look at her. 'It'll be okay. It's not that long since he left the message. We'll be with him in a matter of minutes.'

Much as she was grateful of it, his words of reassurance didn't make things any easier. As far as Brogan was concerned, they couldn't get to Broad View Cottage quickly enough. But they couldn't go any faster due to the wintry conditions on the roads; she had all on to stop herself from getting out and running across the fields to Bert's cottage.

Pulling up in his yard, Brogan flung open the car door. Just as at Pond Farm, the snow on the ground was churned up, prints left by many footprints, including Nell's.

She hurried up the path as best she could, almost losing her footing and snagging the saturated skirt of her dress on a branch with a sickening tear. She beat hard on the door. 'Bert! Bert! It's us!' She rattled the door handle but it didn't budge. She hammered on the door again, harder this time. By now her whole body was shaking. She flipped the letter box up. 'Bert!' she shouted through it, then peered in, relief washing over her when he appeared in the hallway, shuffling more slowly than normal. His breathing seemed more laboured and she could hear him wheezing from this side of the door.

'Brogan? Is that you, lass?' Bert's voice sounded weak.

'Aye, it's me and Nick. We just got your message. Sorry.'

She heard him fiddle with the lock and draw both the top and bottom bolt back. Slowly, he opened the door and out peered a dishevelled version of the elderly man. Brogan's expression fell when she saw him. His wan face was streaked with tears and there was a cut to his head. His thin, grey hair was sticking out all over the place, and his trousers and cardigan seemed wet and muddy down one side. He looked shaken to the core.

'Oh, Bert. Have they done this to you?'

'They've taken her.' He sobbed. 'They've taken my Nell.'

Brogan flung her arms around him, rubbing comforting swirls over his back. 'It'll be all right, don't worry. We'll get her back for you. I promise.' She really hoped it was a promise they'd be able to keep.

Brogan heard the beep of Nick locking his car followed by the sound of him striding over the snow behind her. 'Let's get you inside, Bert. You can tell us what happened where it's warm,' he said kindly.

Once they were in the living room and had settled Bert in his usual seat, Nick asked, 'Have you called the police?'

Bert shook his head. 'They said they'd come back and hurt me if I did.'

'The lousy....' Nick's top lip curled in disgust.

'Bastards!' said Brogan, finishing the sentence for him. Her chest was rising and falling sharply, her insides burning with rage. She glanced across at Bert. 'Sorry for the bad language, but what sort of person does this?' If she could get her hands on them right now...

'Low down scum, that's what sort,' said Nick. He caught Brogan's eye and shook his head in disbelief.

'No need to apologise, lass. That's exactly what they are.' He swallowed. 'The phone was ringing before but I was too scared to answer it in case it was them trying to catch me out.'

'It'll have been me, Bert. I rang a few times after I'd picked up your calls. They wouldn't know your number anyway, so don't be scared to answer your phone.'

'Brogan's right.' Nick sat down in the chair opposite him. 'Are you okay to tell us what happened?'

'Aye.' The elderly man nodded. His hands in his lap, he twisted his fingers anxiously. 'Well, first thing that struck me as suspicious was when I noticed lights flashing around your place.' He nodded towards Brogan. 'I'd spotted headlights making their way along the road, but they stopped just at the end of your lane. Next thing, I noticed what I assumed was torch light shining round your yard. I mean, I know you have the outside light on all the time, but these lights were moving about, going all over the place.' He paused as a bout of coughing took hold. 'Sorry.' He patted his chest, catching his breath.

'Hey, it's okay, Bert, just take your time,' said Nick.

'Yeah, there's no rush.' Brogan gave Bert's arm a squeeze.

'Anyroad, I knew you were out in the village at a party, so it wouldn't be owt to do with you, which is why I called you the first time. Then I felt a bit daft for worrying you. It crossed my mind it might just be someone dropping summat off for you but weren't keen to tackle your track in their car since it had been snowing.' He paused again, inhaling slowly.

Brogan studied his face. He made for a pitiful sight. Her heart squeezed at the sorrow in his eyes, the dried blood in his hair. She couldn't get her head around the sort of person who would do such a cruel thing to an old man.

'Whoever it was didn't hang around for long, which made me think it was just someone you knew calling on the off-chance you'd be in,' he said. 'Which is why I left another message, saying it was a false alarm; I didn't want to call you away from enjoying yourself for no reason.'

'That was very thoughtful of you, Bert.' Brogan smiled gently at him.

'Aye.' He heaved a sigh. 'I kept a look out for a while, but everything seemed okay, so I closed the curtains and made myself a cuppa; me and Nell settled down in front of the fire and watched telly. It'd be an hour later, and I'd just let Nell out for her last wee in the yard when two men appeared, they were grunting something I couldn't work out. One of them, tall, skinny thing he was, pushed me over, which is how I bumped my head, and the other shorter, plumper one grabbed Nell by the collar and threw her in the back of that van. It was awful to see, poor lass.' Tears began pouring down Bert's cheeks. He sniffed and wiped them away with the back of his hand. 'That's when they said if I called the police they'd come back and—' Before he could finish his face crumpled and he was gripped by another chesty cough.

'Oh, Bert, that must've been awful for you.' Brogan's eyes welled with tears and she quickly blinked them back.

'I'm just so worried about Nell,' he said once he'd recovered. 'Why do you think they took her?'

Brogan didn't want to say she'd heard reports of dogs being stolen to order by unscrupulous individuals who sold them on. There was nothing to be gained by adding to his distress. And there was still a chance they could get her back.

'Right, despite what the thugs told you, I'm pretty certain they were bluffing, and I think we should call the police right now. There's a good chance they could catch them,' said Nick.

'I agree,' said Brogan. Not wanting to upset him further, she resisted telling Bert that it would appear he'd been right, that they had paid a visit to Pond Farm. It made her blood run cold to think they could've been after Wilf and Maudie too.

Bert nodded. 'Aye, I reckon you're right.' His bottom lip wobbled and a sob escaped. 'I just hope they're being kind to my Nell. She's a gentle lass.'

'I'm sure she'll be fine. They have nothing to gain by hurting her,' said Brogan.

Nick stood up and headed out into the hallway. Minutes later he returned with the news that PC Snaith was on his way. The police officer had apparently been kept busy throughout the evening with several reports of a similar nature.

'I wonder if we should call Zander? Ask him to pop over and take a look at that bump on your head, Bert? I know he won't mind.' Brogan also thought it would be a good opportunity to mention the elderly man's cough.

'I don't think there's any need to trouble the doctor. It's just a little bump; I landed in the snow. Looks worse than it is.'

'We'll leave it for now then, if you're sure.' Brogan wasn't convinced, but she knew she couldn't force Bert, and other than looking shaken, he wasn't displaying any of the obvious signs of concussion.

'Aye. I'm sure, lass.' Bert gave a weary nod of his head.

'Tell you what, why don't I make a nice pot of tea?' That way she could add extra sugar to Bert's mug which would help with the shock. And once he was on the other side of a warm, sweet drink, she'd sort out some clean, dry clothes for him to change into; it couldn't be very comfortable for him sitting in cold, wet trousers.

'Aye, that's a grand idea. Cup of tea; the Great British cure-all. Wish that's all it'd take to bring Nell back,' he said sadly.

'I'm sure you'll have her back soon, Bert.' Brogan patted his arm as she headed into the kitchen.

Nick had revived the fire, which had been almost out when they'd first arrived. Flames were now licking up the chimney, throwing out a welcome blast of heat into the room. Brogan had just set the tray on the coffee table when there was a knock at the door. Nick went to answer it, while she went to fetch an extra mug.

PC Snaith listened intently, taking copious notes while Bert recounted what had happened. The officer's assurances that the local police force would do all they could to apprehend the culprits went some considerable way to reassuring the older man.

'I think the vigilance of the local community will pay off. After-all, you've got the registration number of the vehicle as well as photographs. I'm sure we'll have the culprits apprehended in no time,' PC Snaith said, taking a sip of his tea.

'Thank you, officer. I hope so too,' said Bert, a little brighter.

It was just gone midnight by the time PC Snaith left. Nick had taken him to one side in the hall and explained what they'd found at Pond Farm and the reason for not sharing it in front of Bert. PC Snaith had confirmed that there had been a number of thefts from unlocked sheds and dogs taken from yards and gardens. 'They've clearly been watching folks' movements and striking while houses have been empty or while no one's been looking. They're evidently not that bright from the number of reports we've had of them; it's only a matter of time before they're caught,' he said.

Back in the living room, Nick had taken a look at the bump on Bert's head, giving it a quick clean-up. Bert had got changed into his pyjamas and dressing gown, and though he was still distraught about Nell, he'd lost the grey pallor he'd had when they'd first arrived.

Much as Brogan felt bone tired and would have liked nothing better than to head home and go to bed, she wasn't keen to leave him on his own. Sensing her reluctance to leave, Nick offered to stay with the older man, but Bert wouldn't hear of it. 'I'm fine, lad. Like the young bobby said, they've got what they wanted; they're not likely to come back. And you've checked me over, so we know I'm all right. You two need to get yourselves home and get some kip, especially if you're at work tomorrow.'

'You could always come and stay with us,' said Brogan. But Bert refused on the off-chance Nell escaped and ran back home. He wanted to be here, just in case.

Brogan thought that unlikely, but kept it to herself.

When the time came for Brogan and Nick to leave, she said, 'You know where we are if you need us, Bert. Just call, no matter what the time, and we'll be with you like a shot.' She pulled him into a gentle hug. Despite his assurances that he'd be okay, leaving Bert on his own still didn't rest easy with her.

What a roller coaster of a night it had turned out to be, she thought as they drove back, snowflakes swirling around the car. Nick had been brilliant with Bert, calmly reassuring him whenever he got upset about Nell. Brogan couldn't imagine how things would have turned out if she'd been on her own. That thought made her realise how good it was to have Nick around. In fact, it was getting harder to imagine what it would be like without him.

THIRTY-SEVEN

NICK

Relieved that Saturday was the surgery's half day, Nick wandered into the waiting room to see the blinds had been pulled down and the bolt drawn across the door. Jules had changed out of her scrubs and into her civvies. He recalled her telling him she needed to leave bang on the dot of twelve-thirty – something to do with having to get ready for her family's annual trip to the pantomime over in York. She was pushing her fingers into her gloves, chatting to Brogan who looked as tired as he felt after their eventful evening, the usual sparkle in her eyes eluding her today.

When they'd returned to Pond Farm last night they'd both been too wired to sleep and had sat talking in the kitchen for over an hour. For part of that time Brogan had stretched out on the floor, stroking both dogs, who'd thankfully calmed down after their stressful experience. They'd laid beside her, two heads in her lap, as if sensing she needed them close – until the cold from the tiles had started to seep into her bones and she'd been forced to get up. She'd mentioned she was worried that the thugs who'd broken into the shed had probably come with the intention of stealing Wilf and Maudie. 'I'm convinced it was them I heard in the early hours the other night, and I'm certain it was their tyre tracks we saw. None of this weird stuff was happening before they turned up. It's too much of a coincidence.' It troubled Nick to see how anxious it had made her. Thankfully, he'd managed to reassure her, telling her if that had been the case, then they'd have broken into the cottage to get them last night. He'd been glad to see it seemed to calm her a little.

'I suppose you're right, but it's made me realise I should take the security of the place more seriously. I mean, if they'd wanted to be in here, the lock on the porch door is rubbish, it's meant to be for a shed, not a house. It's been the same as far back as I can remember. And the porch itself is hardly sturdy; it looks ready to fall down at any minute. I'll have to make sure I remember to lock the inside door too, which I don't always do,' she'd said.

Their conversation had set his mind working and he'd woken with an idea he hoped would go some way to putting her mind at ease. But, first, he wanted to check with Brogan that it was okay before he went ahead with it.

He waited until there was only the two of them left at the surgery before he broached the matter.

'Before we head off there's something I want to run by you.' He was keen to set the ball rolling.

'Oh?'

'I've been thinking about what you said about the lock on the porch door of your cottage being inadequate.'

'Yeah, it's pretty useless.'

He was relieved to see she looked interested and not wary. He went on to say how he knew of a reliable odd-job man in Middleton-le-Moors who could turn his hand to anything, and wondered how Brogan felt about getting him to fit a new lock to the porch door. 'Everyone I know uses Mike. He's a tidy worker and as honest as the day is long.' What he didn't tell her was that he'd already spoken to Mike earlier that morning, and explained the situation to him. Mike had been sympathetic and told him if Brogan was interested he'd call out the following day and fit a new lock as a favour to Nick. The only proviso was that he let him know by that afternoon so he could stop at the wholesalers and buy a suitable lock.

'So, what do you think?' Nick asked her, hoping it didn't look like he was interfering or overstepping the mark. He was aware how fiercely independent she was and the last thing he wanted was to offend her or get her back up and create an uncomfortable atmosphere between them.

She answered without hesitation, taking him aback a little. 'I really like the sound of that. Shattered as I was last night, I couldn't get to sleep with worrying about it and I can't see that feeling going any time soon. Are you sure you don't mind asking him? Or you could give me his number and I'll ring.'

'I'm happy to do it, if you like?' The relief in her eyes made him glad he'd mentioned it.

She mustered up a smile. 'That'd be great, thanks.' Again, her reaction surprised him.

Nick called Mike while Brogan was getting changed out of her scrubs. It was agreed that he'd call round the following morning at eleven provided the weather wasn't too bad, and he'd also put a new lock on the shed.

'All sorted,' said Nick when Brogan came back into the waiting room. She'd got her hands full of the stuff she'd brought to drop off for Bert who they were going to call in to see on their way back. Brogan had already been on the phone to him that morning, and though he was still understandably upset about Nell, he'd assured her he was all right. That was all well and good, but Nick and Brogan agreed they needed to see her neighbour in person, make sure he really was okay. And besides, without Nell around, he'd be feeling extra lonely.

'Thank you. I really appreciate you organising it,' she said to Nick.

'No problem.' Nick smiled. 'Right, let's go and see Bert.'

They'd been relieved to see the elderly man looking better than he had the previous evening. The bump on his head had shrunk considerably, leaving only a tiny cut visible. However, his hacking cough gave them both cause for concern and Brogan had confided in Nick that she was going to try to work on her neighbour to make an appointment at the surgery in Danskelfe.

Back at Pond Farm, they'd just finished their late lunch of sweet potato and rosemary soup with thickly cut slices of Lucy's wholemeal bread when Nick's phone rang. He picked it up from the dresser, his eyebrows shooting up when he saw the number on the screen.

'Everything okay?' asked Brogan.

'It's the Trotters,' he said, surprised. He'd been beginning to think he was never going to hear from them. 'I'd best take it before they ring off.'

'Good luck,' she said as he pressed the phone to his ear and headed into the living room.

The phone call had gone exactly how Nick had expected, the upshot being Gary Trotter lay the blame for the flood firmly at Nick's feet. 'You must've left the flaming bath running, you daft idiot! Don't think you're going to get away with trying to blame us, that house was in perfectly good condition when you took it on, and we'll be expecting you to cover the full cost of the repairs.' He'd also denied all knowledge of any prior problems with the heating and hot water system. 'Everything was in perfect working order before you moved in, mate.'

'Well, it wasn't by the time I set foot over the doorstep!' Nick had said, exasperated. 'And I'm not your "mate".'

Before the call ended, Nick had managed to get Gary Trotter to agree to meet him at the cottage the following afternoon, albeit reluctantly. He wanted his landlord to take a look at the damage, prove to him that it hadn't been caused by an overflowing bath. There was no way he was going to take the blame for the faults with Willow Cottage and there was no way he was going to hand over money to fix a house that was already in a shocking state of repair before he'd taken over the tenancy. Their conversation left Nick with the impression Gary Trotter was an obnoxious bully who wasn't to be trusted, which was why he planned on taking someone else along as a witness to any underhand stunts Trotter might try to pull.

With adrenalin making his skin prickle, he headed back into the kitchen to see Brogan bent fussing the dogs who were both sat at her feet looking up at her adoringly. She glanced up at him, smiling.

In an instant, Nick felt his stress levels shrink back and his heart rate calm. There was something about her that put his problems and worries into perspective. Yes, the situation with Willow Cottage was one heck of a pain, but in the grand scheme of things, it wasn't as awful as what Bert was going through right now. Being with Brogan triggered something indefinable inside him that managed to override the negative and instil a feeling of calm and a lightness in his heart. He'd never experienced anything like it before. Indeed, his life with Loretta had been something of a roller coaster, with her mood swings and always having to be competing with her sister. He hadn't realised just how exhausting it had been until they'd split up.

He drew in a deep breath and launched into a brief rundown of his conversation with Gary Trotter, telling Brogan of their planned meeting at the cottage.

'That'll be interesting,' she said. 'But watch him, he's a notoriously slippery character.'

'Don't worry, I will. I'm going to ask if Jimby or Ollie will come along as a witness, but I'm not going to worry about Trotter today.'

'My grandma Elsie always used to say worrying doesn't make things any better.'

'She sounds like a very wise lady.'

'She was.' Brogan smiled fondly.

'Anyway, what do you normally do of a Saturday afternoon?' Nick asked, feeling suddenly at a loose end.

'Well, being a former dog-walker I'd normally be walking lots of dogs, but since this is the first Saturday afternoon I've had off since I... oh... um... since a few weeks ago.' Her eyes widened and she pressed her fingers to her lips. 'Actually, I don't know about you but I could do with a cuppa?' She scurried over to the Aga, scooping up the kettle.

Nick observed her reaction with interest. Why had her face suddenly turned a vivid shade of red? Why was she stumbling over her words?

And then it dawned on him. *Of course!* Her last Saturday off must have been *that* Saturday. The day they'd met at the wedding. The day she'd walked into his life and given his world a thorough shaking, before exiting it just as quickly. Which would explain why she was acting like a cat on hot bricks.

Okay. He scratched his head absently as he worked through his thoughts, the clink of crockery in the background as Brogan made the tea. Would now be a good time to bring it up? he wondered. Get it out in the open instead of tiptoeing around it like it had never happened? It really was a bizarre set of circumstances they'd found themselves in. If somebody else had told him this had happened to them he'd think it couldn't be true, that they'd embellished their story. The thought of what his brother had said when Nick had called him the other day crossed his mind. He'd wanted to run the situation by Matt, valuing his opinion, knowing he would tell it how it is.

'So, Nick, let me get this straight, you met a girl – who, by the way, you think is very probably your soulmate, aka *"The One"*– at a wedding where you were both last minute guests?' Matt had asked.

'Yep, that's right.'

'Then you took her back to your room where you had the best sex you've *ever* had in your life?'

'Pretty much sums it up.' *It was mind-blowing!*

'But she sneaks off before you can get her number or find out where she lives?'

'Yes.'

'Cruel.'

'I was gutted.' *Couldn't get her out of my mind.*

'Understandable. Then, at the last minute, you switch your job, she switches her job, and you both find yourselves – totally and utterly by chance, which you believe to be fate – starting work at the *very same* surgery on the *very same* day?'

'We did! It's definitely fate. We were meant to meet again, without a doubt.'

'Oh, come on, mate! Pull the other one, it's got bells on.'

'I'm telling you, it's true! It's way more than a coincidence, surely you can see that.'

'Really? Oh, and did you say, the house you were renting flooded so she invited you to stay with her even though you've only know each other for what, five minutes?'

'I know it sounds crazy, but it honestly feels like I've know her for ages; we've got this amazing connection and I've never felt as happy as I do when I'm with her. I just love being around her.'

'What about the feelings you had for Loretta?'

'They don't even come close. The way I feel about Brogan, I can honestly say, I've never felt this way about another woman before. I'm in love with her, Matt. Madly and deeply.'

'That's beautiful but can you quit with the mush before you have me weeping soppy tears.'

'It's not funny! You've got to take me seriously!'

'Sorry, bro, good story, but it sounds like a cheesy chick flick to me, or a load of old rot.'

'Thanks,' Nick had said despondently.

'No probs. Can I ask, does she know you feel this way?'

'I... er, I think so.'

'You *think* so? You don't know for sure?'

'No.'

'Then don't you think you should find out?'

'I suppose so.'

'Good luck, mate. I'll be rooting for you.'

Nick sighed, lifting his eyes to Brogan who was busy pouring tea, her stunning auburn hair framing her pretty face. Matt was right, he had no idea if she knew how he felt, but he wanted more than anything to tell her. Yes, he decided, now was the time. He felt a ripple of nerves in his stomach.

He was prepared for her to be shocked, *heck*, no one was more surprised than he was to be feeling this way. It had hit him with such a force the moment he'd set eyes on her, it had knocked his senses completely off kilter; then her early disappearance had brought him down to earth with a nasty bump. But he'd known from the struggle he'd had to get her out of his mind after their brief time together at the wedding, that she'd stolen his heart.

Seeing her again, combined with all that had happened over the last week, had brought his feelings rushing back to the surface; had given him hope. And he didn't want to lose her so easily a second time.

Maudie, as if she was reading his mind, shot him one of her withering looks as if to say, 'What on earth has taken you so long?'

Time to bite the bullet, he thought.

He headed over to the table where Brogan glanced up at him shyly. 'There you go.' She handed him a mug of tea.

'Thanks.' He set it down on the table and pulled out a chair. He marshalled his thoughts, making sure he brought up the subject in the best way he could, his heart thumping. He was just about to speak when the familiar rumble of a Land Rover caught their attention. Wilf and Maudie barked and trotted to the door.

Brogan went over to the window, peering out. 'It's Kristy and Noushka,' she said happily.

'Great.' Nick mustered up a smile. What he really meant was "bugger"! That was their conversation scuppered before it even got started. He was beginning to wonder if they were ever going to get round to having it.

Brogan rushed to open the door which she now kept permanently locked. She greeted her friends cheerily. 'Talk about perfect timing. I've just made a pot of tea.'

Nick didn't have anything against the two young women, but right now he'd have to argue that their timing was less than perfect. In fact, he'd say it was quite the opposite.

'Ah, well, you know what Noushka's like, she can sniff out a freshly-filled teapot a mile off.' Kristy gave a hearty giggle.

'It's a skill I've honed to perfection,' said Anoushka, grinning broadly. 'Anyroad, how are you doing, chick?' She flicked her plait over her shoulder and pulled Brogan into a hug, planting a kiss on her friend's cheek.

'Aye, last night sounds like it was awful,' said Kristy, hugging her close once Anoushka had done. 'We needed to come, make sure you were okay, flower.'

'I'm fine. I've got Nick with me.'

'So we see,' Kristy said in a knowing tone, waggling her eyebrows.

Anoushka bit down on a grin.

'Right, tea,' said Brogan decisively. The warning look she shot her friends didn't go unnoticed by Nick.

The two women stayed for just over an hour, their bubbly chat filling the kitchen. They'd come straight from Bert's, having heard what had happened with Nell, and had been tasked with taking him a casserole that Kitty had made and some of Lucy's homemade chocolate biscuits Molly had picked up from the village shop.

'It's unnerving having people like that creeping around,' said Anoushka.

'Aye, it is. There's been no sign of them today, makes you wonder if they'll come back,' said Kristy.

'Well, if they do, let's hope PC Snaith and his colleagues manage to nab them,' said Nick, spotting the worry returning to Brogan's eyes.

THIRTY-EIGHT

NICK

By seven o'clock, the events of the previous evening and subsequent late night, followed by an early morning, were catching up with Nick and Brogan. They were watching television in the living room. Nick was slumped in the armchair, while Brogan was stretched out on the sofa, smoothing Wilf's ears. He'd flopped down on the floor beside her after overheating in front of the fire. Maudie had joined him, nudging Brogan's hand for a share of the attention.

Nick felt his eyelids grow heavy, until his eyes eventually closed. A moment later, he woke with a start to see Brogan rooting around for something in one of the cupboards of the large, dark wood dresser. She returned to the sofa with what appeared to be a photo album in her hands.

'Just came over me to have a flick through this,' she said, smoothing her fingers over the cover.

He rubbed his eyes. 'Can I join you?'

'If you think you can stay awake long enough,' she said with a giggle.

'Cheeky.' He grinned at her as he heaved himself up and wandered over, his limbs heavy.

The first few pages were photos of her grandparents taken

around the farm. It was interesting to see that the place looked pretty much the same, though there was more clutter around the yard then – evidence of her grandparents' hoarding, he suspected. Soon, Nick found himself looking at numerous photos of a little girl with bright red hair and an abundance of freckles. One picture in particular caught his attention. It was taken in front of a barn filled with oblong bales of hay stacked high. The little girl, dressed in shorts and a T-shirt and wellies, was sitting in a wheelbarrow, hens scratting about in the ground around her, and a plump sheepdog puppy in her lap. Her sunny smile revealed she'd lost her two front teeth. But there was no mistaking those sparkly green eyes.

'That's you?' he said, smiling.

'Yeah. I can remember when the photo was taken actually. It was a lovely sunny day. Grandad had been pushing me round the yard in the wheelbarrow 'til he was sweating buckets, which was probably why my grandma came out with ice creams for us. The little puppy there was called Scamp; I'd been allowed to name him. My grandparents hadn't had him long; they'd got him to train up to work on the farm, helping with the sheep.'

'Even from the photo he looks mischievous,' said Nick.

'Oh, he was; had loads of energy too.'

They flicked through more photos until they got to the end of the album. Brogan closed it gently. 'Happy memories,' she said softly.

Nick paused a moment, debating whether now would be a good time to start the conversation he'd hoped to have before Anoushka and Kristy arrived. *Go for it! Grasp that nettle!* Before he could stop himself, he said, 'Talking of happy memories I've got one that includes you.'

He watched as she pondered his words, her brows knitting together. 'You do?'

'I do.' He nodded. 'Actually, just give me a second.'

'Oh, okay.'

Within moments he was back, holding something in his hand.

He was struggling to keep an amused grin from spreading over his face.

'I'm intrigued.' Brogan looked up at him as he made his way towards her, sitting down beside her once more.

'Okay, so my happy memories of you start at the wedding.' He watched her reaction closely.

'Oh, right.' She stole a look at him before quickly looking away, colour rising in her cheeks.

'I know we haven't talked about it since we found ourselves working together, but I kind of think it might be good if we do. To be honest, it feels a bit strange that we haven't; we've been doing this odd kind of dance around it, both knowing it's there, that it happened, but both trying to pretend it didn't. If you see what I mean?'

She gave a quick nod. 'Yeah, I think I do.'

'Anyway, it's probably a good time to return a couple of things you left in my room that night.'

The small wince she gave didn't go unnoticed. 'What things?'

'First of all, there's this.' He opened his palm and her eyes lit up.

'My hairslide! I thought I'd lost it forever! Thank you! Where did you find... oh, yeah, your room.' She grinned sheepishly.

'I wanted to give it to you the other night, but I couldn't remember where I'd put it.'

'It's not like you to lose things,' she said with a hint of sarcasm, quirking an eyebrow at him.

'Says she who also lost these.' He opened his other hand.

She peered at the scrap of dark green satin that sat in his palm, her eyes growing wide as realisation dawned. With a squeal, she snatched the fabric away and hurriedly stuffed it into the pocket of her jeans. Wilf and Maudie looked up, ears cocked. 'Oh, my God! I'm so embarrassed!' She clapped her hands to her cheeks. 'I can't believe I couldn't find them. I mean, I normally fold all my clothes in a neat pile.'

'Not that night you didn't. If I remember rightly, you whipped your knickers off pretty quickly, spun them round your finger and flung them right across the room. I promise you, folding anything neatly was the last thing on your mind.' His mouth twitched as he struggled to contain the laugh that was itching to break free.

'That's so not true!' She covered her eyes with her hands and shook her head, laughing despite herself. Peeking between her fingers, she asked. 'So dare I ask, where did you find them?'

'On the lampshade; the one hanging from the ceiling. Had to call housekeeping to help reach them,' he said, his face straight. 'They had to bring ladders, a safety harness, the works.'

'That is so not true!' She gave him a playful backhander on the arm.

'You're right, I'm teasing,' he said, his laughter escaping. 'They were hidden under my suit trousers, which would've made them hard to find when you were trying to do your flit in the dark.'

'Yeah, sorry about that. I just thought if I left before you woke, it would save you the awkwardness of... well, you know.' She gave a shrug. 'Plus, I was *so* embarrassed; I've never done anything like that before. I promise you, I don't make a habit of jumping into bed with strange men.'

'Are you calling me strange?'

Her face fell for a second and she glanced up at him. 'No, that's not what I mean... oh,' she said with a giggle. 'What I'm trying to say is that I've never done anything like that before. I suppose I'm quite reserved where that sort of thing's concerned really. In fact,' she hesitated, 'you're the first man I've been near since Archie.'

Nick sat, his mind processing what she'd just shared. 'Wow. So it really was a big step for you, that day.' He rubbed his hand over his chin. 'I'll let you into a secret, I'm not in the habit of jumping into bed with *"strange"* women. I prefer to have some sort of connection before I sleep with anyone.' He lowered his head, looking into her eyes. 'I felt a connection with you, and if I'm not mistaken, I think you felt one too.'

His conversation with his brother barged into his mind. How could he go on to say that she'd made him feel something he'd never felt before without sounding cheesy? That he was sure beyond doubt that fate had put them together. The answer was, he probably couldn't. So instead, he said, 'I hadn't been able to stop thinking about you, and then there you were at the surgery. I couldn't believe it.'

'You were thinking about me?' she asked, her eyes meeting his.

He nodded. 'Couldn't get you out of my mind. Still can't.'

'But...'

He reached out, touching her cheek, her skin soft against his fingers. 'No buts, Brogan.' Glancing down at her lips he inched closer, his pulse racing. She closed her eyes, their lips almost touching...

The sound of a phone ringing made them both freeze. Brogan's eyes pinged open. Nick released a groan of frustration. 'You've got to be kidding me.' He pushed his fingers into his hair, making his fringe stick up.

'I'd best check that in case it's Bert.' She pulled an apologetic face as she reached for her mobile, her heart still galloping like the clappers.

'Yeah, course, you're right.'

It was Jimby who apologised for phoning on a Saturday evening but told her he was ringing round all the members of the Village Committee notifying them of a meeting to discuss the plans for Christmas Day. 'It's on Tuesday at half-seven at our Kitty's. It'd be great if you could let Nick know too.'

He went on to tell her about the response they'd had from the notes she and Nick had pushed through the letter boxes in Lytell Stangdale but Brogan was finding it difficult to concentrate, her mind full of the almost kiss with Nick.

When the call was over, she placed her mobile on the table. How easy would it be to pick up where they left off? she wondered. Not that she'd have the nerve to make the first move.

She turned to see Nick looking at her, that same look in his eyes. Her stomach performed a somersault.

In the next moment, his mouth was on hers, kissing her, softly at first before becoming more urgent. *Oh my days!* It felt so good. All the feelings she remembered from that day at the wedding came flooding back in all their glory. What had possessed her to creep back to her room?

Nick was the first to pull away. Breathless, he pushed her hair off her face and looked deep into her eyes. 'Brogan Hopwood, do you have any idea what you do to me? It's been the longest week of my life, being this close to you and not being able to do that. It's just about driven me half crazy.'

'I didn't know you felt that way. I thought you'd tell everyone I was an easy conquest and jumped into bed with you after only knowing you two minutes.' How had she got it so wrong? Probably because she was so out of practice, she told herself.

He tipped his head, looking right into her eyes. 'What? Why would I do that? I'm not in the habit of talking about my "conquests", as you call them, to my mates. And besides, with you it was different. It certainly never felt "easy", it felt right. Which is why I was so gutted when I woke up to find you gone.'

'Is that your explanation for hanging on to my knickers for so long? Are you sure you're not just some weirdo with a knicker-stealing fetish?'

Nick threw his head back and let out a roar of laughter. 'Looks like I've been rumbled. I confess, I have a whole suitcase full of them.' He raised his hands in mock surrender.

'Ah, explains why I was getting low,' she said with a giggle.

'Listen,' he said, his face suddenly serious. 'I got the feeling you were reluctant to talk about what happened that day at the wedding, which is why I've held back; I didn't want to push you. But when I saw you that first day at the surgery, well, I don't remember ever feeling so overjoyed. I realised pretty quickly when I met you at the wedding that I wanted to get to know you.'

'Well, you certainly achieved that.' Brogan shot him a playful look, making him grin.

'I don't mean like *that* – though I'm not denying, it was pretty special. What I do mean is, I wanted to get to know you as a person – though I'd be lying if I said getting to know you in the other way didn't cross my mind before we actually, well, you know? And then when we got talking and I felt that incredible connection, I made up my mind there and then to see if you'd let me take you out on a date. I knew in here that you were special.' He patted his chest. 'Knew I didn't want you to slip through my fingers.'

Her whole body thrummed with happiness. It had been a long time since a man had said anything remotely romantic to her and she had to admit, it took some getting used to. But this? Wow! Did Nick really feel that way about her? And if he did, was she ready to dip her toe in the dating pool? The thought triggered a flutter of nerves in her stomach. She was aware that what had happened with Archie had made her wary. Their breakup had been so unexpected; she really hadn't seen it coming, which is why she found it hard to trust her feelings. But something about Nick told her she should just go with her gut, which is exactly what she'd done at the wedding. And exactly what she decided to do now.

'I felt that connection too; I've never felt anything so strong. But it was easier to ignore it than face rejection. I couldn't have stood it if the feelings I had for you weren't reciprocated. It felt safer not to risk it.'

'If only you knew.' He pressed his forehead against hers before brushing a gentle kiss over her lips.

'Mmm. I'm getting a pretty good idea.'

They spent the rest of the evening cuddling on the sofa, talking and laughing, with a liberal dose of kisses sprinkled in between. They'd agreed to take things slowly and not dive slap-bang into an intense relationship, which they knew it had the potential to be. Brogan took comfort from the fact that Nick wanted to get to know her; he'd suggested that they should go out on dates as they would if they weren't living under the same roof. 'I appreciate our circumstances are a little unusual, and we've done things somewhat back-to-front,' he said, 'but don't worry, I'm not going to assume that our new status means I can stay living here permanently. I'll move out as soon as somewhere comes up.' Despite the flash of disappointment his words triggered, she knew it was wise.

Brogan felt blissfully happy to be cuddled up beside Nick, to have his arms wrapped tight around her. She felt secure and loved. She hadn't felt that way for quite some time. At the back of her mind, she got the sense that this was a pivotal moment in her life, something that was exciting, though she couldn't deny, it scared her a little.

'I'm so glad I took the job at Danskelfe,' Nick said. It had just gone midnight and they were standing in the kitchen, having made sure all the doors were secured before going to bed. Wilf and Maudie were curled up together on the cushions, snoozing. Nick had his arms around Brogan's waist and was smiling down at her.

'Me too.' Smiling back at him, she reached up and wrapped her arms around his neck. He bent to kiss her, sending emotions flurrying around her body. Wow! This was heady stuff. She could feel her resolve weakening by the second. It would be so easy to invite him into her bed, but... No! She'd stand firm; stick to the plan.

Rather than jumping straight into bed, they'd agreed to sleep separately until Brogan felt comfortable for their relationship to head back there – Nick told her jokingly he could be ready at a moment's notice. 'Just putting that out there,' he'd said, making her giggle. He'd gone on to reassure her that he understood that after what had happened with her previous relationship she needed to feel she could trust him. After all, they hadn't known each other long.

Brogan climbed into bed, running her fingers over her lips that were bruised from an evening of Nick's delicious kisses. Happiness fizzed inside her.

If only she hadn't crept out of his room that night she could have been feeling this way a whole lot sooner. But there was no point looking back, she quickly told herself. She had a good feeling in her stomach. This was the start of a new chapter in her life, she was sure of it.

Closing her eyes, she was aware of her grandma's voice in her head, words from a conversation they'd had when Brogan had first come to live at Pond Farm, her heart sore from Archie's cruel words. 'You'll know when you're ready to fall in love again, sweetheart. I promise you. You won't question it, you won't be in any doubt about it. You'll just know.'

It would seem her grandma was right.

FORTY

NICK

Nick was pushing bacon around the pan, whistling cheerfully, when Brogan came into the room. Wilf and Maudie jumped up and greeted her with a vigorous bout of tail wagging. Nick turned, smiling at her dishevelled appearance, her hair standing out around her face like an auburn cloud. 'Morning. Been in a wind tunnel through the night?' he asked with a chuckle.

'Cheeky.' She lifted her hand to smooth her hair down. 'I forgot to put my hair in a plait before I went to bed. I blame you for distracting me.' She smiled, the imprint of pillow creases on her right cheek more obvious as she headed over to him.

'Given half the chance.' He bent his head and kissed her deeply, following up with a wide smile. After the rotten few months he'd had, with just about everything going wrong that could go wrong, it was good to be feeling this full-on happy again. And what a reason for it, he thought. 'Oh, and you might be interested to know the King of Drool has been excelling himself this morning. Maudie is seriously unimpressed. You should've seen the filthy looks she's been giving him.'

Brogan chuckled. 'Oh, Wilf, what are you like?' She bent to smooth his velvety head, his tail beating a tattoo against the floor.

After last night's breakthrough in their relationship, Nick

couldn't help but wish he'd organised for Mike to come over and replace the lock on a different day. Same with the meeting with Gary Trotter. Nick would much rather spend the day with Brogan, just the two of them and Wilf and Maudie. But he knew replacing the lock and meeting Trotter were both priorities that couldn't be put off.

He waited for Mike to arrive before he set off for the village. The handyman got down to the task in hand straight away. He set his tool box down by the door, saying he was keen to get started on account of the snow that was forecast for later in the day. 'By 'eck, this is as old as the bloomin' hills, this thing,' he said as he popped his glasses on and examined the lock on the porch door. 'Anyone who knew what they were doing could have it picked in a minute; that'd have your insurance up the creek straight away.'

'At least we're getting it fixed now,' said Nick, giving Brogan's arm a reassuring rub when he noticed her worried expression.

'True. And I really appreciate you coming out at such short notice, Mike,' Brogan said as she handed him a cup of tea.

'No worries, flower. We'll have a sound one in its place before you know it.' Mike smiled as he took the mug.

En route to Lytell Stangdale, Nick called in on Bert to see if he needed anything picking up from the village shop, telling him he was heading there to collect the Sunday papers before his meeting at Arkleby with the obnoxious Gary Trotter. He really wasn't looking forward to that.

Bert was pleased to see him, quizzing him eagerly to find out if he'd heard anything more about the thugs who'd taken Nell. In truth, though the awful events of that evening had featured regularly in Nick's mind, certain other matters had been occupying a great chunk of his thoughts. Nevertheless, he shared what he knew, that there'd been no further sightings of the van, and no reports of anyone snooping around the farms. Nick reminded the elderly man of PC Snaith's assurances that they would find the criminals and bring Nell back home. His words seemed to brighten Bert whose cough, Nick noted, didn't seem to be as bad.

The roads to the village were as treacherous as Mike had warned. And though Camm had done a thorough job of ploughing them, there'd been a brief thaw which had melted some of the snow on the roadside. Hours later the temperature had plummeted to well below zero, creating a smooth layer of ice which, on ungritted roads, was lethal.

Nick glanced up at the sky where clusters of dense clouds were clumped together. He doubted it would get properly light today. As he drove on, snowflakes started flurrying, settling on the windscreen. He flicked the wipers on, thinking how glad he'd be to get back home to Brogan later that afternoon. It sent a wave of warmth washing over him.

Lytell Stangdale was quiet when he parked up, snow tumbling silently. Nick noticed the family of snowmen on the green had increased in numbers. The local children had been busy! A particularly large snowman was sporting what looked like a rather damp feather boa in a vibrant shade of orange. The amusing sight brought a smile to his lips.

Just as he was about to get out of the car, his phone pinged with a text. He fished it out of his pocket. The message was from Brogan saying she'd had a text from Molly, warning them to be on high alert. Nick's heart rate spiked as he read. The dark-grey van had been spotted fleeing from Low Beck Farm over in Arkleby not five minutes ago and had subsequently been seen heading towards Lytell Stangdale on the Danskelfe road. Molly had told her Camm was going to try and cut them off at the other end of the village. 'Not this again.' His first thought was of Brogan, grateful she wasn't alone at Pond Farm. His next thought was that if the criminals were back in the area, then the police stood a better chance of apprehending them.

He'd just climbed out of his four-wheel drive, turning his collar up against the cold, when the sound of an engine screeching cut through the wintry peace of the village. He turned towards the direction of the noise, his mouth falling open as he saw a dark-grey van heading down the middle of the road. It was them! And they were travelling dangerously fast for the conditions. The noise was quickly joined by the wailing siren of a police vehicle. Nick was just about to jump back in his car and join the chase when the van skidded, clipping a nearby parked car, before righting itself and heading down the road again, slush flying everywhere as its wheels spun. Seconds later, Camm appeared behind the wheel of the looming bulk of the plough which he positioned such that he'd completely blocked the road. The driver of the van braked hard, the vehicle spinning a full three-hundred-and-sixty degrees before coming to a halt perilously close to the pond. As Nick ran towards it he was aware of the police car stopping beside him, parking diagonally across the road. PC Snaith and another officer jumped out, raised voices filling the air as two black-clad criminals fled the van. In the next moment, the ear-splitting squawks of Reg, Jimby's cantankerous cockerel, joined the commotion.

It didn't take long before the disruption brought locals out onto their chilly doorsteps to see what was happening in their usually peaceful village.

With the snow falling relentlessly, Jimby shot by, his arms pumping like pistons, his breath coming out in puffs of steam as he raced towards the van.

In the background, Nick was half aware of the continuous squawking of the cockerel accompanied by angry shouting.

The taller of the men had doubled-back and was now running in Nick's direction, his hood pulled low. Nick lunged for him, but the thug dodged his grasp, and Nick fell hard against a garden wall, a bolt of pain shooting up his arm. Ignoring it, he headed straight after the criminal who glanced over his shoulder, an arrogant smirk on his face. It was short lived as he turned back to see Ollie racing towards him.

In the next moment, the thug made a sideways leap through the open gate of Damson Cottage, almost losing his footing as he did so. He righted himself and ran down the path, hurtling by Big Mary who, thinking quickly, stuck out her foot and tripped him up. Scrambling to his feet, he went to run round the back of the cottage where Gerald appeared, his arms outstretched like a goalkeeper. 'Come on then, lad. Not so clever now, are you?' Gerald gave a gummy cackle.

By now, Nick and Ollie were gaining pace. The thug stopped for a second, his hands on his thighs as he gasped for breath, furtively looking around him. He cursed Gerald who was swaying from side-to-side, his long, shocking-pink beard blowing in the breeze.

In the next moment, Nick and Ollie flew into the garden. The black-clad man made a dash for it but he wasn't fast enough and they tackled him to the ground. He landed face down in the snow, Nick and Ollie on top of him. 'Gotcha,' said Nick, his breathing ragged. The thug snorted, and proceeded to kick out, yelling abuse and doing all he could to free himself from the two men. Nick increased his grip; there was no way he was going to let this ape get away and cause any more heartache.

'Ger off me! Ger off me!' the youth shouted.

'I don't think so, mate,' said Ollie, his breathing heavy as he lay across the thug's legs to stop them kicking about.

Gerald rushed over, waving what Nick could swear was a pair of pink fluffy handcuffs. 'Here, these are our Mary's but she won't mind me using them for this, it being an emergency and all; it'd be doing a service for the local communit— Warghh!' He lost his footing and slipped, landing unceremoniously on his backside in the snow, the fluffy handcuffs going flying. 'Ow! Arghh! Ouch, me bum! Me bum! I can't believe it! Me bloomin' teeth have bitten a chunk out of me bum!'

Nick blinked the snow from his eyes; surely he couldn't have heard right?

'Gerry! Gerry! Oh, heavens above! Are you okay, pet? You know you've got to go canny with that dodgy ticker of yours.' Big Mary went rushing over to him, almost losing her footing in the slippery conditions.

'Mary, pet, I need you to go in my pocket and get my teeth out.

The bloomin' things have taken a bite out of me bum.' Gerald was wincing in pain.

'Gerry man, I keep telling you not to keep your teeth in your pocket. They're no use to you there; they should be in your gob. Will you never learn?' she said, shaking her head.

Nick caught Ollie's eye and gave him a puzzled frown. Ollie shook his head in response. 'Best not to ask.'

Nick could only imagine the explanation.

'This village is full of lunatics! Ger off! I wanna get out of 'ere. I'm innocent. I haven't done owt wrong. Me dad made me do it. I said I didn't wanna, but he made me.' The thug attempted to kick his legs free once more but Nick pushed himself down.

Moments later, PC Snaith and the other officer appeared, swiftly taking over the situation. Nick and Ollie got to their feet as the handcuffed thug was led away to the police van, objecting vociferously. PC Snaith thanked them for their assistance. 'Couldn't have done it without you,' he said, adding before he left, 'I'll let you know how we get on.'

Meanwhile, after a rummage in Gerald's trouser pocket, Mary fished out his false teeth. She gave a groan of dismay. 'Ah, pet, the top set's cracked right down the middle. Look.' She showed her husband his damaged dentures.

'Bloomin' 'eck!' he said as she helped him to his feet with the assistance of Nick and Ollie. 'They were good teeth, them.' He rubbed his injured bottom.

'Don't worry, pet, I've got some good glue that should have them right in no time. Now the excitement's over and done with, let's get you inside where it's warm and I can take a look, see what damage your gnashers have done to your bum.' She gave a good-humoured roll of her eyes as she guided him past Nick and Ollie.

Nick caught Ollie's eye, the two men fighting hard not to laugh.

With the snow swirling around them, they made their way to where people had congregated near the van. Jimby was talking to Camm and when they drew closer, Nick saw Jimby had a bloodied nose and an impressive bruise blooming below his left eye.

'Bloomin' 'eck, mate, what's happened?' Ollie rested his hand on Jimby's shoulder.

'Are you okay?' asked Nick, thinking he and Ollie had got off lightly.

'You should see the other fella,' said Jimby.

'The other one from the van?'

Jimby shook his head. 'No, not him.'

'Oh?' Nick looked at him askance before turning to Camm for enlightenment.

'He had a fight with a snowman,' Camm said with a chuckle.

'A fight with a snowman?' asked Ollie, amusement shining in his eyes. 'Only Jimby could have a fight with a snowman.'

Nick turned to where the family of snowmen were standing to see the one with the feather boa looking slightly worse for wear.

'Aye, well, maybe not a fight as such, but I ended up running into one when I was chasing that scumbag dog thief. It's the one with the daft feathery thing round its neck.'

'Yeah, you can't miss it,' said Ollie. He thought for a second and said, 'Well, maybe you can.'

'Anyroad, turns out the bloomin' thing's made of packed ice and is rock solid, as I found out when I collided with it.' He frowned and gingerly rubbed the bridge of his nose.

'Nice one, Jimby, but at least you didn't end up in the pond for a change.' Ollie chuckled.

'Aye, true.' Jimby nodded in agreement.

'So what happened with the other bloke from the van?' asked Nick. 'The one we were chasing's been taken to Middleton police station.'

'And so's his pal,' said Camm.

Between them he and Jimby told them that the shorter of the two men had run down a snicket between two cottages where he'd come face to face with Reg. He'd done an about turn and come flying out with the outraged cockerel in hot pursuit, flapping his wings and brandishing his spurs in a flamboyant display of machismo. The rooster had taken exception to the unscrupulous man's hood and had attached himself to it, pecking angrily at the thug's head until he'd fallen to the floor, yelling and screaming which only served to enrage Reg all the more. Not long after, the police had arrived and arrested the man.

'Wow! Is there ever a dull day around here?' asked Nick.

'Well, there's usually lots going on, but thankfully it doesn't involve toerags like them that have been causing unease around here. Hopefully, now they're caught, things can get back to normal in time for Christmas,' said Jimby.

'And here's hoping the police manage to trace the stolen dogs,' said Nick. He knew Bert would be interested to hear the thugs had been apprehended. And he hoped for Bert's sake they'd find his beloved Nell. He made a mental note to text Brogan once he was back in his car, tell her what had happened. He knew it would be a massive relief to her knowing that no one was going to be sneaking around in the middle of the night any more.

With all the excitement, no one had noticed that the snow had started falling more heavily until now. They declared it was probably time to head back home to their families. 'At least we have some good news to post on the local social media pages,' Ollie said to various sounds of agreement.

As Nick made his way along the narrow road to Arkleby he hoped Gary Trotter wouldn't be late for their meeting. The snow that was falling was dry, and it was settling fast. He knew Camm would be around with the plough, but it had been an eventful few days and the sooner Nick could get back to Pond Farm, the better. He'd be the first to admit, getting back to Brogan and sampling more of her warm kisses was an added incentive.

As he pulled up outside Willow Cottage, it suddenly struck Nick that he'd forgotten to ask Jimby or Ollie if they'd mind accompanying him to his meeting with Gary Trotter. In all the excitement, it had completely slipped his mind. He told himself it was unlikely he'd need a witness; that nothing untoward would happen. At least, that's what he hoped. While he waited for his landlord to arrive, Nick gathered the remainder of his stuff and packed it into his car, before taking copious photographs on his phone of the damage caused by the flood. By the time he'd done, Gary Trotter was over half-an-hour late. After calling and texting him numerous times but with no success, Nick accepted the man wasn't going to show. He'd had enough of his landlord's attitude; it was time to place the matter in the hands of his solicitor.

FORTY-ONE

BROGAN

'Bert! It's me, Brogan. Have you heard? They've caught them. They've caught the pair that took Nell.' Brogan could hardly contain the excitement in her voice over the phone to her neighbour.

'They've got them? Oh, my... Have they got my Nell? Do they know where she is?' he asked, his voice wavery, tearful almost. Her heart reached out to him.

'I haven't heard anything about Nell, sorry, Bert. But I've just had a call from Nick who said he and some other folk were involved in catching them. It happened in Lytell Stangdale. There was a chase.'

'A chase?' Bert sounded intrigued as Brogan went on to share the details Nick had given her.

'PC Snaith said he'd be in touch to let us know what's happening which hopefully he'll do soon. I'll be keeping my fingers crossed it's good news about Nell.'

'Thanks, lass. I'll be keeping my fingers crossed too.'

Ending the call, she glanced out of the kitchen window onto a sea of white. The huddle of conifers over on the north side of the dale were being rocked hard by the wind that was building quickly. She wondered how Nick was getting on with Gary Trotter, hoped it wouldn't be long before he returned home. She didn't like the thought of him being out in this type of weather. The last few winters had been particularly hard here on the moors, the conditions becoming treacherous in a matter of hours, which was the reason Mike hadn't hung around once he'd got the locks fixed. He was a nice man she mused; she could see why Nick liked him. He'd done a good job, too. And it didn't matter that the pair who'd been sneaking around the place had been caught, the new locks would give her much needed peace of mind for the next time the moors were targeted by unsavoury types.

Forty-five minutes later, Brogan heard the sound of Nick's four-wheel drive pulling up in the yard, her heart thumping with relief. Maudie and Wilf jumped up and raced to the door, leaping around excitedly when he walked in. Brogan rushed to him, throwing her arms around his solid frame, inhaling the cold, wintry air that clung to his clothes.

'Well, this is what I call a warm welcome.' Cupping her face in his hand, Nick gave her a lingering kiss. 'Mmm. I think I might go back out and come in again if this is what I'm going to get every time.' He kissed her again and she hugged him tight.

'I'm just so relieved you're back in one piece. Are you okay? Did you get hurt?'

'I'm fine; I just caught my elbow a bit when I hit the floor, but the snow softened my landing.'

While she'd been waiting for him to get home, her mind had wandered to the risk he and the others had taken in tackling the criminals the way they had. What if the thugs had been armed? What if one of them had pulled a knife out? She'd shuddered at the thought, not wanting to dwell on it too long.

Once Nick had changed out of his wet clothes, they shared a pot of tea as he recounted in more detail what had happened in the village. Brogan held her breath as she listened to how he and Ollie had wrestled the thug to the ground, but had burst out laughing when he'd told her about Gerald and his false teeth.

'What I don't understand is, why he would have them in his pocket,' Nick said, laughing.

'That's where he usually keeps them so he can pop them in when Big Mary tells him off for not wearing them. He's not keen on them, says they're not comfortable.'

'Well, I'm sure he didn't find them very comfortable when they sank into his backside either,' said Nick. They both laughed hard at that.

Before long, the snow had stopped. Brogan glanced out of the window, surprised to see the dense clouds had parted to reveal a splash of bright blue sky.

'Don't suppose you fancy going for a walk, do you?' she asked.

'A walk?'

It was two Sundays before Christmas and the day her grandparents always set aside to get the Christmas tree. It was their tradition and Brogan had been a part of it as far back as she could remember. It had always been a joyous occasion, Brogan and her grandma singing along at the top of their voices to the Christmas CD they played when they decorated the tree. But last year, joy had been thin on the ground. Instead, Christmas Tree Sunday had been filled with heartbreak, with Brogan fighting back tears as she'd selected the tree, sobbing as she'd hung each bauble. The cottage had felt painfully empty despite music from the old Christmas CD filling the room, a cruel reminder that she'd never get to do this with her grandparents again.

Looking back, Brogan could see she'd come a long way since that dark lonely day, and she knew it had more than a little something to do with a certain handsome vet and his adorable dog. She smiled inwardly, a new optimism filling her heart.

'Yeah, but I don't mean just any walk, I mean a Christmas tree fetching walk.' She looked at him, her eyes bright. 'At Pond Farm, today is known as Christmas Tree Sunday.'

'Christmas Tree Sunday?' Nick said. 'Now I'm intrigued; the way you said that I thought for a second you meant we should head out onto the moors with an axe and chop a Christmas tree down.'

'That's exactly what I meant. Well, it's not exactly what I meant; we're going to head out on the moors and chop *two* down. One for here and one for Bert's place.' She flashed him a wide grin.

'Okay,' he said, drawing out the word. 'But aren't there laws about just rocking up on the moors and helping yourself to whatever tree you fancy? I mean, isn't the land owned by the Danskelfe Estate? I'm not so sure Lord Hammondely would be too chuffed about that.'

'Well, yes, I believe there are laws about going out and chopping down random trees. But it's very different if the land and the trees are yours – provided there isn't a tree preservation order involved, of course.'

'Right. I see. I think.' He scratched his head.

Brogan laughed, then went on to explain how before she was born, her grandparents had planted a small area with Christmas trees. Every year, two Sundays before Christmas – which they named Christmas Tree Sunday – Brogan and her grandfather would head to where the conifers grew and select a couple of trees – one for them, and one for Bert. Her grandad would then chop them down and they'd drag them home on a couple of sledges where she'd decorate theirs with her grandma, then they'd head to Bert's and do the same there. Each year, she'd help plant two new trees to take their place. The whole process had acquired an almost symbolic meaning as the years had passed.

'So, how do you fancy giving me a hand?' she asked brightly.

'I'd love to.' He grinned, his eyes twinkling. 'I guess we'd best head out right away while we've still got plenty of light.'

'Fab! I'll just call Bert, tell him to expect us, that way it won't come as a shock when we rock up with a conifer on his doorstep. I think with everything that's been going on he'll have clean forgotten what day it is; I know I had.'

Five minutes later they were heading out of the door. They grabbed the sledges – after the recent break in, Brogan was pleased to see they were still there – and dragged them down the snowy track en route to where the conifers grew, Maudie and Wilf in tow.

Nick reached for her hand as they walked along, the gesture making her heart skip a beat. She savoured how her hand felt encased in his, the feeling of closeness it imbued. Wilf and Maudie ran ahead, leaping about. Maudie watched, her tail wagging, as Wilf rolled about wildly in the snow, his gangly legs kicking about in utter abandon. In the next moment she'd joined him, which made Brogan and Nick hoot with laughter. Nick made snowballs, throwing them into the air, Wilf leaping to catch them, spluttering and sniffing as the snowballs fell apart in his mouth. That game over, the two dogs chased one another, tearing about in circles, their eyes wild with joy.

'Maudie's definitely a different girl since Wilf came into her life. I think she's embraced his high spirits and run with them. She's still got a hint of her haughtiness though, which I must admit I do finding entertaining, and I've noticed it's poor old Wilf and me who seem to be on the receiving end of it.'

'I don't think Wilf cares; he's besotted with her. Look at his face, you'd think he was grinning.' Brogan smiled affectionately, watching the pair of them leap about. 'And let's hope she doesn't pick up his horrible habit of rolling in fox poo.'

'I think that would be a step too far for Miss Snooty Pants.' Nick chuckled.

Arriving at the trees, Brogan felt suddenly overcome with emotion, memories of the times she'd been here with her grandfather flooding back. She blinked back a tear but a rogue one spilled onto her cheek and she tried to dash it away without Nick noticing, but it was too late. He wrapped his arms around her and held her tight. 'It'll hurt less and less every year,' he said, kissing her forehead.

'I know.' She nodded, her voice choked.

Much as she would love to have stayed snuggled up in Nick's arms, she dried her eyes, mustered up a smile and said, 'Come on, let's choose a tree for Bert.'

'Sure you're okay?'

'I'm fine.' She nodded, wiping a gloved hand under her nose.

Nick pressed his lips against her forehead again, giving her one last squeeze.

With the trees selected and chopped, they dropped their tree and a very soggy Maudie and Wilf back at Pond Farm to dry out before heading to Bert's. When they arrived, he was standing at the window, watching out for them. Brogan felt a little tug at her heart. How must he be feeling not knowing if he was going to see Nell again?

'We've got a real cracker for you, here, Bert,' Nick said cheerily as he and Brogan shook snow from the tree before bringing it into the house.

They followed Bert to the living room where the tree stand and the box of Christmas decorations he'd retrieved from the under-stairs cupboard were set on the floor.

Brogan got busy decorating the tree, while Nick made a pot of tea and chatted to Bert, telling him all about what had happened in the village that morning. Bert had listened, wide-eyed.

'Oh, I hope they find my Nell,' he said.

'They seemed pretty optimistic,' said Nick. 'I'm sure we'll have some news soon.

With the tree finished, its lights twinkling prettily in the window, Brogan joined them on the sofa when there was a sharp rap at the door making the three of them start. Brogan almost spilled her tea.

'Who the devil could that be?' asked Bert, startled.

'Would you like me to get it for you?' asked Nick.

'Aye, lad, if you wouldn't mind.' Bert glanced at him, concern in his rheumy eyes.

Moments later Nick returned wearing a huge smile. 'There's someone here to see you, Bert.'

'There is?' Bert asked, looking puzzled.

Brogan turned, wondering who it could be. She knew Bert didn't get many visitors.

'There is.' Nick stepped aside allowing PC Snaith into the room. He was holding a fox red Labrador on a short lead.

'Nell!' Bert's face lit up as the Labrador whimpered excitedly, pulling to get to him. The police officer unfastened the lead and before Bert had chance to get to his feet she rushed to him, wagging her tail so hard her whole body shook. She looked as ecstatic to see him as he was to see her.

'Oh, Nell lass, it's grand to see you. I'd thought I'd lost you.'

Brogan pressed her hand to her chest, emotion clogging her throat.

'Where did you find her? asked Nick. He was wearing a huge smile.

PC Snaith explained how once they'd got the two criminals back to the station in Middleton-le-Moors, they'd questioned them. It turned out the duo were father and son who had a history of targeting villages, particularly around the festive period. Brogan had felt inexorably relieved when he went on to say they had no record of violence.

Apparently, though the father had remained schtum, replying "no comment" to the questions put to him, the son hadn't taken much convincing to talk once he heard it might help reduce the prison sentence he would inevitably receive. He hadn't shown a scrap of remorse and was more annoyed at being caught. But he'd sung like a canary, telling the officers where to find the dogs they'd stolen as well as the other items they'd pilfered. A subsequent search of their abandoned van revealed the bounty they'd helped themselves to that morning, which included a garden seat and two lawnmowers. The dogs had been found at a surprisingly well-to-do house on the outskirts of Middleton-le-Moors – the owners of which were being held for questioning – and had been well-cared for in their short time there. As was suspected, the dogs had been stolen to order and were being kept at the house until they were sold on.

'I brought Nell back as soon as we got her.' PC Snaith smiled kindly at Bert who was busy ruffling Nell's ears.

'That's very good of you, lad,' Bert said, grinning from ear-to-ear.

'I can't believe there are people out there who'd do such a thing,' said Brogan.

'Oh, you'd be surprised what some folk are prepared to do,' the officer said gravely.

Back home, Nick had helped Brogan decorate the tree for Pond Farm. She'd lifted the decorations out one-by-one, each one holding its own special memories. They were a mishmash of styles and colours, and some of the older ones were incredibly fragile, their paint tarnished in places. Others Brogan had made at school, which her grandma had told her were her favourites, said they were precious, though Brogan could never understand why.

'Oh, no! Look at this horror!' She lifted out the angel she'd made from a wooden spoon, handing it to Nick. It had definitely seen better days, with its straggly hair made of uneven strands of yellow wool and tattered gown fashioned from white crepe paper, its wings crumpled paper doilies. It had once been liberally daubed with glitter and plastered with gaudy sequins, little of which remained. Seeing it again brought a smile to her face.

Nick turned it over in his hand. 'I wouldn't call it a horror, but it's definitely the first angel I've seen with a comb-over, so full marks for inventiveness.'

'It's like that because the glue's gone from one side of its head.' A giggle bubbled out of Brogan's mouth as she took it back. 'And horrific as it is, my grandma always insisted on giving it pride of place at the top of the tree.'

'Which I hope you will too.'

'Hmm. While I accept it's the sort of thing a grandparent can get away with, I think it's time this one was retired; she's done her bit. It's time for something else to take its place.' She lifted out a tissue-wrapped object to reveal the angel her grandparents had used before she'd presented them with the "comb-over angel". It had large antique-gold wings and a champagne coloured gown that shimmered in the light. 'I think it's time this one went back there;

she fits the bill far better. Can you do the honours?' She handed the angel to Nick.

'You sure about this?' he asked.

'Positive.'

He set the angel on the top branch, adjusting it until it was straight.

Brogan flicked the switch of the fairy lights, their warm glow filling the room. The heart-warming sight sent a wave of contentment rushing over her.

'I think we've done a grand job.' Nick hugged her close, kissing her hair.

'I think we have,' she said, smiling.

Revisiting her memories of Christmas Tree Sunday hadn't been anywhere near as painful as Brogan had expected. And, even better, she found she'd made some new ones that filled her heart with happiness – Nick's comment about the "comb-over angel" would tickle her for years to come. And maybe next year she'd feel able to keep the ones she'd made wrapped up in the box; even add some new – bought! – ones of her own. But for now she was content with how her first ever Christmas tree with Nick looked.

Her feelings for him were growing stronger by the day, and she hoped with all her heart it would be their first Christmas Tree Sunday of many.

FORTY-TWO

NICK

Nick was tucking into a sandwich in the staff room with Vonnie, Chris and Brogan. They were being entertained by Jules who was sharing details of her family trip to the pantomime and how the dame had got her husband up on stage.

'Honestly, Brad was absolutely mortified but the kids thought it was hilarious. Mind, so did I, much to his...' Her words tailed off as her attention switched to the doorway. 'Can I help?' she asked, her smile falling.

The others followed her gaze to where a glamorous-looking woman with a pinched face was standing. She exuded impatience with a smidge of discomfort thrown in. Behind her, Becky the vet nurse was peering over her shoulder, an apologetic look on her face.

'Loretta!' Nick could hardly believe his eyes to see her there, bold as brass. His heart sank, his body tensing. *What the hell is she doing here?*

'Sorry, Nick, I tried to explain you were having your lunch.' A flash of annoyance flitted across Becky's face.

'I'm not a client. We know each other,' Loretta said sharply. She turned back to Nick. 'I need to talk to you. In private.' Her gaze flicked to Brogan, her eyes narrowing.

Maudie raised her head, giving Loretta a look of pure disdain.

'Right, well, now's not a good time, I'm afraid.' He wasn't going to let her march in here and lay down the law. And he didn't like the frosty look she'd just given Brogan.

'You're hardly busy.'

A low growl emanated from Maudie. Nick sighed and got to his feet, ushering Loretta out of the room, the scent of her perfume irritating his nose.

He stopped in the empty waiting area and turned to face her, arms folded. 'What's so urgent?' he asked coolly.

'I told you, I need to talk to you. Not here though.' She gave a saccharine sweet smile.

'You need to talk?' He didn't think they had anything left to say, not that he'd vocalise that here, with the risk she could kick off.

'Yes.'

He paused, studying her face, taking in the petulant tilt of her chin. She put him in mind of a spoilt child who was using tried and tested ways to get what she wanted. It dawned on him that it was an expression she'd regularly worn when they were together. She'd been high maintenance, only he hadn't realised it at the time.

'Why are you looking at me like that?' she asked, a line appearing between her brows. 'Don't worry, I haven't come to give you a hard time about your stuff.'

'My stuff?'

'You were supposed to collect it yesterday. Remember?'

He hit his forehead with the heel of his hand. With all the excitement, he'd clean forgotten. 'Look, I'm sorry, there's been a lot going on; I forgot.'

'And it's not about my shoes either. I've forgiven you for ruining them.'

Ughh! The shoes. Nick had forgotten about those too.

'So, are you going to let me know when you'll be free to talk?' She placed her hand on her hip.

'Tonight, after I finish here.' His voice remained cool, though she didn't appear to notice.

'Good.' She treated him to a wide smile. 'Come to the house.'

'The house? But I thought, I mean, won't Aaron be there?'

'No. It'll just be you and me.' Her expression faltered for a second but she recovered quickly.

Why did her words sound so ominous? he wondered, rubbing his hand across the back of his neck, an idea forming in his mind. If he went to the house, he'd at least be able to get the rest of his stuff, save her turning up like this again.

'Don't look so worried, I'm not going to bite you.' Loretta leaned in and gave him a peck on the cheek; he felt her breath on his ear. 'Mmm. I love the way that cologne smells on you, it's why I bought it.' She gave his arm a proprietorial squeeze, her eyes locking on his for a second too long. He felt suddenly very wary.

A background thrum of dread troubled Nick all afternoon, his mind going over what Loretta could possibly want to discuss with him. It couldn't be the house; as far as he was aware the sale was proceeding smoothly. Whatever it was, he had a bad feeling about it. He didn't feel comfortable discussing his private life in front of the rest of the staff, so he'd waited until he and Brogan were alone to tell her what Loretta had said. It had been awful seeing the anxious expression Brogan had worn since the visit and it didn't lift once he'd spoken to her.

'I don't intend to stay long,' he said, hoping to reassure her, 'but the sooner it's over and done with, the better as far as I'm concerned. I can kill two birds with one stone and pick up the last of my stuff. There'll be no need for me to go back again.' The worry in her eyes was killing him.

'Okay. Just promise me you'll keep an eye out for the weather, there's more snow forecast later this evening. You don't want to get stranded on the rigg road.'

'I promise. Now stop worrying. Everything'll be fine and I'll be home before you know it.' Nick kissed her tenderly, glad that he'd finally managed to elicit a smile from her.

. . .

Nick pulled up outside his former home, trepidation making his chest feel tight. The weather conditions were far better in Middleton-le-Moors than they were back in Great Stangdale and Danskelfe dale, with most of the snow having been turned to slush in the market town. Before he had chance to get out of the car, the door to the house was flung open and Loretta appeared. She was wearing an inordinately wide smile and a sheer, floaty dress that draped over her slender frame. The garment seemed more appropriate for summer than a wintry evening in December, not that he knew much about these things. Her long blonde hair was styled in what she used to call an "artfully messy" up-do. Anyone would think she was going to a party.

On the step, she leaned towards him as if to kiss him on the mouth, but he quickly turned his head to one side, ensuring their lips didn't make contact. She pretended not to notice.

He followed her down the long hallway to the large kitchen, the white wall-to-floor units gleaming in the light. It looked almost clinical in contrast to the rustic kitchen at Pond Farm. Perching herself on a black leather bar stool, Loretta slid a large glass of red wine across the island to him. 'It's Merlot; your favourite.' A flirtatious smile played over her lips.

'I'm driving,' he said. He got the impression she expected him to pull out a chair and sit down, but he remained standing.

'Oh, don't be such a boring old fart.' She reached up and undid her hair so it tumbled over her shoulders, all golden and silky soft. She shook it out with her fingers so it hung around her face. 'You can at least have a little drink with me.'

The glass of wine was anything but little; it looked to be almost half a bottle's worth. And why was she flirting with him? 'I'd rather not. And anyway, I don't have long. So what did you want to talk to me about?'

'Hey, what's the rush? I thought you'd be keen to have a catch up.' She tipped her head to one side and peered up at him from beneath her sooty lashes.

That look might have worked on him not so long ago, but today it felt like she was trying to manipulate him.

'The rush is that I need to get back home.'

'Home?' She pouted her glossy lips and swirled the wine around her glass. 'Is that how you're referring to that little dump you've been staying at?' She drew in a deep breath, leaning forward and flashing her cleavage. 'Some would argue that this is your home.' She treated him to another coquettish look.

Nick snorted. Was she for real? 'Well, not me, that's for sure. You made it perfectly plain that it was no longer my home when you packed my stuff into boxes and went on to tell me you didn't want to marry me, that you didn't love me anymore, that you'd been sleeping with my best mate, and that you wanted me out of the house.' He counted the reasons off on his fingers, using every ounce of his strength to stay calm.

She flinched. 'People can make mistakes, you know.' She lowered her eyes, her bottom lip wobbling.

Ahh. So that's what this is all about. 'Not that I'm interested, but I'm guessing things aren't going the way you expected with Aaron.'

She shook her head. 'He spent the whole of Saturday night at the function ignoring me and flirting with the new girl from accounts. Had the nerve to tell me I was being paranoid when I challenged him about it. I'm not sure how getting upset about your boyfriend dirty dancing with another woman can be construed as paranoid,' she said bitterly.

This wasn't news to Nick. His ex-best mate had a reputation for womanising; Loretta knew that. But hearing all this still didn't explain why he had to come back to the house. 'Your relationship with Aaron is nothing to do with me. I'm sure you'll make up. So if that's all you've dragged me over here for, then I'm afraid I'm leaving.'

'What if I don't want to make up with him?' She arched a questioning eyebrow.

Nick sighed and rolled his eyes.

Loretta took a large slug of wine. 'What would you say if I told you I was wearing those sexy knickers you used to love, you know the ones with—'

'That's enough, Loretta. What do you think you're playing at? Last week you were making my life hell about a pair of shoes, and tonight you're coming on to me. Just quit with the mental gymnastics and tell me what this is really all about.'

She looked at him, her eyes woeful and swimming with tears. 'When I saw you with that girl, it made me realise it should be me you were having a laugh with, not her. I want to give us another go, Nick. I've missed you. I don't know why we split up.'

He shook his head in disbelief. 'You're unbelievable, you know that, don't you? But your cheating on me with Aaron has actually done me a favour; made me realise we were wrong for each other, made me realise how superficial our relationship was.' He drew in a lungful of air. 'That aside, I'm with someone.' He tensed, waiting for her reaction.

'What?' Her mouth fell open, her expression morphing from shock to anger. 'Are you saying you're seeing someone new?' She snorted. 'You didn't hang around, did you? I thought you said you were heartbroken after we split? Clearly not.'

'I wasn't looking to start a relationship with anyone. We just met and it was—' He stopped himself from saying anything further; he didn't need to explain himself to Loretta, and he certainly didn't want to get involved in a slanging match.

'It's her, isn't it? The dowdy girl from the surgery?' She gave a scornful laugh. 'You won't last five minutes; she's not your type.'

He resisted the urge to react. 'If you could just let me know where my stuff is, I'll be off.'

'It's where I said it would be; it's outside.'

'Right. That's fine. Goodbye, Loretta.' He glanced across at her to see her face set hard. She didn't speak as he left the house.

FORTY-THREE

BROGAN

The grandfather clock chimed nine. It had been just over two hours since Nick had dropped her off at Pond Farm and Brogan hadn't heard so much as a peep from him. She didn't know what to think. She peered out of the curtains, frowning when she saw it was still snowing. It had started a quarter of an hour ago, feather-like flakes tumbling from the sky. She dreaded to think what it would be like on the rigg road where it was higher and more exposed; the stretch regularly got blocked by deep snow drifts. Nick would have to tackle it to get home; it was the only access from Middleton-le-Moors way.

Her stomach had been churning all evening, and not just because of the snow and the potentially hazardous driving conditions. It didn't rest easy that he was going back to the house he'd once shared with his ex-fiancée.

Brogan checked her phone again. She toyed with the idea of calling him to make sure he was okay, but decided against it, not wanting to seem needy. In the end, she settled on waiting another half hour, then she'd send him a breezy text, just asking if he was okay and reminding him to be careful of the roads.

She wasn't sure what to do about their evening meal; they hadn't discussed it before he'd left. She'd just assumed he'd be back in time for them to eat together, albeit a little later than usual. She didn't want to eat on her own only for him to get home shortly after. She didn't feel hungry anyway; anxiety had quashed her appetite.

She'd wait a little longer, kill time by having another cup of tea.

While she waited for the kettle to boil, Brogan's mind wandered to Loretta. She was beautiful and glamorous. What if she wanted Nick back? Brogan's stomach twisted at the thought. He was bound to go running back to a woman like that. All she'd have to do is click her fingers and any man in his right mind would jump to attention, happy to be putty in her fingers. Whereas Brogan always had the feeling someone like herself was ordinary, invisible.

Sensing her distress, Wilf and Maudie ran over to her, Wilf nudging her hand with a whimper. 'Hello, you two. Fancy a cuddle?' She slid down to the floor and two whiskery faces were pushed into hers; Brogan couldn't help but laugh.

She'd been pacing the floor for the last half hour, nibbling at her fingernails, her cup of tea long-since drunk. It was ten-thirty and she'd still yet to hear from Nick. Her mind was in turmoil. She didn't know what to think. Had he set off and hit dangerous driving conditions? Or had he decided to stay with Loretta? A picture of them in bed together pushed its way into her mind, making her feel sick. She covered her face with her hands, hoping to chase the image away.

'This is exactly why I've avoided getting involved with anyone,' she said out loud. Wilf and Maudie looked up from their bed, regarding her while her pacing continued. 'Surely, if he'd set off he would've texted to let me know. Ughh! Nick! Why can't you just get in touch?' She threw her arms up in the air.

Another image sprang into her mind; this time it was of him in his car. It had come off the road and ended up on its roof in a ditch. Tears burnt at the back of her eyes. 'Oh, Nick, where are you?'

She peered out of the curtains again, rubbing a circle clear in the glass to see the snow was getting worryingly deep. 'Camm will be out in the plough. Nick will be fine. Stop worrying,' she said to herself in a bid to calm her jittering nerves.

A thought popped into her head and despite the time, she acted on it before she could think better of it and change her mind. She grabbed her phone and sent Molly a text, asking if Camm had mentioned what the rigg road was like, letting her know that Nick would be heading back from Middleton on it. If he hadn't ploughed it yet, she hoped her message would prompt Camm to prioritise it. She pressed send, feeling a little better.

Midnight came with still no sign nor news from Nick despite her sending yet more messages – which she could see hadn't been delivered – and trying to call his number, which frustratingly went straight to voicemail. Though she felt tired, her brain was too wired to sleep. It somehow felt wrong to go to bed and wait for him, so she brought her duvet downstairs and curled up on the sofa. She flicked the television on, selecting some music programme in a bid to fill the silence. As she lay staring into the darkness, a tear trickled down her face and a sob stuck in her throat. *Please come home, Nick.*

FORTY-FOUR

NICK

Nick had thrown his stuff into the boot and driven off the estate without a backwards glance, telling himself he hadn't had a wasted journey; he'd got the last of his possessions. Loretta couldn't nag him about them now. In fact, there was no need for any further contact apart from matters that concerned the sale of the house and that could be done through the solicitor. That things weren't panning out with Aaron was none of his concern.

Once he was away from the estate, he pulled over with the intention of calling Brogan to let her know he was on his way home. He reached for his phone, only to discover the battery had died. 'Seriously?' He'd meant to charge it at work, but Loretta's visit had chased it from his mind. Remembering the charger he kept in the glove compartment, he rummaged amongst the detritus there, his heart sinking when he couldn't find it. He leaned his head back against the headrest and puffed out his cheeks. 'Can this day get any worse?'

Telling himself there was no point in wasting time, he put his car into gear and pulled away.

The closer he got to the moors, the worse the weather became, and by the time he'd turned off the main road, visibility was virtually non-existent. The snow was falling heavily, the wind driving it right at the windscreen. It eventually got so bad, he couldn't tell if he was still travelling along the road or had strayed onto the moors. He had no choice but to stop the car.

He sat for a moment, wondering as to the best course of action, the wind whistling round the vehicle. It sounded bleak. At a guess, he'd say he was roughly five or six miles from Pond Farm. Should he walk it? Or would he be better off staying in his car until the weather eased? He thought of Brogan, sitting at home worrying about him driving in this. She had tried to warn him. He should have arranged to meet Loretta another time, then he wouldn't have found himself in this situation. If only he'd remembered to charge his phone, he could have called Brogan, put her mind at ease. He knew Camm would be out with the plough – this was one of the main routes – but he didn't know when. Weighing up his options, he decided the best course of action would be to sit it out. Stupidly, he'd forgotten to put his wellies in the back of his car so walking in such deep snow was out of the question. He cursed himself for being so forgetful. At least in the car he could turn the engine on now and then; get a blast of warmth from the heater. That decided, he reached over to the back seat and grabbed the blankets there, wrapping them around him. Pulling one up to his face, he prayed Camm wouldn't be long.

He'd been huddled up for a several long hours when a beam of light shone into his car. He raised his hand to shield his eyes, his body stiff from being in the same position for so long. Seconds later, he was aware of the sound of a tractor engine, the low scrape of the plough on snow. Camm! Nick couldn't remember feeling so relieved. He opened the car door, braving the elements that raged around him, his head bowed against the snow.

Shouting over the howling wind, Camm told Nick that he'd plough the road back to Pond Farm and that Nick should follow. 'Stick in a low gear and you'll be all right,' Camm said.

Concentrating hard and driving steadily, Nick followed the

tractor, snow dancing in the car's headlights. The conditions made the journey take twice as long, and Nick was glad and relieved in equal measure when they finally took the lane to Pond Farm.

Camm brought the tractor to a halt in the farmyard. Nick climbed out of his car and went over to him, blinking snow from his eyes. 'Thanks, Camm. I owe you one,' he shouted up to him.

'No problem. Get yourself in where it's warm.' Camm gave a thumbs up before turning the tractor round and heading out of the yard.

Before Nick got to the door it was flung open and Brogan appeared, her face drawn with worry. Wilf and Maudie shot out, gambolling around him, delighted he was back.

'Oh, thank goodness you're okay!' she said as they embraced.

'Yes, thanks to Camm I am.'

Though she was visibly relieved, the hesitance she'd worn before their heart-to-heart seemed to have returned, which puzzled him.

In the warmth of the kitchen, with Nick practically hugging the Aga, he gradually began to thaw out – he'd used the car engine sparingly to keep warm on the moortop since it was low on fuel. The lateness of the hour meant neither of them could face a big meal. Instead, they dined on buttery toast and mugs of hot chocolate prepared by Brogan as he recounted the events of his evening. She listened intently, pausing her chewing when Nick reached the part where Loretta had got flirty. He noticed her body tense. It struck him that this was more than likely the reason she seemed a little cool.

'Were you tempted?' she asked, anxiety lurking in her eyes.

He shook his head emphatically. 'Quite the opposite. It made me realise how little Loretta and I have in common.' He set the toast he was holding back on the plate. 'Made me realise a lot of things actually. In fact, it made one thing glaringly clear.'

He could feel the weight of her gaze on him as she anticipated his next words. He so wanted to tell her, but he didn't want to sound stupid. After all, they hadn't known each other long. But he couldn't just leave it hanging unsaid. *Okay, here goes.* 'It made me realise...' He hesitated. Was he doing the right thing? Should he wait? *Oh, stuff it!* 'It made me realise how I feel about you.'

'It did?' Her breathing deepened.

He nodded. *Say it!* 'It made me realise I'm falling in love with you.'

FORTY-FIVE

BROGAN

She looked at him, unable to speak as her mind processed his words. Had she heard right? He wasn't going to get back with beautiful, glamorous Loretta? He was falling in love with *her*? 'You are?'

'I am.' He gave a small laugh. 'I hope that hasn't scared you off.'

She cast her eyes down to her plate, marshalling her thoughts. Surely this was a dream?

'I've scared you. I should've kept my big mouth shut,' he said, his voice flat.

Her head shot up. 'No, I'm glad you told me.' A smile broke out on her face. 'I feel the same. It's just taking some sinking in. I mean, after you didn't come home my mind started thinking all sorts, and not just that you'd got stranded or had an accident.'

'You thought I'd got back with Loretta?'

She nodded, feeling suddenly foolish.

He reached across the table and found her hand, his fingers closing over hers. 'Brogan, I promise you, Loretta and I are never getting back together. Tonight confirmed that to me. It's you I want to be with. I don't want anyone else.'

Happiness surged through her; it felt like she was dreaming.

All this with Nick had happened so suddenly, yet nothing she'd experienced before had ever felt so right. 'And I want to be with you.' She beamed at him.

In the next moment, he was standing beside her. He took her hand and pulled her to her feet. Cupping her face in his hands, he looked into her eyes, smoothing his thumbs over her cheeks. Her heart was performing somersaults, and she wasn't sure how much longer her knees would hold out without crumbling beneath her. And then he kissed her.

'Wow!' she said when they finally pulled apart, dizziness making her sway.

'You took the words right out of my mouth,' he said, before kissing her again.

Later, when they went upstairs, instead of Nick heading to his own bedroom, he joined Brogan in hers. They climbed into bed, both too tired to speak. She snuggled into him, savouring the warmth of his body as he wrapped his arms tightly around her. Within moments, they'd both drifted off into a contented sleep.

Brogan blinked her eyes open, memories of the previous evening easing their way into her mind. The bed felt warm and cosy, and from where they lay it looked as if they'd barely moved through the night. She tilted her head so she could see Nick's face, surprised to see him looking back at her. Her heart gave a little ping.

'Morning.' He gave a lopsided smile and kissed the tip of her nose.

'Morning,' she said, her voice husky with sleep.

'Don't know about you, but I think we've got a bit of catching up to do.' He started trailing delicious kisses down her neck that sent her heart racing.

'Mmm. I think we do, but won't this make us late for work?'

'Probably, but it's better than my usual excuse of losing my wallet or my keys.'

His kisses were so distracting. 'Yes, but—' His lips were on hers, silencing her and making her stomach flip. She didn't want to resist any more.

Nick was having the usual hunt for his keys while Brogan was piling the breakfast pots in the sink – it wasn't like her to leave a load of washing up while she was out for the day and she found herself smiling at the reason for it.

'Ah, there they are.' Nick scooped his keys up from behind one of the Christmas cards on the dresser. 'So are we going to make this official then? Are we going to tell the world about us.' He strode over to her and planted a firm kiss on her lips. 'Please say we are. I don't think I'm going to be able to keep my feelings a secret.'

'In that case, I suppose we better had.' Brogan giggled at the earnest look on his face. And besides, she had a strong suspicion everyone would be able to guess without her having to say a word. She couldn't stop smiling and she was sure she was walking around with a ridiculous "I'm feeling loved up" glow emanating from her. Anoushka and Kristy would know as soon as they set eyes on her; that was a given.

'Great.' He gave her another kiss, happiness shining in his eyes.

'I think Bert'll be pleased for us,' she said, winding her scarf around her neck.

'I think he's already guessed. Told me I should get a move on in case someone took you from under my nose. Said I wouldn't get another lass like you if I waited a lifetime.'

'Bert said that?' A feeling of warmth filled her chest.

'He did. It hit home, and with what happened last night, I thought I'd better take heed of his words.' He grinned, holding the porch door open for her, stealing a kiss as she passed. 'I think we should go round after work and tell him.'

'Me too.'

Driving across the moors, Brogan smiled contentedly as she

gazed out at the stark beauty. This time last year she'd felt indescribably sad and lonely, the loss of her grandparents still intensely painful. But today, her heart was brimming with happiness. She felt a new optimism for the year ahead.

FORTY-SIX
BROGAN

Christmas Day brought with it clear blue skies and pale winter sunshine that sparkled over the snow-covered land. It was as if Mother Nature had bestowed a gift on this little corner of the North Yorkshire Moors after the last fortnight of relentless blizzards and icy cold winds.

The Village Committee's Christmas Day plan had been put into action; no one would be alone for the big day. Little Mary was going to Molly and Camm's along with Grannie Aggie who usually spent the day with her family over at Wychwood Farm in Middleton-le-Moors. In light of the treacherous roads, she'd opted to stay local. 'Folk are more fun here anyway,' she'd said to Molly, who'd told her in no uncertain terms that she wasn't to trouble Rev Nev over the festive period.

Brogan had wondered where Nick was planning on spending the big day, not wanting him to feel obliged to spend it with her. 'I usually go to my parents, but I'd much rather be here with you and Bert. I'm sure Maudie would agree too,' he'd said with a smile.

They woke early on Christmas morning, fishing presents from under the tree. Wilf and Maudie were given theirs first. Wilf, in particular, was thrilled with his new squeaky toy in the shape of a large steak. Nick had been delighted with the chunky jumper and socks Brogan had bought for him. 'Just in case you get stranded in the snow again,' she said, giving an amused hitch of her eyebrows.

'And this is for you.' Nick handed her a large box. 'I can't take credit for the wrapping; the lady in the shop did it for me.' He grinned, watching intently as she carefully lifted the lid and opened the tissue paper.

Brogan gasped as she lifted out an emerald-green satin dress. 'Oh, Nick!' It was exactly the same as the one that had been ruined that dreadful night Nell had been stolen. 'I can't believe it. You shouldn't have.' A memory of him asking her where she'd bought the dress floated into her mind.

'I so should, I know how upset you were it got damaged. It's a beautiful dress and you look beautiful in it, so I sneaked a look at the label, took a photo and showed it to the lady in the shop; it was the day we went Christmas shopping in York.' He beamed, looking delighted that his gift had been well received.

'That's so thoughtful, thank you.' She went over to him, wrapping her arms around him and kissing him hard.

'Oh, and there's something else.'

'There is?'

'Two ticks.' He disappeared into the kitchen, returning seconds later, his hand behind his back. 'I just need you here a moment.'

'Oh, okay.' She headed over to him, looking up into his eyes to see them dancing with mischief.

'Tada!' With a theatrical flourish, he produced a sprig of mistletoe, the thrilled expression on his face making her laugh out loud. 'Christmas wouldn't be Christmas without a kiss under the mistletoe,' he said, dangling it above them.

'I suppose you're right,' she said, still giggling.

He gave her a lingering kiss. 'Merry Christmas, darling Brogan.' He smiled down at her, the warm glow in his eyes unleashing a host of butterflies in her stomach.

'Merry Christmas, Nick.' She smiled back up at him, squeezing him tight, savouring the solid warmth of his body. She still couldn't believe how things had turned out between them; couldn't believe it was possible to feel this happy.

After delivering another heart-melting kiss, he said. 'I've got a sneaking suspicion kissing under the mistletoe is going to become my favourite Christmas tradition.'

Before Brogan could reply, Wilf barked. They looked across to see him gazing lovingly at Maudie who was looking at him from the corner of her eye. The sight made Brogan and Nick burst out laughing.

'Are you playing hard to get, Maudie?' asked Brogan.

'Poor Wilf,' said Nick. 'Want to see if the mistletoe can work its magic for you, fella?' Wilf replied with a happy wag of his tail while Nick turned to Maudie and said, 'I'll share some advice I was given recently about matters of the heart. Don't leave this fine young man dangling for too long; you never know when someone might come along and steal him from under your nose – don't forget young Nell's calling round today; just putting that out there.'

He turned back to Brogan. 'Right then, where were we? Oh, yes.' His eyes twinkled at her. 'I do hope you realise I fully intend to get my money's worth out of this mistletoe.'

Smiling happily, she stood on her tiptoes and slipped her arms around his neck. 'I was rather hoping you would.'

A LETTER FROM THE AUTHOR

Huge thanks for choosing to pick up *A Cosy Christmas with the Village Vet*. I hope you were hooked on this next instalment in the Life on the Moors series and getting to know Brogan and Nick – and all their moorland friends. If you'd like to join other readers in hearing all about my new releases and bonus content, you can sign up for my newsletter!

www.stormpublishing.co/eliza-j-scott

We won't share your email address, and you can unsubscribe any time.

If you enjoyed this book and could spare a few moments to leave a review, that would be hugely appreciated. It doesn't have to be long, just a few words would do, but for us authors it can make all the difference in encouraging a reader to discover our books for the first time. Thank you so much.

It's hard to believe this is the eighth book in the Life on the Moors series, and the fourth one set over the Christmas period. Yet again, I found myself writing about moonlit frosty nights and bitingly cold snow blizzards while we were in the clutches of a heatwave – and a hosepipe ban for some of the time! I really had to dig deep and channel my inner festive spirit! Luckily, I have plenty of moorland winters stored in my memory from which I could draw inspiration.

I really enjoyed writing Brogan's story. She may not have been there right at the start of the Life on the Moors series, but all the same, it felt good to delve into her character, get to know her better and find out what makes her tick. I hope you like her as much as I do. And being a dog-lover, it goes without saying that I loved writing about Wilf and Maudie!

www.elizajscott.com

facebook.com/elizajscottauthor

instagram.com/elizajscott

bookbub.com/authors/eliza-j-scott

bsky.app/profile/elizajscott.bsky.social

ACKNOWLEDGEMENTS

So, we've reached the part where I get to say thank you to everyone who's helped in one way or another in the process of getting *A Cosy Christmas with the Village Vet* ready for publication. And since this book, along with the rest of the Life on the Moors series, has been taken on and republished by the fabulous Storm Publishing, I think thanking the team there is a good place to start.

I'm going to begin by saying an enormous thank you to Kate Smith, my wonderful editor. Kate's positivity and enthusiasm is infectious, and her edits are always insightful and delivered with kindness. Working with Kate is a real dream come true!

Next up, the boss, aka managing director Oliver Rhodes. Thank you for setting up Storm, Oliver, and for creating such a wonderful team. Thanks also to Chris Lucraft who is Storm's digital operations director who deals with all the techy stuff that is way beyond me! Thank you for all you've done for my books so far, Chris! Alexandra Begley, who is Storm's editorial operations director, also deserves a huge thank you for prepping my book for publication day, as does new team member Maheen Mehmood for her role in production support and file formatting. Thanks are also owed to Elke Desanghere who is Storm's head of digital marketing. Big thanks for all your hard work on the marketing side of things and for creating such beautiful social media graphics, Elke. And thanks also to publicity manager Anna McKerrow for her fab social media posts. Rose Cooper needs a mention, too, for the beautiful new cover she designed for *A Cosy Christmas with the Village Vet*.

I also owe a warm thank you to three fabulous people for their input in getting this book ready for when I self-published it. They are: editor Alison Williams – thank you so much, Alison; I learnt a huge amount from you. Berni Stevens for the beautiful cover she designed for when *A Cosy Christmas with the Village Vet* was first published, and to Rachel Gilbey of Rachel's Random Resources for organising a fab blog tour for that time.

As ever, I'd like to send out an enormous thank you to the book community, whose kindness and support over social media is heart-warming and humbling. Thank you!

A shout out goes to my writing pals Jessica Redland and Sharon Booth for their unwavering support and kindness. We share a fondness for cheese scones, and we put the world to rights as we chomp away.

Huge thanks also go to my wonderful family for always believing in me. I love you with all my heart!

My final thank you goes to you, the reader, for choosing my book and taking the trouble to read it. Thank you so much for being a part of this exciting journey with me; I really am most grateful. I do hope you'll stay in touch and follow more adventures of the friends in the Life on the Moors series – it's *Christmas at Holly Tree Cottage* next!

Wishing you all a merry Christmas and every good wish for the new year.

Much love,

Eliza xxx